BACKCOUNTRY COVER-UP

DENISE N. WHEATLEY

HOTSHOT HEROES UNDER THREAT

LISA CHILDS

D1137501

MILLS & BOON

First Published in Great Britain 2022
by Mills & Boon, an imprint of HarperCollins*Publishers* Ltd
1 London Bridge Street, London, SE1 9GF

www.harpercollins.co.uk

HarperCollins*Publishers*
1st Floor, Watermarque Building,
Ringsend Road, Dublin 4, Ireland

Backcountry Cover-Up © 2022 Denise N. Wheatley
Hotshot Heroes Under Threat © 2022 Lisa Childs

ISBN: 978-0-263-30368-1

1122

BACKCOUNTRY COVER-UP

DENISE N. WHEATLEY

This book is dedicated to you, the readers!
Thank you for coming along on yet another
suspenseful journey with me.

Keep sleuthing, friends!

Chapter One

Elle Scott dug her fingernails into the steering wheel of her rented silver sedan. She made a sharp right turn, slamming on the brakes as her car skidded over River Birch Park's rocky terrain.

Dusk had fallen over her hometown of Bradford, North Carolina. Gone was the afternoon's bright blue sky. It had transformed into a sea of pinkish gray mist. The low-hanging sun was fading behind a curtain of clouds. That had been Elle's cue to pack up and head back to her parents' house.

A stinging chill crawled along the private investigator's skin. She inhaled slowly, waiting for her breathing to stabilize.

She had just left the crime scene where her best friend, Taylor Jacobson-Hendrix, had been found dead. Taylor's brother, Todd, was the one who'd called Elle a week prior to break the news.

"Taylor is gone," he'd whispered so faintly that she asked him to repeat himself.

"Gone? What do you mean, *gone*? Did she finally run off and leave her husband?"

"No, Elle. She—she's dead."

The words had numbed her limbs and sent her crashing to the floor of her Manhattan apartment. She'd remained there for almost an hour. Todd stayed on the phone with her the whole time. He explained how a park ranger had spotted Taylor's lifeless body lying underneath a massive tulip tree along River Birch Park's running trail.

The coroner ruled her death an accident, blaming her broken neck on a fall caused by the path's jagged ground.

Todd didn't believe it. Neither did Elle.

Taylor could've jogged the park's trail blindfolded. She'd been running it for years. It had been her and Elle's personal track all throughout high school and college. When Elle moved away ten years ago, Taylor continued to utilize it religiously.

Todd was infuriated when the sheriff's department stood by the medical examiner's ruling and closed the case. As a former US marine turned deputy sheriff in training, he felt betrayed by his hometown's law enforcement agency. Todd was convinced that his sister's death involved foul play. He'd begged the sheriff to further investigate the case, but his pleas had gone unanswered.

So he'd turned to Elle, asking that she bump up her plans to return home for the holidays and help him investigate Taylor's death. She'd booked the first flight out.

What really happened to you, Taylor?

A pair of blinding headlights flashed through Elle's back windshield. She peered into the rearview mirror. A black pickup truck was tailgating her down the park's gritty, sloped road.

"Could you back up, please?" Elle grumbled just as her cell phone rang.

Todd's name flashed across the screen, along with the photo of him and Taylor she'd saved under his contact information.

Her chest pulled at the sight. Todd and Taylor had taken the picture last year at the Marine Corps birthday ball.

Taylor's bright, wide-set eyes and signature crooked grin jumped off the screen. She and Todd had their arms wrapped securely around each other, which was how they'd always posed for photos considering how close they were.

Todd's crisp blue uniform was pressed to perfection. He could've passed for a young Blair Underwood with his dark, closely cropped hair, perfectly trimmed mustache, deep brown skin and smile so radiant it could light up a movie set.

Elle had had the biggest crush on Todd when they were younger. But she'd admired him from afar, figuring that he saw her as nothing more than his little sister's bestie. Eventually he'd enlisted in the military and she'd moved away, furthering the gap between them.

Taylor had acted as their liaison through the years, keeping them posted on what the other was up to from time to time.

And now she was gone.

Who knew I'd end up reconnecting with your brother through your death...

Elle's cell phone rang for a third time. She snapped out of her thoughts and tapped the steering wheel's Bluetooth button.

"Hey, Todd."

"Hey, just checking in. How are things going?"

His smooth, deep voice flowed through the speakers. It managed to relax her tense shoulders as she melted into the seat.

"I was just thinking about you," she said. "I'm actually leaving River Birch Park now."

"Really? You were out there for a long time. Sorry I couldn't join you. My weapons use training class went way over. But please tell me that you found some sort of evidence that we can work with. *Anything.*"

Elle's lips twisted in defeat. "Unfortunately, I didn't. And I scoured every inch of the area where Taylor's body was found. The only reason I left is because it started getting dark and I forgot to pack my flashlight. But I was confident that I'd find something. I guess I should've added crime scene investigation tactics to my forensic accounting and surveillance techniques studies."

"Look, don't underestimate your capabilities, Elle. I trust your investigative skills. You are truly gifted. I'm convinced that together, you and I are going to solve this case."

"Thanks, Todd. I appreciate your faith in me."

Elle slowed down when she reached the bottom of the road. The pickup truck that had been trailing her came to a screeching halt inches away from her bumper. The driver pressed down on the horn.

"Oh, come on!" Elle yelled, craning her neck toward the side-view mirror.

The truck's windows were tinted. All she could make out was the middle finger being flipped at her.

Elle waved the driver off. *"Jerk!"*

"What is going on out there?" Todd asked.

"Some jackass has been tailgating me ever since I left the crime scene. Now they're mad because I won't jet off into the intersection and get hit by oncoming traffic."

"I can't stand road ragers. Where exactly are you?"

"At the corner of Birch Street and Livingston Avenue." Elle looked to her right, then left. "The roads are jam-packed. Is there some sort of special event happening tonight?"

"Yep. The Christmas parade. I'm sure everybody is making their way downtown now. The main thoroughfare is gonna be flooded with holiday floats, sleighs, horse-drawn carriages, the whole nine."

"Ugh. I used to love Bradford's Christmas parade. But tonight, I couldn't be in a less festive mood. I have got to get out of here. I need to take a detour—"

Bee-ep!

Elle jumped in her seat as the pickup truck's shrill horn blared behind her.

"All right, all right!" she yelled.

"Listen, why don't you cut through the Everest Forest Preserve? That'll get you back to your parents' house pretty quickly." Todd paused. "Better yet, why don't we meet up for a drink? Sounds like you could use one. I know I could."

"After the day I've had?" Elle replied. "I could definitely go for a nice strong cocktail. Is Cozy's still a good place to hang out?"

"Oh, absolutely. Gigi has already added her signature holiday drinks to the menu, too."

"Okay, cool. I'd love to sit down and discuss our next moves over one of her famous cranberry bourbon blizzards. I'll head that way now."

Elle weaved between the cars blocking the intersection, then made a sharp left turn onto Oak Lane.

The trees lining the dim, narrow road created an ominous arc that loomed overhead. She slid closer to the steering wheel and pressed down on the accelerator.

"I should be at Cozy's in about ten minutes. I'm looking forward to…"

Elle's voice trailed off as a loud engine roared in the distance behind her.

Her eyes darted toward the rearview mirror. The black pickup truck that had been trailing her through the park was back.

"Oh no," she muttered.

"What's wrong?"

"I think I'm being followed."

"What?" Todd asked. "By who?"

"The same truck that was riding my bumper through the park."

Elle heard his phone shuffle, then a door slam.

"Listen," he said, "I'm jumping in my car and heading that way now. Just stay calm and be careful."

"I will." Elle turned on her bright lights and sped up. "Just get here as fast as you can. I'm heading north on Oak Lane."

"Got it. I'll stay on the line with you."

She glanced in the side-view mirror. The truck wasn't letting up. The faster she drove, the closer it got.

Elle slammed on the brakes and made a sharp right turn. Just as her car rounded the curve, the pickup rammed against the back of her car.

She screamed, jerking the steering wheel from right to left as she struggled to stay on the narrow road.

"Elle! What's going on?"

"The truck just hit me!"

Boom!

"It just hit me again!"

Elle pressed down on the accelerator. Her boot's heel tore into the floor mat.

"Hang in there," Todd said smoothly, his calm voice helping to ease her anxiety. "I'm driving as fast as I can. All this damn holiday traffic is slowing me down."

Bang!

The truck pounded into Elle's bumper again. Her car skidded off the road and careened toward a cluster of red maple trees.

Her chest hit the steering wheel. She gasped for air. Her hands ached as she clung to the wheel, struggling to guide the car away from the trees.

Elle tried to call out for Todd. But fear took hold of her vocal cords. A thin wheeze replaced the words she fought to speak.

"Stay with me, Elle. Tell me what's going on. Are you okay?"

Her body jolted uncontrollably as the vehicle bounced

over the forest's uneven floor. Branches scraped against the doors. Bright red and orange leaves slammed against the windshield.

Elle leaned forward, straining to see what was up ahead. "I've been run off the road!" she finally managed to say.

The truck rammed into her once again. The car flew farther into the cluster of trees at full speed. It slid across a pile of mud then crashed into a thick gray tree trunk.

Her body thrust forward. The seat belt kept her from flying through the windshield. But the airbags failed to deploy. Her forehead slammed against the steering wheel.

Elle whimpered softly as blood trickled down her nose.

"Elle! Elle? Talk to me! What is going on?"

"I… I've been hit. Crashed into a tree."

She opened her eyes, watching as the truck sped off, then passed out.

Chapter Two

Todd glanced over at Elle, careful not to turn his head while checking on her yet again. Aside from the slight limp in her right leg and small wound on her forehead, she seemed fine.

They'd just arrived at the coroner's office to review Taylor's autopsy report. Todd was surprised when she'd insisted on going with him, considering she'd been pretty banged up the night before.

He had gotten to the forest preserve just as she was regaining consciousness. Then he'd rushed her to the hospital, relieved to hear that she didn't have a concussion. The doctors had wanted to keep her overnight for observation, but Elle had refused, saying she had work to do.

"I can see you staring at me," she said as they walked through the coroner's office parking lot.

"No, I wasn't," he lied.

But Todd's stoic demeanor broke when he opened the door to the sterile gray cement building. "Actually, you're right. I was staring at you. Because I'm concerned. Are you sure you're okay?"

"For the third time, yes. I'm good." Elle poked him playfully in the chest. "So why don't you divert those beady little eyes of yours elsewhere. They're starting to creep me out."

Todd chuckled softly, glad to hear her crack a joke. The

toughness she'd exuded throughout their childhood was still there.

Despite being a scrawny kid, she had never been afraid to roll around in the dirt while playing flag football with the boys or kill spiders that crept through his sister's bedroom window.

But Elle's wiry limbs, buck teeth, corny jokes and giggly snorts were a thing of the past. She had blossomed into a stunning, poised, intelligent woman, the kind he knew only came around once in a lifetime.

Todd walked alongside Elle through the building's bland white lobby, waving at the receptionist as they approached the front desk.

"Hey, Margaret. We're here to—"

"Good afternoon," Elle interjected firmly into the Plexiglas window. "We're here to meet with Dr. Wu."

Todd watched as she began filling out the sign-in sheet. Elle was working overtime to prove that she'd recovered from the attack. He took a step back and let her.

"Hello, Deputy Jacobson," the receptionist said. She tucked her brunette bangs behind her ear and studied the visitor log. "*Aaand...* Ms. Scott. I will inform Dr. Wu that you're here. Please have a seat. I'll let you know when he's available."

Todd followed Elle over to a row of black plastic chairs. He shoved his hands inside his pockets, struggling to focus on the foggy picture windows overlooking the parking lot as they walked. But his gaze kept drifting back to her silhouette.

Elle's suede camel blazer and fitted black slacks hugged her gym-honed curves. Her slender calf muscles flexed when she strutted across the floor. She turned slightly, her pouty lips parting as she prepared to speak.

Todd forced himself to look away before taking a seat next to her.

"Did you remember to bring Taylor's file?" she asked.

"I did." He pulled it from his worn brown leather messenger bag. "I made two copies. One for me and one for you. I left the original down at the station."

"Smart. Thank you."

Elle slid the file out of his hand. Her finger grazed his thumb while her thigh brushed up against his.

A tingling rush shot up Todd's right side. He shifted in his seat and slid over, leaving a sizable gap between them.

"You all right?" she asked.

Todd kept his eyes on the file. "Yep. I'm good. So… um… I'm really curious to hear what this new coroner has to say about Taylor's autopsy report."

"Yeah, so am I. Especially considering he isn't in thrall to the sheriff's department like Dr. Winston was. I am so glad that man retired. The sheriff's office would say, 'Jump,' and he'd ask, 'How high?' Now maybe we'll get an unbiased analysis."

"I hope so. Because there's no way in hell all those scratches on Taylor's hands, forearms and legs were caused by rocks after she fell to the ground."

Elle flipped to an autopsy photo, studying it closely. "Neither was her broken neck." She handed Todd the picture. "Look, she's got red spots around her eyes, a swollen lip, blue fingernails and faint bruising around her throat. Those are all signs of strangulation. *Not* a fall on a running trail."

Todd turned the other way. "I'm sorry, Elle, but I can't look at that again. I've seen enough of my sister's dead body."

"I am so sorry," she whispered, quickly shoving the photo back inside the file.

"No need to apologize. I know you're just trying to help."

Heavy heels clicked across the dull white tile as the receptionist shuffled toward them.

"Ms. Scott, Deputy Jacobson, Dr. Wu is ready to see you now. Please, follow me."

Todd stood and took a deep breath. Elle patted his arm reassuringly.

"You've got this," she told him. "We are going to get justice for our girl. I promise."

That was all Todd needed to hear. He squared his shoulders and followed Margaret toward the coroner's office.

DR. WU PUSHED a piece of paper across his desk. Todd prayed it wasn't one of Taylor's autopsy photos. He peeked down. Let out a sigh. It was a diagram of a woman's body that had been marked up by the medical examiner.

"So, as you can both see here," Dr. Wu said, "my interpretation of Taylor's cause of death is somewhat different from Dr. Winston's. I've circled the lacerations that could, in my opinion, be defensive wounds. She's got a torn meniscus in her right knee, which is an injury that we usually see in athletes."

"Ow," Todd uttered, grabbing his leg. "I tore my meniscus back in college during a football game after being tackled to the ground by one of the opposing team's linemen. That is an excruciating injury."

"Wait," Elle interjected, "it took you being tackled by someone to sustain this injury?"

"Yes. It did."

She turned to the coroner. "So what does that tell you about Taylor's death, Dr. Wu?"

"Hold on. Before you jump to any conclusions, please note that a torn meniscus can also be caused by a hard fall. So can the broken ankle that Taylor suffered."

"But her ankle injury was pretty severe," Todd said. "She fractured both her tibia and fibula."

Dr. Wu pushed his frameless bifocals up his pockmarked nose without responding.

"Okay, then." Elle pulled a photo from Taylor's police file and placed it in front of the coroner, pointing at her white sock. "You see this?"

"I do."

"There's a muddy footprint on that sock. The pattern is consistent with the type of rubber sole that can be found on hiking boots. Look at the soles on Taylor's sneakers. That tight, grooved pattern looks nothing like the round lug pattern on the sock."

"Nice catch," Todd told her. "I didn't even notice that. So this means someone else was out on that trail with Taylor, wearing a different type of shoe. Possibly an attacker who stomped down on her ankle and broke it."

Dr. Wu eyed the photo. "Or it could've been a member of law enforcement who accidentally stepped on Taylor's ankle and left the print during the investigation. *After* she fractured her ankle during a fall."

Todd threw his head back and stared up at the white drop ceiling.

"What about any physical evidence that could indicate foul play?" Elle asked. "Were there any skin cells found underneath Taylor's fingernails? Was there blood present? Hair follicles? Anything?"

"No," Dr. Wu replied. "There wasn't. But listen, don't get discouraged. I'm not trying to play devil's advocate here. I just want you two to view this situation from all angles. These points that I'm bringing up are the same rebuttals that the sheriff's department will present if we approach them about reopening this case."

Elle slumped forward and thumbed through the photos. Todd noticed the corners of her eyes dampen. She bit down on her bottom lip as if she wanted to say something, but didn't quite know what. The sight of her defeat unraveled him.

"You mean *when* we approach the sheriff's department," Todd told Dr. Wu.

The coroner ran his hands down the sides of his chubby face, focusing on the diagram rather than Todd's piercing stare.

"My biggest concern with Taylor's injuries is her broken hyoid bone," Dr. Wu said while drawing a circle around the figure's neck. "That type of fracture is rare."

"Except in cases of strangulation," Elle added.

"That is correct."

"That's pretty damning, don't you think? I really believe we've got enough evidence here to take to Sheriff Glover and ask that he reopen this investigation."

"I agree," Todd said, his voice cracking with frustration. "What do you think, Dr. Wu? Can we make the meeting with the sheriff's office happen?"

"Look, Sheriff Glover has full confidence in Dr. Winston's findings. So does the rest of the department. Deputy Jacobson, you work with the officers who investigated this case. I don't think they'd take too kindly to either of us butting in and demanding a reevaluation."

"At this point, I'm not concerned with my fellow officers' feelings. My top priority is finding out what happened to my sister. By any means necessary."

"Please, Dr. Wu," Elle said. "We need you. I know this case is personal for Todd and me. But emotions aside, we truly believe that law enforcement got it wrong. You seem to be on the same page as us. Your expert opinion could turn this entire case around."

The coroner looked from Elle to Todd, then down at his folded hands.

"Okay," he finally agreed. "Let's give it a try. I'll request a meeting with Sheriff Glover, present what we discussed today and see where it gets us."

"Yes!" Todd pumped his fist in the air. He stood and

extended his hand. "Thank you so much, Dr. Wu. Elle and I really appreciate this."

"You're both welcome. Again, I am sorry for your loss. I just hope that in the end, you find peace."

"We'll find peace when we get justice," Todd said. "Thanks again for your time."

The moment Dr. Wu's door closed behind them, Elle threw her arms around Todd. He leaned into her embrace. Her warm hands pressed against his shoulder blades, releasing the tension in his entire upper body.

"We did it!" she exclaimed. "We are one step closer to the truth."

"Let's hope so. I'm just glad that you're here, doing this with me. I don't think I could've done it alone."

Elle slowly pulled away from him. "Well, I know I wouldn't have been able to do it without you. So, thank you for bringing me on board, partner."

Todd instinctively reached for her hand before quickly pulling back.

What in the hell are you doing?

"Hey," she continued, "we never did get that holiday drink from Cozy's, thanks to the deranged driver who crashed into me. Why don't we stop by there and grab some lunch and a couple of merry cranberry sangrias?"

"Mmm, that sounds good."

Elle pulled up Cozy's menu on her phone as they walked through the lobby. "Uh-oh. I know I shouldn't do this, but Gigi's grilled cheese and maple bacon sandwich with a side of cinnamon sweet potato fries has my name written all over it. Don't try and talk me out of ordering it, either."

"Why would I do that when I'll probably be ordering the same thing?"

Todd tucked Taylor's file inside his messenger bag. Their mission for the day was complete. Now it was time to take a respite, reconnect and focus on their next move.

Chapter Three

Elle sipped her sangria and glanced around Cozy's Café.

The quaint eatery was brimming with customers who'd taken a break from their holiday shopping to grab a bite. Every rustic wooden table was surrounded by bags and piled high with Gigi's signature sandwiches, seasonal drinks and holiday desserts.

The bright red walls were covered with twinkling string lights, evergreen garland and scented acorn wreaths. Servers bustled about in their Santa hats and reindeer headbands. Gigi, who was dressed in a Mrs. Claus apron, bounced around from table to table making sure her customers were content. Despite her petite stature, her silvery voice boomed over the festive music piping through the speakers.

"So," Todd said, "why is it that I haven't seen you around Bradford during the holidays in, like, years?"

"Ah, it's a long story."

"Well, make it short. Or not. I've got time."

Elle tilted her head, wondering just how much she should reveal. "Well, I was dating a guy named Jayson who lives in New York. He's a hedge fund manager, and—"

"Wait, Jayson Wright?"

"Yes. Do you know him?"

Todd's eyes shifted. He took a big gulp of sangria. "No.

I don't. I uh… I may have seen him posted on your social media."

"Hmm, so you've been stalking my Instagram, huh?"

"Oh, no. Of course not," he replied through a toothy grin.

Elle smiled. "No worries. I kinda like the fact that you've been checking up on me."

She paused, waiting on him to make eye contact.

Todd's gaze slowly rose from his empty plate back up to her. Elle's heart flipped at the sight of his deep dimples. She pressed her hand against her chest and cleared her throat.

"So, anyway, between Jayson's schedule and mine, it was hard to find free time to take vacations. The Christmas season was our only option. I'd travel with him during the holidays, which is why you never saw me here in Bradford."

"But you're here this year."

"Yes. I am. I—I…we…um…" she stammered before choking up.

Todd reached across the table and grabbed her hand. "Hey, listen. You don't have to talk about it if you don't want to."

"No, it's fine. Jayson and I were together for three years. People are going to ask questions. I can't dodge the conversation forever."

"Hello, you two!" Gigi said as she approached the table with outstretched arms. "Elle, it's so good to see you. *Especially* during Christmastime. How have you been?"

Elle stood and embraced her. "Hello, Gigi. It's good to see you, too. I'm doing well."

"How's the food? As good as it's always been, I hope."

"Better," Elle replied. "And the signature cocktails? Incredible."

"Aw, thank you, dear. I'll clear off your table and send over another round. What are you two having for dessert?"

Todd picked up the menu. "We hadn't decided yet. These

peppermint brownies look delicious. But so do the red velvet cupcakes."

"I was thinking about a slice of caramel apple cheesecake with the gingerbread crust."

"I'll tell you what," Gigi said. "Why don't I send over a platter with a little bit of all three? How does that sound?"

"That sounds like Todd is gonna have to roll me out of here on a dolly. But hey, it's the holiday season. Calories don't add up the same during this time of the year. Right?"

Gigi gave Elle a wink. "That's right, sweetie. I'll have those desserts and cocktails brought over in a moment."

Todd turned his attention back to Elle the minute Gigi left the table. "So, back to our convo. You were telling me about what happened between you and what's-his-name."

"Jayson," Elle reminded him despite knowing he hadn't forgotten. "He and I didn't see eye to eye on our future together. He was content just dating me while working nonstop, schmoozing with clients, traveling the world and obsessing over his portfolio. I wanted to settle down. Get married. Start a family. You know, like what we grew up around."

"Yeah, our parents and their friends really seem to have it all figured out."

"They do. That type of loyalty and commitment are hard to come by these days."

"Indeed," Todd agreed. "Nevertheless, I'm sorry that things didn't work out between you and Jeffrey."

"Jayson," Elle reiterated, giving Todd's arm a light pinch.

"I know, I know. Just messing with you. It's actually nice having you back in Bradford for the holidays."

"Thanks. It's nice to be back. But anyway, enough about me. How are you doing? Are you enjoying working for the sheriff's department?"

"It's cool. Just between us, this deputy sheriff training program is kicking my butt."

"How could our little hometown's sheriff's department be kicking a former marine's butt?"

"You'd be surprised. I feel like I'm back in college, pledging a fraternity. These guys are pretty much hazing me. I'm starting to think it's personal."

"I'm not surprised they're giving you a hard time. You're Bradford's hometown hero. All-star high school and college quarterback, medaled marine, boyfriend of the prettiest woman in town—"

"*Ex*-boyfriend," Todd interrupted just as a server came over with their cocktails and desserts.

"Oh," Elle uttered, pausing until the server left. "You and Jasmine broke up?"

"Yep. We did."

"I'm sorry to hear that. When did it happen?"

"Earlier this year. The day after Valentine's Day, to be exact. I gave her a gold necklace, which she didn't like, considering she was expecting an engagement ring."

"You two had discussed marriage?"

"She'd brought up the subject on occasion. But I pretty much avoided the topic."

Elle's gaze fell. "Hmm, so you're not interested in getting married…"

"No, it's not that. I wasn't interested in marrying Jasmine. But I'm looking forward to marriage and starting a family. It just has to be with the right person."

Elle slowly raised her head. She and Todd locked eyes just as Gigi approached the table.

"How's everything tasting?" she asked.

"We've been so busy chatting that we haven't had a chance to dig in yet," Elle said.

"Well, hurry up and try everything out! I added a few new ingredients to this year's recipes, and I'm anxious to hear what you two think. Oh! And before you leave, stop by the coffee counter. I'm experimenting with a new ginger-bread espresso and would love to hear your thoughts on it."

"Mmm, that sounds good," Todd said. "We'll see you on the way out."

The moment Gigi left the table, someone else approached.

"Elle? Elle Scott? Is that you?"

She spun around.

"Rachel! Hey!" Elle said to her former high school class-mate. "How are you?"

"I'm doing well. Just shocked to see you in here in Brad-ford. No exotic overseas vacation this Christmas?"

"Long story, but no. We'll have to discuss all that an-other time. Preferably over cocktails."

"Sounds like a plan." The curvy, green-eyed redhead flipped her hair over her shoulder before giving Todd a sympathetic wave. "Hey, how are you holding up, my friend?"

"I'm hanging in there. It's been tough, dealing with Tay-lor's death and all. But my family and I are doing the best we can to get through it. Having Elle here to support us has been a tremendous help."

"I'm sure it has." Rachel paused. "Elle, are you still working as a private investigator?"

Elle pressed her finger against her lips. "I am. But please, keep that information confidential. Most people in Bradford don't know about my practice. I'd like to keep it that way."

"Gotcha. Well, I have some information that I'd like to share with you two. Confidentially. My sister, Faith, still works at the bank, and she ran by me some interesting transactions that were made by Taylor shortly before her death. And I'm assuming you've already looked into that women's organization Taylor was heavily involved with. The Precious Jewels."

"The precious what?" Todd asked before grabbing his phone and pulling up the Notes app.

"The Precious Jewels. It's a social club of sorts, run by some of the wealthiest, most obnoxious women in town."

"Really?" Elle said. "That doesn't sound like the type of crowd Taylor would normally associate with. I mean, she did always aspire to attain the finer things in life. She just never had the money to do so."

Rachel glanced around the café, then bent down. "Yeah, well, this little club was beginning to change all that for her," she whispered. "It was actually a front for a major pyramid scheme."

A sick feeling churned inside Elle's stomach.

Taylor was keeping secrets from me...

"I didn't know anything about this," Elle said while opening the calendar on her phone. "But we'd definitely like to hear more. When are you available to meet?"

Rachel reached inside her handbag and pulled out a business card. "I'll make myself available whenever you are. The sooner the better. Because unlike the sheriff's department, I don't believe that Taylor's death was an accident."

"Yeah, neither do we," Todd said. "We'll give you a call tomorrow and set something up. Thanks for passing along whatever information you have. We really appreciate it."

"Of course. I'm happy to help in whatever way I can. Talk to you soon."

Todd pushed the platter of desserts toward Elle. "I just lost my appetite. But feel free to dive in."

"At this point, I'll pass as well. This day has been a lot. *Too* much."

"Why don't we get this wrapped up and take it to go? I'll drop you off at home, and we can reconvene tomorrow."

"That works for me."

Elle stood and threw on her red wool trench coat, her mind now racing in a thousand different directions. From the pyramid scheme to whatever other secrets Taylor had been harboring, Elle felt as though she no longer knew her best friend.

Oh, Taylor, what had you gotten yourself into?

Chapter Four

Elle pulled into the parking lot of the Bradford Museum of Contemporary Art and glanced down at her watch. She was running a few minutes late for her meeting with Rachel, who served as the museum's curator.

Her father's old sky blue Toyota Camry backfired loudly the minute she turned off the engine.

Elle ducked down, startled by what sounded like a piercing gunshot. She peered over the steering wheel. Two little boys burst out crying while clinging to their mother's legs. A short, stout security guard hustled toward her car.

"Oh, God," Elle moaned, embarrassed by the commotion she'd caused.

"Ma'am, are you okay?" he asked.

She rolled down the window and forced a smile. "I'm fine. Just dealing with an old car that probably needs a tune-up."

The guard removed his cap and scratched his balding head. "I'd have to agree with you there. Sounds like you've got an issue with the engine belts, too. Why don't you pop the hood and let me take a look at it?"

"Thank you for offering, but I'm actually running late for a meeting," Elle said just as her cell phone rang.

The guard coughed when a cloud of black smoke drifted from the back of the car. "All right. But I'd advise you to go get your vehicle checked out as soon as possible. I'd hate for it to stop on you out here. Especially on one of these dark, desolate roads, late at night—"

"I appreciate your help," Elle interrupted. "I need to take this call."

"Suit yourself…" He lingered for a few seconds longer, staring at her intently before finally walking off.

"Weird," Elle muttered before picking up the call. "Hello?"

"Hey, it's Todd."

"Oh, hey. I didn't recognize the number you're calling from."

"I'm using one of the phones at the sheriff's office. My cell is dead."

"Wait, you're not on your way to the museum?"

"No, that's why I'm calling. We had an extra training session added to the agenda today. A law enforcement officer from Cane County who specializes in human trafficking came in to speak with us. Apparently he's one of the best in the state and hard to schedule. So we had to fit him in."

Elle grabbed the handle and bumped her body against the door three times before it finally opened. "I'm bummed that you can't make it. But I'll be sure to take good notes during the meeting. I really wish you could be here."

"Yeah, me, too. Maybe we can get together once you're done and go over everything you and Rachel discuss. I mean, if you're available," Todd quickly added.

She smiled at the nervousness in his shaky tone. It was cute, coming from such a tough guy. "I'm available. I'll give you a call when I'm leaving."

"Cool. Talk to you soon."

Elle rushed through the parking lot and climbed the curved cement staircase leading up to the museum's carved teakwood doors.

Posted near the entrance, the security guard shuffled his

tiny feet back and forth as he eyed Elle hungrily, his bloated hands hanging from his worn leather belt.

"Don't forget to get that car checked out," he said with a wink. "If you need a recommendation for a good mechanic, I've got just the guy for you."

"I'll keep that in mind. Thanks."

The guard opened the door for her. She quickly slipped inside before he could say another word.

Elle pulled out her phone to text Rachel just as she appeared from around the corner.

Everyone stopped and stared as Rachel strutted through the lobby wearing a gorgeous emerald green wrap dress and six-inch nude stilettos. She waved at Elle, oblivious to the attention.

"Hey, glad you could make it."

"Of course. Thank you for inviting me," Elle said, feeling underdressed in her black leather blazer, jeans and combat boots. "I am so sorry I'm late. My father's car was acting up, then Todd called to tell me that he wouldn't be able to make it."

"So it's just gonna be us girls?"

"Yep, just us."

"That's fine," Rachel said. "Knowing you, I'm sure you'll take meticulous notes for him. Follow me. Let's talk in my office. We'll have plenty of privacy there."

Rachel led Elle through a maze of ten-foot-tall bronze sculptures. They walked down a long, stark white hallway where the walls were covered in bold, colorful, abstract paintings. The museum's subtle Christmas decor consisted of elegant crystal ornaments dangling from the ceilings and large evergreen wreaths hanging from the arched windows.

Elle followed Rachel into a spacious, minimalist office. Soft gray walls matched the hardwood floors. An off-white oval desk sat in the middle of the floor.

"Have a seat," Rachel said, pointing toward a pair of

Eames-style yellow swivel chairs. "Can I get you anything to drink? Water, tea, coffee? Something a little stronger?"

"Thanks, but no. I'm fine. I love your space. This is really cool."

"Thank you."

Elle sensed an immediate change in Rachel's demeanor as soon as they sat down. She stared at her hands while fidgeting with her manicured, chocolate brown nails. Her lips tightened as her eyes grew weepy.

"I know this isn't easy, Rachel. That's why I'm here. Todd and I are going to do all that we can to get to the bottom of Taylor's death."

"I hope so." She fanned her face. "*Whew.* I'd better pull myself together. I've got a meeting with an artist later this afternoon and would hate to scare him off with a swollen crying face."

Elle pulled a couple of tissues out of her tote bag. "Here. Dry your eyes, take a deep breath and let's talk."

Rachel inhaled slowly. "Where should I even start?"

"How about with Taylor's husband, Bryce?" Elle asked, cracking open her notebook. "Even though the sheriff's department declared Taylor's death as accidental, I know they spoke with him. He was working at the car dealership that he manages, Capital Motors, during the time that she died. Not that he needs an alibi or anything, but in the event that he does, he's got one."

"*Allegedly.* Do you know how easy it is for him to slip in and out of that dealership without being seen? He also has access to every car on the lot. He could've driven one of the dealership's vehicles to the park rather than his own. His personal car would've remained in the work lot, making it look as if he was still there when he actually wasn't."

"That's true," Elle replied while rigorously taking notes. "I'll ask Todd whether the sheriff's department watched any of the dealership's video surveillance footage from that day. If Bryce did in fact leave work at any given point, it should've been recorded."

She didn't know if Taylor's marriage was happy or if she and her husband had been having difficulties. It was something she wanted to pursue, but carefully.

Elle took a deep breath and glanced over at the twinkling yellow string lights lining Rachel's window. They resembled the ones she and Taylor would drape along her windowsills and canopy bed during the holidays.

Stop it. Stay in the moment before you burst into tears.

"When I ran into you at Cozy's," she continued, "you mentioned some strange bank transactions that Taylor made. Can you tell me more about those?"

Rachel opened her laptop and tapped on the keyboard. "I sure can. My sister didn't email me the bank statements, because that would've been illegal. But she did send me an email summarizing the activity. On a hypothetical account, of course," she added with a wink.

She spun the computer around. Elle zoomed in on the screen.

"Okay, so Taylor took out a second mortgage on the house. Why is that strange?"

"Because her husband didn't know about it. He came into the bank ranting about how Taylor had forged his signature on the paperwork. The manager reviewed the documents and realized that Bryce's signature didn't match those on the docs."

Elle tapped her fingers against her chin. "How did Taylor pull that off? The underwriter should've caught it before approving the loan."

"Not if the underwriter is a member of Taylor's little social club that I was telling you about. The Precious Jewels."

"Oh," Elle breathed, sitting back in her chair. "I see. Wow. I guess I'd be angry, too, if I were Bryce."

Rachel's right eyebrow arched. "Angry enough to kill?

Because a few months after Bryce found out about the second mortgage, Taylor was found dead."

"Humph." Elle slammed her notebook down on the desk. "I would question why the sheriff's department didn't look into any of this. But I already know. They don't want a stain on Bradford's reputation. It's easier to declare a death as accidental than to admit that there's a killer in the community."

"Which is a scary thought," Rachel said.

"What other transactions did your sister mention in that email?"

"Taylor had been making several random deposits. The personal checks were made payable to her, and the amounts were pretty high. I'm talking in the thousands. I think they were payments coming from women who were entering into The Precious Jewels' pyramid scheme."

"Interesting…"

Rachel slid the laptop closer toward Elle. "Here's a picture of several members at Bradford's holiday charity ball last year."

Elle studied the photo. About twenty women were standing in front of the town's historic cultural center. They were dressed in floor-length ball gowns, with their hair twisted into dramatic chignons and botoxed faces covered in heavy makeup. Each of them held a glass of champagne high in the air.

Taylor was standing off to the side, holding several handbags. Her red knee-length taffeta dress didn't quite fit in with the rest of the group's couture formalwear.

"I guess Taylor wasn't a member back then, huh," Elle said.

"Not yet. But a lot had changed since then. Taylor worked her way in by schmoozing with the right people, then pulling together enough money to pay the entry fee. Once she was in, she recruited other members like nobody's business and rose to the top pretty quickly. But I heard that there was a lot of dissension within the group. Not everyone approved of Taylor's presence, nor her tactics. Especially the ringleader, Sloane Whitlock."

"Wait, how do you know all this?"

"The museum is used for charity events, and I've over-heard things from some in that group."

Elle slowly nodded. "Okay, and who is Sloane Whit-lock?"

"The infamous founder of The Precious Jewels. And one of the richest, most powerful women in Bradford."

Elle wrote the woman's name down, then sighed heavily. "Wow. I've been away for way too long. There is so much going on that I didn't know about."

"That's why I'm here. To help fill in the gaps. If you want to get to the bottom of Taylor's death, you're gonna have to refamiliarize yourself with the town. A lot's changed since you've been gone." Rachel opened her drawer and pulled out a flyer. "I'd suggest you start by attending this year's holiday charity ball. All of The Precious Jewels will be there. Including Sloane. It's where she likes to go and scope out potential new members."

Elle picked up the glossy, red-and-green invitation. "This is taking place next weekend. But it looks like I've still got time to RSVP. Are you going?"

Rachel snorted loudly. "Hell no. That's not my scene. I'd rather have my teeth pulled than spend an evening with those awful women."

"Maybe I can get Todd to go with me."

"I'm sure he'd love that. And not just for investigative purposes…"

Elle scoffed at Rachel's sly grin.

"Will you stop that? Todd and I are just friends. And partners now that we're working together on this case. That's all."

"Yeah, okay, *that's all*. I saw the way you two were acting toward one another at Cozy's. The long stares, the unnecessary touching. Looked to me like there was a lot more going on than just two people working on a case."

Elle's skin prickled underneath her blazer. She tugged at the collar and cleared her throat.

"I should probably get going. You've got a meeting coming up, and I'd like to get these notes organized before I talk to Todd. You gave me a lot of good intel. I can't thank you enough."

"It's the least I could do," Rachel said as she walked Elle out. "I'm happy to help in any way that I can. If there's anything else I can do, or anything else you need, just let me know."

"I will. And I'll keep you posted on the charity gala, too. I have a feeling that event just may open up a whole new angle to this investigation."

"I'm sure it will. Talk soon."

Chapter Five

"We haven't gotten any leads on the black pickup truck that rammed into you at the forest preserve," Todd said.

"That's disappointing to hear," Elle muttered, staring down at the dusty earth beneath her boots.

"The sheriff's department is still working on it, though. So don't lose hope."

"I'll try…"

Todd cringed at the doubt in her low tone. The mood between them was already somber as they walked along the River Birch Park's desolate trail, studying the path that Taylor used to run.

An eerie feeling lingered in the air. Tree branches seemed to move a bit slower. A cold sprinkle of rain fell from the gray afternoon sky. The howling wind was reminiscent of whining, tortured souls.

"I've lost faith in our town's sheriff's department," Elle said. "I still can't believe they didn't put more effort into Taylor's death investigation. So it's not surprising that they have no answers for me."

"My hope is that I can help turn things around now that I'm a part of the agency. It's just gonna take some time. And a lot of effort. Starting with those leads Rachel gave you yesterday."

"Yes, because coming out here time and time again hasn't produced anything new. I've been praying that we'd stumble upon some sort of overlooked evidence. Or a rock stuck in the dirt near where Taylor fell. Or even a small ditch. *Something* that would explain how she could've fallen and broken her neck on a seemingly even trail that she'd been running for years."

Elle looked to the sky as a beam of light shone through two parting clouds.

"I wish Taylor would somehow speak to us," she whispered. "Tell us what really happened to her. Guide us to the evidence so we won't have to keep returning to the place where she was murdered. It's becoming too painful."

Todd wrapped his arm around Elle. "I know it is. But just remember, you're not in this alone. I'm here with you, every step of the way. The answers are going to come."

"Isn't it a shame that so far, our best intel came from an art curator rather than the sheriff's department?"

"In all fairness, the department did talk to Bryce. They just took him at his word when he said he was at work during the time of Taylor's death. And as for that women's group Taylor was a part of, the uh…"

"The Precious Jewels."

"Right. The Precious Jewels. Sheriff Glover thinks they're just a superficial social club filled with gossipy women. I don't think he even knows about the pyramid scheme they're allegedly running."

Elle approached the tulip tree where Taylor's body had been found. She crossed her arms over her chest and turned to Todd. "Yeah, well, that's why I've got to figure out a way to infiltrate the group. See if I can find out exactly what was going on with Taylor before her death. If she was at odds with the group's founder, and there was a lot of money at stake, then that could very well be the cause of her murder."

"Which is why we'll be front and center at that gala next weekend." Todd bent down, studying the tree's bark. "But before that, I'd like for us to stop by Taylor's house and pay Bryce a visit. Because you're right. There may be more to his involvement now that we know about that second mortgage."

"Do you think you could get ahold of his car dealership's surveillance footage from the day Taylor died?"

"Possibly. I'll look into the list of employees and see if I know anyone who works there. I would try and go through the sheriff's department. But at this point that wouldn't be a good look considering the case is technically closed. I'm sure it'll remain that way until we can present enough evidence to Sheriff Glover convincing him to reopen it."

Elle reached inside the pocket of her black yoga jacket and pulled out her cell phone. "Do you see anything down there?"

"Nope. Nothing."

"I'm gonna call Bryce and see if he's home. If he is, I'll tell him I want to stop by and give him my condolences in person."

"Good idea. Because this crime scene isn't giving us anything."

"Except a morbid feeling of dread," Elle replied as she dialed Bryce's number.

THE FIRST THING Todd noticed when Bryce opened the door was his puffy red eyes. He looked to have dropped a good ten pounds from his five-foot-ten-inch frame.

Todd opened his mouth to speak, but nothing came out. The shock of Bryce's appearance took hold of his brain.

"Bryce, I am so sorry for your loss," Elle said, giving him a warm embrace.

"Thank you," he croaked. "It—it's been tough."

"I can imagine."

Bryce sniffled into a tissue and stepped aside, letting them enter.

The living room was in complete disarray. Half-empty

take-out containers and dirty dishes were strewn about. A pillow and blankets covered the taupe suede couch. The Christmas decorations Taylor normally hung up right after Thanksgiving were still in boxes, scattered around the room.

"Sorry, guys," Bryce said, quickly clearing the sofa. "As you can see, I have been living out of this room. I've barely stepped foot in the bedroom since Taylor..."

His words transitioned into a long sob. Todd reached over and grabbed his shoulder.

"I am so sorry, man."

"Thanks. I just—I miss my wife. How are you and the family doing? I tried calling your mom this morning, but she didn't pick up."

"Yeah, she's having a tough time. Don't take it personally. My father and I are the only two people she's been able to talk to."

"Understandable. Please, have a seat. I did manage to make a batch of that sweet Christmas tea Taylor loved, with the apple cider and cranberry juice mix. It was our holiday tradition. Even though this year, I've been adding quite a bit of vodka to mine. But anyway, would either of you like a glass?"

"I'd love some," Elle said. "Thanks."

Todd slowly sat down. "I would, too. I'm pretty thirsty. Elle and I just came from the park's hiking trail where Taylor's body was found."

Bryce froze, staring straight ahead as if digesting what Todd just told him. Several moments of silence passed before he shuffled over to the dining room table and poured their tea.

Todd watched his hands closely for signs of nervous trembling. There were none.

"Did you all find anything out there?" Bryce finally asked.

"No, unfortunately. But we're gonna keep looking until we do."

Bryce handed them their glasses, then paced the floor a few times before sitting on the edge of the love seat. "I've actually gone to the scene to see what I could find. I came up empty, too. Then when I went into the station to speak with Sheriff Glover, he told me that his guys combed the area thoroughly. They didn't come up with any evidence proving Taylor's death wasn't accidental."

"So you're okay talking about Taylor's passing?" Elle asked. "Because if not, we won't—"

"No, no," Bryce interrupted. "I'm fine talking about it. I actually *want* to talk about it. Especially with you two. I'd love to get your take on the whole thing."

"Good," Todd said. "You and I haven't really had a chance to discuss any of this. And I honestly feel more comfortable having this conversation outside of the sheriff's department."

"So do I. Because, trust me, it hasn't gone over my head that some folks in Bradford think I had something to do with this. The scrutiny only gets magnified when I'm sitting in the station being questioned by authorities."

Todd propped his elbows onto his knees. "Well, we're not here to interrogate you. We go too far back for all that. We just wanna hear what you think, and try to figure out what really happened to the woman we all loved dearly."

"Absolutely," Bryce choked, pressing his knuckles against the corners of his eyes.

"I know this is hard for you," Elle said softly, "but do you really believe that Taylor stumbled and fell on the trail? Or do you think there's more to her death?"

"At this point, I don't know what to believe. Taylor ran that path almost every day for years. She knew it so well. For her to fall and break her neck on it doesn't make sense to me. Is it possible? Yes. But is it likely? I don't believe so."

Todd observed him closely, looking for any signs of suspicion.

Bryce had broken eye contact the minute Elle asked what he thought really happened to Taylor. He licked his lips several times while rubbing his right palm against his knee. He stared down at the floor, pausing in between sentences as if searching for responses within the fibers of the beige carpeting.

Todd glanced over at Elle. She stared back at him, her eyelids lowered. He had a feeling they were thinking the same thing. Bryce's body language seemed suspicious even if he was agreeing that Taylor's death didn't look accidental.

"So you believe there's a possibility that Taylor's death wasn't accidental?" Todd asked.

"Yes. I do think that's a possibility."

"But who would want to kill Taylor? And why?"

Bryce's breathing quickened. He swiped his hand across his creased forehead, which suddenly appeared damp.

"Look," he began, "I don't wanna wrongly pin my wife's death on anyone. But I will say this. Taylor had been hanging out with this group of women who were involved in some type of money grabbing scheme. I don't know much about it, because Taylor kept a lot of what was going on hidden from me. What I do know is that some of the women were making a lot of money. And in order to make money, you have to spend money, which is where my problem with Taylor came into play."

Todd paused, almost spilling his tea as he raised his glass to his lips.

"Taylor was doing a lot of spending?" Elle asked.

"Yes. To the point where she took out a second mortgage on our house behind my back."

Bryce's cell phone rang. He grabbed it off the coffee table. "I need to take this. Could you please excuse me?"

"Of course."

Todd turned to Elle as soon as Bryce sauntered into the kitchen. "I'm surprised he told us about the second mortgage," he whispered.

"*And* that he had a problem with Taylor's spending. I guess he doesn't think we'd ever suspect him of hurting her."

"It's so convenient that he's pointing the finger at The Precious Jewels. Plus he's supposedly got an alibi. I really need to try and get ahold of his dealership's surveillance footage."

"Yeah, you do," Elle agreed. "Because if Bryce's sweating, heavy breathing and lip licking are any indication of guilt, that man is far from innocent."

Todd glanced down at a pile of bills that were hanging off the glass end table. The word *OVERDUE* had been stamped in red across several of them.

He took a closer look. Charges ranging in the hundreds, a few in the thousands, were highlighted in yellow.

Todd quickly straightened up when Bryce walked back into the living room.

He appeared to have more pep in his step. A bit of a bounce even. The creases in his forehead were gone, as was the sheet of perspiration covering his deep brown skin.

"Sorry for the interruption," Bryce said. "That was my agent calling about Taylor's life insurance policy."

Todd and Elle sat silently, waiting for him to elaborate. He didn't. Instead, he poured himself a glass of tea and took a long sip.

"So," Bryce continued, "like I was saying, Taylor had gotten involved with this secretive women's group that had some sort of strange money scheme going on. She wouldn't tell me anything about it. But when I started seeing all these charges on my credit card bills for extravagant new clothes and shoes, and large charitable donations being made, I knew something was up."

"Hmm, that's interesting," Elle said. "You know, Taylor told me about several of the get-rich schemes she'd invested in over the years. All the work-from-home opportunities, multilevel marketing services, promises to help her open a business. The list was never-ending. But she always had to put money up before she made anything back. Most times, she never turned a profit."

Bryce snorted. "Yeah, tell me about it. My salary was financing all those schemes. Including this last one she was involved in before she died."

Todd noticed a glint in Elle's eyes. He knew she was egging Bryce on in hopes that he'd start spilling more than he intended.

In that moment, he was overcome by a strong mix of admiration and attraction. Seeing Elle in action had him smitten.

"So, Todd," Bryce said. "Has the sheriff's department looked into The Positive Gems yet?"

Todd hesitated.

Don't reveal too much...

"The Precious Jewels," he corrected. "And um…yes. The sheriff's department has looked into the group. As far as I know, nothing suspicious came up."

"Humph." Bryce slammed his glass down onto the coffee table, then stood. "Well, I appreciate you both coming by to check on me. But I need to get going. I was supposed to be at the dealership thirty minutes ago."

They followed him to the door. Elle placed her hand on his arm.

"Thanks for letting us stop by on such short notice. Hang in there. Todd and I are doing everything in our power to get justice for Taylor."

Bryce's body stiffened up. Elle quickly snatched her hand away.

"That—that's good," he stammered. "Keep me posted on whatever you find out."

Both Todd and Elle ignored the request.

"If you think of anything that could help with our investigation," Todd said, "give me a call. No lead is too small."

Bryce nodded as his chin began to quiver. "I will. Oh… wait!" He ran toward one of the end tables and shuffled through the pile of bills.

"What is he doing?" Elle muttered.

"I have no idea."

Bryce pulled out a notebook and handed it to Todd.

"What is this?" he asked.

"A book that Taylor used to track the new members she recruited into The Positive Gems."

Todd opened his mouth to correct him again.

Don't even bother. Just let him finish.

"She kept up with all the names, initiation fees that were paid and what I'm assuming are levels that members reached over time. It's weird. They referred to themselves as different gemstones. Rubies and Emeralds and whatnot. I don't know. I couldn't make sense of it all. But I figured it might offer up some new leads. So I'm handing it off to you two."

"Good looking out," Todd said. "We'll definitely check it out."

"If I think of anything else that might help with the investigation, I'll give you a call."

Todd and Elle said their goodbyes. They didn't speak a word to each other on the way to the car.

As soon as the doors were closed, he turned to her.

"I'm still not convinced that Bryce is innocent in all this."

"Neither am I. He seems to be harboring a lot of anger over the way Taylor mishandled their finances."

"You should've seen the pile of overdue credit card bills

sitting next to the couch. Maybe that's why his mood suddenly lifted after he got that call about Taylor's life insurance policy. I wonder if he's expecting a big payout."

"Could be." Elle closed her eyes and pressed her hand against her forehead. "As far as I'm concerned, Bryce is still a suspect."

"Absolutely. But aside from that, I'm looking forward to attending the charity gala and finding out what The Precious Jewels are all about."

Chapter Six

Elle stood in front of the mirror hanging from the back of her bedroom door. Her hair was slicked back into a flawless bun. Her shimmery nude makeup had been expertly applied by a Lancôme specialist at the mall. The strapless midnight blue dress she'd borrowed from her cousin fit as if it had been designed just for her.

Everything appeared perfect. Except that it wasn't.

"Get your head on straight," Elle told herself.

She sat down on the bed and slipped her feet inside a pair of sparkly silver pumps. Taylor's notebook was lying next to her. It was still open to the page that read more like a journal entry than a recruitment registry.

It was dated five days before her death.

Elle was certain that Bryce had overlooked it. Had he not, maybe he would've thought twice before passing the book on.

She grabbed it and reread the haunting admission for a third time.

I'm afraid. Too afraid to share this with anyone. So I'm pouring it all out right here on these pages. Maybe writing it down will put an end to the harassment. Somehow...

Someone is after me. Messaging me. Emailing me. Following me. Trying to scare me. I know it's one of my recruits. Maybe Sloane was right. Maybe I did open my circle up too wide. Let too many people in. People who weren't right for The Precious Jewels organization.

My recruits are angry with me and I feel terrible about it. But what can I do? They knew what they were getting themselves into. It isn't my fault they haven't been able to enlist new members, move up in the ranks and earn the treasure chest. I've worked my ass off to get to where I am. I earned that treasure, and I shouldn't feel guilty now that it's my turn to collect it. And not half of it this go round. ALL of it. My recruits should be inspired, not bitter.

But someone is angry. Angry enough to threaten my life. They don't want to see me win. They'd rather see me dead.

I can't go to the police. They'll dig too deep and find a way to disband our organization. I refuse to ruin this opportunity, for myself or my fellow sisters.

I'm finally where I want to be in life. It's my time. I deserve this. I will get rich or die trying. Scared or not, I refuse to let empty threats stop me.

I am going to press on toward the goal. Collect the treasure chest. Then move on to bigger and better things...

A teardrop fell onto the page, smudging the black ink. Elle didn't realize she'd been crying.

Stop it. Put the book away. Focus on tonight and the mission at hand.

But Elle was having a hard time following her own advice. Taylor's message was so unsettling. Especially the ending.

What bigger and better things were you moving on to?
Elle's phone buzzed just as she picked up her clutch.

Her heart thumped. She checked the caller ID. It was Todd.

She sighed with relief.

"Hey," Elle rasped. "What's up?"

"I'm heading your way now. Are you ready to hit this gala and do your thing?"

Elle's eyes fell to the floor. She cleared her throat. "Yep. I'm ready."

Todd went silent for a moment.

"Wait, what's going on?" he asked. "Are you okay?"

"Yeah!" she blurted out too eagerly. "I mean, yes. I'm good. Why?"

"Because you sound strange. Like something's bothering you."

Just tell him...

Elle stood and began pacing the floor. "I...um... I received a weird phone call today. Voice mail, actually. Someone called me anonymously and I didn't pick up. So they left a message."

"*Okay...*what did the message say?"

"That they know what I'm doing. And if I don't stop, I won't make it out of the next attack alive."

Todd grunted into the phone. "The next attack? What the hell is that supposed to mean?"

"That whoever called had something to do with the crash at the forest preserve, and they're planning the next move against me."

Elle's legs trembled uncontrollably. She stumbled over to her vanity and slumped down onto the white wooden stool.

"Was it a man or a woman?"

"I couldn't tell."

"Well, what did the person's voice sound like?" Todd asked.

"Very eerie. And deep. But cartoonish. Like they were speaking into one of those devices that disguise your voice."

Elle grabbed a tissue and dabbed it along her forehead. "Isn't it ironic that I got that call right after we went to visit Bryce?"

"It is. Or it could just be a coincidence. Either way, we'll get to the bottom of it. But in the meantime, you need to be careful. Somebody's obviously watching you. Keep your eyes open. Be mindful of how you move around town. Of course I'll be looking out for you, as well."

"Thanks, Todd. I'm just… I'm nervous."

"That's understandable. But trust me, you and I will get to whoever is behind this before they get to you. You're a highly skilled private investigator. I'm a former marine turned deputy sheriff. Together, we're a force to be reckoned with."

A surge of confidence shot through Elle's chest. She stood, grabbed her clutch and headed to the living room. "I need that reminder, Todd. Sometimes I forget to stand in my power."

"Never forget that, my friend. Listen, I'm pulling up to your house now. Are you ready?"

"I am. Let's do this."

TODD WRAPPED HIS arm around Elle's waist and led her up the Bradford Cultural Center's winding marble staircase. She held on to the railing, careful not to disrupt the decorative cedar garland.

All eyes were on the pair when they reached the landing. Elle glanced around the vast lobby, taking in the elegant Christmas decor. Snowy wreaths hung from the walls, and large red poinsettias stood at each ballroom entryway.

A twelve-foot-tall Douglas fir stood in the corner. Its twinkling lights and crystal ornaments shone brightly as guests took photos in front of the majestic tree.

Elle was surprised when Todd's hand remained on the small of her back. His touch caused a tingling sensation to dance across her skin. She forced herself to ignore it and focus on the smiling faces greeting them while they walked through the atrium.

This is not a date. Stay focused on why you're here...

But that wouldn't be easy. Elle had almost forgotten the reason they were attending the gala the moment Todd showed up at her house.

His freshly trimmed hair and goatee framed his handsome face perfectly. His slim-fitting tuxedo accentuated his muscular physique. The sexy scent of bergamot lingered on his neck. The sensual way in which he'd clutched her hand while helping her to the car was reminiscent of a date night versus an investigative mission.

It didn't help matters when Todd kept telling her how beautiful she looked.

"*Hello*, Earth to Elle."

She snapped back into the moment as Todd led her inside the grand ballroom.

"Did you hear me?" he asked.

"No, I'm sorry. What'd you say?"

"I asked if you'd like a glass of champagne." He stopped and turned to her. "Are you sure you're okay?"

"I'm fine." She gazed out at the crowd, watching as partygoers laughed, danced and drank with one another. "I was just thinking about how nice it would be if we were here under different circumstances. More pleasant circumstances. With Taylor by our side."

Todd inhaled sharply. "I know. But she's here with us in spirit. Seems like I can feel her presence everywhere I go."

"Same here. I'm just hoping her spirit will lead us in the right direction with this investigation."

"Knowing Taylor, I'm sure it will."

A server walked by carrying a tray filled with glasses of champagne.

"Would either of you like a cocktail?" she asked.

"I'd love one," Elle said. "Thank you."

She and Todd took two flutes, then slowly circled the room.

"Why don't we go and check out the items that are up for auction?" he asked.

"Good idea. I think some of the women standing over by the jewelry table were in that photo of The Precious Jewels Rachel showed me." Elle ran her hands along the sides of her dress and squared her shoulders. "Time for me to go and work my magic."

"I'm right beside you."

They strolled over to the far end of the ballroom, past the oil paintings of the town's past politicians hanging on the carved wood paneling.

Elle casually approached the table and gazed at the sparkling earrings, necklaces and bracelets. She pretended to read through the descriptions of each piece while listening in on the women's conversation.

"Did you put in a bid for the vacation in Oahu?" one of them asked.

"The one that Suzanne and her husband donated? Absolutely not. You couldn't pay me to stay in that run-down shack they like to call a picturesque plantation home."

The trio burst into a fit of cackling snorts.

"Wow, tough crowd," Todd murmured.

"They sound more like a herd of laughing hyenas than a group of sophisticated ladies. I can't believe Taylor would've wanted to be around women like that."

"You know my sister. She was a wonderful person who had a penchant for the finer things in life. Unfortunately, she was willing to go to any length to attain them."

"Ladies!" someone shrieked. "I am so sorry I'm late! The couture seamstress I hired to alter my dress made a complete mess of it. I had to pull this old rag out the back of my closet at the last minute. I am so embarrassed!"

Elle watched through the corners of her eyes as the woman ran her perfectly manicured hands, which were draped in vintage cocktail rings, over her size zero frame. Her floor-length black silk dress appeared to be brand-new. A stunning pearl and rhinestone belt cinched her tiny waist.

"So," she continued, "please, pardon my tardiness."

"Oh, come on, Sloane," one of the women said. "You know you look marvelous."

"And I'm sure you don't need any of us to tell you that," another chimed in.

Elle leaned in and whispered in Todd's ear, "Sloane Whitlock is the founder of The Precious Jewels."

"Got it."

Sloane flipped her sleek platinum blond bob over her shoulder and waved her friends off. "You all are just saying that to make me feel better. But keep going. Because it's working!"

A rotund brunette came waddling over to the group.

"Ladies!" she wheezed while tugging at her tight floral gown. "Have you seen any new prospects here tonight? The Precious Jewels are in desperate need of new members."

"I just arrived not too long ago," Sloane told her. "So I haven't had a chance to make my rounds just yet. But my eyes and ears are definitely open."

Elle grabbed an onyx choker off the table and held it to her neck. "What do you think of this piece?" she asked Todd. "It's gorgeous, isn't it? I've got some extra cash to play around with, plus the proceeds will go toward a good cause, so…"

The group of women fell silent. Elle could feel their eyes on her. She acted as if she didn't notice.

Todd reached out and touched the delicate stones. Her skin shivered beneath the warmth of his fingertips.

"I think it looks beautiful," he said. "Let's bid on it."

Sloane pushed her friends aside and slowly approached Elle.

"Excuse me, but I don't think we've met. My name is Sloane Whitlock. I'm on the board of directors here at the cultural center. And you are?"

"Elle. Elle Scott. It's nice to meet you."

"Likewise," Sloane purred, gently shaking her hand. "And your husband is right. That choker looks absolutely stunning on you."

"Thank you. But this isn't my husband. He's actually—"

"Todd Jacobson," the chubby redhead interrupted. "Taylor's brother. I remember meeting you at the funeral." She grabbed his hand. "Oh, honey, I am so sorry for your loss. How are you and your family holding up?"

"We're hanging in there. Thank you for asking."

Elle peered over at Sloane. Her gaunt cheeks reddened underneath streaks of bronzer. Her overly plumped lips parted, then tightened, then parted again, as if she wanted to say something but couldn't find the words.

What are you holding back?

"So," Elle said to her, "you think I should bid on this choker?"

Sloane pressed her hand against her bony chest. "I certainly do. It's gorgeous. *You're* gorgeous. I'd say you two are a match made in heaven."

"Aw, how sweet. Thank you."

"I don't believe I've ever seen you here at our charity event. Is this your first time?"

"Yes, it is. I grew up in Bradford but moved to New York years ago. I rarely get back to town for the holidays. But this year was different. I'm so glad I was able to come home and spend it with my family."

"Ah, very nice. New York is one of my favorite cities in the world. What is it that you do there?"

"I...um—I'm a consultant," Elle lied. "An image consultant."

"And how long will you be in town?"

"I'm not sure. Right now, indefinitely. I haven't seen my family in quite some time, so I'd like to stick around for a while."

Elle could feel Sloane scrutinizing her. Making sure she was someone worthy of an invitation into her fold.

Keep doing what you're doing. It's working.

"I'm also looking forward to reconnecting with old friends," she continued. "But so many of them have moved away or are too busy preparing for the holidays to socialize. I'm glad I was able to attend this event tonight. Maybe I can connect with some new people."

Sloane's Cheshire-cat grin widened. "Speaking of this event, how did you find out about it? Through your friend Todd?"

"No, actually. An old friend from high school. Rachel Bennett. You may know of her."

"Oh, yes. Rachel Bennett. The Museum of Contemporary Art's curator. I do know of her. We've actually met several times. I've invited Rachel to tea on numerous occasions. But she's a very busy woman. Unfortunately, we haven't been able to connect. Yet..."

"I may be able to help you with that," Elle said while filling out her bid sheet.

"That would be lovely."

The women were interrupted when a man walked over and tapped Sloane on the shoulder.

"My apologies for the interruption, ladies. Mrs. Whitlock, our chairman would like for the board of directors to join him onstage."

"Thank you, Fredrick. I'll be there in a moment."

Sloane reached inside her black Judith Leiber clutch and pulled out a business card.

"It was very nice meeting you, Elle. I'm hosting a private event at my home next week and would love for you to attend. My phone number is on the card. Call me. I'll share the details then. Feel free to invite Rachel, as well."

"That is so nice of you, Sloane. Thank you. I'll be in touch."

"By the way," Sloane whispered, "don't spend all of that extra cash you mentioned here at the auction. I've got a lucrative opportunity that'll provide a hell of a lot more than anything you'll find here."

She gave Elle a wink, then slunk off. The other women hurried behind her.

"Um, what just happened?" Elle asked Todd.

"Looks to me like your introduction to Sloane and The Precious Jewels was a success. That's what happened."

She clinked her glass against his. "We came. We saw. We conquered. I can't believe I got an invitation to one of their events that quickly."

"Of course you did. You're amazing."

The spark in Todd's eye told Elle he wasn't just referring to her investigative acumen.

"Thank you. Now that our work here is done, why don't we head over to our table and relax?"

Todd held out his arm. "Let me lead the way. I've been looking forward all day to that $250 filet mignon they're serving up."

Elle took his arm and together they walked across the room. "You know what? For the first time since arriving in Bradford, I feel good. I'm getting inside information from Rachel, we've got Bryce on our radar and now I'm in with The Precious Jewels. We're getting closer to finding out what really happened to Taylor."

Todd gave her arm a squeeze. "Yes, we are. And I cannot thank you enough."

"I keep telling you. You don't have to thank me. Taylor meant a lot to me, too. There's no place I'd rather be than here with you, working this case."

Todd stopped at the edge of the dance floor and kissed Elle softly on her cheek. "I appreciate you."

"Same. Now, before I burst into tears, let's do our best to enjoy the rest of the evening."

"Deal."

Chapter Seven

Todd peered around the corner. Sheriff Glover's office lights were out. It was almost 7:00 p.m. Todd assumed he'd gone home for the evening.

There were several deputies scattered around the station, either talking among themselves or focused on their computer screens.

Todd slipped inside the evidence room and closed the door behind him.

Earlier that afternoon, he'd seen a digital file in the department's database titled River Birch Park. There were no documents attached. Todd was determined to find the paperwork connected to the file, considering it was the location where Taylor's body had been found.

During the day, the evidence room was monitored, but after hours, whoever was on shift was supposed to keep an eye on anyone going in and out. The other deputies hadn't seen him slip in.

The evidence room's aisles were arranged in alphabetical order. He peered up at the signs, stopping when he reached the lane marked P-R.

Todd scanned the row of boxes containing files beginning with the letter R. When he tried to grab the first one on the shelf, it jammed between two others. He gave it a good yank. Several boxes went crashing to the floor.

"What the hell was that?" a deputy yelled from the main floor.

Dammit!

Todd froze, praying no one would come back and investigate the noise. Several moments passed. No one showed up.

Thank you.

He eyed the mess he'd made. Files were scattered everywhere. Paperwork had spilled out of several of them.

Todd kneeled and began shoving documents back inside the folders, making sure to keep a lookout for the River Birch Park file.

"One box down, three more to go," he said while placing it back on the shelf. He bent down to refill another when his cell phone rang.

The volume was still turned all the way up from earlier that morning, when he'd been at the gym.

Todd jumped up and snatched the phone from his back pocket. He fumbled with the buttons until the ringing ceased.

"Dude, pull it together," he muttered to himself. "Deputy Jacobson speaking."

"Hey, it's Elle. You got a minute?"

He hesitated. "I do, but I've gotta make it quick. What's up?"

"I just spoke with Sloane. She extended an official invitation to a gathering at her house tomorrow evening. I think it's going to be some sort of Precious Jewels informational. Either way, I'll be there with my checkbook, ready to sign up."

"Excellent. I'm actually in the evidence room right now. I found a digital file labeled River Birch Park that didn't have any docs attached, so I'm trying to find the actual papers."

"River Birch Park, huh. Interesting. Why would the documents be missing? Is someone trying to hide something?"

"Maybe," Todd said. "If they are, I'm determined to find it. I'll search this place all night if I have to."

"Good. I'll let you get back to it. I have to call Rachel and beg her to attend this event with me. You know how she feels about The Precious Jewels. But since this is really a ruse that's for a good cause, I'm hoping she'll agree to it."

Todd stooped back down and shoved more files inside a box. "I'm sure she will. Let me know what she says."

"Keep me posted on your end, too. Let me know if you find anything."

"You got it. Talk soon."

As soon as Todd disconnected the call, he saw a file labeled RBP. He grabbed it and shuffled through the contents.

A white envelope slipped out and fell to the floor. Todd picked it up. The envelope was sealed. He hesitated, then tore it open.

A piece of paper was folded neatly inside. It contained a stack of photographs. The first two were images of the River Birch Park's hiking trail. The third was a picture of a massive tulip tree. It looked to be the exact same tree near where Taylor's body had been discovered.

Todd's hands shook as he shuffled through the photos. They appeared to be duplicates of those he'd already seen.

He reached the last pictures, then gasped. His muscles froze as the stack of photos hit the floor.

Todd fell back against the shelf. The cold metal edge dug into his back. He couldn't feel the pain. He was too numb.

He slid to the floor, forcing himself to look at the photo. The gruesome image of a woman's dead body, sprawled out underneath the tulip tree, glared back at him.

It wasn't Taylor.

Flashbacks of his sister's body lying in that very same spot flooded his mind.

"Stop it," he muttered, rubbing his head vigorously in hopes of wiping away the memory.

Todd flipped the picture over. He grabbed the file and shuffled through its contents. The sheriff's death scene report was stuck against the back of a coffee-stained list of evidence collected.

He pulled the papers apart and began reading the report.

The victim's name was Harper Mitchell. Her body had been found on the River Birch Park's hiking trail a little over a year ago. The manner of death was marked accidental. The cause of death—a broken cervical vertebra.

A fractured neck.

Todd slammed the report down and grabbed his phone, frantically dialing Elle's number.

"Hey," she said.

"You're not gonna believe this."

"Not gonna believe what?"

"Another woman died on the same hiking trail where Taylor's body was found."

The other end of the line went silent.

"Elle? Are you still there? Can you hear me?"

"I—I'm here. And I heard you. I'm just…*shocked*. Who is the woman?"

"Her name is Harper Mitchell. Does that ring a bell?"

"No, it doesn't. What happened to her? Is the cause of death listed?"

"Are you sitting down?"

"Uh-oh."

"A broken neck."

"Oh my God," Elle moaned. "What in the world are we dealing with here? Some sort of serial killer?"

"We could be. At this point, I'm not ruling anything out. What concerns me is that I never heard anything about this case. I was still on active duty when Harper died, so I was away from Bradford. But I don't like the fact that no one has mentioned this possible connection to Taylor's death. The cases are so similar. But the department just swept it under the rug."

"It sounds like the report had been hidden away on purpose. Those documents should have been attached to the digital file. Why weren't they?"

Todd flipped through the death scene report. "Good question. I don't know. We need to find out who Harper Mitchell is and what she had going on at the time of her death."

Todd could hear Elle typing away on her keyboard. The tension in his pounding head suddenly eased up.

"Already putting together a master plan, huh?" he asked.

"Of course."

"I've said this before, and I'll say it again. I am so glad to have you on my team."

"And I'm glad to be on it. Now, why don't you make a copy of Harper's file, and I'll contact Rachel to find out if she knows anything about her?"

"Good idea. I'll run a background check on her, too. See what comes up. And on that note, I'd better get the hell out of the evidence room before somebody sees me and I get hit with a bunch of questions."

"Be careful, Todd."

"I will."

Chapter Eight

Sloane stood in front of her Victorian-style great room's bay window, next to the massive Fraser fir Christmas tree. She ran her hands down her cream tweed dress then tapped her fingernail against a champagne glass.

"Ladies, if I could please have your attention."

The chatter ceased immediately. A jazz quartet playing their rendition of "Let It Snow" out in the foyer stopped the music.

Elle and Rachel sat down on a pewter silk love seat positioned near the back of the room.

"First of all," Sloane said, "I'd like to thank everyone for being here today. To all of the new faces in the crowd, welcome. And to those of you who are already members of The Precious Jewels family, welcome back. I'm hoping that our new attendees have had an opportunity to meet their assigned mentors and learn more about our illustrious organization."

"What assigned mentors?" Elle whispered to Rachel.

"I have no idea. I guess we weren't given one."

Elle felt a tap on her shoulder. She spun around and watched as a woman she'd never seen before tiptoed around the love seat and sat down next to her.

"Sorry I'm late," the woman murmured. She gave Elle and Rachel a quick once-over. "I'm Chloe Hale. Your mentor."

"Oh, we were just wondering about that," Elle said, scooting over as the woman continued inspecting them.

Elle was glad she and Rachel wore almost identical navy wool suits. Judging by Chloe's intense scrutiny, appearance was a priority in her book.

"It's nice to meet you. I'm Elle Scott, and this is my friend Rachel Bennett."

Chloe slid forward and waved. "Yes, Rachel and I know one another well. She recently curated a friend's art show at the museum. I'm surprised to see her here. I've invited her to numerous events, but she's always turned me down."

"Hmm…" Elle gave Chloe a polite smile, watching as she pulled her long, honey-blond hair over her shoulder.

Chloe appeared to be in her mid-thirties and was quite beautiful. A violet sheath dress hung from her petite frame. Her porcelain skin was covered in very little makeup. Just a dusting of pale pink blush over her high cheekbones and a layer of sheer lip gloss.

"If anyone has questions," Sloane continued from the front of the room, "please feel free to speak with me or any of our other members. In the meantime, continue to enjoy the Christmas jazz quartet along with the hors d'oeuvres and cocktails."

Sloane rushed over to Elle as soon as she was done speaking.

"Hello! I'm so glad you could make it. And, Rachel, thank you for joining us. As you know, you're high on the list of Precious Jewels' potential members."

"So I've heard," Rachel replied through clenched teeth. Elle discreetly nudged her arm.

"But I'm so happy to have finally found the time to attend an event," Rachel continued, sweetly this time. "From what I've gathered, it's a wonderful organization."

"Why, thank you. That means a lot, coming from someone as impressive as you. I've assigned Chloe as a mentor for both you and Elle. You'll be under the tutelage of one of our finest members. Chloe, have you had a chance to tell these ladies about The Precious Jewels and all of its great benefits?"

"Not yet. I arrived a bit late. But I'm planning to do so right now."

"Excellent. I'll leave you three to it. Elle, Rachel, be sure to see me before you leave."

"Thank you again for having us."

Chloe took a sip of her cranberry-orange mimosa. "Listen, ladies, I'm going to give you the real scoop on The Precious Jewels. This organization is amazing. It's filled with wealthy, accomplished women who have provided me with endless networking opportunities. The social aspects are great, too. These women know how to throw a party. And then there are the generous charitable contributions. So heartfelt, and so satisfying." She held her hand to the side of her mouth and added, "Not to mention they're a nice tax write-off."

"That all sounds fantastic," Elle said.

"Trust me, it is. But that's not even the best part."

"Ooh, there's more?" Rachel asked.

Her tone dripped with sarcasm. Elle resisted the urge to give her another nudge.

"Yes," Chloe breathed. "Much more. The Precious Jewels also offers its members an opportunity to generate a nice stream of residual income. But as they say, you have to pay to play. Entry into The Precious Jewels will cost you."

"How much, exactly?" Elle asked.

"Five thousand dollars."

Elle reached over and pinched Rachel's thigh before she could say a word.

"And in order to gain membership, you're required to bring in at least one recruit. That's how the organization grows and builds what we call the treasure chest."

Chloe drained her glass. "So, does that sound like something you two would be interested in?"

Elle reached inside her purse and pulled out her checkbook. "Yes, it certainly does." She turned to Rachel. "And you'll join with me as my recruit?"

"I sure will."

"Yay!" Chloe squealed, frantically clapping her hands. "So, here's a quick breakdown of how all this works. You ready?"

"Ready," Elle replied enthusiastically while Rachel followed with a lackluster "Yep."

"Okay, so Elle, once your membership is accepted, you and Rachel will be initiated into The Precious Jewels and considered what we call Sapphires. As you recruit new members, and your recruits bring in new members, you'll climb up the pyramid, going from Sapphires to Emeralds, then Rubies, and finally, *Diamonds*. Once you reach Diamond status? That's when you'll become eligible to cash out on your investment and receive the $150,000 treasure chest."

"Wow," Rachel uttered. "That's a lot of money. What is your current status?"

"Right now I'm back to being a Sapphire."

"Really?" Elle asked. "How is that? Haven't you been a member of the organization long enough to have reached a higher status?"

Chloe smiled stiffly. "Let's step out onto the deck. Where we'll have a little more privacy."

She stood and strolled through the great room. Elle and Rachel threw one another inquisitive looks before following her.

On the way to the kitchen, Chloe was stopped by a fellow group member. As they chatted, Elle tugged Rachel's sleeve.

"Hey," she whispered, "I've been meaning to ask, were you able to find anything out about Harper Mitchell?"

"Oh, yes! I was so caught up in trying to get here on time that I forgot to mention it. My sister was familiar with Harper because she banked at Bradford Financial. Harper was originally from North Carolina, but traveled back and forth between here and Florida for her husband's job. Then she filed for divorce and got her own place in Bradford. Harper shared that she was expecting a generous settlement. But she died before the divorce was finalized."

"Oh, wow. That's interesting. I wonder if Todd received the results on her background check. They may be delayed since she was living state to state—"

Elle stopped abruptly when Chloe walked back over.

"My apologies for the interruption, ladies. Please, follow me."

She led them through a luxurious all-white kitchen out onto the deck.

"This yard is beautiful," Elle said, eyeing the vast area. Sparkling icicle lights hung from the tall bamboo privacy fence. Bright blue viburnum shrubs and yellow winter jasmine plants surrounded a stunning gazebo. Solar fairy lights filled the deck's glass lanterns.

"Please, have a seat," Chloe said, pointing toward a set of sleek beige lounging chairs. "There are some things I'd like to share with you both. First of all, to answer your questions, Elle, I did in fact reach Diamond status not too long ago. Then I cashed out on my investment and received the treasure chest. After that happened, I dropped back down to Sapphire status and started the process all over again. That's how the income cycle works."

"Okay," Rachel said slowly. "Why would you need privacy to tell us that? Isn't it known knowledge among the members of the group?"

Chloe looked away and began fiddling with her platinum tennis bracelet. "It is. But the way that I attained the treasure chest was somewhat controversial."

"Why is that?" Elle asked.

"Because... Taylor Jacobson was my mentor."

Elle gripped the arms on her chair.

Don't say a word. Just let her finish.

"Taylor was the one who recruited me into The Precious Jewels. I came in with her, just like Rachel is coming in with you, Elle. Taylor should have collected the treasure chest instead of me. She'd worked *so* hard to get there, too..."

Chloe's voice trailed off.

"It's okay," Elle told her. "Please, go on."

"I'm not sure how much you two know. But...um... Taylor was out for a run one afternoon and stumbled on the hiking trail. She fell and broke her neck. I still can't believe she's gone."

Chloe dropped her head. Tears trickled down her cheeks, streaking her pale pink blush. "And that's how I collected the treasure chest. It was really Taylor's money. She should still be here, enjoying her earnings."

"She really should," Rachel interjected. "How unfortunate that she isn't."

Sloane appeared in the doorway. "Excuse me, ladies. I'm sorry to interrupt, but we're ready to begin the initiation process. Elle, Rachel, are you two prepared to become official members of The Precious Jewels?"

"Yes, we are," Elle said, quickly dabbing at her damp eyes.

"Wonderful!" Sloane pressed her hands together. "Once we're done, we'll all celebrate over Veuve Clicquot and eggnog crème brûlée. I'll meet you ladies in the living room in a moment. Chloe, could you please join me and the other Precious Jewels in the dining room?"

"Yes, of course."

Elle and Rachel hung back on the deck while the women went inside the house.

"I do not have a good feeling about these women, Elle. Especially this Chloe chick. There's something sinister going on here. I can literally feel the underlying current of greed, jealousy and superficiality running through this entire operation."

"So can I. Isn't it interesting that Taylor died right before she was set to collect that treasure chest?"

"Of course it is! It took everything in me not to dig deeper and interrogate Chloe. *Taylor stumbled on the trail. Girl, please…*"

The two friends slowly walked back inside the house.

"I'm glad you didn't interrogate her," Elle said. "We've got to remain low-key and play the game. Not show our hand. Maintain that poker face of yours while we infiltrate this group and get some answers."

ELLE'S CELL PHONE buzzed on the way home from Sloane's house. She stopped at a red light and swiped open her home screen.

A text message from Sloane appeared.

Thank you again for attending our event, and welcome to The Precious Jewels! Remember, ladies, discretion is key. What goes on within our organization stays within our organization. Please do not share any information with anyone. That goes for husbands, family members and friends alike. Again, welcome to the club. You're going to love it here. All my best, Sloane Whitlock

A horn blasted behind Elle. She looked up, realizing that the light had turned green.

Elle hit the accelerator and sped down the dark road. She approached a stop sign and glanced in the rearview mirror. The car that had blared its horn came careening toward her.

"Stop!" Elle screamed just as the driver slammed on the brakes inches away from her bumper.

The vehicle's screeching tires pierced her ears. Its headlights flooded inside her car.

She was triggered.

Elle squeezed the steering wheel, twisting her palms along the smooth leather.

This cannot be happening again...

She glanced to her right. Bright lights shone down on Green Avenue, illuminating the shiny new cars parked throughout the Capital Motors lot.

Elle made an abrupt turn down the street and prayed that the looming vehicle wouldn't follow her.

She sped toward the dealership, quickly glancing in the rearview mirror. The car's engine roared. It peeled off and kept straight.

"Thank God." Elle sighed, pressing her hand against her heaving chest.

She let up on the accelerator. All of the lights were out inside the dealership's offices. It was already after eight o'clock. Business was closed.

Elle stared up at the surveillance cameras positioned throughout the lot. Several of them hung from the pole lights. As she drove closer toward the sales office, Elle noticed cameras lining the corners and center of the roof's edge.

Todd had yet to retrieve surveillance footage from the day Taylor died. Bryce's movements were still unknown. While they waited, Elle figured it would be helpful to know where the cameras were positioned throughout the dealership.

She parked her car along the side street and stepped out. The cool night air was still. And unnervingly silent.

Elle pulled her phone out of her beige trench coat and shuffled toward the lot. Her thin high heels skidded along the grainy asphalt. She wished she'd brought a more comfortable pair of shoes.

But who knew I'd be participating in an impromptu assignment?

Elle climbed through the metal railing and snapped several photos of the sales office's surveillance cameras.

Just as she turned to take pictures of the ones hanging from the pole lights, a pair of headlights appeared.

They crept toward her. Elle tried to get a better look at the vehicle, but she couldn't. The side street was too dark.

Make this quick, then get the hell out of here.

She walked to the back of the lot. Stood in the middle of an aisle and aimed her phone up toward the pole light.

An engine roared loudly.

Elle spun around. A black pickup truck sped into the lot. It resembled the one that had crashed into her at the forest preserve.

No. No. No!

She tried to jump in between a row of cars. But she couldn't move. Her legs were laden with fear.

The truck raced toward her. Elle screamed, unable to budge.

Come on. Come on. Move!

She closed her eyes and braced herself.

This is it. This is how I'm going to die...

She opened her eyes. The pickup was a few feet away from her.

"Stop!" she screamed.

Right before the truck made impact, the driver swerved around Elle.

The passenger door brushed up against her body. Elle fell to the ground and rolled over, clutching her arm in agony.

Get up. Get up!

She attempted to stand. But her legs were too weak. She dragged her body in between two cars. The rough concrete scraped against her bare legs. Elle ignored the pain and focused on getting to safety.

The truck circled the lot. It sped up, then slowed down, then sped up again, like a predator tormenting its prey.

Elle struggled to get a look at the license plate. But there were none mounted on the front or back.

"Please leave me alone," she pleaded. "*Please* leave me alone…"

The driver gunned the engine. Elle recoiled, sliding further in between the cars.

My phone!

She held up her cell, anxiously waiting for the facial recognition to register.

The pickup truck flew around the corner and raced down the aisle where Elle was hiding.

"Come on. *Activate*!" she yelled at the screen.

The truck came to a screeching halt right in front of Elle's hiding spot. She looked up at the black tinted windows, straining to peer inside.

Her phone rang. She jumped at the shrill chime.

Anonymous Caller.

Elle looked back up. She had a feeling that the call was coming from inside the truck.

She tapped the accept button.

"Yes?" she whispered.

"Ah, you answered."

A cold chill seeped through her skin. It was that voice. That deep, creepy, cartoonish voice of the person who'd called the night of the charity gala.

Be strong. Don't back down…

"Who the hell are you? What do you want?"

"First things first. Are you okay? Or did you scar those gorgeous legs of yours when you fell to the ground?"

"I'm fine. Is your truck okay? Or did I dent it when you

hit me? Unfair advantage, using a pickup as a weapon. Why don't you step out and show your face?"

"Oh, you would love that, now, wouldn't you? But no. I'll pass. By the way, I'm the only one making demands tonight. My advice to you? Stop your little investigation and go back to New York before you get yourself killed. Because next time I see you? I won't spare your life like I did tonight."

Elle thought about Taylor. A surge of courage shot through her. She jumped up and ran toward the truck.

"Get out!" she yelled, slamming her hands against the window. "Get out and show your face, you coward!"

The driver revved the engine. Smoke billowed from the tailpipe and surrounded Elle. She choked, barely able to see through the thick fumes.

The truck sped off. Elle stumbled backward, wincing as the rear tire grazed the tip of her shoe.

She struggled to stay on her feet. "You *maniac*!" she hollered.

Elle whimpered as she limped back to her car. She finally unlocked her phone and dialed Todd's number. It went straight to voice mail.

"Todd," she moaned, "I've been attacked again. Meet me at my parents' house as soon as you get this message."

Chapter Nine

"I don't know how much more of this I can take, Todd."

"Come on, Elle. You can do this. *We* can do this. Don't give up on me now."

The pair were sitting on his backyard's Asian-inspired heated deck. Several days had passed since her attack, and she was still shaken up.

Todd had hoped that inviting Elle over for grilled Cajun shrimp and sausage kebabs would help lift her spirits.

She did seem to appreciate the fresh orchid arrangement that served as the centerpiece, the slim bamboo waterfall gurgling softly in the corner and the stone lanterns shining brightly along the yard's pathway. But despite the soothing ambience, Elle still appeared frazzled.

She pulled her wringing hands apart long enough to re-fill their glasses with Chablis.

"Don't get me wrong," she began. "I'm not saying that I'm giving up. But I *am* getting tired. Law enforcement can't seem to find my attacker, who's doing an excellent job of finding me. I'm still mad over the shoddy investigation into Taylor's death. Then we find out that a similar death occurred in the exact same location almost a year to the day Taylor died. I feel like that case was deliberately kept from you. I mean, what's really going on with our sheriff's department? Is it just sloppy work or something else?"

"I have no idea. But you're absolutely right. Seems like

we can't catch a break. I still haven't heard back from Dr. Wu on whether or not he's reached out to Sheriff Glover. I'll call his office again tomorrow morning and see if I can get through to him."

"What about the surveillance from the car dealership? Any luck in contacting someone about footage from the day Taylor died and the night I was attacked?"

Todd shook his head. "I'm so sorry, Elle. I've been waiting for the right time to tell you that all of the footage was taped over before anyone had a chance to review it."

"On both occasions?"

"Yes."

"Ugh!" Elle groaned. "How the hell did that happen? And how did you find out?"

"Deputy Cross knows a security guard who works at the dealership. I talked him into reaching out and asking for his help. The guard admitted that the staff is very lackadaisical when it comes to reviewing the surveillance. You already know the sheriff's department never requested footage from the day Taylor died. As for the night you were attacked, by the time it was ordered, it had already been recorded over."

Elle dropped her head in her hand. "I feel like we're fighting a losing battle here."

"Come on, E. Don't give up hope. Trust me. We will get to the bottom of all this. It's just gonna take some time. Don't forget, you and I are going at it alone. We don't have the power of law enforcement behind us. But we're still a force. We can do this."

She looked up, her expression softening. He reached over and squeezed her hand.

"You're right," she said. "We can do this. I won't give up."

"That's my girl." He paused, slowly releasing her hand. "Listen, there's something else I need to say."

"I'm listening," Elle said before plucking a shrimp off a bamboo skewer and popping it inside her mouth.

"I don't want you going out on any more of these solo missions. It's too dangerous. I could've easily gone to the dealership with you to take photos of the cameras."

"I know. But it was a last-minute decision that I made on a whim."

"Which is even more dangerous, Elle. Trying to pull off an unplanned operation like that just isn't wise. Especially now that you know someone is following you. You've got to be more careful. I need to keep a closer eye on you, too."

She gave him a salute. "Sir, yes, sir. I hear you, Deputy Jacobson. Loud and clear."

"Oh, so you're gonna go all formal on me now? Don't tease me, woman. I'm being serious."

"I know you are. I'm just being respectful of your orders. But anyway, what's going on with Harper's background check? Any updates?"

"I reached out to a former marine buddy of mine who works for Miami-Dade County Corrections Department. He's gonna run the checks on Harper and her estranged husband. See if anything comes up since they were spending a lot of time in Florida. I'm hoping to hear from him by the end of the week."

"If anything substantial comes back, would you feel comfortable presenting that plus all of the other evidence we've collected to Sheriff Glover in hopes that he'll reopen Taylor's case? Even without Dr. Wu's recommendation?"

"I most certainly would."

"Good." Elle reclined in her bronze wicker chair and stared out at Todd's ranch-style home, which he'd inherited once his parents moved into a nearby retirement community. "You know, it feels good being back here. I spent so many years running around this yard, playing with Taylor and the rest of our little crew."

"Yeah, I remember those days well. Life was good back then, wasn't it?"

"It really was…"

Elle's expression fell as her downturned lips began to tremble.

Say something. Anything!

"You know," Todd said, "there is one thing that's missing around here."

"What's that?"

"Christmas decorations."

Elle sat up and looked around. "I hadn't even noticed. This house used to be the most festive on the block. Your parents went all out during the holiday season. What did they do with all those ornaments?"

"They're still here, tucked away in one of the spare bedroom closets. I thought about setting them out, just to brighten up the place. But this year, I haven't been in the merriest of moods. For obvious reasons."

"Of course. Neither have I."

Todd drank the last of his wine, then stood. "I have an idea."

"And what might that be?"

"Why don't we decorate the place? I mean, we don't have to go all out like my parents did. Maybe just put a few things up. I kept the faux Fraser fir stored in the basement. All of the lights, ornaments and wreaths are boxed up inside that closet I mentioned. And I was gonna save this for later, but, I went to Cozy's this afternoon and picked up some gingerbread hot chocolate and butter snowflake cookies for dessert."

A slight smile crept across Elle's lips. "Are you really trying to seduce me with Gigi's delicious desserts in order to get your house decorated?"

"Ha! I might be. Is it working?"

The pair burst out laughing.

"Whatever your intentions are," Elle said, "they worked." She picked up her plate and glass. "Come on. Let's clear these dishes and get to work."

"Yes, ma'am."

Todd's body felt lighter as he followed Elle inside the house. While they were both grieving the loss of Taylor, having Elle there was certainly making the process much easier.

TODD CRACKED OPEN a plastic container filled with silver bells, crystal icicles and iridescent snowflake ornaments.

"Ooh, these are gorgeous," Elle breathed.

"Taylor and my mom handpicked all of those." He stood back and crossed his arms over his chest. "We're doing a hell of a job on this tree, aren't we?"

"We are. It looks stunning."

"I'm sure you remember how much Taylor loved Christmas. You hadn't been home for the holidays in years, so you never attended one of her tree trimming parties. She'd host two of them. One at her place, and one here. That woman went all out for both, too. She handpicked most of these orname—"

Todd's voice broke. He closed his eyes. "I still can't believe she's gone," he whispered.

Elle wrapped her arms around him. Her soft, warm touch eased the strain running through his tense shoulder blades.

"I know," she said. "I can't believe it, either. But look at us, cherishing her memory by continuing her tradition. How ecstatic would Taylor be knowing that we're celebrating the season together and hanging her decorations?"

"She'd love it."

Elle grabbed their mugs of hot chocolate and handed one to Todd. "Gigi really outdid herself with the holiday treats this year."

"Yes, she did," he replied, appreciating her attempt to lighten the mood.

"I think I ate about six of those butter cookies."

"That's okay." His eyes roamed Elle's body. Her curves were accentuated in a fitted mint green sweater and black leather leggings. "You look great. A few cookies won't hurt. Plus, it's the holidays. Calories don't count during this time of year, remember?"

She bent down and pulled a snowflake from the container. "I wish that little joke of mine was true. Try telling it to my waistline."

A warm sensation stirred below his black leather belt. Todd turned away and took a gulp of hot chocolate, burning his tongue in the process.

"Once we hang this box of ornaments," Elle said, "I think that's it. There won't be an inch of free space left on this tree."

Todd grabbed a handful of silver bells. He approached the tree just as Elle spun around. Her breasts brushed up against his chest.

She jumped back, almost falling into the tree. Todd caught her just in time.

"Ooh!" Elle squealed, clutching his shoulders. "I am so sorry. I wasn't paying attention and didn't see you coming when I—"

"Hey, calm down. It's okay. The tree is still standing and we're both fine."

Her hands drifted from his shoulders to his forearms. "Thanks. I need to relax. I freaked out imagining this gorgeous tree crashing to the floor."

"We'd just have to pick it up and start all over again."

Todd felt drawn to Elle's vulnerability. It was a side of her that he rarely saw. She was always so tough.

"So you're good?" he asked.

"I think so. Just a little flustered. Maybe I drank too much wine…"

"Or maybe it's me," he boldly suggested.

Their mouths were inches apart. Todd could smell the sweet scent of gingerbread on her breath.

Go for it…

He gently pulled her toward him. Their lips lightly touched, and he waited, silently asking for permission. Within seconds, the kiss intensified. All of Todd's worries melted into that moment.

His cell phone buzzed inside his pocket. They both jumped back, startled by the vibration.

"I am so sorry," he panted, digging for it. "Just give me a minute."

Elle's hands fell to her sides. "No worries."

He could hear the disappointment in her tone. The disruption made him want to punch a hole in the wall.

"This is Jacobson," he barked into the phone as Elle fiddled with a miniature snow globe.

"What's up, Todd? This is Ryan. Listen, I got the results on those background checks you requested."

Todd signaled Elle over and put the call on speaker.

"Really? That was fast. What'd you find out?"

"Harper's came back clean. But her ex-husband, Keaton? Not so much. He was arrested for domestic violence and disorderly conduct early last year."

"Were there any details attached to the charges?"

"There were. According to the report, Keaton violated the order of protection that Harper had taken out on him while they were in the middle of their divorce proceedings. He showed up at her place of residence. A struggle ensued, and he allegedly tried to strangle her. A neighbor saw what was going on and called the authorities."

"Damn," Elle whispered. She grabbed her phone and began taking notes.

"Did law enforcement note Keaton's motive behind the attack?" Todd asked.

"They did. According to Harper, he was angry over the divorce settlement."

"Got it. Thanks, Ryan. That'll definitely give us something to work with. Would you mind emailing that report to me?"

"Make sure he sends it to your personal email address," Elle whispered.

Todd gave her a thumbs-up.

"I'll text you my personal email address. You can send it there."

"Will do. If you need anything else on my end, just give me a holler, brother. Oorah."

"Oorah."

Todd disconnected the call. He and Elle stared at each other in disbelief.

"Unreal," Todd uttered. "On one hand, we've uncovered a possible motive behind Harper's death. But on the other hand, if her estranged husband murdered her, that wouldn't have anything to do with Taylor's case."

"Right. But how weird is it that their bodies were found in the exact same location and their causes of death matched?"

"It's very weird."

"This case is getting more and more twisted by the day." Elle glanced at her watch. "It's getting late. I should probably get going."

Todd hesitated. He was hoping they would pick up where they'd left off before Ryan's call. Clearly the mood had shifted. At least for Elle.

"Okay," he muttered reluctantly. "Let me get you home."

"Thank you again for dinner. And dessert. And the impromptu tree trimming party."

"The pleasure was all mine," Todd said, wishing the night didn't have to end.

Chapter Ten

Sloane approached the portable cherrywood podium positioned in the front of her great room and banged her gavel against the sound block. "Ladies, please. Let's settle down. I'd like to call this meeting to order."

The room fell silent.

"Good morning. Welcome to The Precious Jewels' sisterly sit-down. I'd like to extend an especially warm welcome to all of our new members."

A round of applause ensued. Seasoned Jewels smiled and waved at the newbies. Elle and Rachel nodded their heads politely.

"Ew, this is so phony," Rachel mumbled through her stiff grin.

"Just play the role and remember that it's only temporary."

"Now," Sloane said, "let me start by saying how proud I am of our group's growth. We have recently initiated several outstanding women into our distinguished organization. Our recruitment efforts have afforded us endless opportunities. Whether you're looking to enhance your social circle, charitable footprint or financial status, The Precious Jewels can turn those goals into a reality."

Elle heard someone sitting behind her snort loudly.

"Yeah, speak for yourself, sweetie," the woman muttered. Elle glanced over her shoulder. A slender brunette with a spiked pixie haircut and face full of chalky makeup was slouched down in her chair, picking at her bright red acrylic nails.

"While we may all have different objectives in mind," Sloane continued, "there is one thing that each and every one of us cherishes. And that is our *sisterhood*. What do I mean by sisterhood?" She stepped away from the podium and walked around the room. "I mean bonding. Providing support for one another. Being a shoulder to lean on. Cry on. Whatever our fellow Jewel may need at any given moment."

"Are you kidding me with this crap?" the brunette ranted under her breath.

Rachel nudged Elle's arm. "Whoever this woman is sitting behind us, we need to talk to her."

"Mmm-hmm," Elle agreed, keeping her eyes glued to Sloane.

"For those of you who have moved to the next levels toward that treasure chest, congratulations. And for those of you whose movement has stalled, don't give up. Keep working hard to recruit new members. If you're having trouble doing so, book a training session with one of our highly skilled recruitment specialists who can help you—"

Sloane was interrupted when the brunette burst out cackling. "Yeah, and how much is that session gonna cost us?"

Sloane stopped in the middle of the floor. "Sara, we have not yet reached our Q and A segment. Once we do, feel free to ask any questions that you may have. But until then, please respect those who are speaking. Thank you."

"Whatever. *Little Miss High-and-Mighty...*"

Sloane threw her a look before continuing. "As I was saying, if you're having trouble recruiting new members, schedule a meeting with one of our specialists. Their track records speak for themselves."

A woman sitting near the bay window waved her hand

in the air. "I don't mean to toot my own horn or anything, but *beep beep!*"

Everyone laughed and applauded.

"That's right, Linda!" Sloane exclaimed. "You deserve to toot that horn of yours. You are one of our top recruitment experts. And I've got the receipts to prove it!"

"Oh, so that bitch can interrupt Queen Sloane," Sara grumbled, "but I can't. Got it."

The room fell silent. Sloane cleared her throat.

"Linda, could you please make the big announcement about our fellow Jewel, Michelle? I need to speak with Sara privately."

"Yes, of course."

Linda jumped up and hurried toward the podium while Sloane marched over to Sara. On the way there, she stopped in front of Elle and Rachel. "Ladies, I am so sorry for the rude interruption. Trust me, this is not a normal occurrence." She glared at Sara. "Nor will it ever be."

"You don't have to apologize on my behalf," Sara shot back. "Just give me back my initiation fee since I'm never gonna cash in on it. What do I have to do? Join your little circle of flunkies over there?" She pointed toward the group of women who'd attended the charity gala with Sloane. "*That'll* never happen. I refuse to kiss your—"

"Sara!" Sloane interrupted. "In the kitchen. Now!"

Sara jumped out of her seat and stormed off.

"Lord, please help me not strangle this woman," Sloane whispered under her breath before going after her.

Elle and Rachel elbowed one another. The room buzzed with hushed chatter.

Linda pounded the gavel.

"Ladies, please! Let's all settle down and get back to the business at hand. We're supposed to be celebrating Michelle Ingram's promotion to Diamond status. Woot woot!"

Linda burst into applause. Her glossy orange lips spread into an exaggerated, joker-like smile.

The rest of the women slowly followed suit, still reeling from Sara's outburst.

"Congratulations, Michelle," Linda continued. "We are all *thrilled* that you're next in line to receive the treasure chest. Now, why don't we take a break and enjoy the cocktails and hors d'oeuvres until Sloane returns?"

Linda stepped away from the podium, her smile quickly fading as she rushed toward the kitchen.

"Girl!" Elle whispered to Rachel, "what have we gotten ourselves into?"

"I have no clue. But had I known The Precious Jewels were this entertaining, I would've joined a long time ago."

"Can you believe Sloane said something about strangling Sara?"

Elle cocked her head to the side. "That was an interesting choice of words. Trust that I made note of it, too."

ELLE AND RACHEL teetered down Sloane's winding driveway, holding on to one another so as to not topple over in their five-inch pumps. When they reached the curb, Sara waved at them from across the street.

"Hey! You two got a sec?"

"We sure do," Rachel replied, grabbing Elle's hand and shuffling over the asphalt.

Sara took a long pull from her cigarette, then leaned against a run-down gray sedan. "You all look nice."

"Thanks, so do you," Elle lied, eyeing her ill-fitting mustard suit and beat-up ballet flats.

Sara tugged at her blazer's tattered hemline. "You, um, you don't remember me, do you?"

Elle squinted, then shook her head. "Your face looks a bit familiar, but no. Have we met?"

"Sort of. We went to high school together. I was a few

years behind you. And…let's just say we didn't run in the same circles, if you know what I mean."

"Oh…okay." Elle opened and closed the flap on her tan suede clutch, racking her brain for a subject change.

"So, Sara," Rachel said, "how did you end up becoming a member of The Precious Jewels?"

"Ha!" Sara chortled. "Good question. I know what you're thinking. I know I don't fit in with these hoity-toity bitches. But I needed some money. *Bad.* I met this really cool chick who promised she could help me make some quick cash. So, like a fool, I believed her. I did what she suggested, took out a second mortgage on my house and joined the group."

"I heard you mention that you haven't earned any money back on your initiation fee," Elle said.

Sara blew a stream of smoke in the air, then tossed her cigarette butt. "Nope. I haven't. And honestly, how could I? Everybody I know is just as broke as I am. I haven't been able to recruit a single soul into this shady-ass pyramid scheme. And Sloane refuses to refund my money so I can just quit altogether. So basically, I'm screwed. Do you all know my husband would kill me if he found out about the second mortgage? Which is why I have got to get my money back. I wish—"

Sara paused. Her eyes glazed over.

"You wish what?" Rachel asked softly.

"I wish the woman who recruited me was still around. She's the one who got me into this mess. Too bad she can't help get me out of it."

"Who recruited you?" Elle asked.

"Taylor Jacobson."

Elle's stomach dropped.

"She died not too long ago." Sara pointed at Elle. "Wait, weren't you two pretty tight? Seems like I remember you all hanging out a lot during high school."

Elle swallowed the lump of grief creeping up her throat. "Yes. We were."

"Sorry for your loss," Sara muttered.

"How did Taylor convince you to join The Precious Jewels?" Rachel asked.

"Funny story. I was at Capital Motors trying to buy a car. Taylor just so happened to be there, getting chewed out by her husband for whatever reason."

Rachel coughed lightly. Elle threw her a look. The comment hadn't gone over either of their heads.

"Taylor heard that I didn't get approved for a loan, so she chased me down on my way out and told me about this so-called money-making opportunity that would change my life."

Sara paused. She pulled another cigarette out of her pocket and lit it. "If only I knew then what I know now. I would've turned that woman down immediately. This mess has me so stressed out that I started smoking again after quitting three years ago."

"Bye, ladies!" Elle heard someone call out.

She looked up.

Chloe drove by in a silver Range Rover, performing her best beauty pageant wave. "See you all next week!"

Elle and Rachel waved back.

Sara rolled her eyes and flicked her cigarette ashes. "I'd better get out of here. I've gotta pick my husband up from work. We're down to one car, and unfortunately, it's this piece of junk."

"Thanks for being so open with us," Elle said. "I'm looking forward to hearing more of your story."

"No problem. I'm like an open book. As you can see, I don't hold back. With that being said, I'd watch out for that Chloe chick if I were you two. I know she's your little mentor and all, but I don't like her."

"Why not?" Rachel asked. "She seems cool."

Sara wrapped her thin lips around the tip of her cigarette and took a long pull. "I just don't trust her. That whole caring, sugary-sweet act is as fake as Santa Claus. Chloe is all about money. She'll do anything to get it. And I do mean anything."

Elle peered over at Rachel, her brows creased with curiosity.

"Has she done anything illegal that you know of?" Rachel asked.

Sara threw her head back and laughed. "Girl, this whole damn operation is illegal. But that's a conversation for another day. For now, I'll just say that it's awfully coincidental how Taylor died right before she was set to receive the treasure chest. And who got the money instead? *Chloe.*"

"Well, coincidence could be all that there is to it," Elle debated.

"Yeah, okay. Maybe that argument would hold up better if the same situation hadn't happened before."

Elle almost dropped her purse. "What do you mean, if it hadn't happened before?"

"Oh, you sweet, innocent newbie. You two don't even know the half of it. The woman who recruited Taylor into The Precious Jewels died right before she was set to receive the treasure chest. Since Taylor and Chloe were next in line to reach Diamond status, they ended up splitting the money. Then, when the rotation came back around, and Taylor had reached Diamond status again, she died right before she could collect. Who received the money instead? *Chloe.*"

"Wait," Rachel said, "we never heard about another death being linked to The Precious Jewels."

"Of course you didn't. The women in this organization are powerful. And well-connected. Whatever they want swept under the rug *stays* under the rug."

Sara's cell phone buzzed.

"Dammit. That's my husband texting me. We both work

down at the meat processing plant and he took my shift so I could attend this meeting. I was supposed to pick him up twenty minutes ago. I gotta go." She handed Elle her phone. "Here. Add your number. There's a lot more I wanna share with you two."

"Thanks," she said, taking the phone and adding her info. "We'd appreciate that. It'll be good for us to know both sides of The Precious Jewels."

"Both sides? Uh-uh. There's only one side to this. And it ain't good. If I had time, I'd tell you all about how Sloane and Taylor fell out right before Taylor died."

"Excuse me?" Rachel said.

"Look, this situation runs way deeper than you know. Sloane had pretty much cut Taylor off a couple of weeks before her body was found."

"Why?" Elle asked. "Wasn't Taylor one of The Precious Jewels' biggest recruiters? What could she have possibly done to make Sloane that mad?"

Sara's lips curled into a smirk. "That's the problem. Taylor became *too* good of a recruiter."

"That doesn't even make sense. The Precious Jewels are all about bringing in as many members as possible. More members, more money. Right?"

"Right. But in Taylor's case—"

Sara was interrupted when her cell phone buzzed again.

"Listen, I've got to get outta here. Call me. We'll get together somewhere far away from the prying eyes of these women, and I'll tell you everything I know."

She climbed inside the car and attempted to start her engine. It sputtered loudly, then stalled. She punched the steering wheel.

"*Man*, I need a new car! Come on. Not now. Come on!"

Sara turned the key and pressed down on the accelerator. After two more attempts, it finally started.

"Wait!" Elle said right before Sara closed the door. "Before you go, tell us. Who was the other member of The Precious Jewels who died?"

"Her name was Harper. Harper Mitchell."

Chapter Eleven

Todd strolled inside the sheriff's department with Taylor's evidence file tucked securely under his arm.

Be cool. Be confident. Kill!

He ran the Marine Corps motto through his head over and over again on the way to Sheriff Glover's office.

"Good morning, guys," he said to a group of deputies huddled near the break room. "How's everybody doing?"

The men ignored him and continued chatting among themselves.

Todd stopped and turned around. "I said good morning."

A couple of them grumbled something inaudible while the others sipped from their coffee cups, barely looking at him.

Todd waved them off and kept it moving.

He approached Sheriff Glover's office, took a deep breath then knocked on the door.

"Come in!"

Todd stuck his head inside. The sheriff's normally cluttered desk appeared neat and tidy. It was a good sign. Maybe he wasn't too busy for an impromptu chat.

"Good morning, boss. You got a minute?"

He glanced up from his laptop. The handsome, six-four, former Ironman triathlon champion looked more like a professional athlete than a law enforcement officer.

Framed photographs of him crossing finish lines at

triathlons around the world hung from the walls, next to certificates of achievement and pictures with various dignitaries.

"Jacobson," he growled, his full lips twisting into a slight snarl. "Just the man I need to see. Have a seat."

Todd's legs grew heavy with apprehension as he sat down. "You need to see me? What's going on?"

Sheriff Glover ran his hand along his salt-and-pepper goatee. "You tell me. I got a call from the medical examiner's office this morning."

"Really? That's great. So what did you think of Dr. Wu's—"

"That's great? No. That's *not* great. What in the hell would possess you to go behind my back and meet with the coroner? About a closed case that you didn't even work on, no less?"

"I can explain—"

"Hold on. Before you do that, let me say this. I understand that Taylor was your sister. I can only imagine how painful her death has been for you and your family. You're frustrated. You want answers that make sense to *you*. But you have got to respect our department's investigative process and final reporting on the matter."

Todd's knee bounced rapidly. *"On the matter,"* he repeated. "Meaning my sister's death." He stared down at the thin gray carpeting, struggling to choose his words wisely.

"Sheriff Glover, I do respect the department's final reporting. I just don't agree with it. And it's not that I'm studying this case through an emotional lens. Nor a personal one. I'm taking an objective look at the evidence. According to it, we are not dealing with an accidental death here."

Todd's chest swelled with hope when Sheriff Glover sat back and nodded his head.

I've got him. He's hearing me out. Keep going.

"According to Dr. Wu's findings," Todd continued, "Taylor's neck injury could've been caused by manual strangulation rather than an accidental fall. That fractured ankle? It was severe. That plus the muddy footprint left on her sock proves someone may have stomped Taylor's—"

The sheriff held up his hand. "Son, let me stop you right there. First of all, Dr. Wu wasn't able to fully present his findings to me because he called during the middle of my deputies' meeting."

"Did the deputies happen to hear your conversation with him?"

"Yes. They did."

"Interesting. I guess that explains the collective cold shoulder they gave me when I walked in this morning."

"Well, can you blame them? These guys don't like being second-guessed, Jacobson. Especially by a rookie. You think an attacker caused Taylor's neck and ankle injuries? Where's the proof? I can't reopen this case based on a muddy sock. My deputies didn't uncover one shred of physical evidence from that hiking trail proving another person was involved."

Maybe that's because the attacker outsmarted your deputies...

"Not only that," the sheriff continued, "but our former medical examiner, who'd been on the job for over forty years, declared Taylor's death an accident. That just confirmed our team of investigators got it right."

Todd bit the inside of his cheek and pulled out Elle's report on The Precious Jewels. "Have you heard of this organization?"

Sheriff Glover slipped on his black-rimmed glasses and flipped through the pages. "Yeah, I have. It's some sort of social club. A few of the members attend my church. Why?"

"Taylor was a member of the group. It's way more than just a social club. It's actually a pyramid scheme."

Todd waited for the sheriff to say something. He responded by closing the report.

Keep pressing...

"There's a lot of money being funneled through this organization, Sheriff Glover. And it's causing problems among the members. Major problems. There's jealousy, infighting, backbiting—"

The sheriff snickered. "Sounds a lot like game night at my house."

Todd showed no signs of being amused.

"Listen, Jacobson. I'm familiar with these women. They're just a bunch of bored, superficial housewives who don't have anything better to do than to sit around gossiping and eating crumpets. They're harmless."

"Harmless? I'm sorry, sir. But I have to respectfully disagree." Todd pulled out the notes he'd taken on Harper Mitchell's death. "Taylor isn't the only person linked to The Precious Jewels who's dead. Do you remember the case of Harp—"

Todd was interrupted by a knock at the door.

Please tell whoever it is to come back later.

"Come in!" the sheriff called out instead.

Major Dixon cracked open the door. Todd acknowledged him with a wave. Dixon ignored him.

"I'm sorry to interrupt, Sheriff. But we've got the video call set up in the conference room. Our virtual briefing with the mayor starts in five minutes."

"Thanks. I'll be there in a second."

Sheriff Glover pulled a brush out of his drawer and ran it over his short dark hair. "Look, son. If I were you, I'd keep my head down and focus on my current workload. Again, I'm sorry for your loss. But there just isn't enough evidence here to justify reopening Taylor's case."

"I appreciate that, sir. But you didn't even give me a chance to finish presenting what I've—"

The sheriff stood. Todd knew what that meant. The meeting was over.

"Do me a favor, Jacobson. Don't go behind my back and pull another rogue stunt like this again. You're a former marine. You know loyalty. Give this department the same amount of respect you gave your infantry brothers."

"Yes, sir."

Todd's skin burned with anger. He shoved the evidence back inside the folder, forcing himself to stand tall on his way out the door.

SHERIFF GLOVER HEADED to the conference room while Todd made a beeline toward his desk. Fellow law enforcement officers glared at him. A disgruntled buzz floated through the air.

Todd blocked it all out. He didn't care if the entire department turned against him. If getting justice for his sister meant ruffling his colleagues' feathers, so be it.

He collapsed into his chair and pulled out his cell phone. A text message from Elle appeared.

Good morning! Excited for your meeting with Sheriff Glover. Let me know how it went as soon as you get a chance!

Todd hit the reply button so hard that he almost cracked the screen.

Went horribly. Dr. Wu called Sheriff Glover this morning and the sheriff shut us both down. The rest of the department caught wind of the situation and they've iced me out. We need to come up with another course of action.

He sent the message. Within seconds, the cell rang. It was Elle.

Todd spun around in his chair, making sure no one was hovering near his desk.

"Hey," he murmured in the phone.

"Hey, I know it's probably easier for you to text since you're at the station. But I was so shocked when I saw your response that I had to call. I'm sorry you got shut down and are being ostracized like that."

"Yeah, it's unfortunate. But I'm tough. I can handle it. My number one concern is Taylor. I'm still all in on our investigation."

"So am I. As far as taking another course of action is concerned, I've already got one. You know that defiant member of The Precious Jewels I was telling you about, Sara?"

"The one with the beat-up car who took out a second mortgage on her house behind her husband's back?"

"Yes. Her. She invited Rachel and me to some retro country music bar for a line dancing event tonight. Rachel can't go because she's hosting an opening at the museum. I asked if I could bring you instead. Sara was a little hesitant at first."

Todd ran his fingertips along the lines in his forehead. "Really? Why?"

"Because you're a deputy sheriff. And the crowd she runs with doesn't usually associate with law enforcement. But I convinced her that you're cool and just looking for some answers."

"All right. So, am I in?"

"Yes. You're in."

Todd opened his laptop and pulled up the internet. "What's the name of the bar?"

"BB's Two Step."

"Hmm. Never heard of it." He entered the name in the search engine. A distressed wooden shack popped up on the screen. "Ooh, this place looks pretty run-down. More like an oversize outhouse than a bar."

"Ew," Elle uttered. "Where exactly is it located?"

"Right outside of Bradford, in Old Creek. Not my usual stomping grounds, that's for sure."

"Mine, either. It's a pretty rough area. But we're not going for the ambience. This is about business. We can step out of our comfort zone for one night if it means getting a new lead on Taylor's case."

"True. What time do we need to be there?"

"Around eight p.m."

"All right, cool. I'll pick you up at seven fifteen—"

Todd paused when a couple of deputies walked past his desk.

"Sellout," one of them muttered in his direction.

Todd jumped up from his chair. The deputies stopped and turned around.

"Is there a problem?" one of them asked.

"I don't know," Todd shot back. "You tell me. Is there?"

"Nah, man. We're good. You good?"

"I most certainly am."

The men stared each other down for several moments. When Todd didn't back down, the deputies shook their heads and walked away.

"What is going on?" Elle asked.

"Looks like I'm being challenged by my fellow law enforcement officers." Todd slowly sat back down. "These dudes have no idea. I'm just getting started. And I won't stop until I get justice for my sister."

"Neither will I. Keep your head up. If nobody else has your back, you know I do."

"Thanks, Elle. I appreciate that."

"Deputy Sheriff Jacobson!"

Todd almost dropped the phone. He spun around in his chair. Sheriff Glover was standing directly behind him.

"Yes, sir?"

"It is nine forty-five a.m. You were supposed to be in the conference room for the crisis intervention training session fifteen minutes ago."

"I'm on my way, sir."

"Uh-oh," Elle said. "Sounds like I'd better let you go."

"Definitely. I'll see you tonight."

Chapter Twelve

"Ooh," Elle breathed. "This place is worse than I thought it'd be."

"I couldn't agree with you more."

Todd led Elle inside BB's Two Step. It took her eyes a minute to adjust to the darkness as she searched for Sara.

The stench of stale beer filled the smoky air. Shania Twain's "Any Man of Mine" blared from the speakers. Peanut shells crunched underneath the soles of Elle's black riding boots. The atmosphere was a far cry from her normal social scene.

She noticed Todd bobbing his head to the beat of the music.

"Already enjoying yourself, huh?" she asked.

He shrugged and cracked a sexy smile. "Hey, what can I say? I like Shania's music."

Elle's gaze traveled down to Todd's hips as they rocked back and forth in his slim-cut jeans. Her mind drifted to that kiss they'd shared in front of his Christmas tree. She wondered what it would've led to had they not been interrupted by his cell phone.

Stop it, she thought before quickly turning away.

"Do you see Sara anywhere?" Todd asked.

"I don't. But she texted me saying that she's here. We should do a lap and find her."

"Let's do it." Todd placed his hand on the small of her

back. "Why don't we stop by the bar first and grab a drink, then look for her?"

"Sounds good. I'd love a vodka tonic."

"One vodka tonic, coming right up."

Patrons threw them strange looks as they walked by. Elle pulled her fitted denim jacket over her black bodysuit, covering the cleavage peeking over her top's neckline.

"Two of these kids do not belong," Todd sang in her ear.

His soft lips nipped at her earlobe. Elle ignored the tingles that shot down her neck. "Yep. It's pretty clear that we're not members of BB's clique."

A woman at the other end of the bar waved her arms in the air.

"Elle! *Elle!*" Sara yelled while dancing toward them. "Hey, you two made it!"

"Hey, yes, we did."

Sara's ruby red-lips were spread into a bright smile. She was dressed in an army green tank top and skinny jeans that were ripped at the knees. Her dark brown cowboy hat matched her dusty steel-toe boots.

She held her arms out at her sides and spun around. "See, I'm in my element here. Not at some stuffy ass Precious Jewels meeting. Now you'll get the *real* me." Sara took a step toward Todd and held her hand in the air. "Nice to meet you. Elle says you're cool, so I'll break my cardinal rule and hang out with law enforcement for a night."

He gave her a high five. "Why, I'm honored. Thank you. Can I get you a drink?"

"No, thanks. I've already had three beers and two rum and Cokes. I'd better pace myself. Come on. Grab your cocktails and let's go over to my table so we can talk."

They trailed Sara through the throng of plaid shirts and cowboy boots. She led them to a high-top table near the edge of the dance floor.

"Sara!" someone yelled as they sat down on rickety

wooden stools. "Get your ass out here! This is our favorite song."

"Gimme a minute! I've got some business to tend to."

Sara drained a half-empty bottle of beer that was sitting on the table. Her eyes darted back and forth between Elle and Todd. She threw her head back and laughed.

"Clearly this place isn't your thing, huh?"

Elle smiled sheepishly. "I mean…it's fine. I'd never even heard of it until you mentioned meeting up here."

Sara tipped her hat at Todd. "What about you, Bradford's finest? Have you been here before?"

"No, I haven't. But it's cool. I may have to hit the dance floor and try my hand at that two step they're doing out there."

"Yes!" Sara exclaimed. "You should. First things first, though. My girl Elle here wants to know what I know about your sister, Taylor. I'm sorry for your loss."

"Thanks. I appreciate that."

"So, Sara," Elle said. "You mentioned that Taylor and Sloane fell out right before Taylor died. What exactly happened between them?"

"Long story short, Sloane felt like Taylor was recruiting a lower caliber of women into The Precious Jewels than she wanted. I'm sure I was included in that mix. You know Sloane and her *image*. But, whatever. Bottom line is Taylor was all about quantity. That girl was trying to collect as much money as she could. Sloane, on the other hand, was all about *quality*, i.e. fake, bougie women."

"And Sloane confronted Taylor about all this?" Todd asked.

"She sure did. During one of our meetings, right in front of all those *lower caliber women* that she didn't want in the group. They were so offended. I was the only one who spoke up, along with Taylor. Everybody else was either too intimidated or blind to the fact that Sloane was refer-ring to them."

Elle sipped her drink, mulling over this new informa-tion. "What happened after the big fallout?"

"All hell broke loose, that's what happened."

"Meaning?" Todd asked.

"Meaning The Precious Jewels started to crumble. It got so bad that Taylor decided to launch her own group. She secretly approached a lot of fellow Jewels asking if they'd leave Sloane's organization and join hers. Everybody knew Taylor was pulling in a lot of money. She was a hustler. So most of them said yes."

Todd held up his hand. "Wait a minute. I thought The Precious Jewels were about sisterhood. And charity. And female empowerment. Where was that whole philosophy in all this?"

Sara threw her head back and laughed. "That's all a farce, man. The Precious Jewels are all about money, sta-tus and more money. Period. That's why so many mem-bers were willing to run off with Taylor. She was making some major promises. A real sisterhood with better money-making opportunities, in a relaxed, judgment-free zone."

Sara paused. She grabbed the napkin from underneath her beer bottle and pressed it against her eyes.

"Take a minute if you need it," Elle said.

As she waited for Sara to regroup, something dawned on her. Taylor's notebook. That last paragraph in the jour-nal entry that had left her so confused.

I am going to press on toward the goal. Collect the trea-sure chest. Then move on to bigger and better things...

Maybe Taylor's plan to launch her own group was that bigger and better thing. And it ended up getting her killed.

"You look like something's on your mind," Sara said to Elle. "What is it?"

Keep it to yourself. At least for now. You still don't know who's played what part in all this...

"Oh, nothing. I was just waiting on you to finish your point. Please. Go ahead."

"Taylor was just getting started. She had some great ideas. She and one of her recruits named Audrey decided to name the new group The Blossoms. Each tier would be represented by a different flower. Once you reached rose status, you'd cash out on the garden, which was equivalent to The Precious Jewels' treasure chest. But none of that ever happened..."

Sara's voice trailed off. She sniffled inside of her napkin.

"Audrey, Audrey..." Elle murmured, tapping her fingernails against the table. "That name doesn't ring a bell. Was she at the last meeting?"

"No. She's no longer a member of the group. Audrey and Taylor were really close. Like, best friends. When Taylor died, Audrey was too distraught to stay on board. So she left. I really miss her, too. She was a super cool chick."

Todd pulled out his cell phone and scrolled through the contacts. "I've never heard Taylor mention anyone named Audrey. I have most of her friends' numbers, too."

"She hasn't been in Bradford for that long. Audrey moved here when she got a job at the car dealership where Taylor's husband works. That's how she and Taylor met." Sara wiped away the stream of black mascara that had trickled down her cheek. "But anyway, back to shady Sloane. I can't let her win, guys. I wanna see her get locked up for whatever role she played in Taylor's death."

"So you think Sloane had something to do with this?" Elle asked.

"You bet your ass I do. You have no idea how...how *arrogant* that woman is. Imagine someone like that being dethroned by a member of a group that *she* started. Trust me, Sloane wasn't gonna let Taylor ruin her reputation by dismantling her organization. So yeah, I believe she fought to the death before that could happen."

A somber silence fell over the table. Elle felt the urge to get up and leave the bar.

"All right, ladies and gents!" the DJ yelled into the mic. "It's time for my favorite part of the evening."

Melodic guitar chords blasted through the speakers. The crowd went wild. A sea of cowboy hats and boots bum-rushed the dance floor.

"Tonight's cowboy cha-cha is being sponsored by one of my favorite duos, Brooks & Dunn," the DJ continued. "It's time to hit the floor and get to spinning to the tune of their greatest hit, 'Neon Moon.'"

A tall, slender man dressed in all black came two-stepping toward their table. He spun around in front of Sara, then held out his hand.

"May I have this dance, darlin'?"

"Not now, Pete. I'm in the middle of something here."

He sized up Elle and Todd, his beady eyes narrowing.

"Aw, come on, Sara," he pressed. "This is your favorite song. Plus your husband's not here tonight, which means you're free to dance with me." Pete nodded his long, narrow head in Elle and Todd's direction. "You don't look too happy sittin' over here with these two anyway. What do you say? Just one dance? And maybe one drink afterward?"

Sara hesitated.

"I do love this song…"

"Go on," Elle told her. "Enjoy yourself. You probably need a break from us anyway."

"Are you sure?"

"Positive," Todd chimed in. "I think we could all use a quick break."

"Yeehaw!" Pete howled through a snaggletoothed grin. He grabbed Sara by the waist and helped her off the stool, then practically carried her onto the dance floor.

"I'm glad Sara's husband isn't here," Elle said.

"If he were, I doubt that Pete would've even approached the table." Todd threw his head back and drained his bottle of beer. "What do you think of that info Sara just shared?"

"It was pretty insightful. Especially the new intel on Taylor and Sloane's relationship. You know, the more I learn about this situation, the more I realize just how much Taylor was keeping from me."

"Yeah, me, too. Even though I'm her big brother, she was usually open about what was going on in her life. But she kept all this to herself."

"Which tells me she knew it was wrong and didn't want either of us calling her out on it."

"Hey, Elle! Todd!" Sara yelled from the dance floor. "Come on out here and get your cowboy cha-cha on with us!"

Todd extended his hand. "What do you say, cowgirl? Should we take a shot at this cha-cha thing?"

Elle watched as Sara and Pete took three steps forward, rocked back, did a half turn and cha-cha-cha'd to the side.

"And make a complete fool of myself in front of all these people?" she asked. "I think I'll pass."

"Oh, please. You know how to do the Electric Slide, don't you? This isn't much different. Come on. Let's give it a try."

Todd didn't give Elle a chance to respond. He grabbed her hand and pulled her onto the dance floor.

"There they are!" Sara exclaimed. "All right, y'all. Show us what you're working with."

Elle shuffled her feet, stumbling about as she tried to keep up with Sara and Pete.

Todd caught on right away. When Elle almost fell into him, he grabbed her hips until her steps matched his.

"There you go," he said. "You got it."

His hips pressed against hers as they stepped from side

to side. A tingling heat crept up Elle's thighs. She considered pulling away from him, but he was holding on to her too tightly.

Just relax and enjoy yourself...

Sara shuffled over to Elle and twirled around her. "You know what I forgot to mention?"

"What's that?"

"As much as I can't stand Sloane, I think Taylor's shady-ass husband could've had something to do with her death."

"What makes you think that?"

"Well, thanks to Chloe, practically every Precious Jewel knew that Taylor and her husband were having marital problems. Taylor thought Chloe was her friend. She confided in her about how she'd taken out the second mortgage on the house behind Bryce's back, ran up their credit cards buying all those designer clothes and purses. I wouldn't be surprised if he got fed up and offed her."

"Interesting theory," Elle said, not letting on that she and Todd shared the same sentiment.

"Motive!" Sara yelled, pointing over at Todd. "I learned all about that watching true crime shows on the Investigation Discovery channel. If Bryce did it, he had a *motive*. Right, Sergeant?"

"You got it," Todd said, giving her a thumbs-up while throwing Elle a look.

"Ladies and gentlemen," the DJ shouted over the music, "you all are killing this one! The bartender wants me to remind you that drinks jump to full price in ten minutes. When you're done cha-cha sliding, head over to the bar and show Katt and her crew some love. Tell 'em I sent you, and don't forget to tip!"

Pete tapped Sara on the shoulder. "Let's go grab a drink before the prices go up."

"Let's do it!" Sara turned to Elle. "I'm gonna get a beer. Wanna reconvene after that?"

"I'm actually pretty tired. My days of partying are long gone. Why don't we make plans to get together again sometime soon?"

"Yes, please! And in the meantime, if I think of anything else you need to know, I'll reach out."

Pete grabbed Sara's arm. "We'd better hurry up. The bar is getting crowded."

"Bye, guys!" she yelled, waving wildly before rushing off.

The DJ switched things up and threw on a love song. Couples headed to the dance floor as the cowboy cha-cha-ers departed.

Todd took Elle's hand and led her through the crowd toward the exit. "You're not too tired to come by my place for a nightcap, are you?"

That tingling in Elle's thighs shot straight up to her chest. "No. I'm not."

"Good. Because I've got an amazing bottle of rosé that I've been dying to pop open. Tonight seems like the perfect evening to do it."

"It does. The night was a success. We accomplished what we came here to do. So yes. Let's toast to our progress."

Todd gripped Elle's hand a little tighter as they stepped outside.

Through the corners of her eyes, she noticed a flash of silver speed out of the parking lot.

Tires screeched. The stench of rubber filled the air.

Elle caught a glimpse of a silver truck before it disappeared behind a convenient store.

Was that Chloe's Range Rover?

"What's wrong?" Todd asked her. "You look like you just saw a ghost."

"I—I actually think I just saw..." Elle paused. "Wait!"

She took off running toward the parking lot's entrance. Stared down the street.

The truck was gone. Its only trace was the squeal of shredding tread.

Todd ran over.

"Elle! What is going on? Did you see something?"

Did I?

"I—I thought I did."

"What was it?"

Elle's head spun with uncertainty. She didn't want to appear paranoid. So she lied.

"No. I didn't see anything. There's just so much going on. I guess my mind is playing tricks on me."

"What is it that you *thought* you—"

"Don't even worry about it," she interrupted, locking her arm in his. "Let's just go back to your place and enjoy that rosé."

Chapter Thirteen

Elle took a sip of her sparkling wine. The fruity bubbles lingered on her tongue. She swallowed slowly, watching as Todd lit the firepit out on his deck.

His biceps flexed underneath his fitted green shirt. Elle crossed her tingling legs, willing the heat, which had never quite gone away, to simmer down.

"How's the wine?" Todd asked.

"Delicious, as promised." Elle reached for a cube of cheddar cheese and popped it inside her mouth.

"And the charcuterie board? How'd I do with that?"

"You did amazing," she said, eyeing the large wooden round filled with cured meats, various cheeses, dried fruits and crackers. "Who knew the former quarterback turned decorated marine turned deputy sheriff could whip up such a fancy display."

"Hey, what can I say? I'm a man of many talents."

The light from the firepit's flame glowed against Todd's handsome face. He grabbed a chair and pulled it closer to Elle's than necessary. When he reached for his glass, his arm brushed up against hers. His touch warmed her skin.

He tapped his glass against hers.

"Are we toasting to something?" she asked.

"We are. To us getting that much closer to solving Taylor's case. Thanks to Sara, I think we've got a pretty solid new lead."

"I agree. Sloane has risen to the top of the suspects list. But what about Bryce? Do you still think he may have been involved?"

"Oh, absolutely. Bryce is still on the list. So is your mentor, Chloe. Honestly, and this may surprise you, so is Sara."

Elle's head fell to the side. "*Sara?* Even after tonight? She's doing so much to help us."

"Maybe that's her tactic. To try and throw us off by offering up her assistance. As long as she's pointing the finger at somebody else, we'll be too occupied to look at her. Right?"

"Possibility. She does have a motive. Sara's pissed about the initiation fee that she can't get back. Deep down, I think she blames Taylor."

Todd emitted a low groan. He slowly piled slices of prosciutto and smoked gouda onto a rosemary cracker, hesitating before taking a bite.

"You know, our parents didn't raise us to be materialistic. And self-serving. Taylor had to have known that Sara couldn't afford to be a part of The Precious Jewels and keep up with the recruiting demand."

"That's why I believe Sara felt used. It was as if Taylor recruited her just to elevate to the next level, knowing she wouldn't be able to follow suit. Sara was destined to fail."

The loaded cracker Todd had been holding fell onto the plate. "I wish I'd known about all this. If I had, Taylor would still be alive. I'd have sensed the trouble brewing and insisted she walk away."

A vein pulsated down the middle of Todd's forehead. Elle reached out and clasped his hand. "Do not blame this on yourself. Taylor chose to keep us both in the dark for a reason. All we can do now is try and figure out what happened to her."

"You're right," he whispered, intertwining his fingers within hers.

They sat silently. Despite their worry over Taylor's death, Elle was overcome by a calming sense of peace. Being in Todd's presence helped ease the burden of grief.

She inhaled. The cool night aired rushed through her lungs, clearing her mind.

Elle sat back and stared up at the sky. Twinkling stars shone against the velvety dark blue sky. There was one that sparkled brighter than the others. She observed its glimmering rhythm, feeling Taylor's presence in the glow.

"We're going to solve this case, Todd. Don't lose faith."

His grip on her hand tightened. She turned to him, surprised by the soft, hopeful expression on his face. The creases in his forehead had faded. His mouth was no longer twisted into a scowl.

"I won't lose faith," he declared. "With you by my side, how could I? Together we can do anything."

Todd's words shot straight through Elle's chest and penetrated her heart. Waves of heat settled into her skin. As streams of smoke floated through the air, she knew it wasn't the crackling firepit causing her body to burn. It was him.

He slid toward her. She leaned in. Their bodies pressed against each other's. Her lips parted.

Bang!

Elle jolted forward. Todd fell back so fast that he almost toppled out of his chair.

"What the…"

Bang! Bang!

They stood and stared up at the sky.

"Are those fireworks?" she asked.

The only thing flashing up above was the stars.

"What is that noise—"

Todd stopped abruptly at the sound of smashing glass.

"Gunshot!" he yelled. *"Get down!"*

Todd grabbed Elle and pulled her underneath the table. He covered her body with his as shots continued to ring out.

She clung to him, flinching with every blast of the gun.

"Sounds like somebody's shooting inside my living room. Where the hell is my cell phone?"

"I think you left it inside the house."

Todd frantically patted down his blue jean pockets. "I did. It's on the kitchen counter. Right next to my Glock. Dammit!"

Elle's head swiveled from right to left. "My phone is out here somewhere. I think I left it on the table."

Todd reached up to grab it.

Bang! Bang!

"Wait!" she shrieked. "Just leave it. No phone call is worth you getting shot over."

He hunkered back down underneath the table.

Elle's limbs trembled with terror. Todd wrapped his arm around her tightly. "Come on. I got you."

"What if the shooter comes back here?"

"I've got the backyard's security gate locked. By the time he gets through it, we'll be back inside the house." He paused. "Wait. Listen…"

Silence filled the air. Then police sirens blared in the distance.

Elle gripped her chest, releasing a heavy sigh. "Thank God. One of your neighbors must have called the police."

"Good. Maybe now the department will start taking this entire situation more seriously."

A blaring engine revved loudly.

Elle froze. She recognized that roar.

The black pickup truck!

"Todd!" she screamed. "That's my attacker! They must've followed me here."

"What makes you think that?"

"I'd know the sound of that engine anywhere. Trust me. The person who's been after me just shot up your house."

The sirens drew nearer. Brakes screeched out front.

"This is the sheriff's department," someone yelled over the loudspeaker. "Deputy Jacobson, are you home?"

"We're in the back!" he called out. "Is the coast clear?"

"We're surveying the scene now. Stay put. We'll update you shortly."

Elle's cell phone buzzed against the glass tabletop.

"I should see who that is."

Todd ran his hand along the edge of the tabletop.

"Got it."

He handed the phone to Elle just as someone knocked on the fence.

"Deputy Jacobson? It's Deputy Cross. Are you all right?"

"Yes, we're fine."

"Looks like the coast is clear. Can you come and unlock the gate? Tell us what happened?"

Todd jumped up and ran to the front of the yard.

Elle was slow to stand. When she did, she fell against a chair. Her quivering legs were still weak with fear.

She sat down and willed her shaky hands to unlock her cell phone. A text message appeared from an unknown number.

Back off your investigation and get the hell out of town before you end up like Taylor!

The message sent a bolt of adrenaline straight through her.

Elle quickly rose to her feet and charged through the yard, anxious to show it to Todd.

Chapter Fourteen

Todd sat in the back of the sheriff department's conference room with his arms crossed over his chest and a scowl on his face. He was only half listening to the Force Option Training Unit's director, who was reviewing firearm and de-escalation techniques. Todd couldn't focus on anything except the attack on his home.

Who in the hell would have the audacity to shoot up my house?

It had been a week since the assault. While the sheriff's department hadn't produced any leads, Todd did notice a change in his colleagues' demeanor. The silent treatment and snubs were replaced with concern. Their "good mornings" and "how are things going" appeared genuine.

More importantly, the shooting proved that Todd wasn't being paranoid. He was on to something.

Todd's cell phone buzzed. It was Elle calling. He declined the call and sent her a text message.

Hey, can't talk right now. In a training session. What's up? Everything okay?

Everything's fine. Just checking on you and sharing some new intel. I spoke with Sara, and she brought up that woman Audrey whose name she'd mentioned at BB's. Remember her?

Todd hid his phone underneath the table so as not to get called out by the training director.

She's the one who was helping Taylor start up the new organization, right?

Right. Sara suggested we talk to her since she and Taylor were so close. Audrey knows all about the beef between Taylor and Sloane, and the issues Taylor was having with Bryce. What do you think?

Todd glanced around the room. The instructor was busy writing on the whiteboard while his colleagues took notes.

Sounds like Audrey could be an asset to our investigation. We should definitely talk to her. How do we get in touch?

Audrey's been off the grid since Taylor's death. If she's not at work, she's at home. Sara suggested we stop by her house tonight, introduce ourselves then go from there. Said she'd be happy to help figure out who killed her friend.

"Deputy Jacobson!" the director shouted from the front of the room.

Todd shot straight up. "Yes, sir?"

"What's got you so preoccupied that you can't focus on this whiteboard?"

"I was…um…"

"Could you please answer the question I just asked the group?"

A sheet of sweat formed along the back of Todd's neck.

The short, stocky director came strutting toward him. His bulky arms swung by his sides as if he were marching in a military parade.

Deputy Cross, who was sitting next to Todd, held his fist to his mouth and quickly muttered, *"Name one of the top gun safety rules."*

The director stood over Todd, heaving like a bull ready to storm a rodeo.

Todd's nose wrinkled at the stale stench of coffee on his breath. "Handle any weapon as if it were loaded, sir."

The trainer's narrow gray eyes darted back and forth between Todd and Deputy Cross.

"Good," he finally said. "Now get your head outta that phone and pay attention."

"Yes, sir."

As soon as he walked off, Todd turned to Cross. "Nice save. Thanks."

"Don't mention it. I know where your head's at. I hope you find the bastard that killed your sister."

The words almost knocked Todd out of his chair. It was the first time anyone in the department had shown him some support for his investigation.

"I appreciate that, man. I'm trying."

He sent one last text to Elle while the trainer's back was turned.

Gotta sign off. I'll pick you up at six and we'll head over to Audrey's.

Todd MADE A right turn onto Kenilworth Lane and let up on the accelerator. He turned on the windshield wipers, clearing a layer of foggy mist.

"We're a couple of blocks away from Taylor's house, aren't we?" Elle asked, peering out at charming cottage-style homes.

"Yep. Three to be exact."

The quaint residential street was filled with festive Christmas decorations. Streetlamps were wrapped in candy cane garland. Twinkling lights and wreaths adorned the entryway of each home. Children ran in between Santa and snowman figurines lining their perfectly manicured lawns.

Todd's chest pulled at the sight. He couldn't connect with all the merriment. His mind was focused solely on catching his sister's killer.

"You have arrived," the navigation system announced. "Your destination is on the right."

Todd parked in front of a dark gray vintage bungalow. A tall, slightly overweight woman dressed in black workout gear stood out front, wrapping string lights around the porch's white wooden railing.

"Here we go," Todd said. "Let's see what we can find out."

The woman he assumed was Audrey stared at them as they climbed out of the car. When the pair walked up the driveway, she froze.

"Uh-oh," Elle muttered. "Please don't freak out…"

The bundle of string lights fell from her hand. She tucked her honey-brown bob behind her ears, her dark, close-set eyes squinting curiously.

"Todd? Elle?"

They paused.

"I'm sorry," Elle said. "Have we met?"

"No. We haven't. I'm Audrey. A friend of Taylor's. And I could point you two out in a crowd. Taylor talked about you both incessantly. Between her scrolling through your social media and sharing stories about the good ole days, I feel like I've known you for years."

Her words warmed Todd's heart. "That's nice to hear. And it's good to meet you."

"You as well." She pointed at them. "Wait, let me guess. Sara sent you over here to check on me, didn't she?"

"She did," Elle replied. "She shared with us how close

you and Taylor were, and how devastated you've been since her death."

"Elle and I were actually hoping you'd be willing to talk to us about what was going on in Taylor's life before she passed."

Audrey pressed her hands against the sides of her face. "Taylor was going through a lot. And I do mean *a lot*. But yes. Of course. I'll share with you everything I know. Hopefully it'll help get us closer to finding out what really happened to her."

"So you don't believe Taylor died from an accidental fall, either?" Todd asked.

"Absolutely not. Somebody wanted that woman dead. I think I know who it is. And I don't think that person acted alone."

Elle nudged Todd, her eyes gleaming with hope.

"We'd love to get your take on all this," he said. "Do you have time to sit down and speak with us now?"

Audrey looked at her watch. "I have to hop on a virtual therapy session in about thirty minutes. But please, come inside. I just made a pot of hot chocolate. We can have a quick cup and talk until my therapist calls."

"Great. Thank you."

The pair followed Audrey inside. Her contemporary, neutral-toned living room was packed with plastic bins, each of them stuffed with colorful Christmas decorations.

Audrey hurried over to the russet tweed sofa, snatched up several rolls of wrapping paper and propped them in a corner.

"Please excuse the mess. In case you couldn't tell, I've been drowning my grief in holiday decor. Have a seat. I'll go and get the hot chocolate."

Todd turned to Elle as soon as they sat down. "Who do you think is at the top of Audrey's list of suspects?"

"Sloane. Definitely Sloane. But she mentioned the suspect having help. I wonder who that could be."

"Maybe one of Sloane's cronies. I remember them from the charity gala. I get the impression that if Sloane told any of those women she wanted someone dead, they'd be begging to pull the trigger. But who knows. Audrey may surprise us and say she suspects Bryce."

Elle pulled out her cell phone and opened the Notes app. "We'll soon find out."

Audrey came back carrying a green ceramic tray topped with red mugs and a plate of gingerbread cookies. "I hope you two like whipped cream in your hot chocolate. I got overly excited that you're here and didn't even think to ask. Blame it on me not having company very often these days."

"All good," Todd said. "Elle and I both love whipped cream."

Audrey served the refreshments, then took a seat on an ottoman. "So, where should I start?"

"Wherever you feel most comfortable," Elle told her.

She stared down at her mug, her sunny disposition dimming. "I'm guessing you're both aware of Taylor's involvement in The Precious Jewels organization."

"We are. And we know that you and Taylor were in the process of leaving the group to start your own."

"We were. Actually, it was going to be Taylor's group. She was the driving force behind it all. I just acted as her wing woman. During that transitional phase, Taylor made quite a few enemies."

"Was that because she was working to pull members away from The Precious Jewels?" Todd asked. "Or was there more to it?"

"Oh, there was definitely more to it. Sloane was infuriated that Taylor had attempted to disband the organization she'd worked so hard to build. She wasn't the only one who was angry, though. A lot of Taylor's recruits were mad when she approached them about leaving the Jewels and joining her group, since they had yet to receive the money she'd promised they would earn."

Todd set his mug on the acrylic coffee table and rubbed his hands together. "Was Taylor expecting these recruits to pay another initiation fee in order to join her group as well?"

"She was. Needless to say, that didn't go over very well. And before we were able to come up with an amiable solution, Tay—"

Audrey paused. She held her hand to her mouth, sobbing softly.

"Taylor died."

Todd glanced down at the plate of cookies, quickly looking away when his stomach turned.

"I am so sorry, Audrey," Elle said softly. "I know this is hard for you considering how close you and Taylor had become. And I understand that there were a good number of people upset with her. But who would've wanted to take her life?"

"Sloane Whitlock."

"And you mentioned her having help," Todd interjected. "Who else do you think was involved?"

Another long pause.

He twisted his watch around his wrist, anxious to hear her response.

"Sara," Audrey whispered.

"I'm sorry, who?" Elle asked.

"Sara," she repeated, louder this time. "She was more upset with Taylor than anyone else. That money she put up to join The Precious Jewels was all she had. Sara realized she'd never cash in on her investment, and felt that Taylor stepped on her back to reach the next level. Most of Taylor's recruits felt that way. But it hit Sara the hardest. I don't think she could cope with the betrayal."

"I'm surprised at your response," Todd said.

"Why? You don't think that makes sense?"

"No, that's not it. I was under the impression that you and Sara were friends."

"When it comes to The Precious Jewels, there is no such thing as friends. Those women aren't trying to create genuine bonds. They're trying to make money and enhance their social status. That's why I was so willing to jump ship and join Taylor's group. Hers would've embodied a *real* sisterhood."

"So you don't think Taylor's husband had anything to do with her death?" Elle asked.

"*Bryce?* No. I mean, I knew he wasn't happy about Taylor's wild spending habits. But he loved her. Bryce wouldn't have harmed her over money issues—"

Audrey was interrupted when her laptop pinged.

"Oh, that's my therapist. Give me a quick sec," she said before jumping up and rushing into the dining room.

Todd rubbed his temples as his head began to throb. "I guess I'm not the only one who thinks Sara could be involved."

"I didn't see that one coming. This case just keeps getting more and more twisted."

"And the list of suspects keeps getting longer and longer."

The pair stood when Audrey returned.

"Thank you for speaking with us," Todd said, "and for being so open." He pulled a business card from his wallet and handed it to her. "If you think of anything else that might assist in our investigation, please don't hesitate to reach out."

"Thanks for stopping by and asking my opinion. I hope what I shared was helpful."

"It definitely was."

Audrey opened the door, her expression hardening.

"Trust me. The truth behind Taylor's death is hidden within The Precious Jewels. Just be careful. Those women are dangerous."

"We'll keep that in mind," Todd said as he and Elle exited the house.

They headed to the car in silence. Audrey's ominous words ran through Todd's mind.

"That was pretty damn sobering."

"It was," Elle agreed. "We've got a lot to unpack. I think I'm gonna need to do so over something stronger than hot chocolate."

"Drinks at Cozy's?"

"Sounds good to me."

Todd opened the passenger door. Elle stepped off the curb, stopping before climbing inside the car.

She pressed her hand against his chest. "You were great in there. Keep it up. We're getting closer to the truth."

"Thanks, E. I hope so."

And just like that, Todd's somber mood lifted.

Chapter Fifteen

Elle adjusted the hem of her lavender cocktail dress and glanced around the room. The Museum of Contemporary Art was filled with the major players of Bradford, who'd come for the opening of an exhibition of works by North Carolina's own Pilar Samuels. Even the mayor had shown up to celebrate the artist, who had recently been featured at Art Basel in Miami.

As she wandered through the event, Elle's thoughts drifted to her evening at Cozy's with Todd. They'd talked about the case, but they had also enjoyed some much-needed laughs as they reminisced about growing up in Bradford. A smile crept to her lips as she thought of him squeezing her hand across the table, and the sweet kiss they'd shared at night's end.

Elle approached one of Pilar's sculptures. The life-size, all-black clay figure of a woman lying in the fetal position was depressing to say the least. The work wasn't Elle's cup of tea, but major curators from around the world seemed to love it.

"So, what do you think?" Rachel asked, handing Elle a glass of champagne. "Would you shell out six figures for this masterpiece?"

"Um, no, ma'am."

"Well, believe it or not, five of Pilar's pieces have already sold. I'm guessing the other three will sell before the end of the night."

"Good for her," Elle muttered, only half listening as she scanned the room once again.

Rachel had personally invited The Precious Jewels to the opening, along with Audrey, whom she'd met at a previous art exhibition. She and Elle were interested to see how they'd all interact with one another. Maybe hidden secrets would be unearthed and unspoken truths revealed once the champagne kicked in.

"Looks like Sloane and her cronies aren't here yet," Elle observed.

"Of course not. You know they like to make an entrance. Seems like they're a good hour late to every event they attend."

"They really think they're A-list celebrities, don't they?"

"Around here, they are," Rachel rebutted, smoothing the collar on her cream tuxedo dress. "The real housewives of Bradford."

The museum's heavy wooden doors opened. Elle stood on her tippy toes, peering over the heads of the sea of guests. Two unfamiliar faces entered the lobby.

"Ugh," Elle groaned. "None of our guests are here yet. They'd better show up. It took a lot of convincing for Audrey to agree to come. She doesn't even wanna be in the same room as The Precious Jewels. Especially Sloane. But I told her that seeing them might be therapeutic. All that hate she's harboring is unhealthy."

"Well, can you blame her? She believes they had something to do with her friend's death."

"True. I can relate to that. But I'm funneling all my anger into this investigation. Maybe she'll find comfort in knowing that Todd and I are working overtime trying to solve the case."

"Speaking of Todd, is he coming tonight?"

"He's gonna try. He and a couple of other deputy sheriffs are meeting up to try and figure out who's behind all these attacks. So while he works that angle, I'll be working this one."

Rachel placed her empty glass on a server's tray and pick up a full one. "Way to tag-team. I like the two of you together."

"We do make a good team."

Rachel's right eyebrow arched. "I'm not talking professionally. I mean, don't get me wrong. You and Todd obviously work well together. I just think you'd play together even better."

"Mmm, maybe," Elle murmured coyly. "But first things first. Taylor's investigation supersedes all of that."

"Of course it does. But come on. You can't deny the connection between you and Todd."

Elle gazed at the champagne bubbles shooting through her glass. "There's definitely something brewing between us. We…uh…we actually kissed the other day."

"Oh, *did* you now? Exactly when did this happen? Where did this happen? And why are you just now telling me about it?"

"It happened the night Todd and I were at his house trimming the Christmas tree."

She deliberately withheld the information about their good-night kiss after the evening at Cozy's. One kiss was enough info to share with her exuberant friend.

Rachel clapped her hands. "Eek!"

"Hold on. Don't get too excited. It wasn't that big of a deal. We'd probably just had too many glasses of wine…"

Elle's voice trailed off when she saw Sara shuffling toward them.

She was staring down at the white marble floor, clutching a beat-up brown tote bag. Her black-and-white houndstooth dress appeared two sizes too big, and her run-over loafers were riddled with scuff marks.

"Hey, Sara," Elle said. "Glad you could make it."

"I cannot believe you convinced me to come to this thing," Sara scoffed, her wide eyes darting around the room. "I feel so outta place. I don't belong here. Was that the *mayor* I saw on the way in? I think I should leave. *After* I get a drink."

"Sara," Elle said. "Relax. You're fine. You belong here just as much as anyone else."

"Absolutely," Rachel assured her. "It's nice to see you again. How've you been?"

The straps on Sara's tote slipped off her shoulder. The bag fell to the floor. She didn't bother to pick it up.

"*Terrible*. I'm exhausted. My boss made me work a double after three truckloads of pork came in unexpectedly. That's why I look a mess. I had to borrow this tent dress from my next-door neighbor because I didn't have anything to wear, and…" She spun around. "Where's the bar?"

Rachel pointed toward the back of the room. "In the corner. Right next to that statue of the man falling to his knees."

"Ew," Sara muttered. "He is creepy as hell. But not creepy enough to keep me away from the alcohol. You two good with your champagne or do you want something stronger?"

Elle nodded her head. "We're good. Thanks."

"Cool. Be right back."

The moment Sara walked off, Sloane came strolling toward the women.

"Hello, ladies," she purred, tossing her hair back and greeting them with air kisses.

"Hello, Sloane," Rachel said. "I'm so glad you could make it."

"Thank you. I'm excited to be here. I never would've

missed a Pilar Samuels art opening. I am a huge fan. My husband and I actually own a few of her pieces."

Of course you do, Elle almost blurted out.

Sloane twirled around, and the hem of her red silk dress fluttered through the air. "The turnout is wonderful. Looks like all of Bradford's elite showed up. I saw several of the cultural center's board members when I walked in. And I had a lovely chat with the mayor before making my way back here."

"Oh, nice," Rachel replied, her squeaky voice reeking of insincerity.

Elle held her glass to her lips, hiding a snicker behind the rim.

"One person I was surprised to see," Sloane continued, "is *Sara*. How did she even know about this event?"

"I invited her," Rachel said. "I didn't want to leave her out considering she's one of our fellow Jewels."

Sloane shot her a look through the corners of her eyes, then turned up her nose.

"Well, I did make an oath to honor our sisterhood during the initiation process," Rachel added.

Sloane's matte red lips snarled in disgust. "Speaking of the devil. *Literally...*"

Sara came dancing toward them, her feet shuffling to the beat of the DJ's jazz record.

"Mmm!" she exclaimed. "This is the best rum and Coke I have ever had. Just between us, it's my second," she mumbled through the corner of her mouth. "I threw the first one back while I was chatting with the bartender. I coulda sworn I knew him from somewhere. BB's maybe?"

Sloane gritted her teeth as Sara slurped loudly from her glass.

"*Heeey*, Sloane," Sara sang. "What's going on, girl?"

"Good evening, Sara."

"Look, lady. It is so obvious that you can't stand me. Know how you can get rid of me for good?"

"No, but I'm sure you're going to tell me."

Sara took several steps toward Sloane, stopping inches away from her.

"Pay me back the money I—"

"Ladies," Rachel interrupted, attempting to slide in between them. "Please, let's all just calm down."

"Hello, everyone," Audrey said as she approached the group. "Is everything okay over here?"

Sloane and Sara were too busy staring each other down to respond.

"Not really," Elle whispered in Audrey's ear.

Rachel wrapped an arm around Sara and pulled her back. "Come on. This isn't the time or the place. Why don't you two table this discussion and revisit it at the next Precious Jewels meeting?"

"What did I miss?" Audrey asked Elle.

"A lot. We'll talk about it later."

Sloane ran her fingers through her hair and squared her shoulders. "You're right, Rachel. My apologies. This is a dignified, classy affair, and we should all act as such. Those of us who know how, at least."

"I should throw this drink in your face," Sara spewed.

"Looks to me like that glass is already empty," Sloane countered. She turned her back to Sara and faced Audrey. "Hello there. How are you? I haven't seen you since—well, you know."

"I'm hanging in there. Thank you for asking. How have you and the rest of The Precious Jewels been?"

"I'm doing well. We all are, for the most part. Aside from a few bad seeds sprinkled here and there." She cut her eyes at Sara before turning to address Audrey. "Listen, dear. I know you and I didn't end our relationship on the best of terms. But I hope we can make amends. Maybe you'll even consider rejoining The Precious—"

"Are you *serious*?" Sara interrupted. "Woman, you have no shame. Can't even lay off the recruiting for one night, you money-hungry hag."

"How *dare* you!"

Rachel nudged Elle as the women bickered back and forth. "Maybe putting these two in the same room together wasn't such a good idea."

"Maybe not. But let's stay tuned. Something interesting might come of it."

No sooner than the words were out of her mouth, Sara lunged toward Sloane.

"Look, *bitch*," she spat. "I did everything you asked me to do. *Everything.*"

"What are you talking about? You're drunk."

"I'm not drunk. You know exactly what I'm talking about. And unless you want everybody in this room to know, too, you'd better gimme back my money!"

Sara poked Sloane in her bony chest. Sloane stumbled backward. Rachel grabbed her arm right before she crashed into a praying hands statue.

"Security!" Sloane screamed. "I've been assaulted! Security? Help!"

Rachel steadied Sloane while Elle held Sara back.

"Come on, Sloane," Rachel said. "You're okay. Why don't we step away for a minute? Go to my office and regroup."

Sloane stood straight up and smoothed her hair. "Fine. I'll follow you."

Sara lunged at her again when she walked by. Elle pulled Sara back right before her fist connected with Sloane's jaw.

"You'd better stop before Sloane calls the police on you," Elle warned.

"All right, all right. Fine. I'm good. You can let go of me now."

Elle waited until Sloane and Rachel were gone before releasing her.

Sara somehow managed to hold on to her drink. She drained the glass, then set it on a white marble pedestal.

"I need to get the hell outta here. That snitch probably is gonna call the cops on me. The last thing I need is another charge on my record."

Another charge?

Audrey, who'd managed to distance herself from the drama, threw Elle a knowing glance.

"It's been real, ladies," Sara said, throwing up a peace sign. "I'm gonna slip outta one of these side doors. Next time we meet up, it'll have to be at one of my spots. Deuces!"

Audrey waved feebly as Sara shuffled toward the back of the museum.

"See what I mean about her? That woman is trouble. Did you catch what she said about doing *everything* Sloane asked of her? What do you think she was talking about?"

"I have no idea. But I'm certainly going to find out."

"I bet you and *I* know what it's about. I'm telling you, Elle. Sloane had something to do with Taylor's murder. And she pulled Sara in to help her. She preyed on that poor woman. Now Sloane won't hold up her end of the bargain and pay Sara whatever she's owed. The whole situation is just shameful."

Elle's mouth went dry. "The thought of that even being a possibility makes me sick."

"Me, too! I think it's worth you and Todd looking into."

"So do I…"

Elle peered down the hallway, wishing she could hear what was going on in Rachel's office.

"And can you believe Sloane had the audacity to suggest I rejoin The Precious Jewels?" Audrey asked, her tone rising. "She must be out of her mind. This is too much. I *knew* I shouldn't have come here tonight."

"I'm glad you did. Because I never would've been able to recap all the drama we just witnessed."

Elle surveyed the room. Guests were busy chatting and studying the artwork. "I'm glad Sloane and Sara's altercation didn't disrupt the event. I guess we have the DJ to thank for that."

"True. He's kept the Christmas jazz going nonstop."

Elle's cell phone buzzed. A text message from Todd popped up.

Hey, the guys and I are still at it. Got an update. I reviewed the crime scene report taken after you were hit by the pickup at the forest preserve. Didn't realize there were photos of the truck's tire tracks. I emailed them to you for our personal file.

Excellent, Elle replied. Find anything else noteworthy?

Unfortunately, no. We combed the hiking trail again, where Taylor's and Harper's bodies were found. Got nothing. Now we're back at my house looking for shell casings or anything linked to the shooting. How are things going there?

Interestingly, to say the least. Sloane and Sara got into a huge argument. Sara said some incriminating stuff. Will share with you later. Guessing you won't be able to make it to the museum?

Doesn't look like it. Let me know when you're done. I'll give you a ride home and we'll catch up then.

"Hey," Audrey said, nodding toward the hallway. "Here come Sloane and Rachel. Looks like Sloane's pulled herself together."

The women approached.

Play your part. Show Sloane some support.

Elle placed a hand on her shoulder.

"Are you okay?"

"Yes. I'm fine. I just need to be kept away from that little degenerate." Sloane swiveled from side to side. "Where is she? Gone, I hope."

"She is."

"*Good.* Ladies? I'm going to brush that whole incident off as if it never happened. I'll also have mercy on she who shall go unnamed and won't press charges. Now, if you'll excuse me, I'm going to go over and say hello to Pilar."

Audrey grabbed Sloane's arm. "Wait, before you go, tell me. What was Sara talking about when she mentioned doing everything that you'd asked of her?"

Elle's eyes darted from Audrey to Sloane. She held her breath, anxious to hear her response.

"Oh, please. Don't listen to that delusional woman. She's just bitter. And intoxicated. Nothing was expected of her that wasn't asked of the other Jewels. Honor your commitment to the organization. Respect your fellow sisters. Make an effort to recruit new members..."

Audrey's head lowered as she ticked off the oaths.

"Sloane, you and I both know that Sara doesn't associate with women who can afford to join The Precious Jewels. That's why she feels so used. It's as if you stole her money and left her with nothing but false promises."

"You can thank your friend Taylor for that, may she rest in peace. Don't forget, she's the one who recruited Sara and made all of those false promises. Not me."

Linda, Sloane's right-hand woman, came rushing over. "Sloane! Senator Butler just arrived. He's talking to your husband and asked about you. You'd better get over there. *Stat!* Now would be the perfect time for you to discuss the idea of him planting a botanical garden on Jefferson Boulevard instead of building that wretched playground."

"Good idea. Ladies, if you'll excuse me."

Sloane and Linda bolted toward the front of the room. Elle turned to Rachel and Audrey, pressing her palm against her damp forehead. "What in the hell just happened?"

"Utter chaos," Rachel said, sighing heavily. "That's what happened. As much as I'd love to stand here and dissect that fiasco, I need to go and check on the guests."

Audrey embraced her. "I'm glad those two didn't ruin your event. Thank you again for inviting me. But I think I've had enough for tonight. I haven't been to a social outing in, gosh, I don't know how long. This one proved that I've been doing the right thing by staying home."

"Thank you again for coming. I wish it could've been under more pleasant circumstances, but…"

"No worries," Audrey said. "Maybe we can all get together for lunch sometime and make up for it. We'll talk soon."

Once Audrey was gone, Elle linked arms with Rachel. "And then there were two."

"Yeah, two who need something stronger than champagne after all that. Why don't we go grab another drink, then I'll introduce you to Pilar?"

"That sounds good. Can you give me a quick sec? I wanna send Sara a text. Make sure she's okay."

"How sweet." Rachel hesitated, peering at Elle through squinted eyes. "Wait, why do I get the impression you're up to something more than just checking on her?"

"I'll meet you over by the bar and tell you all about it."

"Suit yourself, secret squirrel."

Elle pulled her cell from her overstuffed clutch and began composing a message.

Hey, just checking on you. Hope you're okay. Sorry things went left at the opening. Quick question, what were you referring to when you told Sloane you'd done everything she'd asked, yet she didn't uphold her end of the bargain? Just curious…

Elle sent the text, then headed toward the bar, hoping Sara would be sober enough to respond.

Chapter Sixteen

Todd pulled up in front of Elle's house.

"Thank you for the ride."

"You're welcome. Thanks for providing the entertainment the whole way here. I can't believe a Pilar Samuels art opening got that wild."

Elle pressed her hand against her forehead. "Neither can I. I'm just glad to be home."

"You know, I haven't seen your parents since you got to town. Are they here?"

"No, they're at the teachers' union's annual holiday party. They never miss it, even though my mother retired years ago."

"Aw, nice. Well, I'll try and catch them next time."

"You can still come in if you want."

Todd looked at the dashboard's clock. It was after 11:00 p.m.

"Are you sure it isn't too late?"

Elle threw her head back and laughed.

"What?" Todd asked, enamored by her bright smile. He fought the urge to lean over and kiss her.

"Sir, we are grown. Not only can I have company when my parents aren't home, but I can also do so whenever I want. Plus, you're not even considered company. You're family. Which means you're welcome anytime."

Just reach inside my chest and steal my heart, woman...

"That's a sweet thing to say," Todd murmured.

"It's the truth. I should also mention that my mother made a pot of her famous gumbo, which, if I recall correctly, you used to devour back in the day."

He turned off the engine. "Oh, you should've just led with that. Did she throw in everything that I love?"

"If you're referring to crab legs, chicken wings, shrimp, oysters and lobster, then yes. She did."

"Now I'm drooling. I'd love a bowl. Or three."

The pair climbed out of the car and headed toward the house.

"What if I told you she made hot water cornbread and peach cobbler, too?"

Todd pumped his fist in the air. "If you're trying to make me snatch your mother away from Mr. Scott so that *I* can marry her, it's working," he joked as Elle opened the front door.

"Please. There is nothing you could do to steal my mother from—"

She stopped midsentence. She stood in the doorway, staring into the dim living room.

"Todd. Something's wrong."

Elle ran her hand along the wall in search of the light switch. She took a step forward and stumbled over something. Todd quickly grabbed her.

"Are you okay?"

"I'll know as soon as I turn the light on," she breathed.

Elle flipped the switch then emitted a guttural scream.

The living room had been ransacked. The couch and love seat were overturned. The midnight blue upholstery had been ripped apart.

Broken mosaic lamps were strewn across the hardwood floor, lying among shattered glass from the coffee and end tables.

"Oh my God," Elle sobbed into her hands. Tears rolled

down her cheeks. She crept through the room, her legs shaking as she surveyed the damage.

Anger burned in the pit of Todd's stomach. He pulled out his cell phone and called Sheriff Glover. It went straight to voice mail.

"Sheriff, it's Jacobson. I need for you and the team to meet me at the Scotts' house as soon as possible. It's been vandalized."

He sent an emergency group text message to the sheriff's department, alerting them of the attack, then turned his attention back to Elle.

She was now frantically moving about, taking pictures of the damage with her cell phone.

"I am so sorry, Elle. The team will be here shortly. In the meantime, let's see what we can find without disturbing any possible evidence."

She approached him and collapsed. He caught her before she fell to the floor.

Elle's entire body trembled against his.

"I don't know how much more of this I can take, Todd. It's too much. Attacking me is one thing. But my *parents*?"

"I know, Elle. I know."

His cell phone rang.

"Hello?"

"It's Deputy Cross! Are you all okay?"

"Yes, we're fine. But you and the team need to get here immediately."

"We're already on the way. Just hang tight."

"Will do."

Elle clung to Todd tighter as he disconnected the call.

"Was that the sheriff's department?"

"It was. They're on the way. Once they get here, we'll examine the scene thoroughly and hopefully collect some evidence—"

"Wait!"

Elle pulled away from him and darted through the dining room.

Todd ran after her. "What's wrong?"

She was too busy hopping over the toppled oakwood chairs to respond.

He sped up, clipping his shin on the overturned dinner table's leg.

"*Ouch!* Elle, where are you going?"

"To my bedroom!"

Fragments of broken porcelain plates crunched underneath her pumps.

"Watch your step!" Todd insisted, grabbing her waist just as she slipped on a cream chair cover.

They ran up the stairs two at a time. Elle flung open her bedroom door. The room was in shambles.

The bed had been torn apart. Her silver comforter was balled up in one corner while the mattress lay in the other. The dresser drawers had been dumped and thrown about. Lamps were knocked to the floor. Makeup and toiletries were scattered everywhere.

Elle jetted toward her toppled desk and fell to her knees.

"Please be here." she panted. "*Please* be here…"

Todd bent down next to her. "What are you looking for?"

"My laptop. All the information we've collected for Taylor's case is on it. The police report, the research, our personal findings, theories…*everything*!"

Elle's breathing quickened as she ripped through the drawers.

"I'm about to have a panic attack. It's not here. It's not here!"

Todd placed his hands on her shoulders. "Elle, listen. Calm down. It's okay. I'm sure all the information was saved in the cloud. Plus, you've got a hard copy of the file, I've got everything saved on my computer—"

"That's not the point! Our attacker has the upper hand

now. They know it all. Who our suspects are, what we're presenting to Sheriff Glover—"

Her voice broke. She fell back, slamming against her mirrored closet door.

Todd sat down and wrapped his arm around her. She leaned against his chest.

"Change in strategy, then," he said. "Let's meet with Sheriff Glover sooner than we'd planned. Since these attacks are only getting worse, law enforcement will have no choice but to step up and go all in on this investigation."

"Let's hope so. They should've done that a long time ago." Her head slumped. "After what happened tonight at the art opening, Sloane is looking more and more suspicious. To be honest, so is Sara. She really showed out. *Bad.* Her bitterness toward The Precious Jewels is something vicious. I think she'd do anything, and I do mean anything, to recoup that initiation fee."

"Didn't you say she left the event early tonight?" Todd asked.

Elle glanced around her ravaged bedroom, then slowly sat up. "Yes. She did."

Todd felt her body tense. She turned to him.

"Do you think Sara did this?"

"I think it's a strong possibility. If she did, let's just hope she left evidence behind to prove it."

Elle's cell phone buzzed.

"Oh, how convenient. This is Sara, finally replying to my text from earlier tonight."

"What'd she say?"

"She wrote, Hey Elle, sorry I'm just getting back to you. I went straight home after leaving the museum and passed out."

"Hmm. Already setting up her alibi possibly?"

"Could be. Then she wrote, To answer your question, I did something that I'm not proud of. Sloane offered me money to spy on the new group Taylor was putting together, and pass on whatever info I could. So I did. But Sloane never paid me. I'm still pissed about it."

"Damn," Todd muttered. "I feel so bad for my sister. Here she was, thinking Sara was her friend. And I know Taylor made some missteps. But that was just low-down. I hate that she was surrounded by so many awful people before she died."

Elle leaned her head against his shoulder. "Me, too. Taylor may have done some questionable things, but she didn't deserve this."

"How did Sara end the text?"

"By asking if I could keep everything she shared to myself."

"That's not gonna happen. I'll be passing that intel on to Sheriff Glover along with everything else we've collected."

Sirens blared in the distance.

"They're here!" Elle exclaimed.

The pair jumped up and jetted downstairs.

"I'd better call my parents and tell them what happened. I would hate for them to drive up and see all this without knowing."

"Good idea. In the meantime, I'll get together with the other officers and start collecting evidence. There's gotta be a fingerprint, droplets of blood from all this broken glass, *some* form of evidence that'll lead us to a suspect."

"Let's hope so this time."

Elle watched as Todd went to let his fellow officers inside.

Thank God I've got you here...

She walked back to the kitchen. It hadn't been touched. She turned on the light.

There, scrawled along the wall over the breakfast nook, was a message spray-painted in black.

Consider this your final warning. Leave Taylor's case alone and GET OUT OF BRADFORD!

Chapter Seventeen

The next evening, Todd and Elle sat across the street from The Ravenswood Lounge, which was a hot spot for Bradford's second-shift factory workers.

Sara was known to frequent the seedy bar often. Elle suggested to Todd that they fake an unexpected run-in and catch her off guard, hoping the mix of surprise and alcohol would lead to some answers.

"So it's official," Todd said. "Sara and Sloane are running neck and neck on your list of suspects."

"Yep. They sure are."

"If Sara is involved in Taylor's murder, I'll have to admit, she's pretty damn clever. Remember the way she interacted with us at BB's? Her behavior didn't exactly scream out suspect."

"She may just be a good actress. As well as an evil human being."

"As the famous poet Charles Baudelaire once said, the finest trick of the devil is to persuade you that he does not exist."

"Hmm, good one," Elle remarked. "With that being said, I still haven't ruled out our other suspects just yet. Along with Sloane and Sara, Chloe is still on my list. So is Bryce."

"Yeah, I haven't forgotten about that life insurance Bryce will be cashing out any day now."

"Neither have I. But do you know what I can't seem to shake?"

"What's that?"

"The comment Sloane made during The Precious Jewels meeting about wanting to strangle Sara. When I heard it, my mind immediately went to Taylor being choked to death."

"I thought you were going to say the break-in at your parents' house was what you couldn't shake. How'd they take it?" he asked.

"I think they were more worried about how I took it. They're staying with friends while the place is searched for evidence before the cleaning service comes in to get it back in order."

"And you?" he said, concern coloring his voice. "You feeling safe?" He'd dropped her at the local five-star hotel on that awful night after she talked to the officers in charge of the investigation.

"I am, thanks. I told my parents I'd go back home and check things out for them as soon as the house is in order again."

A run-down gray sedan pulled in front of the lounge.

Elle leaned into Todd and stared out of his window. "I think that's Sara's car."

"Are you sure?"

"Positive. I saw her driving it at Sloane's house."

Four men climbed out of the vehicle. No Sara.

"Doesn't look like she's with these guys," Todd said.

"No, she isn't. But the driver is her husband."

"Wait, which one was driving?"

"The big guy with the bald head and the scraggly beard."

"You know him?"

Elle pulled out her cell phone and opened Facebook. "Only through social media. Sara friended me last week. Her profile pic is a photo of them on their wedding day."

Todd eyed the phone screen. "Yep. That's definitely him. Gunnar Ross. Hmm, where do I know that name? Wait, didn't he go to Bradford High?"

"He did. He and Sara were a few years behind me."

Todd glanced out the window, studying Gunnar's bloodshot eyes and potbelly. "Yeah, it's coming back now. He was an all-star pitcher on the baseball team. There were write-ups on him in the local paper every week. He damn near made it to the majors. Until he got caught up in drugs."

"Wow. What a waste." Elle paused. "I wonder why Sara isn't with them tonight."

"You think she may have stayed late at the factory? Picked up an extra shift?"

"And missed out on a night of drinking with her buddies? I seriously doubt it. But hey, you never know. Maybe she's working extra hours to recoup the money she lost with Sloane and The Precious Jewels."

Todd's cell phone buzzed. He checked the message then grasped Elle's hand.

"Deputy Cross just got a call from the crime lab. Forensics lifted half of a bloody fingerprint from a porcelain plate at your parents' house."

"*Really?* That is awesome! At the rate we were going, I didn't think our suspect would ever screw up and leave any evidence behind."

"Hold on. Don't get too excited. They don't know how good the quality of the print is just yet. Forensics is hoping they can lift it from the porcelain using the powder, brush and tape method."

"It'll work. It has to. And when it does, I pray the print matches a DNA profile in the FBI's database."

Todd watched the entrance to the lounge. Factory workers continued to pour inside. But still no Sara.

"What do you think?" he asked. "Should we just go in and grab a drink? Wait to see if she shows up later?"

"Might as well."

Todd stepped out of the car. He paused when Sara's husband and his friends came charging out of the bar.

"Wait, what's going on?"

"I have no idea." Elle walked around the car. "Is Gunnar crying?"

"Looks like it."

Gunnar jumped inside the car. His coworkers followed suit. He revved the engine, then sped off.

"Get back in the car," Todd said. "Let's follow them!"

His door was barely closed before Todd peeled away from the curb and flew to the corner. He slammed on the brakes. His head swiveled from right to left, then right again.

"Dammit! Did you see which way they went?"

"Left. Left!"

Todd turned onto Washington Boulevard and pressed down on the accelerator as they approached a yellow light.

"There they are!" Elle said, pointing toward Shoreham Street. "Make a right."

"I'm on it."

He turned the corner, careful to keep some distance between his car and theirs.

Todd peered into the car's back window. Everyone's heads were bobbing around frantically.

"Do you see them?" he asked. "They all look like they're freaking out about something."

"I wonder what's happening. Why'd they leave the bar so abruptly?"

"And where are they going?"

Gunnar blew through a red light and made a sharp right turn onto Piedmont Drive. Todd slowed down, making sure no cars were driving through the intersection before running the light and continuing after them.

Streams of smoke billowed from a tall, skinny chimney in the distance.

"Are they going to the factory?" Elle asked.

"That's what it looks like. But why would they be going back to work? Didn't they just leave from there?"

"That's what I thought."

Todd steered the car along the winding, narrow road. Ackman's Meat Packing Plant appeared up ahead.

Gunnar swerved into the massive parking lot. He slammed on the brakes right in front of the dingy gray building.

The group climbed out and ran toward the entrance.

A security guard stopped them before they went inside.

"What in the hell is going on?" Todd asked before pulling into a nearby space.

"I don't know. But we're about to find out."

Todd pulled her back. "Wait. Don't get out just yet. I don't want Gunnar to see us and realize we were following him. Let's hang back and see what happens."

He rolled down the windows, listening in as Gunnar pointed a finger in the guard's face.

"Where is my wife?" he yelled. "I wanna see my wife!"

The guard gripped Gunnar's shoulder. "Just hold on, sir. The ambulance is on the way."

"Ambulance," Elle said. "Todd, I think you should—"

His cell phone buzzed just as sirens rang out.

"Deputy Cross is calling me."

"Good. Maybe he knows what's going on."

He picked up the call. "What's up, Cross?"

"Jacobson, I know you're off the clock. But I wanted to let you know that a woman's been attacked over at the meat processing plant."

Todd put the call on speaker. "Do you know the name of the victim?"

"Yes. Sara Ross."

"What?" Elle gasped, gripping the door handle. "What happened?"

"Is she alive?" Todd asked.

"Barely. I don't have all the details just yet. But from what I've gathered, she's in critical condition. I'll know more once I get down there."

"My God," Elle whispered, covered her mouth. "I cannot believe this…"

"I'm actually at the plant now," Todd told Deputy Cross. "The victim must still be inside."

An ambulance sped through the lot and drove around to the back of the factory. Several squad cars followed.

"No," Deputy Cross said. "She was found outside. Around back, in the employee parking lot. It's been reported that she was taking a smoke break. My guess is that someone snuck up on her. Caught her completely off guard."

"Let's get back there," Elle whispered. "Now!"

"All right, Cross. I'll see you when you get here."

"Ten-four."

Todd disconnected the call and turned to Elle. She stared straight ahead, her eyes filling with tears.

"Are you okay?"

"Not really. I—I am in complete shock. I guess we can cross Sara off our list of suspects."

"And then there were two."

"Three," Elle rebutted. "Don't forget Chloe." She slouched down in her seat and jammed her hands underneath her arms. "This case is getting so twisted that I can barely keep up anymore."

Todd drove around to the back of the factory. Security had blocked off the entrance to the lot. He flashed his badge and was let through.

The scene was chaotic. Frenzied factory workers crowded the sidewalk, craning their necks to see what was happening. Law enforcement struggled to keep them at bay.

Deputies swarmed the parking lot. Paramedics were standing over Sara's body, transporting her onto a stretcher.

Todd crept past the scene. Sara's eyes were shut, and a brace had been secured around her neck.

"Oh no," Elle whimpered. "It looks like she's gone!"

"Stay calm. Sara is not dead. If she were, they wouldn't be giving her oxygen."

Elle patted her heaving chest. "You're right. I just wonder how she managed to stay alive. Our suspect's modus operandi seems to be death. Every time."

"My guess is that one of her coworkers entered the lot before the suspect could finish the job."

Sheriff Glover spoke with paramedics as they placed Sara inside the ambulance.

"Just get her to the hospital!" he yelled, frantically waving his hands. "Do everything in your power to keep that woman alive!"

Todd parked near the back of the lot. "I have never seen the sheriff lose his cool. Maybe he's finally realizing that there's more to this situation than he'd originally thought."

"Good. Hopefully that'll motivate him to reexamine Taylor's and Harper's deaths. He's gotta know that they're all connected."

"Listen," Todd said before stepping out of the car, "you're gonna have to lay low and stay here while I find out what's happening."

"I can do that. Hey, is it okay if I call Rachel and update her on all this?"

"Yeah, just make sure she keeps it to herself. I don't see any media here, so I'm guessing word hasn't gotten out yet. I'd like to keep it that way until Sheriff Glover is ready to release the information to the public."

"I will. We can trust Rachel."

"I'll be back soon."

"Take notes!"

Todd gave her a thumbs-up and headed toward the scene.

Elle's fingers trembled as she dialed Rachel's number. Her friend picked up on the first ring.

"Hey!" Rachel panted, sounding out of breath. "I was literally just dialing your number."

"You were? Why?"

"You haven't heard the news? Sara was attacked down at the factory."

"I did hear the news. That's why I was calling you. I'm actually at the factory right now with Todd. But wait, how did you find out?"

"My cousin Al is their quality control manager. He called and told me. Do you know whether or not Sara's still alive?"

"She is. But she's in critical condition. The ambulance is taking her to the hospital now."

"Oh my God," Rachel moaned. "I pray that she'll be okay. What in the world is happening to our town?"

Elle's entire body went numb as she watched paramedics work on Sara. "Somebody is wreaking havoc all over Bradford. That's what's happening."

"Have you talked to Audrey?"

"No. Why? Have you?"

"I ran into her at the grocery store last night. She said that Sara came storming into the car dealership yesterday afternoon, demanding to see Bryce. When he came out of his office, she confronted him about the money she paid to join The Precious Jewels."

"Why would she do that?" Elle asked.

"According to Sara, she thinks Bryce should reimburse her initiation fee since Taylor's the one who convinced her to join the group, and she's no longer here to do it."

"*What?* You have got to be kidding me."

"Unfortunately, I'm not."

"It sounds like she was really starting to unravel. I wonder what prompted her to barge into the dealership and confront Bryce like that."

"It could be the fact that her husband found out about that second mortgage she took out on their house," Rachel said.

Elle shot straight up in her seat. "Oh no. Did he?"

"He sure did. And he told Sara that if she didn't get their money back ASAP, he would divorce her. Audrey said things got so heated at the dealership between Sara and Bryce that he had to call security and have her escorted off the property."

"So Sara pops up unexpectedly at Bryce's job yesterday and confronts him over the whole Precious Jewels debacle. Then today, someone attempts to murder her."

"Yep," Rachel chirped. "That's it in a nutshell."

Elle watched as Todd and the other officers huddled in a circle, having what looked to be an intense conversation. A few deputies were busy interviewing some of the workers. A forensic investigator was picking up items off the ground and placing them in plastic bags.

"It is taking everything in me not to get out of the car and go share this with Todd. But I'm not supposed to be here, so I'll wait." She bit down on her thumbnail. "Bryce just got bumped up to the *top* of my suspects list."

"Rightfully so."

"I think it's time for Todd and me to pay him another visit. Oh, speaking of Todd," Elle said as he headed toward the car, "here he comes. I'll brief him on everything, then figure out what's next. Thanks for the info."

"Anytime. Keep me posted."

Todd's expression was grim when he climbed inside the car.

"Any word on Sara's condition?"

"She's alive. Unconscious, but alive. The bruises around her neck are an indication that she was strangled. Paramedics don't know how long she may have gone without oxygen. So the doctors will run tests and see if there's any brain activity."

Elle pressed her hands against the sides of her face, struggling not to choke up.

Deep breath. Suck it up. Now is not the time for tears. You've got a case to solve.

"We need to go to Bryce's house," she said. "I'll explain why on the way there."

"Right now?"

"Yes. *Right* now."

Chapter Eighteen

Todd turned down Bryce's block. As they drove toward his house, Elle noticed that the front door was open.

Bryce stepped outside. Someone hovered behind him in the doorway.

"Looks like Bryce has company," Elle said. "I wonder who that is."

Todd slowed down. "I can't tell from here. But we're about to find out."

"Let's do so discreetly. Don't let him see us."

Todd pulled over near the curb on the opposite side of the street, creeping slowly toward the house.

Whoever was standing in Bryce's doorway wrapped their arms around him.

"What in the world is he doing?" Elle asked.

"Looks to me like he's hugged up on some woman." Todd's acidic tone was filled with venom. "My loathing for that man just keeps on growing. Right along with all the reasons he wanted Taylor dead."

Elle's stomach churned in disgust. "Taylor hasn't been buried a good two months and he's already out here dating. What happened to the mourning? And the tears? And the claims that he misses his wife so much?"

"I know, right? He was just putting on a show for us."

Bryce stepped to the side. Opened the door wider. A red high heel attached to a long leg hit the porch.

"Wait, here she comes," Elle whispered, as if someone might hear her.

She and Todd peered through the windshield.

The woman stepped outside.

It was Audrey.

What the...

Elle emitted an audible gasp. Her limbs shook with fury. She grabbed the door handle.

Todd pulled her back.

"Don't," he warned. "Be cool. Let's just wait and see how this is gonna play out."

As soon as the words were out of his mouth, Audrey pressed her body against Bryce's. He wrapped his arms around her waist. The pair indulged in a long, deep, passionate kiss.

"I think I'm gonna be sick," Elle choked.

Several moments passed before the pair finally pulled away from each other. They glanced up and down the street before sharing one last kiss. She then hurried toward her car, which was parked several houses down from his.

"Oh, please!" Elle said. "If your plan was to be discreet, you failed. *Miserably.*"

Todd hit the accelerator and made a U-turn, parking right in front of Bryce's house.

"Time to go and get a confession."

BRYCE SAT ON the edge of the couch, staring down at the floor. Elle was seated next to him, and Todd was on the adjacent love seat.

They had him boxed.

"I cannot believe what I just saw," Elle said. "You know, we were originally coming here to ask about your confrontation with Sara Ross at the dealership yesterday."

Bryce remained silent.

Elle studied his body language. Looked for a sign of guilt. Fidgeting. Twitching. Shifting in his seat. *Anything*.

Bryce was perfectly still.

"Why didn't you call the sheriff's department and report the incident with Sara?" Todd asked. "Better yet, why didn't you call us while she was there so that we could pick her up for disturbing the peace?"

"Come on, man," Bryce said, waving Todd off. "I wasn't worried about that silly woman and her ridiculous claims. That situation was between her and Taylor. It had nothing to do with me. I didn't even want to waste the authorities' time on it. So I handled the matter myself."

Elle and Todd exchanged curious glances.

"What do you mean, you handled the matter yourself?" she asked.

"I called security and had her removed from the premises."

"Did you do anything else to *handle it*?" Todd probed.

Bryce finally looked up, staring Todd directly in the eye. "What do you mean?"

"Exactly what I asked."

Bryce hesitated. "Um…no. All I did was call security. They came right away and escorted Sara off the property. She complied, *reluctantly*, but she complied. Nothing else needed to be done."

Todd nodded his head discreetly at Elle. It was her cue to let it go.

"Listen," Bryce said. "There's something I haven't told you all."

"Humph," Elle uttered under her breath. "Ya think?"

"And what would that be?" Todd asked.

"This…this is tough to talk about—" Bryce sputtered before his voice broke.

"Look, whatever is going on here," Todd said, "it's time

for you to get it off your chest. I know this entire situation has been weighing heavily on you. Just release it. Free yourself from the burden of your secrets and admit the truth."

Bryce extended his legs and bent over, as if trying to catch his breath. His brown skin had turned a pale shade of gray. His cheeks were smeared with tears.

The look of a guilty man...

"Taylor knew that she was going to die," he blurted out.

Elle and Todd stared at each other blankly, both completely dumbfounded.

"Excuse me?" Elle asked. "How did she know that?"

He just sat there, quietly weeping.

"Bryce," Todd said firmly, "what do you mean? How did Taylor know that?"

"A couple of weeks before her death, Taylor told me that she was having dreams and visions of someone wanting to kill her."

"Someone?" Todd asked. "Who exactly was it?"

"I don't know. I got the feeling that *she* knew. But when I asked, she wouldn't say."

Elle thought about Taylor's journal entry in her Precious Jewels notebook. "Did she ever mention being followed, or harassed?"

Bryce's eyes closed as he pressed his fingertips into his forehead. "Not that I can recall."

"Do you remember her saying anything about receiving threats?"

"No. *Wait*...no. Only in the visions. Or the dreams, or... whatever the hell they were. All this chaos has me confused."

Bryce slammed his hand against the arm of the couch.

Elle jolted forward, startled by the gesture. She wondered if it was a sign of pain. Or guilt. Or both.

Either way, she and Todd were determined to keep going until they got some answers.

"Did my sister know that you were cheating on her, Bryce?"

Silence.

Elle tightened her jaws, willing herself not to reach over and slap Bryce across the face. Regardless of their financial woes, his infidelity was inexcusable.

Bryce turned on the waterworks again.

"No," he sobbed. "She didn't."

Elle dug her fingernails into her thighs as her frustration grew. If Bryce's tears were a call for sympathy, he wouldn't be getting any.

"How long has this affair between you and Audrey been going on?" she asked.

He shrugged. "A few months or so. Maybe four or five. I don't know."

"Of all the women you could've cheated with, why would you choose one of Taylor's friends?"

"No. That is not how it happened. Audrey and I were already involved before she and Taylor became friends."

"Oh, okay, cool," Todd interjected smugly. "That makes it all right, then."

Bryce ignored the comment. "Taylor practically forced herself on Audrey, pressuring her to hang out and whatnot. And it was all so superficial. Taylor just wanted to recruit Audrey into that—that Positive Gems group or whatever."

Elle didn't have the energy to correct him. Instead she pressed on toward getting a confession.

"Audrey seems to think that she and Taylor shared a genuine friendship. Aside from the fact that she was sleeping with her husband, of course. But I digress."

Bryce held his hands in the air and opened his mouth.

Elle kept going, uninterested in hearing his defense.

"So did you and Audrey meet when she started working at the car dealership?"

"No. We, uh, we met before that. At a car show. *Damn*, this is embarrassing," he whimpered before burying his face in his hands.

"Well, the cat's out of the bag now," Todd said. "So you may as well keep going."

"I'm so sorry, you guys—"

Todd leaped from the love seat so abruptly that Elle thought he might pounce on Bryce. But instead he began pacing the floor. "Look, save the apology. Just tell me what the hell was going on between you and my sister before you killed her!"

Bryce hopped up and marched toward Todd. "What did you just say to me?"

Todd placed his hand behind his back.

Elle knew what was there, propped inside his waist-band. His gun.

"You heard me," Todd said. "But I'll repeat myself since you wanna play dumb. What was going on between you and Taylor before you—"

Bryce lunged at him before he could finish.

Elle quickly swooped in, wedging herself between the two men just as they made contact.

"Hey!" she yelled. "Stop it. Relax. Both of you!"

They leaned into her, neither wanting to back down. Her hands were pressed against their chests. Both of their hearts pounded erratically.

"Todd, Bryce, please. Let's sit back down and talk this out like adults."

Bryce reached over Elle's head and pointed his finger in Todd's face. "That's what I was trying to do until he accused me of murder!"

Elle heard the click of Todd's gun being cocked. He pushed Bryce's hand away.

"If you ever stick your finger in my face like that again," Todd spat, "I swear I'll kill you."

"Go ahead, man. Do it!"

Elle pushed them both away and pulled out her cell phone. "How about I call Sheriff Glover and let him settle this situation for us. Huh? How does that sound?"

"Sounds good to me," Bryce said. "That way I can file a report stating that Deputy Sheriff Todd Jacobson just threatened my life—"

"And I can write you up for assaulting an officer!"

Todd's cell phone rang.

"Saved by the bell, *bitch*," he muttered.

"Man, you'd better—"

"Bryce!" Elle interrupted, pulling him toward the couch. "Come on. Let it go. Have a seat."

"Deputy Jacobson," Todd barked into the phone. "Wait, slow down, Cross. I can't understand you. What happened?"

Bryce took a seat. "I'm cool," he told Elle. "I'm actually glad everything's out in the open now. I feel like a weight's been lifted off me."

"This is not good," Todd grumbled. "At all…"

Elle spun around. "What's wrong?"

He looked up at her, his face twisted with frustration. "Sara is dead."

Chapter Nineteen

Sloane stood at the podium in front of her great room, banging the gavel down hard on the block.

"Ladies! May I have your attention, please? I would like to call this emergency meeting to order."

The room continued to buzz with frantic chatter.

"Ladies!" she screamed. "I would like to call the meeting to order. Now!"

An abrupt silence filled the air. All eyes turned to Sloane, who was visibly shaking.

Elle hadn't recognized her when she arrived at the meeting. Gone was Sloane's sleek hair, overdone makeup and perfectly tailored suit. Her hair was pulled back into a severe bun. Her face appeared pale, almost sickly, without the filled-in eyebrows, false eyelashes and overlined lips. A black velour leisure suit had replaced the Chanel blazer and skirt. Satin slippers covered her feet rather than designer stilettos.

Rachel tilted her head toward Elle. "Looks like somebody is crumbing underneath the weight of their actions."

"Thank you all for coming on such short notice," Sloane said. "I do wish that we were here under more pleasant circumstances. But unfortunately, we're not. As you all know by now, we lost one of our fellow Precious Jewels. Our sister Sara Ross."

Whispers swept through the room. Sloane held up her hands.

"Please, everyone. Let me finish. I will allow questions once I'm done. But for the time being, I've got the floor. Now, I'll be the first one to admit that Sara and I did not have the best relationship. We certainly weren't on good terms when her life was cut short. But I've heard the rumors. And frankly, I am…"

Her voice cracked. She pressed her unmanicured hand against her chest.

"I am appalled. I would have never harmed that woman. Let alone *killed* her."

"That woman," someone mocked from the back of the room. "But didn't you threaten to strangle *that woman* at our last meeting?"

"Exactly," another member chimed in. "And what about that fight you two had at the art museum? Did you really slap Sara and have her arrested?"

Sloane picked up the gavel and slammed it down so hard that it broke.

An audible gasp swept across the room.

She stood at the podium, her back erect as she trembled from head to toe. "How sad is it that you people don't know me better than this. My character. My servitude. Look at all that I've done for this town. For all of *you*! I made you somebody. I lined those designer pocketbooks of yours with thousands of dollars."

"Not all of us!" someone shouted.

"Shut up!" Sloane screamed so violently that she stumbled backward.

Linda ran over and helped steady her.

"Get away from me!" Sloane insisted, pushing Linda so roughly that she almost fell into the Christmas tree. "I'm fine."

Rachel nudged Elle's arm. "Oh my word. That lady is far from fine."

"She is completely unraveling, right before our very eyes."

Sloane grabbed her highball glass and took a long sip of Scotch and soda. It was a far cry from her normal meeting drink of choice—a mimosa.

"Please excuse my outburst," she sniffed. "I am in mourning, as are all of you. It isn't easy losing two women you consider sisters, despite being on rocky terms."

"Three," Elle muttered. "Let's not forget Harper Mitchell."

Sloane clapped her hands. "Quiet!" she hollered in Elle and Rachel's direction. "Now, as I was saying, I have heard the rumors. And I am taking this moment to tell all of you that I had nothing to do with Taylor and Sara's deaths. *Nothing.*"

She pointed over at Linda, who was standing nearby but keeping a safe distance.

"We would now like to open up the floor for questions," Linda said. "But before we do so, please, ladies, be respectful. Also, note that after today, Sloane does not plan on addressing this unfortunate situation again."

Rachel held her hand to her mouth. "That is until she gets called down to the station for questioning."

"Elle? Rachel?" Linda called out. "Do either of you have questions?"

"No, ma'am," Rachel replied. "I was just telling Elle that I need to get back to the museum soon."

Emma Green, a newer member of The Precious Jewels, stood up. "I have a question. Sloane, why wouldn't you just give Sara her initiation fee back and let her out of the organization? That wasn't very sisterly of you. Maybe she'd still be alive if you weren't being so selfish and greedy, and—"

"*Excuse* me," Linda interrupted. "Did you not hear the part where I asked for everyone to be respectful?"

"Do you hear how she is speaking to me?" Sloane asked Linda. "The anger in her tone? And the hostility?"

Linda patted her on the arm. "Yes, I know. You're right. It sounded awful…"

Chatter among the group picked up.

Sloane pointed at various women sitting around the room. "And do you notice a pattern here, Linda? All of these members who are disrespecting me are Taylor's recruits. They have truly brought down the integrity of my organization. Maybe one of *them* had something to do with the deaths—"

"Does anyone else have a question?" Linda asked, quickly interrupting Sloane.

Rachel nudged Elle. "You should ask Sloane where you can find your laptop."

"Better yet, why don't we sneak off and do a search of the house? I'm sure it's around here somewhere."

Several women stood and began talking at once.

"Uh-oh," Elle uttered. "This meeting is about to turn into a riot. Sloane should have hired a security company to keep things in order. Because she and Linda alone aren't cutting it."

Sloane picked up her glass and threw it across the room. It shattered against the gold frame of an oceanic oil painting.

All eyes turned to her.

"Meeting adjourned," she said before fleeing the room.

Half of the members chased after her while the other half tried to hold them back.

"Welp, it looks like Sloane has completely shut down," Rachel said. "I don't think anything else is going to come of this meeting. Should we leave?"

A shoe went flying through the air.

"Yes!" Elle declared. "Let's get the hell out of here."

The women hurried past the chaos and slipped out of the house.

"Whew!" Elle sighed. "That was a lot."

"Too much. Should we unpack it all over eggnog cocktails at Cozy's?"

"Most definitely."

They climbed inside of Rachel's white two-seater and headed to the restaurant.

"At this point," Rachel said, "Sheriff Glover has got to realize that all of these murders are linked. Haven't you and Todd gathered enough evidence to convince him that Sloane needs to be investigated?"

"Yes. We have. But it's all circumstantial. Todd wants to wait until we've gathered solid, direct evidence that supports our claim before we present anything to the sheriff." She also knew the sheriff had rebuffed Todd before, so he was determined to be extra sure before going to him again.

"Plenty of people have been convicted based on circumstantial evidence."

Elle's lips twisted with doubt. "Not when you're Sloane Whitlock, also known as the queen of Bradford."

"What about the bloody fingerprint that was found at your parents' house? Have the results come back on it?"

"Yep. And it didn't match up with anyone's in CODIS."

"Wow. So you mean to tell me that this maniac, who's committing all these heinous crimes, has managed to stay out of the system?" Rachel asked.

"That's exactly what I'm telling you."

"We are dealing with a certified psychopath here."

Rachel made a right turn down Steward Avenue. A silver Range Rover pulled in front of them. "Hey, is that Chloe?"

Elle craned her neck, squinting through the windshield. "I don't think so. Looks like an older woman. But speaking of Chloe, I'm surprised that she wasn't at the meeting."

"Me, too. I texted her yesterday to find out if she'd heard about Sara, but she never responded. I didn't make a big deal out of it since I thought I'd see her today."

"That's strange. She stays on top of her phone and usually responds to texts within minutes."

Rachel tapped her palm against the steering wheel. "She never misses a Precious Jewels meeting, either. I hope she's okay."

"I have a feeling that Chloe is perfectly fine. Might just be keeping a low profile."

"Hmm, interesting. Wait, I see where you're going with this. And if that's the case, then you and Todd need to keep her close on your radar."

"We definitely haven't ruled her out." Elle rolled down her window, letting the crisp afternoon air cool her overheating skin. "Chloe still has a permanent spot on my list of suspects."

Rachel turned into Cozy's parking lot. Christmas music piped through the outdoor speakers. A four-foot-tall mechanical Santa Claus waved at customers as they entered the restaurant. A server stood near the doorway, passing out dessert samples.

"I can't remember the last time I was in Bradford during the holidays," Elle said. "I really wish I could enjoy all the festivities this year."

"You'll get to enjoy them again. You and Todd are on the cusp of solving this case. Where do you think you'll go from here?"

Elle paused as she fidgeted with her pearl drop earring. "I think it's time for us to take a deeper dive. Maybe pay Harper Mitchell's husband a visit. See what he might know."

Chapter Twenty

Todd let up on the accelerator as he crossed into Madison, which was two towns over from Bradford.

"How long has it been since you've visited this place?" he asked Elle.

"It's been years. And from the looks of it, the town is nothing like it used to be."

The main thoroughfare, once lined with quaint mom-and-pop shops, now housed a slew of chain restaurants, clothing stores and hotels.

"Yeah, a lot's changed," Todd said. "The town's population has doubled over the past few years. You should see it during the summer. Tourists everywhere."

"I guess that explains all new lodging along Hartford Boulevard."

Todd tapped the navigation screen. "It's also what brought Harper's husband back to North Carolina from Florida. I heard he's the primary builder behind most of this new construction. He's putting up a multiplex entertainment center at the site where we're meeting him. It's gonna be huge. Movie theaters, a beer garden, live concert venue. The works."

"I'm actually surprised he agreed to talk with us considering his tumultuous history with Harper."

"Well, he was never named a suspect in her death. Plus he doesn't know what we know. As far as he's concerned, we aren't aware of their pending divorce and his criminal record."

"Never even named a suspect," Elle muttered, "despite violating Harper's order of protection and trying to strangle her. That's a damn shame."

Todd stopped at a red light, watching as a group of high schoolers dressed in elf costumes crossed the street. "It'll be challenging not to bring any of that up. I'm not promising that I won't, either."

"Neither am I," she said. "But I think we should focus on what Keaton knows about Harper's involvement with The Precious Jewels."

"Agreed. If it does creep into the conversation, however, I'll make an effort to at least be decent."

"In one thousand feet," the voice navigation announced, "make a left turn. Your destination will be on the right."

"Have you gotten any updates on Sara's investigation?" Elle asked.

"Last I heard, Sheriff Glover was looking into one of her coworkers. Apparently, Sara was in the middle of a battle with a fellow lineman who'd suffered a shoulder injury. He didn't want to take an unpaid leave and heal up properly, so he kept coming to work but wasn't pulling his weight on the assembly line."

Elle held up her hand. "So wait, the sheriff's department is trying to pin this on a coworker?"

"That's what it's looking like. Sara and this team assembler got into a huge altercation the day she was attacked. And it just so happens that he was unaccounted for during the time of the assault."

"Was he able to explain his whereabouts?"

"He claimed that he'd left the floor and gone to cool off in one of the meat freezers. The deputies are looking through surveillance footage to see if it'll back his statement. This isn't the first time he and Sara have had an altercation, either. They got into a minor scuffle earlier this year over a similar issue. Sara ended up getting hit with a simple assault charge."

Elle thought back on the event at the art museum. "So that's the charge Sara was referring to the night she fought with Sloane. *Whew*. And the plot continues to thicken."

Todd turned down Cobb Court. The framework of a massive structure appeared up ahead.

Grassy knolls were filled with piles of dirt, wood and steel beams. The street was packed with dozens of bulldozers. A sea of construction workers milled about, hauling materials and reviewing sets of drawings.

"How in the world are we supposed to find Keaton in all this chaos?" Elle asked.

"I told him I'd send a text when we got here. I'm not gonna even attempt to drive any farther down this road."

Just as Todd began composing the message, there was a knock at the window. He and Elle jumped in their seats.

"Sorry, didn't mean to startle you!"

Todd rolled down the window. "No worries. You must be Keaton."

"I am. Deputy Jacobson?"

"Yes, and this is Elle Scott."

"Good to meet you both. Why don't you leave your car here? We'll walk over to our makeshift coffee shop and talk there."

"You bet."

As Todd pulled closer to the curb, he noticed how different Keaton looked from the photo posted on his company website. With his scruffy beard and dark, shoulder-length hair, he appeared more like a rugged cowboy than a business owner.

His blue eyes were dull, and his bowlegged gait was slow. While still handsome, Keaton appeared weighed down. Grief-stricken, even.

"I'm a little surprised by this guy," Todd said when he and Elle stepped out of the car. "He seems pretty pleasant. Sad, but pleasant."

"Yeah, well, people who've encountered Jeffrey Dahmer have said that he was pleasant, too. Yet he killed and ate people. So keep your guard up."

"Touché."

Keaton approached with hard hats in hand. "Safety first."

He led them to a white, heated tent. Evergreen garland hung from its sloped roof. Folding tables and chairs were set up near the back. A barista wearing a Santa hat and snowman apron stood behind the wooden counter, passing out hot drinks and doughnuts.

"As you can see, I'm trying to keep things festive around here," Keaton said. "I really appreciate how hard my guys are working to complete this project. During the holiday season, no less."

Todd studied the development's intricately designed, multilevel buildout. "Looks like it's gonna be a spectacular complex."

"That's the plan." Keaton paused. "Building this entertainment center was actually Harper's idea. I just wish she were here to see it." He pulled a handkerchief from his jeans back pocket and ran it across his face. "Why don't we grab a coffee and have a seat?"

Todd tapped Elle's hip. She nodded discreetly. They were both on the same page—surprised by the way Keaton spoke of his estranged dead wife.

The barista had already poured three drinks for the group by the time they reached the counter.

"Thanks, Lisa," Keaton said. He handed Todd and Elle their cups, then led them to a table near the back of the tent.

"We really appreciate you meeting with us," Elle said.

"I'm happy to do so. Bradford PD really dropped the ball on my wife's case. Her death was no accident, and no one can tell me otherwise. As far as I'm concerned, it's a cold case. So, nice to know someone cares enough to look into it a year later."

"What do you think happened to Harper?" Todd asked.

"Honestly? I think someone in that women's group she'd joined killed her."

"Are you referring to The Precious Jewels?"

"Yes. That…that cult."

"Why do you think they were involved?"

Keaton pushed his coffee cup to the side and folded his hands. "Harper and I had a great marriage before she joined that group. But then, once she became a member, everything changed. She was brainwashed into thinking they were all about sisterhood, and charity, and prosperity. In reality, those women are a bunch of scam artists. Harper paid out a huge sum of money to become a part of their scheme."

"From what I've heard," Todd said, "a lot of the members' husbands have a problem with the money their wives pour into the group. Did you?"

"Of course not. Look around you. I'm rich. Why would I care about that? My problem was that The Precious Jewels became an obsession for Harper. She loved competition, which turned into an addiction. The woman who ran that group touted it as a family. But she pitted the members against one another. It was all about who could bring in the most recruits. Level up the fastest. Gain the most status among Bradford's elite. Just ridiculous."

Todd took a swig of his coffee. He watched Keaton over the rim of the cup, expecting his expression to appear distorted with anger. But it was neutral. His eyes, however, drooped with sadness.

Keaton had caught Todd off guard. The man was actually making sense. Even more surprising was the fact that Todd felt sorry for him.

"What's the name of that group's ringleader again?" Keaton asked.

"Sloane Whitlock."

He snorted loudly. "Yes. Sloane Whitlock. *Man*, that woman is evil."

"Why do you think that?" Elle asked.

Todd almost chuckled at the airy innocence in her tone.

"Sloane has bad intentions. She's all about money, power and prestige. That woman is willing to do whatever it takes to attain all three. Like I said, she's running a cult. She uses her charm to possess those women, to the point where she can control them. Once she gains that control? They start to worship her."

"And you believe that Harper fell victim to Sloane's beguiling ways?"

"Absolutely. Full disclosure? I lost my wife to The Precious Jewels way before she died. Back then I was in Florida a lot for work. Harper chose to spend more time here with them rather than there with me."

Todd was tempted to interrupt him and address Harper's abuse allegations. But he bit his tongue and let Keaton finish.

"And I'm not proud to admit this, but at one point, I started seeing other women. I was chasing after what was missing in my marriage. Harper eventually found out. Rather than leave The Precious Jewels behind and work on our relationship, she filed for divorce."

Now's the time. Ask about the restraining order...

"Have you heard about the other deaths that are linked to The Precious Jewels?" Elle interjected before Todd could speak up.

"I have. I told Todd how sorry I am to hear of Taylor's passing. Just like Harper, I understand that law enforcement ruled her death as accidental. But a lot of people suspected her husband had something to do with it. Isn't that usually the case, though? The husband's always guilty, right?"

Todd shrugged, tilting his head back and forth. "Well, in many cases, yes. He is."

"It wasn't in mine," Keaton shot back, snatching off his hard hat and slamming it onto the table.

Todd winced at the loud thud.

"I don't think that was the case in Taylor's death, either," Keaton continued. "If you wanna find Harper and Taylor's killer, take a closer look at that cult."

Elle turned to Keaton and gently placed her hand on his arm. "Let me ask you a question. Don't you find it odd that there are now three women linked to The Precious Jewels who were murdered, and they were all having trouble in their marriages?"

"Wait, what do you mean *three*? I thought the woman who was attacked at the factory survived."

"She did initially. But she didn't make it."

"Damn," Keaton mumbled, balling up a napkin and tossing it across the table.

"You know," Todd said, "you seem like a decent guy. But Elle and I have heard some things about your marriage that are pretty alarming."

"Oh, really? Like what? The restraining order she took out on me? And how I allegedly violated it?"

"Allegedly?" Elle chimed in. "The record shows that you did violate it. By strangling Harper, no less."

Keaton sat back and tucked his hands underneath his arms. When he began snickering, Todd almost reached over and snatched him up by the collar.

"Oh, is that funny?"

"Actually, yes. It is."

Todd and Elle both sat in silence, stunned by Keaton's response.

"Let me explain. When Harper left Florida and went

back to Bradford, she took a very expensive antique scarf that belonged to my mother. My mom had passed away a few months prior. That scarf meant the world to me. Harper knew that. So I flew to Bradford to get it back."

"But Harper's neighbor reported that she saw you strangle her," Todd said.

"I did not strangle her. I'd asked her to please leave the scarf in the doorway. My plan was to get it, then go on about my business. Harper decided to come outside with the scarf wrapped around her neck, prancing around the parking lot and trying to provoke me. She refused to hand it over. So… I'm not gonna lie. I got upset and tried to remove it myself. Harper made a big scene. Started screaming and whatnot. The neighbor came outside and saw what was going on. Thought I was trying to choke Harper. So she called the police."

"Okay," Todd said, tapping his finger against the table. "That's uh…that's a lot. But let me ask you this. Why did Harper file the order of protection in the first place?"

"Because she'd found out about my affairs and got angry. So angry that she lied to the courts claiming that I'd been violent toward her. It was simply payback for my infidelity."

"My goodness…" Elle whispered, clasping her hands together.

Todd could tell by the look in her darting eyes that she was overwhelmed. Hell, he was, too. Keaton could be lying. But if so, he was damned good at it.

"What about the divorce settlement?" Todd asked. "Were you upset with the amount and fighting it in court?"

"I wasn't upset with the amount. I was concerned over what Harper planned to do with the money. I wanted her to invest it wisely, not blow it all trying to keep up with that women's group. I tried to work out some sort of monthly payment plan where she wouldn't receive the entire settlement at once. But Harper fought me on it, insisting she get it in one lump sum. That money would've been gone in less than a year."

"What about the scarf?" Elle asked. "Did you ever get it back?"

"I did. Eventually…"

Todd observed Keaton's demeanor once again. His posture was tall. Eye contact was direct. Nothing about him appeared deceptive.

"I'm glad we came here to meet with you," he said. "I had a completely different perspective on this situation before today. I think Elle and I both have a lot more clarity now."

"Good. I'm happy to hear that. Thank you for giving me the opportunity to tell my side of the story. Do you think anything I shared will help in your investigation?"

"Absolutely," Elle replied. "You've just confirmed that Todd and I are on the right path."

"The path to take down The Precious Jewels, I hope," Keaton said, slamming his hand down onto the table.

A worker came over and tapped him on the shoulder.

"We need you over by the main water fountain, boss. We're getting a slow trickle rather than a full flow."

Keaton grunted loudly. "Ugh. Sounds like a leak in the seal or the suction lines. I'll be over in a minute."

Todd stood and extended his hand. "We'll let you get back to work."

"Deputy Jacobson, Elle, thanks again. I look forward to reading all about how you two disbanded The Precious Jewels and threw the crooked members behind bars."

Todd smiled slyly while removing his hard hat. "Have a good afternoon."

He and Elle headed back to the car.

"Welp, that was pretty damn eye-opening," she said.

"It most certainly was. Now it's time to go even harder. Catch this killer before someone else loses their life."

Chapter Twenty-One

Elle sat at her parents' kitchen table, scrolling through the Cuban Cigar Specialty website. Last time she was at Todd's house, she'd noticed that his Spanish cedar humidor was practically empty. So she'd decided to surprise him with a box of Romeo y Julieta Wide Churchills for Christmas.

"You're buying Todd a *Christmas* gift?" Rachel had asked when Elle went to her for cigar recommendations.

"Yes. Why? What's the big deal?"

"What's the *big deal*? When was the last time you bought a Christmas gift for a man you weren't in love with?"

The question was valid. Elle had never bought a present for a man who wasn't her relative or significant other.

"Girl, please," was the only response she could come up with.

Elle wasn't ready to verbalize her feelings for Todd just yet. Plus she needed to remain focused on Taylor's investigation, not on making a love connection.

Just as she added the cigars to her cart, Elle's cell phone rang. She didn't recognize the number.

Oh no...

She reached for the phone, her hand jittery with apprehension.

"Hello?"

She winced at the quiver in her voice.

"Hello, Elle?"

"Yes?"

"This is Keaton. Keaton Mitchell."

"Ah," Elle sighed and slumped into the back of her chair. "Keaton, hey. What's going on?"

"I'm sorry to bother you. I tried phoning Todd but the call went straight to voice mail."

"He's down at the station in an all-day training session. Is there something I can help you with?"

"I hope so. I was going through some of Harper's things to donate to the Salvation Army, and I found a file that contained an interesting letter."

Elle stood up and walked over to the window. "What type of letter?"

"It was from her attorney. Apparently one of the women Harper had recruited into The Precious Jewels went to the IRS claiming that members were committing wire fraud and filing false tax returns."

"*Really.* So much for that sisterly bond."

"You should see all the emails, text messages and social media posts that the plaintiff turned over."

Elle put the call on speaker and began composing a text to Todd.

"Harper was in the process of cutting a deal with the feds. In exchange for providing information on Sloane Whitlock and Linda Basco, she would avoid jail time."

The phone almost fell from Elle's hands. "In the process, meaning she never cut the deal?"

"No. She didn't. She died the day before the meeting with the federal agent was scheduled to take place."

A cold chill swept over Elle. She tried to take a deep breath. But shock had blocked her airways.

"Can you send me a copy of that letter and the accompanying correspondence?" she asked. "I want to include it in the report that Todd and I are presenting to Sheriff Glover."

"Of course. Text me your email address. I'll get everything over to you ASAP."

The phone buzzed. Todd was calling on the other line.

"Keaton, I need to go. I'll keep an eye out for that information."

She swapped calls.

"Todd! Did you—"

"Yes. I just saw your text message. I had to excuse myself from the training session and I've only got a few minutes."

"Then I'll make this quick. We have got to take our case to Sheriff Glover. *Now.* Time is running out. If we don't see to it that The Precious Jewels are dismantled ASAP, they're going to end up killing each other until there's only one woman standing."

"I hear you, Elle. But we still don't have a smoking gun. I know I said I wanted to go to him sooner rather than later, but we have to have something nearly airtight when we do go. Glover won't listen otherwise. What direct evidence is there to argue our case? Clearly Sloane is using her high-power status to fly under law enforcement's radar. If Chloe is involved in this, she's taking advantage of that as well. I suggest we stay the course and keep our investigation going until we've got solid proof of guilt."

The chill Elle had been feeling transformed into heated frustration. "You know what? Maybe I need to wear a wire and set Sloane up so that she thinks I'm preparing to rat her out to the feds. Then when she comes after me, you can catch her in the act and arrest her."

"Hold on, hold on. The feds might be on this case right now if Harper was about to sit down with an agent," he said.

"If that were true, don't you think we would have picked up on it by now? If the feds are involved, they're moving at a snail's pace. C'mon, I can do this."

Todd sighed audibly. "You'll do it anyway, won't you?" he asked. "No matter what I say."

She smiled. "Yes."

"All right. Desperate times call for desperate measures…"

"Deputy Jacobson!" someone called out. "We need you back in here."

"Listen," Todd said, "I've gotta return to my session. Why don't you start brainstorming some ideas? I'll do the same. We'll reconvene tonight."

ELLE SLID A piece of salmon sashimi around on her plate. She and Todd were sitting in a far corner inside The Freshwater Grill. Todd was friends with the owner, so he'd allowed the pair to dine in a closed-off section of the restaurant for privacy.

"Here's what I'm thinking," Elle said. "I'll tell Sloane that I need to have a private, in-person conversation with her. When we meet up, I'll explain that a federal agent reached out to me asking if I'm a member of The Precious Jewels, what do I know about the group, etcetera etcetera. If Sloane asks, I'll use the same agent's name that was working with Harper—"

"But you won't mention knowing anything about the Harper situation, right?"

"Of course not. I won't make any mention of Harper at all."

"Good. And you'll wear a wire when you meet with Sloane?"

"Yes, I'll wear the wire, and we'll record the conversation. I can use the information that Harper gave her attorney and make it seem as if I received it from the federal agent. That should get her to talking."

Todd refilled their cups of sake. "And when she asks whether or not you're going to meet with the agent?"

"I'll tell her that I am. I'll share the date and time, too."

"Then that, my friend, will set the trap."

Elle raised her drink in the air. "It certainly will. Because on that day, Sloane will come after me, you'll go after her, and she will finally be arrested."

"Cheers to that," he said flatly.

They clinked their cups together and sipped their rice wine.

"You don't sound enthused," she said to him.

"I don't like using you as bait. It could be dangerous."

She smiled at his concern. "I'll be careful. And you'll be watching. And listening."

"I wish there was a better way."

"It's all we've got right now."

"And you'll do it even without my involvement," he said, as if the matter was settled.

"Let me ask you this," Elle said as she poured soy sauce over her dragon roll. "Where does Bryce stand in our investigation at this point? I mean, we're so focused on Sloane and The Precious Jewels. Is he still in this?"

"Absolutely. The Precious Jewels are just at the top of the suspects list. For the time being, let's focus on them, primarily Sloane. When she goes down, Chloe will automatically follow suit, and so will everyone else involved."

"The domino effect."

"Exactly."

Todd reached across the table and dabbed his napkin against the corner of Elle's mouth.

"Wasabi sauce," he said.

"Oh…" Her cheeks burned under his piercing gaze. "Thanks."

"I think we've had enough talk about the investigation for one night," Todd said. "Why don't we switch gears? Lighten up the mood a bit?"

"I'd like that. Because we have been talking about this case incessantly."

"That we have." Todd ran his fingertip along the rim of his cup. "So, have you heard from your ex?"

Elle almost choked on her sashimi. "Wait, is that what you call lightening the mood?"

He chuckled. "I guess not. I…uh… I was just curious. That's all."

"Well, to answer your question, no. I have not heard from my ex. As a matter of fact, a mutual friend told me he's already seeing someone else."

"Was that upsetting to hear?"

"Not really. It was just further proof that we didn't belong together. He never even tried to fight for our relationship. He just nonchalantly agreed when I suggested we part ways."

"Had he fought to keep you, would you have stayed?"

"No. Because I know there's better waiting out here for me."

"I couldn't agree more. And it just might be closer than you think."

Todd's cell phone buzzed. He and Elle held their gaze for several moments before he checked the text.

"Deputy Cross and some of the other deputies are heading over to Bradford High's football game. They're playing their biggest rival tonight."

"Duncan Tech?"

"Yep. You wanna go after we're done with dinner?"

Elle didn't immediately respond.

"I hear the marching band is gonna be playing Christmas carols during halftime," Todd continued. "Not to mention we could both use a break from all this investigative work."

"That's true. I haven't done anything just for fun since I've been back in Bradford."

"And Taylor would *not* be pleased with that. So, what

do you say? Let's take a night off and go enjoy ourselves. Stuff our faces with churros and cheap chocolate candy bars like we used to do back in the day."

"You know what?" she said. "Yes. Let's go."

Chapter Twenty-Two

Elle pulled in front of Sloane's house. Checked the rearview mirror. Watched as Todd rounded the corner and pulled over at the end of the block.

Her cell phone rang. It was him.

"Hey," she said as he flashed his headlights. "I see you back there."

"Good. I'll be here the whole time. How are you feeling?"

"Nervous, but ready," Elle said, adjusting the collar on her suede lilac blazer.

Nervous was an understatement. Her heart thumped so forcefully that it practically rattled her silver chain necklace.

Nevertheless, it was showtime.

Time to face Sloane, one-on-one...

"Do you have the recording device secured inside your jacket?" Todd asked.

"I do," she said, patting her pocket. The slender recorder, which was two inches long and wide, was tucked deep inside. "I just get so anxious thinking Sloane might see it, or it might fall out, and she'll realize what I'm really up to."

"She won't. Just be cool, don't fidget with your blazer, and stick to the script. You'll be fine."

"Thanks for the encouragement." Elle glanced at the

clock. It was five minutes to seven. "I'd better go on in. I don't wanna be late."

"Good luck. Like I said, I'll be right here when you come out."

Elle double-checked to make sure that the device was turned on, then stepped out of the car.

Just as she slammed the door shut, Chloe came bouncing out of Sloane's house.

What are you doing here?

Elle hadn't wanted anyone to know that she was meeting with Sloane privately. The Precious Jewels were messy, and they loved to gossip. Especially Chloe.

The less they knew, the better.

"Elle?" Chloe said. "Is that you?"

"Yes, it is me. Hi."

Chloe came sashaying toward her, looking like the quintessential sorority member in her pale pink petticoat-style dress and string of pearls. "Hey, girl, hey! What are you doing here?"

"I…um—I just need to talk to Sloane about…about tips on how to recruit new members."

"*What?* You should've just come to me! I'm like, the *queen* of recruitment. Plus, I'm your mentor. You're gonna have Sloane thinking I'm not fulfilling my leadership duties!"

Elle waved her off. "Please. I'm sure she won't think that. I hadn't seen you at the last couple of events, so I figured you were busy and didn't have the time."

"Listen, I'm never too busy to coach my mentees. I've been traveling a lot, but I will always make time for you. We can email, text, chat over video conference. Whatever you want."

"Thank you. I'll remember that next time."

Chloe glanced up at Sloane's front door. "I actually stopped by to check on our fearless leader after hearing about that epic meltdown she had at the last meeting. I wish I had been here. I feel like I could've done something to stop it."

"It was pretty bad. So bad that I don't think anyone could've stopped it. Linda certainly tried."

"Yeah, well, Linda's not me. She's weak." Chloe moved in closer. "Just between us, I'm hoping to knock her out of that number two spot. *Soon.* I've got a plan, too."

Elle's ears perked up. "You do?"

"I do. And I ran it by Sloane tonight. She liked it. I'll share the deets with you if you promise not to say anything."

"Of course I won't. It'll stay between us."

"Awesome. So, I asked Sloane if she'd like to cohost a tea party with me this weekend, which would be sponsored by The Precious Jewels. We'd invite a select group of prominent women from Bradford and a few surrounding counties. Nothing too fancy. Just something casual at Sloane's place. It'll be a push to recruit new members, and of course bring in more money."

"That sounds like a great idea, Chloe. I'm sure it'll help to lift Sloane's spirits, too."

Chloe bounced up and down on her high heels. "That is exactly what I was thinking! Of course we'll charge an entry fee, which is only fair considering how amazing it will be to have all these VIPs in one room together. Can you imagine all the networking opportunities? And the added bonus is Sloane and I are gonna make a huge profit off this."

"Oh, so…you and Sloane are going to split the proceeds among yourselves?"

Chloe's head bobbed from side to side. "I mean, we'll probably donate a small portion of it to charity. Which of course we'd write off on our taxes. Speaking of taxes, that's the beauty of being a Precious Jewel. I haven't had to report any of the money I've made to the IRS. So I'm just out here making a killing!"

Elle's eyes squinted as she watched Chloe readjust her rhinestone Chanel broach. "Wait, isn't that illegal?"

Chloe's lips curled into a knowing smirk. "I don't know. Is it?"

Sloane's porch light came on. Elle looked up the driveway. Ivory Chantilly lace curtains parted as she appeared in the window.

Elle pulled her cell out of her purse and checked the time. It was ten minutes after seven.

"Anyway," Chloe continued, "I just figured Sloane could use a boost since some of our fellow Jewels are questioning her involvement in those deaths. What better way to do that than to generate some cash—"

"Elle!" Sloane yelled from her veranda. "You're late! What are you doing out there?"

"Sorry! I'll be up in a sec."

Chloe grabbed Elle's shoulders and gave an air kiss on each cheek. "You'd better go. Be on the lookout for Sloane's tea party invitation. She's going to email it out tonight. It'll contain all the deets on the event. Be sure not to share it with anyone!"

"I won't. Thanks!"

When Elle reached the front door, she was greeted with an angry glare.

"The one thing you will not do," Sloane snarled, "is disrespect my time. My calendar is jam-packed, Elle. Yet I was gracious enough to clear a spot for you at the last minute. And what do you do? You insult me by—"

"Sloane, please," Elle interrupted. "I am so sorry. I was actually here on time. But I ran into Chloe on the way in, and we started chatting about all of the exciting things that are going on with The Precious Jewels. Time just got away from me. Again, my apologies."

Sloane stepped to the side and held out her hand. Elle entered the foyer reluctantly, feeling the angry heat coming off Sloane as she walked past her.

Elle was surprised to see her dressed in yet another velour leisure suit, this one a pale shade of yellow. From the looks of her loose ponytail and bare face, Sloane was still in meltdown mode.

"Excuse is the tool of the incompetent," Sloane said while leading them into the great room.

What in the hell is this woman talking about?

"A monument of nothingness," she continued. "And those that use it are not wise. Have you heard that quote, Elle?"

"No. I have not."

"Words to live by, spoken by Pastor Paul Adefarasin. Keep them in mind *the next time you run late for a meeting with me then make excuses for it*. Now, have a seat and tell me what's so urgent that you *insisted on coming here* on such short notice."

The glare in Sloane's steely eyes made Elle want to get up and leave. Her dark aura was chilling. Elle felt as though she was looking into the face of a killer.

Time to take you down...

Elle cleared her throat. "I wanted to let you know that I received a call from a federal agent."

Sloane's scowl fell into an open-mouthed gape.

"Wh-what did he want?" she asked, her overly plumped bottom lip quivering. "What did he say?"

Elle felt her body relax. She crossed her legs, unable to resist finding pleasure in Sloane's fear.

"*She*. The agent is a woman."

"Okay. What did *she* want?"

"To know whether or not I'm a member of The Precious Jewels."

Sloane slapped her hands against her thighs. "*And?* What did you tell her?"

"I told her that I am."

"*Dammit*, Elle!"

Sloane jumped up and began walking in circles, her UGG slippers sliding across the white glass mosaic tiles.

"What else did she ask?"

"Um…let me think," Elle stalled. She bounced her knees rapidly, feigning nervousness. "She asked whether or not I was required to pay an initiation fee in order to join."

"What'd you say?"

"That I was."

"Ahh!" Sloane spun around and fell against the quartz fireplace mantel. "You are killing me, Elle! Are you that daft? Why the hell would you tell her that?"

"Because it's the truth! And I—I was nervous. Plus they're the *feds*, Sloane. They already know the answers to their questions before they even ask them."

Sloane dropped her head and turned her back to Elle. "First Harper and now you," she muttered under her breath.

"Wait, what did you just say?" Elle asked, hoping that her recorder had picked up the comment.

"I said, first Harper, and now you!" Sloane pivoted and rushed toward Elle, her wide eyes darting with fury.

Elle recoiled, gripping the arm of the couch.

"You'd better not speak another word about The Precious Jewels," Sloane spewed. "To anyone!"

"So…so what am I supposed to tell this agent when I meet with her?"

A guttural howl pierced Elle's ears. She thought it'd come from one of Sloane's dogs. But it had come from her.

"*Meet* with her? You actually agreed to meet with the feds, Elle? To discuss *my* organization?"

"Yes, of course! What was I supposed to do? Tell them no?"

"When is the meeting?"

"Next week. Monday. At nine a.m. to be exact."

Sloane grabbed Elle's arm and yanked her off the couch.

"Ouch!" Elle shrieked, stunned by the petite woman's strength.

"Get out," Sloane insisted as she dragged Elle toward the door. "Get the hell out of my house! Expect a call from my attorney first thing in the morning. And if you speak one word about The Precious Jewels to a single soul, I swear I will sue you for slander and take everything you own. Not that it appears to be much."

Sloane threw open the door, then leaned in so closely that Elle could smell the whiskey on her breath. "I do not go down without a fight. And I never fought a battle I didn't win."

"Wh-what do you mean by that?"

"Take it however you want. Now get out!"

Sloane pushed Elle onto the veranda and slammed the door.

Elle just stood there, breathing heavily, struggling to regain her composure. And then, she broke into a fit of elated laughter.

"I just got everything I need, and then some."

She hurried down the driveway and stared down the street in search of Todd's car. It wasn't there.

That's strange...

Elle pulled out her cell phone to dial his number. When she unlocked the screen, a text message from him appeared.

Hey, there was a robbery over at Ingram's Grab N Go. Deputy Cross asked me to meet him there and check out the scene. I should be back at Sloane's before your meeting ends. So hang tight. I'll be back soon.

"Yeah, not gonna happen," Elle muttered to herself as she responded to the message.

Things at Sloane's didn't go as planned. Long story short, she kicked me out. I'll just head back to my parents' house. Meet me there when you're done. I'll tell you all about it then.

Elle sent the message and hopped inside her car.

She started the engine and slowly pulled away from the curb. A pair of headlights flashed behind her. She called Todd to see if it was him. The call went straight to voice mail.

Elle drove to the corner and stopped. A twinge of queasiness pierced her stomach.

Something didn't feel right.

She glanced in the rearview mirror. Darkness blanketed the street. The car's headlights had been turned off.

The tension in Elle's joints slackened.

Stop allowing your imagination to get the best of you. You're fine. No one is following you...

She turned down Austin Lane and sped through a yellow light. Glanced in the side-view mirror. The road was empty.

"See? You're good."

Elle switched on the satellite radio and turned to the twenty-four-hour Christmas jazz station. Duke Ellington's rendition of "Jingle Bells" piped through the speakers. She bobbed her head to the beat of his lively remake while heading into downtown.

A traffic controller resembling a slightly taller Danny DeVito stopped her as she approached Livingston Avenue. She rolled down the window.

"What's going on?"

"Happy holidays, ma'am. We closed off the street for the Taste of Christmas Carnival."

"The *what*?"

"The Taste of Christmas Carnival. It's something new that the restaurant owners are doing this year. Everybody's cooking up their most popular holiday dishes and serving them at individual booths all along Livingston Ave. You should do yourself a favor and check it out, especially Patty's merry mac and cheese—"

"I'm sorry," Elle interrupted, "but I'm gonna have to miss out this year. I really need to get home. Is there a detour I can take?"

"Where are you headed?"

"Kenwood Street."

"Oh, that's easy. Just head over to Oak Lane and cut through Everest Forest Preserve. That'll get you to Kenwood in no time."

Elle's jaws clenched. She thought back on the moment that black pickup truck rammed into her car at the forest preserve.

Just pull over. Wait for Todd to finish up at Ingram's...

A horn blew behind her.

"Give me a minute, will you?" Elle yelled out the window.

The traffic controller tapped her door frame. "I'm sorry, ma'am. But I'm gonna have to ask you to either pull into the parking lot or take the detour. You're holding up traffic."

Stop being paranoid. Just take the detour and get home. You'll be fine.

Elle made a U-turn and headed toward Oak Lane. She stopped at a red light and tried calling Todd again. It went straight to voice mail again.

"Hey, it's Elle," her voice quaked.

Shake it off...

"Wanted to let you know that Livingston Avenue is closed off for an event. I'm being rerouted through the Everest Forest Preserve. So...um...yeah. Just thought I should share that. Hope everything's okay at Ingram's and no one got hurt. I can't wait to tell you about the craziness that happened at Sloane's. Call me back. Or, if you can't, I'll see you at my parents' house or whatever."

You're rambling. Hang up the phone.

The light turned green. Elle disconnected the call and glanced in the rearview mirror. No one was behind her.

She hit the accelerator and made a right turn into the forest preserve.

"Come on, Todd. Call me back."

Hearing his voice would help calm her nerves. Convince her that she was overreacting.

Elle turned down the radio as if that would help, then switched on her bright lights. She checked the side-view mirror. No one was there.

"See? You just being—"

She paused when a car appeared behind her.

Relax. It's a public thoroughfare. Other people are allowed to drive on it.

The vehicle remained at a safe distance.

Elle focused on the road ahead. Safe distance or not, she was desperate to get to the other side.

The lampposts that were sporadically placed along the street appeared to be out. The forest preserve felt more like an abysmal black tunnel than a roadway. There didn't appear to be an end in sight.

But you know that there is. Just get to the other side.

Elle was hit with an eerie sense of vulnerability. The massive evergreen trees looming overhead took her breath away. They felt monstrous. As if they were closing in on her.

The car behind her had the same effect as it got closer. And closer.

Not again. No. Not again!

She slammed down on the accelerator until it hit the floor-board. Her car jolted forward, flying through the darkness.

Elle could barely see what was up ahead. She didn't care. She was determined to escape her attacker this time.

Headlights flashed in her rearview mirror. The car tailing her sped up. Its engine roared loudly as the horn blew erratically.

"What in the hell are you doing?" Elle screamed. "Leave me alone!"

Elle drove faster. The vehicle behind her followed suit.

Fears of a deer or fallen tree in the road crossed her mind. Elle pushed out the thoughts.

Just focus on the other side. Focus on the other side.

Her cell phone rang. It was Todd.

She pounded the Bluetooth button.

"Todd! I'm being chased through the forest preserve again!"

"Stay calm, Elle. I got your voice mail and I'm heading that way now. Are you still on Oak Lane?"

"Yes! Please hurry. Somebody is trying to run me off the road!"

The headlights shone so brightly behind her that Elle could barely see up ahead.

"Hang on. I'm almost there. Can you tell what type of vehicle it is?"

"No," she whimpered. "It's too dark. All I can see is lights."

"Okay. Stay on the line. I'm turning down Oak Lane now. You're heading north toward your parents' house, right?"

"Yes," she breathed, her eyes darting back and forth between the rearview mirror and the road.

The car wasn't letting up. The faster she drove, the closer it got.

"I see lights up ahead," Todd said. "I'm coming up the rear."

"Please hurry!"

"I'm catching up. Listen, I want to pin this car in between us. So, start slowing down."

Elle sat up in her seat, craning her neck in search of him. "Are you sure?"

"I'm positive. I can see your car. Just trust me. Start letting up on the accelerator."

Please let this work...

She said a quick prayer, then gradually lifted her foot off the pedal. The car chasing her slowed down.

"You see that side road up ahead?" Todd asked.

"I do."

"Make a quick right. It's a one way. We'll jam this maniac in between our cars."

"Okay."

Elle quickly steered her car down the road. Sure enough, the vehicle followed.

"I'm right behind you two," Todd said. "Keep going about a hundred more feet, then stop."

"I am so nervous," she said, her stomach churning uncontrollably.

"Just stay calm. You got this. Okay, now...stop!"

Elle slammed down on the brakes. The car behind her came to an abrupt halt, inches away from her bumper.

Todd jumped out of his vehicle and approached the attacker's door.

"Get out of the car with your hands up!" he yelled with his gun and flashlight drawn.

Elle spun around in her seat, anxious to see who would step out of the unfamiliar burgundy sedan.

The door slowly opened. A bare leg swung out. A nude Mary Jane pump hit the dirt.

Who the...

Elle's hand trembled as she pulled the door handle. She stepped outside, watching Todd move toward the suspect.

The woman climbed out of the car. Todd flashed the light in her face.

It was Chloe.

"Elle!" she squealed. "I hope I didn't scare you."

Elle marched toward her, stunned.

"What the hell do you mean, *you hope you didn't scare me*? Of course you did! Why are you chasing me through the forest preserve?"

Chloe turned to Todd. "Um, excuse me. But could you please put that gun away and stop shining that light in my face?"

"Not until you tell us what you're doing."

She reached inside of her car.

"Keep your hands where I can see them, Chloe!" Todd warned.

She stood back up and handed him something.

"What is that?" Elle asked, taking a step toward her.

"Your debit card. You dropped it while we were standing outside of Sloane's house."

Elle almost fell to her knees. *"Chloe,"* she snapped, snatching the card. "You went through all of that just to return this?"

"Of course! I didn't want you looking for it, then panicking when you couldn't find it. I waited outside of Sloane's house for you instead of knocking since she was so angry that you were late. Then you left so soon after you got there that I wasn't able to catch you."

"Yeah, that's because she kicked me out."

"She did? Why?"

Elle paused. She glanced over at Todd, who discreetly shook his head.

"Long story," Elle told her. "Anyway, now that I've recovered from the massive heart attack you just induced, I need to get out of here. Thank you for returning my card."

"You're welcome. Sorry for the scare."

Todd wrapped his arm around Elle. "Are you okay?"

She inhaled sharply, leaning into his chest. "I will be. I just wanna go home and relax. Shake this whole experience off."

"Understood. I'll follow you and make sure you get there safely."

"Would you mind staying with me for a while?"

"Of course not. I'll stay with you for as long as you want."

The intensity in his lively eyes told Elle that he wasn't just referring to that night.

"Aww, look at the two *lovebirds*," Chloe sang. "How cute."

Todd threw her a look. "Be safe getting home, Chloe."

"Oh, wait, no police escort for me, too?"

"I'll make sure you get back out onto the main road safely," he replied through tight lips before turning back to Elle. "Hey, I'm so sorry I missed your calls earlier. I couldn't get any reception inside of Ingram's. This should have never—"

"You do not owe me an apology, Todd. This was my fault. I should've just waited for you. But you got here right on time."

"Thank God it was a false alarm. Now let's get out of here."

Chapter Twenty-Three

Elle handed Todd a mug of hot chocolate topped with whipped cream and cinnamon.

"Ooh, that looks so fancy. Thank you."

"Hold on. I'm not done yet."

She grabbed two candy canes from her mother's crystal snowflake-shaped bowl and slid them inside their mugs. "Now it's really fancy."

The pair were back at Elle's parents' place, relaxing on the tan leather couch inside the family room.

She'd lit the brick fireplace as soon as they had arrived, to take the chill out of the air. Its flames crackled softly in the background. A large evergreen wreath hung over the mantel, the scent of its pine cones wafting through the air.

Being back at the Scotts' house felt warm and tranquil, now that the broken furniture had been removed and replaced, and the home cleaned from top to bottom, insurance covering it all. Elle had just moved back in, he knew, while her parents stayed with friends for a while.

Being in Elle's presence felt like home.

Todd was glad to see that she had finally calmed down after the evening's fiasco.

"Mmm," he said after taking a sip of hot chocolate. "It tastes as good as it looks."

"Thank you. Have you forgotten that Taylor and I mastered the art of crafting hot chocolate during our junior year of high school? That's when we started selling it out of my parents' garage."

"Really? No, I don't remember that. I must've been on one of my massive workout-slash-healthy-eating binges that year. Otherwise I would've guzzled your entire supply before anyone could buy a cup."

Elle threw her head back and laughed. Todd gazed at her. She still appeared radiant, despite her traumatic night.

Loose curls framed her smiling face. A faint trace of pink gloss covered her supple lips.

Todd felt the urge to lean in and kiss them. But he resisted. The romantic gesture didn't seem fitting in the moment.

"So Sloane put you out of her house, huh?" Todd asked.

"Like Martin did Pam on almost every episode of his sitcom."

"Ha! I'm glad you're able to joke about it."

"Sometimes you just gotta laugh to keep from crying, right?"

Todd gave her arm an affectionate nudge. "Ah, come on. There's no crying in criminal justice. We are so close to solving this case, Elle. You were great tonight. You did what you set out to do. Planted the seed in Sloane's mind that you're meeting with a federal agent."

"Yeah, but I'm not gonna lie. That run-in with Chloe at the forest preserve has me shaken up. I know it was a false alarm and all, but it gave me a taste of what may happen if Sloane comes after me. That was scary."

"I know it was. But the difference is I won't leave your side next time. Getting called to Ingram's was an unexpected fluke. No matter what comes my way the day of your fake meeting with the feds, I'll be there. Period. Got it?"

"Got it." Elle stared down at her cup, poking at the whipped cream with her candy cane. "You know, it just dawned on me that Chloe wasn't driving her Range Rover tonight. I've never seen that car she was in before. I wonder who it belongs to. And where's her truck?"

"Good question. I was so discombobulated by all the chaos that I didn't think to ask. Maybe you can find out when you see her at that Precious Jewels tea party this weekend."

"I will. That should be an interesting event. We'll see if Sloane can get back to her normal, glamorous self. Maybe she'll show up in something besides a tracksuit and avoid having another meltdown."

"I would hope so since it sounds like she's inviting the who's who among all of North Carolina."

Elle dug inside of her pocket and pulled out the recording device.

"Damn," Todd said. "In the midst of all the madness, I forgot that you recorded your conversation with Sloane. Did you get any useful information?"

"Nothing that could land her in jail. She did mention Harper being contacted by the feds. And said something about not going down without a fight. The juiciest bites were of her freaking out over my meeting with the federal agent."

"I guess you got kicked out before you could really dig for some dirt."

"Exactly."

Todd gently swiped a lock of hair away from Elle's eye. "Is it okay if I shift gears for a minute? Talk about something outside of the case?"

Elle turned, her lips brushing slightly against the palm of his hand. "Of course."

He took a long sip of his hot chocolate. "How do you feel being back in Bradford? I mean, aside from working Taylor's case. Are you enjoying spending time in your hometown?"

Elle sat back, her head tilting to the side.

"You know, I am. I live a fast-paced life in New York City. Being back here has reminded me that there's an easier pace. One that may be better suited for me now that I'm getting older and tired of that jet-setting lifestyle."

"Hmm, interesting. I'm sure it helps that you've returned during the holidays. I don't know about you, but as far as I'm concerned, there's no place in the world that does Christmas quite like Bradford."

"Oh, I totally agree. There's something about this town during the season that can't be replicated. The warm sense of community coming together to curate all these amazing events. The unique, handcrafted decorations and elaborate lights festivals. And don't even get me started on the delicious food. It literally feels like the most wonderful time of the year around here."

Todd slid closer toward her. "It does. Especially this year, having you home. This has been nice. Really nice. The time we've spent together has been primarily about Taylor, but being around you just feels…*good*."

"Thank you, Todd. I feel the same way about you. But… there's something that I have to ask."

"Ask away."

Elle pulled at a string hanging from the couch cushion. "What about your ex? Is there a chance that you two might get back together?"

Todd shook his head adamantly. "No. Absolutely not. That relationship had run its course. I've been looking forward to the next chapter in my life ever since."

"Have you been dating since the breakup?"

He set his hot chocolate down and tugged at his sweater sleeve, avoiding eye contact.

"Wait, what are you doing?" Elle asked. Her shrill tone was filled with amusement. "Did I hit a nerve asking that question?"

Todd smiled sheepishly. "Maybe…"

"Okay. Spill it. What type of dating disasters have you gotten yourself into? At least give me one good story."

Todd fell against the back of the couch and covered his face. "Man, I do have some stories to tell. But the wildest one has got to be the time I connected with a woman who lives in Florida through a dating app."

"Wait, you've tried online dating?"

"I have. And it was a nightmare. But let's not dwell on that. I'll just hurry up and share this *one* story so that we can hurry up and change the subject."

"Okay, fine. Let's hear it."

"So I met this woman who lived in Tampa. We clicked immediately. We'd text, talk on the phone and video-chat whenever we could. After about a month of that, I decided to fly to Tampa and meet her in person."

Elle snickered into her hand. "Oh no. Please don't tell me you went all the way to Florida and got catfished."

"No, no. I didn't. When I met her in person, she looked exactly like her photos."

"So, what went wrong?"

"Well, after an amazing seafood dinner at Ocean Prime, then a wine tasting on the Tampa Riverwalk, I was ready to call it a night. But my date had other plans. She insisted that we stop by one last spot before I went back to my hotel…"

Todd's voice trailed off. He stared up at the ceiling, clenching his teeth together.

"Hey, you can't just leave me hanging like that!" Elle insisted. "Come on. Finish the story."

"Ugh," Todd groaned. "The memory of it all just turns my stomach." He sat back up. "So anyway, after this woman begged and pleaded, I agreed to go to this one last spot. I pull up to the address and see that it's a private residence. We go around to the back of the house, enter through a sliding glass door, and are led to the basement by a woman dressed in all black leather from head to toe. Oh, and she was wearing a cape, too."

"A *cape*?"

"Yes. A cape."

"What was this, some type of costume party?"

"Not quite. When we got down to the basement, I realized that it was a swinger party."

"Excuse me," Elle said, turning her ear toward Todd. "It was a what?"

"A *swinger party.*"

"Oh my word. I have heard it all. What happened next?"

"I got the hell outta there, that's what happened next. My date insisted on staying, so I left her there. Flew back home the next day and never spoke to her again."

"*Wow*. If this were a dating disaster competition, you'd win first place. Hands down."

"Thanks. I think…" he said before finishing off his hot chocolate. "Lucky for me, the days of random dating are behind me now. I've taken myself off the market."

"Really? Why?"

"Because I'm done wasting my time. Until the real thing comes along, I'm cool just being single."

"That's understandable. I feel the same way."

Elle yawned, stretching her arms high in the air.

"Looks like somebody is getting sleepy," Todd said.

"I am. But I'm also really enjoying your company."

"Same here. But it's getting late. And we've had a long, challenging day. We should probably get some rest."

"We should." Elle stood and held out her hand. "I'll walk you to the door."

Todd took her hand in his and followed her to the living room.

Her tender touch was soothing. It made him think twice about going home and sleeping alone.

"I'll call you tomorrow," she said.

"Please do."

Todd leaned down and kissed her gently on the forehead. She gazed up at him, then pressed her mouth against his. He closed his eyes, relishing the feel of her soft lips.

Todd felt his jeans tighten near the zipper. He quickly pulled away and opened the door.

"Talk to you tomorrow," he said, rushing out the door.

Chapter Twenty-Four

Elle looked around Sloane's great room. It was packed with some of the wealthiest and most uppity women she had ever seen.

The Precious Jewels tea party was in full swing. Despite the last-minute email invitation that Sloane sent out, she'd gotten a huge turnout.

The room was filled with a sea of perfectly coiffed bouffant hairstyles, designer duds, pricey handbags and surgically enhanced faces. Conversations ranged from summer home purchases to husbands' affairs, booming businesses to gossip on who'd filed for bankruptcy.

Elle could not have felt more out of place. Her feet were beginning to ache inside her spiked-heel ankle boots, which she shouldn't have worn considering they hadn't been broken in yet.

She let out a deep breath just as Rachel walked back over and handed her a porcelain teacup.

"One pumpkin spice tea with a dash of raw sugar for you, and one peppermint tea with two packets of stevia for me."

"Thank you, ma'am."

"So why are you standing over here looking so disgusted?" Rachel asked.

"You know, I'm getting tired of being around all these superficial, overbearing women. And I don't feel comfortable being back inside this house after Sloane kicked me out the other day. I know that none of this is real, and I'm working undercover to solve Taylor's murder. But this entire situation is getting to me. I'm ready for it to be over."

"Well, from what I can tell, you and Todd are almost there. So keep going, sis. You got this."

"I hope so." Elle tugged at the collar of her plain black A-line dress. "I feel so underdressed next to all these other women. Chloe said this party would be casual."

Rachel stepped back and pointed at her denim jumpsuit. "Yeah, tell me about. And look at Sloane. Is she about to serve as somebody's bride in that gold silk mermaid dress?"

Elle snickered. "Looks like it. She's doing way too much. I guess she finally snapped out of that slump she'd been in. I was expecting to see her in yet another velour tracksuit."

"Same. And her little sidekick Chloe's been flitting around here like she's the belle of the ball."

"Yeah, she's making her bid to take over Linda's spot," Elle said before taking a sip of tea.

"Well, it appears to be working. Sloane and the rest of these women are eating up her little corny jokes and kiss-ass compliments."

"Spcaking of thc dcvil, hcrc shc comcs…"

Chloe came strolling toward the women, her powder blue cocktail dress swaying from side to side.

"Hello, ladies," she purred. "I'm glad you two were able to make it. I love that my mentees are showing so much enthusiasm."

"You know us," Rachel said. "We're all about female empowerment, which The Precious Jewels clearly embodies."

Elle almost snorted at her sarcasm.

"Good," Chloe gushed. "That means we must be doing something right."

The group fell silent. Elle racked her brain for something

to say. But her mind was blocked. Being around Chloe was triggering an odd sense of discomfort.

Maybe you're still not over that incident at the forest preserve...

Chloe turned toward her.

"*Sooo*, how are your recruiting efforts coming along?"

"They're...uh...they're coming along great. As a matter of fact, Rachel and I met several women at Pilar Samuels's art opening that are interested in joining The Precious Jewels."

"Oh, really? That is awesome! Have you invited them to our upcoming social yet?"

"We were planning on sending out invitations this week," Rachel chimed in. "Elle and I are determined to work our way up to Diamond status and cash out on that treasure chest. Right, E?"

"Absolutely."

Chloe squealed and bounced on her tippy toes. "Ah, this is all music to my ears!" She twirled around and then took a bow. On the way back up, she turned her ankle. "Ouch!"

Elle grabbed her arm. "Are you okay?"

"I think so," she said, bending down and rubbing her shin. "But I'd better go and sit down for a minute. Take the weight off. I'd hate to end up with a fractured fibula like our girl Taylor."

Elle almost dropped her drink. "You'd—you'd *what*?"

"Let's reconvene later, ladies. My ankle is on fire," Chloe said before hobbling toward the couch.

"Elle?" Rachel said. "Why do you look like you just saw a demon?"

"Because I think I just did."

"What are you talking about?"

Elle turned to Rachel, so rattled that her teeth were chattering. "No one knew about Taylor's fractured fibula except for law enforcement. That information was never revealed to the public."

Rachel's head dropped. "Excuse me?"

"The sheriff's department only revealed that Taylor suffered an accidental neck injury."

Elle pulled out her cell phone and began texting Todd. "That's it. I'm over this. Todd has got to speak with Sheriff Glover about Taylor's case. Between Chloe, Sloane and Bryce, one of them killed her. And they need to find out who."

"Hell, at this point, maybe all three of them were involved."

"I'm asking Todd if he can try and talk the sheriff into bringing them all in for questioning. I mean, seriously, how much more evidence do we need to show that they are viable suspects? Just pull out the lie detector test so we can get to the truth!"

"Amen, sister. But considering all the political crap that goes on in this town? Good luck with that—"

Rachel was interrupted by the sound of a finger tapping against a microphone.

"Testing, testing, one-two, testing, one-two."

They turned to the front of the room. Sloane was standing at the podium with Linda to her right and Chloe to her left.

"I guess Chloe wasn't too injured to run up to her fearless leader," Elle muttered.

"Hello, ladies," Sloane said. "Welcome to The Precious Jewels' first annual holiday tea party. I am aware that you all lead such big, busy lives, which is why I'm so grateful that you took the time to celebrate the season with us."

The group gave Sloane a polite round of applause.

"This event is such an extraordinary networking opportunity," Sloane continued. "I'm trusting that you've all had a chance to mingle, converse and exchange contact information. More importantly, I hope that each of you has spoken to the members of The Precious Jewels and gotten to know more about our illustrious organization."

As Sloane schmoozed the crowd, Chloe pulled out her cell phone and began typing away.

"I'm sorry," Rachel whispered, "but could Chloe be any ruder? She is literally texting someone during the middle of Sloane's speech!"

"Um, have you met Chloe? She doesn't care about anyone except herself. She's just glad to be standing up there next to her idol. Next she'll be trying to knock Sloane out of her spot and take over The Precious Jewels."

Sloane leaned into the mic and cleared her throat. "I would love to introduce to you my cochair of this event, Chloe Hale. But it looks like there's something more important going on with that cellular phone of hers!"

The partygoers burst out laughing.

"Oh, no, no!" Chloe insisted, dropping her phone down by her side. "My apologies, Sloane. Please, go ahead."

"Thank you. Ladies, Chloe is one of the most dynamic members of The Precious Jewels that you could ever meet. She is ambitious, caring, and most importantly, *loyal*. As we all know, that is a hard trait to come by these days."

Sloane shot Elle a look.

Elle stared back at her, crossing her arms defiantly.

"Showdown at the Whitlock estate," Rachel hissed, struggling to contain her laughter.

"From Chloe's community service efforts to her passion toward our sisterhood," Sloane continued, "this woman's dedication to our organization is unmatched. She has made quite an impact on the Bradford community, as well as a ton of money, thanks to The Precious Jewels!"

Everyone broke into laughter once again.

"Oh, come on, Sloane," Chloe said, embracing her tightly. "You're too much. You're simply *too much*!"

"Ugh, I think I'm about to barf," Rachel said.

"So," Sloane said, "without further ado, I present to you one of The Precious Jewels' brightest stars, and a woman I'm proud to call my sister, Miss Chloe Hale!"

Cheers and applause filled the room while Chloe stepped up to the podium.

Elle rolled her eyes. "Here we go. This woman has been waiting for this moment all her life."

"Thank you so much for that wonderful introduction, Sloane! My goodness. How could I ever top that?" She held her finger to her chin and stared up at the ceiling. "Oh! I know. By telling you who I really am. My name isn't Chloe Hale. It's Kendra Duval. And I'm not a member of The Precious Jewels. I am a special agent with the Federal Bureau of Investigations. Sloane Whitlock, Linda Basco, you are both under arrest for defrauding the IRS."

Audible gasps swept through the crowd. Elle grabbed hold of Rachel as her knees gave way.

"Am I losing my mind," Elle shrieked, "or did Chloe just say she's with the FBI?"

"No, *Kendra* just said she's with the FBI."

Elle's breathing grew shallow. "This is too much. I think I'm about to pass out…"

"Don't you dare fall out on me and miss all this good action!"

Sloane whimpered as Kendra, formerly known as Chloe, spun her around and put her in handcuffs.

"You—you *traitor*!" Sloane screamed. "How could you betray me like this?"

Kendra ignored her, remaining stone-faced as she moved on to handcuffing Linda.

Sloane's housekeeper came rushing into the great room, followed by several FBI agents.

"Mrs. Whitlock!" she yelled. "I tried to stop them, but they just came bursting through the door like a herd of *animals*!"

"Agent Keller!" Kendra yelled across the room. "Can you please take over the arrests? I need to show the other agents where they can find Mrs. Whitlock's computer and files."

"Absolutely, Agent Duval."

Two of the other agents began directing guests out of the house.

"Okay, ladies, the party's over. We're gonna have to ask you to leave. Please do so as quickly as possible."

Elle and Rachel clung to each other as women rushed past them, their faces twisted in horror and their high heels screeching across the tile.

"Look at all these guilty women," Rachel said. "Charging out of here before they get arrested, too."

Elle held her hand to her spinning head. "This is unreal. I cannot believe that Chloe... I mean *Kendra* is a special agent!"

"Yep. She is. And it looks like she's heading our way."

Kendra walked over and extended her hand. "Ladies, please, let me formally introduce myself. As you just heard, I'm special agent Kendra Duval, and I've been investigating The Precious Jewels over the past year." She handed Elle a business card. "I get the impression that you're really here to find out what happened to Taylor. Am I correct?"

"Yes. You are."

"I thought so. I was assigned to this case in order to investigate the organization's suspected tax and wire fraud activity. But that doesn't mean Sloane's crimes stop there." She looked over her shoulder at the retreating crowd of shocked women. "We did this publicly to send a message to the rest of the Jewels. We might shake some informers out of the group." Her eyes focused once again on Elle. "I do think that you and Deputy Jacobson are on to something."

"Wait, you know about that?"

"Of course I do. Let's stay in touch. I'll be reaching out to Sheriff Glover as well."

"*Good.* Maybe all this will convince him to reopen Taylor's case." Elle paused, tapping Kendra's card against her palm. "You know, for a minute there, I thought that you might be the killer."

"I know you did. That was intentional. If you thought I was a murderer, you'd never suspect me of being a special agent."

"Agent Duval?" someone called out. "We need you in the library."

"I'll be there in a second!" She turned to Elle and Rachel. "Ladies, take care."

Kendra walked away, her usual peppy gait transforming into a stern stride.

"Do you see this?" Rachel asked. "That woman just sauntered off like Keyser Söze in *The Usual Suspects.*"

"I do. And just like that character in the movie, Kendra had me completely fooled."

Elle stepped back as Sloane and Linda were led outside, both blabbering about their innocence through mascara-soaked tears.

"And now," Elle continued, "I don't have to put myself at risk by faking that meeting with the feds on Monday—"

She was interrupted by her buzzing cell phone. It was a text message from Todd.

Hey, I think calling Sloane and Chloe down to the station for questioning is a great idea, followed by Bryce. I'll go run it by Sheriff Glover and let you know what he says. How are things going at the tea party?

"Oh no. I've gotta call Todd and update him on what just happened here!" Elle said before grabbing Rachel's arm and rushing out the door.

Chapter Twenty-Five

Elle stood along the edge of the River Birch Park hiking trail. She'd gone there on a whim, motivated by Todd's plan to interrogate Bryce down at the station that evening.

After Sloane's and Linda's arrests, Sheriff Glover had finally agreed to reopen Taylor's case. He wanted to take a look at all possible suspects, including Bryce.

Elle had forgotten how quickly the sun set on December days. Gone was the dusky lavender sky that was present during her ride to the park. It had been replaced by blankets of heavy, gray clouds.

The scattered lampposts that lined the trail had been turned off. The park district must've assumed that the town's holiday-obsessed community would rather go ice skating or Christmas shopping than take a jog along the chilly trail.

And they would be right...

The trail was empty. And now dark.

Elle pulled a flashlight from her green nylon backpack and turned it up to the brightest setting. She was beginning to second-guess her rash decision to go out there. But she couldn't quiet her urge to revisit Taylor's crime scene once again.

Elle was still determined to uncover some sort of direct evidence linked to Taylor's murder. And now that Sloane was behind bars, Chloe had come out as a special agent and Bryce was at the sheriff's office, she felt safe knowing all their suspects were accounted for.

Elle approached the tulip tree near where Taylor's body had been found. She shined the flashlight toward the base of its trunk, studying the deep grooves in the brown, furrowed bark and inhaling its sweet, musky scent.

Elle wondered what had gone through Taylor's mind as she was being attacked in that very spot.

Why didn't you leave us a clue, friend? A clump of hair. Smear of blood. Set of footprints...

A blast of chilly wind blew straight through Elle's pink yoga jacket. She bowed her head and pulled the zipper toward her chin. The gust blew a small pile of dried orange leaves away from the tree trunk. They landed near Elle's gray sneakers, then swirled through the air as if caught in a tornado.

The spot that the leaves evacuated was covered in a cluster of twigs. Elle focused her light on the shoots.

One of them caught her eye. She took a step closer. It appeared to be covered in droplets of deep burgundy stains.

It couldn't be... Could it?

Elle's entire body began to shake. She bent down, her breathing quickening at the thought of finally uncovering a piece of evidence.

Her cell phone rang. She jumped up, almost falling backward from the shrill buzz.

"Calm down, girl," she told herself, accepting the call without bothering to check the caller ID.

"Elle Scott speaking."

"Hey," Todd said. "Are you okay?"

"I'm more than okay. I'm ecstatic. I think I just found a piece of evidence out at River Birch Park."

"River Birch Park? Elle, it's practically pitch-black outside! What are you doing out there? *Alone* no less?"

She pulled a pair of gloves and a plastic baggie out of her backpack.

"I know, I know. It wasn't this dark when I came out here. I felt compelled to revisit the crime scene while you were interrogating Bryce. Something was urging me to take another look. And I'm glad I did. Because guess what I see?"

"What?"

"A stick that looks to be covered in blood."

"Wait, you found *what*?"

"A twig, speckled in blood!" she repeated while slipping her hands inside the gloves.

"Are you sure, Elle? We combed that entire area several times over and came up empty on every occasion."

"I'm telling you what I see. I'll collect it, and you can send it off to the forensics lab for testing. If the stick is in fact connected to Taylor's murder, then that means my instincts were right. I was called to come out here for a reason."

"We'll see…"

Elle could tell by the sound of his low tone that Todd wasn't pleased. But she didn't care. Her actions would be justified if the potential evidence helped solve their case.

Elle's fingers trembled as she picked up the twig and slowly placed it inside the baggie.

"Got it," she declared, securing it inside her backpack.

Elle paused.

"Hold on, Todd. Shouldn't you be questioning Bryce right now?"

"Yes, I should be. That's why I was calling. To tell you that he didn't show up."

"What?"

"Bryce never came to the station. I called, texted and emailed him. Even sent a squad car by his house to see if he was there. He wasn't."

"That is so weird. One thing about Bryce, he's always been dependable. I wonder why he—"

She stopped midsentence. Turned her head to the side.

"Elle? You still there?"

"I'm here," she whispered. "Sounds like I may not be alone. I think I heard footsteps sliding across the dirt."

"Have you seen anybody out there running on the trail?"

"Not a single soul."

She pulled the phone away from her ear.

Silence.

"I don't hear anything now. Maybe it was just my—"

Bam!

Stinging pain hit the side of Elle's face. She toppled over onto her side.

A blurry figure dressed in all black hovered over her.

She screamed.

"Elle?" Todd yelled. "*Elle!* What's going on?"

Her phone was down by her side. But she could still hear his voice.

"Todd! I'm being atta—"

Slap!

The shadowy figure whacked her across the face again, then kicked the flashlight from her hand.

A rock came crashing down toward her chest. Elle rolled over right before it made contact. The stone hit the dirt instead, leaving a deep dent.

Elle grabbed hold of the tulip tree trunk, scrambling to her knees. Jagged bark scraped her palms as she struggled to stand.

She made it onto her feet. But a kick to the stomach knocked her back down.

Elle's body hit the dirt hard. Her whole left side went numb.

The attacker pounced. Black leather gloves went straight for her neck.

"Get away from me!" Elle screamed, reaching up and grabbing hold of the attacker's black ski mask.

The assailant grabbed her wrists and pinned them to the ground. Steely brown eyes glared down at Elle.

She squinted. Peered into them. Those eyes looked familiar.

"Who are you?" she grunted, writhing about to free herself. "Who are you!"

Silence.

"Somebody help me!" Elle screamed.

Her pleas echoed into the distance, then faded. The trail was empty. She was left to fend for herself.

You should've brought a weapon. Why didn't you bring a weapon?

Elle knew why. She hadn't expected to be assaulted. All of their suspects were accounted for. All except…

Bryce!

Elle kicked her leg high in the air, attempting to knee him in the groin. He jumped up, avoiding the impact before slamming back down on top of her.

She cried out in agony.

"Bryce! I know it's you. Get off me!"

He didn't budge. She choked underneath the weight of his body.

"Now I know why you didn't show up to the station," she wheezed. "You were too busy following me! You won't get away with this. I was just on the phone with Todd. He knows where I am. And he heard you attacking me! He'll be here any minute—"

"You'll be dead and we'll both be gone before he gets here…"

Elle cringed at the sound of his raspy, whimpering voice. The same voice that left the messages on her phone.

"You sound disgusting, you…you *maniac*. What is that,

your serial killer voice? Because that's what you are. A serial killer!"

"Shut up!"

Whack!

Bryce punched Elle square in the jaw. She screamed out in agony. Her entire face throbbed as if it had been shattered into a thousand pieces.

She lay there, unable to move. Bryce pounced once again, going straight for her neck.

His clammy leather gloves clung to her throat. Elle grabbed his wrists and pulled. Bryce's hands didn't budge.

"Please," she gasped. "Stop...*please!*"

His grip tightened.

She pulled harder, gagging from the pressure of his suffocating grasp.

Her eyes bulged, then glazed over.

"Die," he wheezed. "That's it. Die!"

Elle's eyelids lowered while her heart raced. She struggled to take in thin streams of air. Oxygen evaded her lungs.

Her limbs began to convulse. Bryce squeezed her legs between his knees, showing no mercy.

"Aww, look at that," he hissed. "Two best friends, dying the same death. Is your throat closing up, just like Taylor's? Are you losing consciousness? Is your windpipe getting crushed?"

Elle felt herself slipping away.

A man's voice rippled through the mountain air.

"Stop!"

Despite being half-conscious, Elle felt her eyes fill with tears of relief.

Todd!

Bryce's grip let up.

Elle took advantage of the reprieve. Made a feeble attempt to push him off her. But she was too weak.

"Get away from her!" Todd yelled as his voice drew nearer.

Bryce didn't budge.

"Get up! *Now!*"

Pounding footsteps approached, then skid across the dirt path.

Elle blinked rapidly, straining to clear her blurred vision. Her dilated eyes gradually regained focus. And then... Confusion hit.

Bryce stood over Elle. *And* her attacker.

Who is this?

"Get up!" Bryce yelled, pulling the assailant by the arm.

The assailant didn't budge.

Bryce kicked the attacker in the back.

That did the trick. Elle was finally freed.

She rolled over, choking on a rush of air.

Bryce pounced on the assailant. A tussle ensued. Punches were thrown amid screams and grunts.

Elle pulled herself up, watching as Bryce got the upper hand.

He grabbed hold of the ski mask and tore it off. Shined his flashlight in the assailant's face.

Elle recoiled, falling back against the tulip tree.

She screamed, nearly fainting from shock.

It was Audrey.

"It's over, Audrey," Bryce said. "You're done. Do you hear me? *Done!*"

"No!" Audrey screamed.

She shoved Bryce to the ground, then went straight for Elle. Took hold of her throat and squeezed. Her twisted expression filled with rage.

"Die, bitch. Die!"

Elle gasped, clawing at Audrey's arms. The deranged woman refused to let up.

Bang!

A gunshot blasted overhead.

"Everyone on your knees with your hands up!"

Todd! For real this time!

Audrey squeezed harder despite the warning shot. She was possessed, determined to crush the life out of Elle.

Todd rushed the group.

Audrey released Elle and scrambled to her feet, attempting to make a run for it.

Todd grabbed her by the collar and pulled her back, holding his gun to her head.

"If you do not stand down, I will shoot."

Audrey finally relented, sobbing as she fell to her knees, and buried her face in the dirt.

"Just kill me now," she cried. "Just kill me now!"

Todd placed her in handcuffs. "Audrey Bingham, you are under arrest. You have the right to remain silent. Anything you say can and will be used against you in a court of law…"

Bryce rushed over and helped Elle to her feet.

"I am so sorry," he said. "Are you okay?"

She ran her hand down her throat, wincing in pain. "I—I think so…"

"Elle," Todd said, "I've got backup and an ambulance on the way. Hang in there. You'll be fine. Bryce, can you help get her down to the bottom of the trail while I escort Ms. Bingham?"

"Sure thing."

Elle and Todd shared a long glance. In it was everything they felt. The relief, the gratitude, the resolve. But most importantly, the love.

Chapter Twenty-Six

Todd sat next to Sheriff Glover inside the station's tiny interrogation room. Audrey was seated across from them, slumped down in her gray metal chair with her arms folded tightly over her chest.

A fluorescent white lightbulb flickered overhead, buzzing loudly. Todd tuned it out while focusing on Audrey, who was staring down at the dingy beige carpet with her lips puckered smugly. She hadn't spoken a word since they'd left the hiking trail.

Todd turned on his tape recorder while Sheriff Glover cracked open his notebook. "There's a lot to unpack here, Audrey," Todd began. "Where should we start?"

She snorted loudly and shrugged her shoulders. "F it. What've I got to lose? I might as well tell you everything. Then you'll realize that I'm the victim in all of this. Not Harper. Not Taylor. Not Sara. *Me*."

"Oh," Todd said, leaning into the table, "so you're admitting to killing Harper and Sara, too?"

Audrey turned away and bit her cheek.

"Got a little ahead of yourself there, didn't you?" Sheriff Glover asked. "Said too much. I'll tell you what. Since you wanna to tell us everything, why don't we start here—why did you kill Harper Mitchell?"

She sat straight up and looked the sheriff directly in the eyes. "Because I was having an affair with her husband."

Todd forced his poker face to remain intact as he remembered Keaton mentioning his extramarital affairs.

"So you killed her?" the sheriff probed. "Over an affair?"

"Yes."

Her boldness almost knocked Todd out of his chair.

"Why?"

"Because her husband was miserable in that marriage. Keaton was trying to part ways amicably, but she refused to sign the divorce papers. The greedy bitch kept begging for a bigger settlement. Then she really pissed me off when she stole a scarf that belonged to his mother. So, that's when I stepped in."

"Exactly how did you step in?" Todd asked.

"By getting the scarf back. But not before I strangled her to death with it."

Todd went cold. Sitting face-to-face in front of a psychopath was bone-chilling, to say the least.

"Wow," Sheriff Glover uttered while wiping sweat from his brow. "Never in my thirty-plus years…"

"Look," Audrey said, "I was just trying to fix the situation. You know, do the right thing. For Keaton. For *us*. But then…"

"Then what?" Todd asked.

The veins in Audrey's neck pulsated. "He refused to marry me. And I found out that he was seeing other women. I wanted to kill him, too. Then I met Bryce. We just…we clicked. He's the reason why I moved to Bradford. He got me the job at the car dealership, helped me find a home near his."

Todd's hands curled into tight fists underneath the table. Bryce had conveniently left all of that out when they'd spoken.

Deal with him later. Focus on Audrey's confession for now.

"Deputy Jacobson," Sheriff Glover said, "I know this case is personal for you. Are you sure you're okay listening to this?"

"Absolutely, sir. I'm here to get justice for my sister. I want to see investigation all the way through." He turned to Audrey. "Now, why did you kill Taylor? Because Bryce wouldn't divorce her?"

"Nope," she said, cocking her head to the side. "That's not the reason at all. Those two were in financial ruin. A divorce would've put Bryce further in the hole. Getting rid of Taylor meant he could cash in on her life insurance policy, get out of debt, and live happily ever after with me. But then Sara and Elle started interfering in my plan. So I tried to get rid of them before they figured me out. Unfortunately, I was only fifty percent successful."

"And look at what ended up happening," Todd said. "The very man you killed for helped assist in your arrest."

The smirk on Audrey's face fell.

"How did Bryce know you were at River Birch Park this evening?" Sheriff Glover asked. "Did you tell him what you were planning to do?"

One lone tear trickled down Audrey's cheek. It was the first time she'd shown any sign of emotion.

"No," she admitted. "He didn't. And that's where I messed up. We were both at the dealership, and I knew he was supposed to meet Deputy Jacobson at the station for questioning. The walls were closing in on me. So I snuck out of work in one of the dealership's cars and went to Elle's house. Followed her to the hiking trail. But I forgot that some of the cars on the lot have trackers. Bryce must've realized I was gone and traced the whereabouts of the vehicle."

There was a knock at the door.

"Come in!" Sheriff Glover called out.

Deputy Cross stuck his head inside. "Excuse the interruption. Sheriff, can I please speak with you for a second?"

Todd and Audrey glared at one another silently while the two men shared a brief exchange.

"Good work," Sheriff Glover told Deputy Cross. "Thanks for the update."

He closed the door and took a seat. "We found the black pickup truck you'd been driving around town at a private garage over on Astor Street. You were renting the space from a woman named Mrs. Wilson?"

Audrey dropped her head down onto the table.

"The description matches the one that Elle Scott had given us. And the tire tracks match those that were photographed at Everest Forest Preserve the day you crashed into Ms. Scott's car." The sheriff turned to Todd. "Oh, and the *deputies* found Elle's laptop wrapped in a blanket inside the truck's cargo bed."

"Good. She'll be glad to have that back."

Sheriff Glover opened a file that Deputy Cross had given him and slid it across the table. "I'm not done yet. Look at what's behind door number three. Your fingerprints match the one that was found at the Scotts' residence."

Todd tapped Audrey's shoulder. She sat back up. He stared into her cold, vacant eyes.

"Were you the one behind all of the stalking? And the threatening messages? The shooting at my house?"

She nodded.

"Audrey, do you understand how many lives you've ruined?"

Her mouth opened and closed several times as she pulled at the handcuffs binding her wrists. "I just—I just wanted someone to love me…"

Sheriff Glover stood and walked around the table. "We've heard enough. Deputy Jacobson, I'm sure you wanna get to the hospital and check on Elle. I'll take over from here."

"Thank you, sir."

The sheriff stopped Todd before he left the room. "Listen," he whispered, "I owe you an apology. I should've listened to you on this one and reopened Taylor's case a long time ago. You single-handedly got it solved. Excellent job. I'm proud of you."

"Thank you, sir. Elle was a huge help in all of this, too. I couldn't have done it without her."

"I'll be sure to share those same sentiments with her as well. Oh, and I'll be looking into the shoddy investigation into Harper Mitchell's death, too. As for you, let's talk promotion once the dust settles."

"That would be great, Sheriff. Thanks again."

Todd ran to his desk and grabbed his keys, his mind now focused solely on Elle.

On the way out the door, his cell phone buzzed. It was a text message from her.

The doc just examined me. I'm fine. No serious injuries. Just a little bruising and soreness. I'll be released tonight.

Relief almost knocked Todd to the floor.

I am so glad to hear that, he wrote back. I'm on my way there now. See you soon. Love you.

Love you, too.

Chapter Twenty-Seven

"Merry Christmas, Elle."

"Merry Christmas, Todd."

The pair clinked their glasses together and took sips of strawberry Bellini as they sat underneath Todd's Christmas tree.

"I've got another gift for you," he said.

"But you already gave me the most beautiful silk robe. Why are you spoiling me like this?"

"No, *I'm* the spoiled one. Those fancy cigars you gifted me are hard to come by. But hold on. This is a different type of present. You know that twig you recovered from the crime scene?"

"I do."

"The forensics came back on it."

Elle propped herself up onto her elbow. "And? What were the results?"

"Taylor's DNA was present. So was Audrey's."

"Yes!" Elle exclaimed. "Time to update my business card. Which sounds better? Elle Scott, crime scene investigator? Or Elle Scott, forensic investigator? Or—"

"Hold on, hold on, let's not get ahead of ourselves," Todd said with an amorous chuckle. "You do deserve your accolades, though. I don't know how law enforcement could've missed that twig time and time again. Leave it to my eagle-eyed girl to find it."

He ran his finger across her cheek.

"I definitely think I should be rewarded," she murmured.

"Oh, you should absolutely be rewarded."

Todd wrapped his arm around the small of her back and pulled her close.

"There's something I've been wanting to say to you in person as opposed to text," he said.

"Oh, really? What's that?"

"I love you."

Elle's breath caught in her throat. Her lips parted.

Before she could speak, Todd continued.

"I knew that I loved you the minute you arrived back in Bradford. You've been here by my side during the hardest time of my life. You rode with me nonstop, determined to help solve Taylor's murder. Through the ups, the downs, the triumphs and the disappointments, your support never wavered."

"Thank you, Todd. I can say the same for you. I am so proud of the work we've done together. Partnering with you has proven one thing to be true."

"Which is?"

"That I lo—"

Todd pressed his lips against hers before she could finish.

Elle melted into his kiss, growing dizzy from the joy swirling inside of her.

Several moments passed before they pulled away from each other. And when they did, Elle responded with a breathless "I love you, too."

* * * * *

HOTSHOT HEROES
UNDER THREAT

LISA CHILDS

With great appreciation and love for my hotshot husband, Andrew Ahearne, who is always my inspiration – especially for this series!

Prologue

They were all watching him. Hell, they'd been watching
him from the moment he'd joined the Huron Hotshots
firefighting team. They were either waiting for him to
prove himself worthy of joining or for him to betray the
real reason he was here in Northern Lakes, Michigan.

But they couldn't know the real reason, or he would
never find out the truth. So he had to prove that he belonged, which wouldn't be hard. The son of a smoke
jumper trainer, Patrick "Trick" McRooney probably
knew more about fighting fires than any other Hotshot
on his brother-in-law's elite team. Except his brother-
in-law...

For his ability to sense when a fire was about to start,
Superintendent Braden Zimmer was nearly as legendary as Trick's father was for all the smoke jumpers he'd
trained. So maybe Trick should have heeded Braden's
warning.

"You don't need to do this," Braden murmured, keeping his voice low—probably so that nobody else would
overhear them, since other members of the team were
gathered around the area where they were working.

But Trick was already climbing into the bucket on

the US Forest Service boom truck. He assured his boss, "It's no big deal."

Cutting off some treetops hanging low over the power lines was a hell of a lot safer than the other assignments Braden had been giving him. Of course the transformer had been shut down so that there was no electricity in the wires where they were working. The power was the least of his worries, though. The trees were tall, so tall that he would need the crane extended to lift the bucket to the maximum height. He clipped the hook of the guard cable onto his harness so he wouldn't fall out of the bucket if he leaned over too far with the chain saw.

To reduce the noise and block out Braden's worried comments, Trick clamped on his earmuffs and then his hard hat before he gave the thumbs-up signal for the bucket to start ascending. Even with the muffs on, he heard the ominous creak and groan as the crane rose, taking him higher and higher. The bucket rustled through the tree branches, which slapped and tore at his clothes.

The truck operator could have parked the rig a little farther away from the trees and angled the crane so that Trick wouldn't be getting dragged through the branches. He suspected the operator knew that as well, but didn't give a damn how beat-up Trick got. Maybe she even preferred if he got a little roughed up.

Since Trick had joined the team several weeks ago, Henrietta "Hank" Rowlins had been giving him a hard time—both intentionally and unintentionally. She had no idea how she affected him, and he had no idea why she did.

He had never been attracted to anyone he'd worked with before, and he'd been paired with other female Hot-shots in the past. But none of them had looked like Henrietta, with her long black hair, honey-toned skin and big dark eyes. Preoccupied with thoughts of her, he took a moment to remember why the hell he was up in the bucket.

Then the weight of the chain saw in his gloved hands reminded him, and he set to work trimming the high branches. He was careful to cut them so that they fell away from the wires to the ground below. But he had to lean against the edge of the bucket, and as he did, he felt the metal give way and the bucket tilted.

He yelled out as the chain saw slipped from his grasp, and he catapulted over the side of the bucket after it. He waited for the harness and cable to stop his fall, but what if it had been tampered with like the bucket? Then he'd hit the ground and his assignment would end. That had to be what whoever had sabotaged the bucket truck had intended. To stop him from investigating…

…forever.

Chapter One

His image reflected back from the side-view mirror, his desperate grasp on the side of the bucket that dangled from the crane. A scream rose in the back of Henrietta's throat, but it stuck there, burning. She couldn't utter it. She couldn't even open her lips. All she could do was murmur.

What the hell had happened? How had the bucket come loose? And Trick...

Why hadn't his harness stopped him yet? How long would he be able to hold on before he fell?

The bucket had a control panel on it that Trick could operate, if he wasn't holding on for dear life. But there was another control panel inside the cab, where she sat, frozen. She reached for the control to bring down the bucket. But before she could move the mechanical arm that would lower it and Trick, he moved. His gloves must have slipped because he fell back, arms spread wide— almost like he'd been pushed off the side. Why wasn't the harness stopping him?

Finally she took action, throwing open the driver's door to rush to his side. The bucket had been high, the crane extended nearly the entirety of its seventy-five-foot height. He'd fallen so far...

And onto the saw…

She dropped to her knees beside him, and not just because her legs had been shaking so badly that they'd folded beneath her. Horror knocked her to the ground.

Horror…

Trick McRooney stared up at her, his beautiful green eyes wide with shock. The fall had knocked the hard hat from his head, and his thick auburn hair was tousled and damp with perspiration. He was so damn good-looking that it wasn't fair.

And it wasn't fair what had happened to him.

That he was gone…gone just like Dirk Brown, the dead Hotshot whose place he'd taken on their team.

Dead.

And the scream that had been burning the back of her throat tore free.

She couldn't stop screaming…until strong hands grasped her shoulders and gently shook her awake. Henrietta opened her eyes and stared up into his face, into his unfairly handsome face.

His green eyes gleamed in the dim light of the bunkroom of the Northern Lakes firehouse. "Are you okay?" he asked, his deep voice gruff with concern.

She nodded but wondered aloud, "How—how are you okay?" Almost of their own volition, her hands rose to his face. She ran her fingertips along his strong jaw, over the soft stubble that darkened his skin. A jolt traveled up her arm to her heart, making it pound even faster than it had from the dream—from the nightmare.

It was the same dream she'd been having every night since that day three weeks ago when the bucket had mysteriously come apart, like so many of the other equipment failures they'd experienced over the past seven or eight months. Was it all just bad luck like the rest of the team seemed to believe?

"But I—I saw you fall," she murmured. It was always so real—more a memory than a dream—because the horrible event of that day had actually happened, and Trick could have died. So in her dreams, he always did... just like Dirk Brown had died. Which had opened up a spot on their team for Trick. Dirk's death had seemed like the result of another equipment failure, when a cable on the winch of a logging truck had snapped and cut the man...

She shuddered and tried to shut that memory out, that image. She hadn't actually seen it happen; only Owen James from their team had been with Dirk in that moment. But afterward she'd run to help, even though it had been too late. That had haunted her for weeks until Trick had nearly died, too. In another accident?

But what had happened to Dirk had been no accident; his wife had just set it up to look that way so she could collect double on the life insurance policy with the accidental death rider she'd recently taken out on him.

Trick had no wife. When they'd gotten called out to a wildfire a week ago, Hank had heard from the other Hotshots that Trick went from team to team and never stayed anywhere for long. It didn't sound like he'd ever had much of a serious relationship. Maybe that was for the best, though, so that nobody had gotten hurt. Unlike her situation...

Trick shook his head, and Hank's hands fell away from his face. "I didn't fall," he said, "because of you. You lowered the boom before I fell completely out of the bucket. You saved me."

Not in her dream. In her dream she wasn't able to move fast enough, wasn't able to stop him from dying.

"No…" She shuddered. "You died…just like Dirk. That's what I saw in my dream…" There had been no way to save Dirk, and in her dream she hadn't been able to save Trick either.

"The harness stopped me from hitting the ground. I'm alive," he said with a gruff chuckle. "But if I have to prove it to you, I can do the whole Sleeping Beauty thing…" He leaned forward then as if he intended to kiss her.

She jerked back and gasped with shock and maybe a little excitement. She still wasn't fully awake yet, but she was aware enough to know not to give in to temptation. And Trick McRooney was tempting—so tempting that she closed her eyes to shut out the sight of him. She didn't trust him, so there was no way she was going to let him kiss her. But at that moment, with awareness rushing through her body, she wanted to kiss him, wanted to see what it would be like, how it would feel.

A loud cough jolted her fully awake. When she opened her eyes, Trick was still there. And someone stood in the open doorway, clearing his throat.

The heat in her body rushed up to her face now as embarrassment overwhelmed Henrietta.

Even though her boss hadn't caught them kissing, she was even more embarrassed than when her grandfather had caught her actually kissing her high school sweetheart on the deck all those years ago.

A pang of loss struck her heart over the thought of Grandpapa. He'd been the sweetest man…and the bravest, choosing to raise her after her parents died in a car crash even though he'd already been in his midseventies and widowed. Maybe he'd needed her as much as she had needed him.

She still needed him. But he was gone now, and all Henrietta had was her job—one she would be putting at risk if she got romantically involved with a team member. The superintendent had a strict rule against that kind of fraternization. Not that she could get romantically involved with Trick McRooney anyway. With all these accidents befalling the team, they had to stay alert. Trick McRooney was a distraction she couldn't afford, one that might cause her pain or worse…

"WHAT THE HELL do you think you're doing?" Braden had waited until he closed his office door before he fired the question at his brother-in-law. It had been killing him to hold it inside, to say nothing until Trick had followed him from the bunkroom on the second floor down to his office on the first. But he hadn't wanted to have this conversation in front of Henrietta Rowlins.

He'd been hoping he wouldn't have to have this conversation at all, but his wife, Sam, had warned him about how many women found her brother attractive. She'd even had to contend with a college roommate who'd crushed on him. With a slight smile curving her lips, she sat on the corner of his beat-up metal desk. Petite and blonde, she looked nothing like her muscular, hulking, auburn-haired brother.

Trick leaned against the cement-block wall behind him. He crossed his arms over his massive chest and reminded Braden, "I'm doing you a favor."

"I didn't ask you to put the moves on Hank," Braden said. "And what really worries me is that she probably didn't ask either." The last thing he needed right now was an allegation of harassment on his team. He was already in enough trouble with his superiors over all the damaged equipment and accidents.

Trick's face flushed. "I wasn't putting the moves on her. She was having a nightmare, and I just woke her up."

Braden snorted. Not that he doubted Hank could have been having a nightmare. After what had happened to Dirk, and what had nearly happened to Owen and Luke and Trick and then to him and Sam, he'd been having nightmares, too. But he'd also felt the tension and the heat in that bunkroom all the way out in the hallway, so he reminded his brother-in-law, "You know I have a strict rule about no relationships between team members."

Trick shrugged his massive shoulders. "Doesn't seem to be a problem right now. Nobody trusts anybody else on the team—least of all me."

"I meant no romantic relationships," Braden clarified. "And you know that."

But Trick wasn't wrong. The other relationships were strained as well. Everybody had once been so close that they'd acted more like family than coworkers. But that closeness was gone now, just like Dirk Brown.

Since his death and Trick's addition to the team, nothing with the Huron Hotshots was the same. But then, it hadn't been good for a while before that—since the accidents had started. Since that damn note that Braden had received—the one warning him that someone on his team wasn't who he thought they were.

Who the hell was that?

The note had arrived long before Trick, so it couldn't pertain to him, but Braden wondered now if his brother-in-law was who he thought he was.

As if she'd read his mind, Sam reminded him, "I warned you."

Trick arched an auburn brow. "What did you warn him about, sis?"

"Your propensity for breaking hearts wherever you go," Sam said, and her slight grin curved into a teasing smirk directed at her older brother.

Trick's arched brow lowered along with the other one, and he glared at his sister. "I don't break hearts." He shuddered. "I don't want anything to do with anybody's heart."

Sam snorted. "That's exactly how you break them—because you don't care. Just ask Colleen…"

"You ask your old college buddy," Trick said. "She'll tell you that I didn't do anything to her. I never even took her out. And I'm not a womanizing ass—" Trick tensed and stepped away from the wall.

"That's enough," Braden told his brother-in-law. As superintendent of his team, he was used to playing peacemaker. But his teammates treated each other with more respect than the McRooneys did. Or at least his team used to…before everything had gone so wrong. Before the accidents had started, before Dirk had died and Owen had nearly been killed and Luke had been accused of being complicit in all that…and the team's trust in each other had eroded.

Braden needed *it* right again—needed his team back to the trusting family they once had been. He needed Trick's help to do that because Braden himself was too close to them all to see clearly who might be destroying their cohesion. Because Trick never stayed long enough anywhere to get close to anyone, he'd have more perspective.

"Sam recommended you for this job," Braden reminded them both, "because she thought you could objectively investigate everyone." Braden was too emotionally invested in every member of his team.

Trick nodded. "And I can do that—no problem."

Braden arched his brow now. "Really? You can be objective about Hank?"

Trick's face flushed again, but he nodded. "Yeah, like I said, that was nothing."

"Really?" Sam asked, and she was smirking again. Despite the ribbing they gave each other, the siblings were really close; they'd had to be after their mother had abandoned them, leaving their busy father to raise them alone. "Sounds like you were just about to kiss her when my husband busted you. What was that, Trick? Some new investigation tactic?"

"You're the investigator," Trick said. "I'm just checking everybody out to give my brother-in-law my honest opinion about them." He turned back toward Braden. "Your wife's a jerk, by the way."

Instead of being offended, Sam giggled and Braden chuckled. He rose from the chair behind his desk and slipped his arm around her slender shoulders. "My wife is amazing," he said, "and I'm so damn lucky she chose to be with me."

Trick acted as if he was gagging. "I'm not here for all this mushy stuff."

"No, you're not," Braden agreed. "So be careful with Hank." He loved the female Hotshot like a little sister, like Trick loved Sam.

Trick nodded. "That was…" And again, he seemed at a loss to label what it was, the moment of near intimacy in the bunkroom with Hank.

"Be careful with everyone," Braden added. They were all like his family. "I asked you to meet me here tonight because I got the report back on the boom truck."

Sam picked up the file from his desk. "Bolts were loosened on one side."

Trick nodded. "We knew that. The bucket wouldn't have suddenly come off the crane like that if they hadn't been."

Sam's slight body trembled against Braden's as she shuddered in remembered horror. And she hadn't even been there. But Braden and Trick had described to her what had happened to her brother—apparently in too much detail. "You could have been killed."

"Whoever was in the bucket could have been killed," Trick said.

"You don't think it was meant for you?" Braden asked.

Trick shrugged again. "Nobody knew for sure I'd be the one getting in that bucket."

The tightness in Braden's chest eased slightly. "True…" So maybe his brother-in-law hadn't been the intended target, but that didn't change the fact that someone had once again sabotaged his team's equipment. There had been so many instances of sabotage over the last several months: chain saws tampered with, brake lines cut, oxygen tanks emptied…

"And I didn't get hurt," Trick added. "So stop worrying."

"He won't stop until these incidents stop," Sam answered for Braden. She knew him so well. "You need to find out who's causing these."

Trick didn't argue with her, and this time he didn't point out that he wasn't an investigator like his sister was. He just nodded in agreement and with determination. "I will." Then he started for the door. "First, I'm going to need some rest to do that."

Braden couldn't argue with that; nobody had caught up on their sleep since that wildfire call out West a week ago, which was probably why Hank had been crashing in the bunkroom before driving back to her apartment. But he felt compelled to add again, "Just be careful."

Trick gripped the doorknob for a long moment before turning it. Once he opened the door, he turned back and glanced at them over his shoulder. Then he grinned and assured them, "Always am."

"Liar," Sam accused him, but her voice was gentle with affection and she chuckled. When the door closed behind her brother, she released a ragged sigh.

"You're worried," Braden said.

"You are, too."

"I don't want your brother getting hurt," Braden said.

"You should probably be more worried about Hank," Sam said with another heavy sigh. "I warned you before that women fall hard for my brother."

"Like Colleen?" he asked. He'd heard about Sam's friend from college before; he'd also heard the woman call and ask about Trick.

Sam sighed. "She still has a crush on him. Sometimes I wonder if she only keeps in touch with me to keep tabs on him."

Braden felt that tightness in his chest again, but he assured her and himself, "Hank doesn't even like him." The minute Trick had joined the team, Hank had made her opinion of him pretty damn clear, and it hadn't been complimentary at all. Just like everyone else, she didn't believe he'd earned the privilege of taking Dirk's spot.

"That's good," Sam said, "because I doubt he's sticking around once your saboteur is caught."

"Why doesn't he ever stay in one place for long?" Braden asked.

Sam sighed. "It's better to be the one who leaves rather than the one who's left." When Sam and her brothers were young, their mother had divorced their father and given up custody of her children. Apparently Sam wasn't the only one of the McRooney children who'd suffered from that abandonment.

A pang struck his heart as he remembered aloud, "That was why you left me."

"But you found me," she said. "You brought me home." She leaned closer to him and brushed her lips across his throat. "You're home for me." Her mouth skimmed along his jaw now. "Wherever we are…"

She knew about the letter he'd received, the warning that he might lose his position as superintendent if the safety of his team was further compromised. But losing his job was the least of his concerns. He was worried about something happening to her brother while Trick was helping him.

She pressed her mouth to his, and as if she'd read his mind again, she murmured against his lips, "Don't worry…"

But he felt the tension in her body as he closed his arms around her. And he knew that he wasn't the only one worrying.

HE WAS WORRIED. So damn worried.

What the hell had he been thinking to flirt with Henrietta Rowlins like he had, teasing her about kissing her? Wanting to kiss her…

And what the hell was he thinking that he wanted to go back upstairs to see if she was still there, to see if she would change her mind and accept his kiss?

Knowing she was not about to change her mind, he forced himself to walk past the stairwell, past the garage bays filled with fire engines, and then to push open the service door to the street.

He hesitated a long moment before stepping across that threshold and into the night. And it wasn't just because he was tempted to go back to Henrietta.

It was because of that feeling…

That feeling that he was being watched.

He'd had it since he'd shown up in Northern Lakes seven weeks ago. But then, he'd figured it was just because he was the new guy. He was usually the new guy, the one who filled a sudden open spot on a Hotshot team until the superintendent could hire a permanent replacement.

Trick was never permanent. When he was just a kid, he'd learned that nothing was ever permanent. Not a place nor a family.

So he knew it was a waste of time looking for permanence. Hell, he avoided anything that might become permanent. He couldn't understand why his sister was trying to put down roots. Sure, Braden Zimmer was a great guy and Northern Lakes was a nice enough town…

But he shuddered, and it wasn't because the temperature had dipped low, as it often did at night in northern Michigan, even this late in the spring. He shuddered at the thought of staying here, or anywhere.

He'd already been here longer than he liked to stay in one place. He needed to find out soon who was behind the accidents happening to Braden's team and their equipment. And not just because he could have been killed in that boom truck. If not for Henrietta reacting as quickly as she had, the safety line clipped to his belt could have broken like the bucket if it had been tampered with, too.

Hank had saved his life.

But that wasn't why he'd been so tempted to kiss her. He hadn't just been trying to comfort her after she'd awakened from what had sounded like one scary-ass nightmare. He'd also wanted to kiss her because she'd looked so damn beautiful with her long hair tumbled down around her shoulders, falling nearly to her waist. And her eyes had been so big and dark and...

Vulnerable...

That had shaken him, and he was rarely shaken—even when he'd fallen out of the bucket on the boom truck. That hadn't rattled him like Henrietta had. Because in the vulnerability in her eyes, he'd felt his own. That he could have nearly died, and worse yet, that he was getting attached to this place, to these people...

He needed to find out who was causing problems for Braden fast, so he could get the hell out of Northern Lakes and the hell away from Henrietta Rowlins.

The steel door snapped shut behind him, bringing him out of his reverie. He glanced around then—in the shadows beyond the light of the streetlamps.

Somebody was out there.

He could feel them watching him.

But he wasn't intimidated, not like he'd been by that kiss. He straightened his shoulders and let a slight grin curve on his lips. Nobody was scaring him off.

Not even Henrietta...

But he did walk a little faster as he headed toward his

truck. He pressed the key fob to unlock it. Then, when he reached for the door handle, he noticed the slip of paper tucked under his wiper blade.

He knew it wasn't a parking ticket. He wasn't sure Northern Lakes had any parking enforcement. Until recently, they'd had a state trooper who, because of his resentment of Braden, had harassed the Hotshots. But he'd lost his job, and his freedom, when he'd taken that harassment to the extreme and tried to kill one of the team, Luke Garrison, and his wife, Willow.

The note wasn't from former trooper Gingrich.

But Trick wished he knew who the hell was sending them. The same person who'd sent the note to Braden?

He doubted it.

The notes Trick had been receiving had a different tone to them. They felt personal. He unfolded the paper and, in the glow of the streetlamp, read the words printed on it in crude block letters: *You're not going to get away with this...*

What the hell was this?

Get away with what? Taking the spot that Dirk Brown's death had opened up? Investigating the team?

Or what...?

He had no idea what it meant or if it had anything to do with his investigation for Braden. That was why he hadn't shown them to his brother-in-law—and because Braden already had too much to deal with. Even his recent surprise honeymoon had turned into a nightmare. Trick would deal with the notes on his own. They'd all said essentially the same damn thing.

You've made a huge mistake coming here...
You're going to regret what you're doing...

How? What was the mistake? How was he going to regret whatever the hell it was?

He'd lied to Braden and his sister when he'd implied that the bucket sabotage hadn't been meant for him. Someone must have known he would be going up in the bucket. And that someone must have realized what his real job was—investigating the team—and intended to make Trick stop by either hurting him or killing him.

Chapter Two

Henrietta wasn't the only one pretending that moment in the bunkroom hadn't happened the night before. That moment when she'd let Trick McRooney get too close, when she'd been tempted to kiss him. Fortunately, her boss hadn't mentioned it at all when she'd seen him this morning at the firehouse. And even better, Trick was totally ignoring her. He hadn't looked at her during the meeting that morning, which Braden had convened to review their recent call out West, and now he didn't look at her in the bar around the corner from the firehouse that the Hotshots frequented at shift's end in the evening.

They owed their patronage to Charlie Tillerman, the owner, after an arsonist who'd been targeting them had set the Filling Station on fire last year. Fortunately, the structure had been restored quickly and almost exactly as it had been—with scuffed-up hardwood floors and wood-plank walls reclaimed from an old barn.

The bar was nearly full, since that meeting had required the attendance of every Hotshot on the team. Only a handful of the twenty members were actually assigned to the Northern Lakes Fire Department. Others were rangers in national forests, like Ethan Sommerly and Rory VanDam, or firefighters in other areas of Michigan, like Trent Miles and Michaela Momber and Hank. While Trent worked out of Detroit, she and Michaela worked out of a closer firehouse. It was just twenty miles north in an even smaller town than Northern Lakes. They had a gas station, a church, a corner store and nothing else, so she and Michaela spent their off-duty time in Northern Lakes.

Fortunately, they were both off duty tonight. Or maybe unfortunately—since Michaela had followed her into the bathroom to grill her.

"Where were you last night?" Michaela asked the minute Henrietta stepped out of the restroom stall. The blonde leaned against the sink; she must have not even had to use the bathroom.

"You know what they're going to say about us coming in here together," Henrietta said. They had it tough enough being the only two females on the team; they didn't need to give the guys any more reasons to tease them.

"They're not going to say anything," Michaela said, "because they respect us too much to give us any grief."

Henrietta snorted. "Yeah, right..."

"They do," Michaela insisted. "Well, all of them do except Trick McRooney." She snorted now. "Not that we respect him either since he hasn't done a damn thing to earn it."

Most of the team thought he'd gotten the job because of nepotism. But was that really the case?

He had more experience than a lot of the team members, except for Braden and Carl Kozak, who was even older than the superintendent—so old that he had retired from his off-duty job and only worked when called up with the Hotshots. So Braden probably would have hired

Trick even if he wasn't his brother-in-law. But everybody thought their relationship gave him an unfair advantage over the rest of the team—not that he seemed to use it to his advantage.

He had volunteered to get into the bucket and cut back those limbs from the power line. He'd held his own last week when they'd been called up to the wildfire out West, and he hadn't shied away from any other tough assignment he'd been given either. Some of the things he'd done at Braden's request, like following around a couple other team members, had everybody wondering what his real job was. Hotshot or something else? Spy?

And it was that something else that made everybody wary of him. Well, everybody but the two guys he'd followed around; Owen James and Luke Garrison seemed to appreciate that he'd been there for them during their recent hard times. They often sat with him at the bar instead of joining the rest of the team in the corner booth that had always been theirs. Nobody had asked Trick to join them in that booth. And he must have been astute enough to realize sitting there was by invitation only.

Henrietta quickly washed and dried her hands, but before she could reach for the door, Michaela stepped in front of it. Although the blonde was much shorter than she was, Henrietta knew the woman was freakishly strong. So even if she'd been so inclined, she wouldn't have tried to push her out of the way. "What?" she asked.

"I asked you a question," Michaela reminded her. "And you dodged it. Where were you last night? Who is he?"

Heat rushed to Henrietta's face as she thought of Trick and how close she had come to kissing him. But he wasn't the reason she'd been sleeping in the bunk-room the night before. Well, not exactly…

"There was that meeting this morning," she reminded Michaela.

Michaela shrugged. "Yeah, and I wasn't late for it, even though I slept at our place last night."

"I didn't come back to the apartment because I didn't want to wake you up again," Hank admitted.

Michaela's blue eyes filled with sympathy. "You should talk to somebody about those nightmares you keep having about that damn accident with the boom truck. It wasn't your fault."

She'd been operating it, so ultimately it was her responsibility to make sure it had been functioning properly. She still couldn't figure out what had gone wrong with it.

But she didn't want to concern Michaela with how worried she'd been, so she just shrugged. "I'll be fine. It's just losing Dirk, and nearly losing Owen and Luke…"

She shuddered as she remembered how many close calls the last two Hotshots had had, how many times they had nearly died. But those close calls hadn't been due to real accidents. Dirk's widow had been trying to kill Owen so he wouldn't realize she'd been responsible for her husband's murder. Then her lover, Trooper Gingrich, had tried framing Luke, and unfortunately too many of them had believed it. That distrust and uneasiness hadn't left the team yet. It was between them now, creating a distance…even between Hank and her roommate.

Michaela nodded. "That makes sense—more sense than you having nightmares over Trick McRooney." The blonde sighed. "Although I guess his joining the team is a nightmare."

It was—because his spot had only opened up due to Dirk's death. That wasn't his fault, though. But in the beginning, before they'd known Dirk's wife had been responsible for his death, it had been easier to blame Trick than acknowledge what had really happened.

Now Henrietta wasn't sure what to think of Trick, not that she wanted to think about him at all. She wanted to put him far from her mind.

At least he was sitting far from the booth the Hotshots occupied near the bathroom. He was all the way across the room at the bar. When she followed Michaela from the bathroom, she couldn't help but glance his way. Every time she'd looked in his direction earlier, he hadn't so much as glanced back. It was as if he'd been completely unaware of her presence.

And she'd been glad—relieved, really—that he had seemed to forget all about that moment in the bunkroom the night before.

If only she could do the same…

But this time, when she looked at him, she found him staring back. And despite the distance between them, she felt a jolt—like she had when she'd touched his face, when she'd thought she'd been dreaming and he was dead. And she worried again about all those accidents and if someone else on the team might die.

"WHY DON'T YOU join us in the corner booth?" Owen James asked as he walked up to Trick at the bar.

Maybe the Hotshot, who also worked as a paramedic, had noticed Trick staring longingly in that direction. But he hadn't been looking at the booth; he'd been gazing at Henrietta Rowlins.

In slim-fitting jeans that encased her long, long legs,

she seemed more like a runway model than a Hotshot. But while her body was willowy, it was also damn strong, which made her even sexier to Trick. She wore an oversize white sweater with the jeans, which set off her naturally tan skin with a radiant glow. She was so beautiful.

Even when she was glaring at him…

Which she did now before she slid into the booth beside Michaela Momber. The petite blonde was glaring at him, too, but then she always did.

He faked a shiver and chuckled. "I don't want to risk frostbite."

"They'd thaw out if they got to know you," Luke Garrison said. He sat at the bar next to Trick, working his way through an enormous burger.

Trick chuckled, then asked, "What about you? Why are you sitting here with me instead of with them?"

Luke's face flushed slightly. "It's not because I'm holding a grudge or anything…"

Most of the team had fallen for the frame-up job state trooper Marty Gingrich had pulled to make Luke look guilty of crimes that the trooper's mistress had committed. Even Trick had had his doubts about the guy. But to his credit, he hadn't known him long—not as long as the rest of his teammates had.

"You should be holding one," Trick said. "They shouldn't have doubted you." Luke was a good guy. Trick suspected that was why Luke was sitting at the bar with him. He knew what it was like to be the odd man out, since he'd been ostracized himself when team members had believed Trooper Gingrich's false claims about him.

Luke's wife, Willow, a nurse, was working her night shift at the hospital, or else he would have been home with her. Since their reconciliation, he spent every moment he could with her.

Luke snorted. "Everybody's been on edge after what happened to Dirk." His brow furrowed. "But even before Dirk died, weird things were happening."

"The arsonist," Owen said.

Luke shook his head. "Not just the arsonist, and you both know it."

And maybe that was why he was sitting beside Trick—because he knew why Trick was really there. It wasn't to take Dirk's job. It was to find out who was causing some of the problems the team had had.

Trick grinned. "I don't know what you're talking about."

And both men cursed him.

He laughed, and there was a sudden lightness in his heart. Maybe he was just relieved that at least two members of his new Hotshot team didn't hate him anymore. Then he glanced back at the booth in the corner of the bar and found Henrietta glaring at him.

She still hated him, despite that moment in the bunkroom when she'd touched his face with such wonder that he was alive.

Luke leaned closer and lowered his voice. "Owen and I know your real job is investigating these 'accidents,'" he said. "But you shouldn't have been investigating so closely that you had one of your own three weeks ago." He shuddered. "You might have died if Hank hadn't gotten that broken bucket down so fast."

She had saved his life. He wished she had let him kiss her to show his gratitude. But she wasn't interested in him.

He glanced over at her again, at all that thick black hair lying around her shoulders. She was so damn beautiful…

He really needed to kiss her. Just to thank her, of course…

Unless she'd been the one who'd caused his accident in the first place. She could have loosened the bolts holding that bucket on to the crane. The person causing the accidents had only caused minor injuries before—not deaths.

So Trick wasn't looking for a killer now. The murderers involved in Dirk Brown's death had already been caught. He was looking for a saboteur. And that could be any of them—but for Luke and Owen.

After what they'd been through, he trusted them. He couldn't make the mistake of trusting anyone else, though. Not even Henrietta…

"Maybe you two aren't the only ones who've figured out why I'm here," he mused. That had to be what those notes were about, had to be what he wasn't going to get away with: the investigation.

"A lot of people think it's because of nepotism," Owen said with a chuckle.

Irritation gnawed at him. Apparently, they didn't care about all of his experience, about how the single parent who'd raised him had also trained most of the smoke jumpers in the US, about all the other teams he'd worked with. None of that mattered to them because he'd never worked with *their* team before, and he wouldn't have, if not for their friend dying. Maybe accepting Trick would have made them feel like they were betraying Dirk somehow.

"I'm sure they think it's nepotism," he acknowledged

with a sigh. "That's why I'm sitting over here instead of over there. Nobody's invited me to join them."

"I just did," Owen reminded him. "And if you really think one of us is responsible for the accidents, then you should be over there—investigating everyone."

He should. Even Braden, albeit begrudgingly, believed the saboteur was a member of the team—because of the note he'd received, warning him that someone on the team wasn't who Braden thought they were.

What kind of person sent notes like that?

His mother had left a note for them when she'd left. As if any words, written or spoken, could justify abandoning her family. Nothing could have, and maybe that was why she hadn't tried to explain in person. That was why she had taken the coward's way out…

Leaving a note…

A coward was the kind of person who left notes like that, instead of directly confronting the person. But how could any Hotshot, who had no problem confronting deadly wildfires, be a coward?

But maybe it wasn't cowardice; maybe it was just self-preservation, like his mother had claimed. That staying with them would have destroyed her, that she wasn't the person she wanted to be—that she needed to be—with them.

She'd left to save herself. And maybe that was why the person had left a note, to warn Braden without getting caught themselves. To save themselves…

Trick would catch whoever was responsible. Not just because he'd promised his sister and brother-in-law that he would, but also because he was pissed now.

He could have been killed when that bucket broke

loose from the crane. He had to find out who had sabotaged the equipment before someone was killed.

He slid off the bar stool. "You're right," he told Owen. He couldn't investigate the other Hotshots from afar. He needed to get up close and personal.

Except with Henrietta Rowlins. He shouldn't risk getting any closer to her, or he might be in even more danger than he already was. And not just for his life...

But Trick didn't always take the safe road or do the smart thing, or he wouldn't have accepted this assignment in the first place. So since he'd already put himself in danger once...

HE WASN'T LISTENING. The notes had obviously had no effect on Trick McRooney at all. He was still here—in Northern Lakes, Michigan.

Why?

He never stayed anywhere; that was what he'd always claimed. So why here?

Because of his sister?

Or because of another woman?

It didn't matter what his reason was for not listening to the warnings. He wasn't going to get away with it.

The notes might have been too subtle for someone like Trick. It would take more to get his attention—to make him aware of the mistake that he'd made.

The one he wouldn't be allowed to repeat...

Chapter Three

Henrietta glared…at Owen. He was the one who'd gone over to the bar and convinced Trick to join them in the corner booth. Instead of pulling up a chair like Owen had, Trick had pushed his way into the booth, next to Hank.

His thigh pressed tightly against hers, so thick and muscular and hot. Heat coursed through her—from where their bodies touched to her flushed face and her core. What was it about him that affected her so much?

Sure, he was good-looking, but he wasn't the only good-looking Hotshot on the team. Owen, a former Marine, was handsome even with the jagged scar on his cheek. He was also just about engaged, as were so many of the team. But she wasn't envious. Despite their good looks, none of them particularly attracted her as anything more than friends. Of course, she had known everybody else for so long that, even though she was an only child, they seemed like brothers to her. She couldn't imagine being attracted to any of them—even if Ethan Sommerly shaved his bushy beard and cut his overgrown hair.

Maybe if she worked with Trick more, her attraction to him would wear off. He wouldn't make her pulse quicken and her skin tingle anymore—like she tingled now because of his closeness. And her pulse wasn't just quick—it was pounding so fast and hard that she could feel it, just like she could feel him pressing against her.

His thigh was taut next to hers, his skin hot even through his jeans and hers. And when she glanced down, she noticed that his thigh wasn't the only taut thing on him. Something pressed against the fly of his jeans.

So he was attracted to her, too? He wasn't just teasing her? She glanced up at his face now and caught him staring at her—just like she'd caught him doing so many times when he'd been sitting at the bar, after first conspicuously ignoring her when she'd entered.

She wished he was ignoring her now—as embarrassment flooded her face. Because when she'd caught him, he'd caught her looking at him, too. And she hadn't been looking at his face...

What the hell was wrong with her?

"What the hell is wrong with you?" a voice whispered in her ear.

She jumped and pressed closer to Trick. But the voice in her ear wasn't his deep and rumbly one. It was husky but feminine.

Michaela addressed him now. "You need to get out of our way. We have to go."

Trick hesitated a moment before moving—maybe because he didn't want everyone else to notice his erection. Just her? When he finally slid out of the booth, Michaela pushed Henrietta out after him. Her legs a little shaky, she might have landed on the floor if not for Trick wrapping one of his big hands around her arm to help her straighten up.

"Can't have you falling for me," he murmured, his green eyes twinkling with amusement.

Michaela snorted and answered for her. "Like that would happen…"

Henrietta should have answered for herself, but the words were stuck in her throat. All she could do was glare at him.

Trick grinned. "I've been told I'm the stuff of some women's dreams."

She sucked in a breath—that he had the audacity to allude to her admission that she'd been dreaming about him in the bunkroom. She narrowed her eyes and reminded him, "Nightmares. You're the stuff of women's nightmares."

Michaela and the other Hotshots chuckled, and the tightness in Henrietta's chest eased a little. Maybe she had no reason to feel embarrassed. Maybe nobody else had caught on to her attraction to Trick McRooney.

But she and Michaela barely made it to the door of the bar before her friend remarked, "This is a bad idea."

"You're the one who wants to leave," Henrietta reminded her, "which you could have done alone since we drove here separately." And that was because Henrietta had actually driven into town the night before the meeting to sleep at the firehouse. But she'd had very little sleep thanks to him, both before and after she'd awakened from that nightmare.

"Leaving is a good idea," Michaela said. "You and Trick McRooney is the bad idea. The very bad idea."

Henrietta shook her head. "It's not an idea at all." It was just a dream.

Michaela's blue eyes were narrowed as she stared up at Hank. "I hope that's true."

"Of course it is," Henrietta insisted.

"It better be," Michaela said. "For your sake. Who do

you think will be leaving the team if you hook up with the boss's brother-in-law? Not *him*."

Henrietta glanced at the booth in the back of the bar. Trick hadn't sat down again. Maybe that was because the only team member talking to him was Owen. Why had he come back to the booth?

To speak to the team? Or to her? He hadn't protested her leaving. He wasn't even looking at her now. So his interest hadn't been her. Maybe he was trying to be part of the team. Maybe the person at the wildfire who'd been gossiping about his never sticking around hadn't realized that Trick had a reason to stay in Northern Lakes—his sister. And brother-in-law.

"Nobody's hooking up with anybody," Henrietta assured her friend.

Michaela glanced toward the bar now and sighed. "Sad but true."

Henrietta followed her friend's gaze. Luke Garrison had been sitting there earlier, but he was gone now. He was also very happily married. So who…?

Before she could ask Michaela, her friend had pushed open the door and stepped outside. She dangled her keys from her small calloused hand. "I forgot we both drove. See you at home." And she rushed off before Henrietta could ask her any questions.

Maybe Henrietta wasn't the only one struggling with an unwanted attraction to someone unsuitable. And Trick was definitely unsuitable. Hooking up with him could cost Henrietta what mattered most to her. And since her parents and Grandpapa had passed away, and she'd ended her relationship with Greg, it was really all she had: her job.

HE HAD A job to do. But he wasn't doing it very well. He hadn't made any progress yet on figuring out who was behind the accidents. It didn't help that the only people who would talk to him were the people he no longer suspected.

Luke and Owen. Luke had left, though. And Michaela and Henrietta were leaving, too. The door swung shut behind them as they stepped out of the bar. A compulsion to follow overwhelmed him and even had him moving toward the door.

"Where you going?" Owen called after him.

He turned back toward his new friend and lied, "Got a meeting with Braden…"

"Another secret meeting," someone else in the booth murmured. It might have been Ethan Sommerly. With his bushy beard concealing most of his face, it was hard to see if his lips had moved. What else was he concealing?

Trick had been wondering about that for a while. There was just something about the guy…some kind of fugitive-hiding-out-from-the-law vibe that Trick picked up from him. Ethan was so hard to read; even now Trick couldn't tell if he had uttered the remark or…

It might have been Trent Miles who'd made the resentful comment. The firefighter from Detroit had given him nearly as much attitude as Henrietta had since his arrival. Luke Garrison had briefly suspected Miles of being behind the attempts on his life. Apparently the guy had known Luke's wife before him and might have wanted her for himself. Trick figured a guy like Miles, who was rumored to have once been a gang member in Detroit, wouldn't let much get between him and what he wanted. What did he want? Trick out of his way so he could keep messing with his team?

But why?

He wasn't the only one who might be harboring a grudge against the Hotshots, though. The owner of the bar, Charlie Tillerman, had nearly lost everything because of them. The arsonist had targeted his bar since it was where they hung out. Luke had suspected Charlie, too, of framing him. Trick had been wrong to think either man guilty, but what about the others…?

The incidents that hadn't been solved, the sabotage…

Trick grinned at the team members left in the booth. "Not much of a secret meeting when I just said that's where I'm going," he pointed out to whoever had made the remark. Of course he was lying, but they didn't need to know that. It might have been smarter to tell the truth, but he wasn't sure what that was until he walked out of the bar and discovered the two women had parted on the sidewalk. His pulse quickened with excitement. One woman walked toward the parking lot around the corner, and the other toward the firehouse.

He should have followed Michaela. She was the better suspect of the two of them. Henrietta had helped him survive the bucket sabotage. He didn't know if Michaela would have done the same. And she was the one who'd insisted on leaving once he'd joined them in the booth.

Henrietta hadn't tried to stay either, though. She was no bigger fan of his than Michaela was. In fact, she'd been the most vocal of all the Hotshots in her disapproval of his taking Dirk Brown's spot on the team. So he shouldn't have just been grateful that she'd saved him, but surprised as well.

And maybe it was that surprise that compelled him to

follow her. Or maybe it was the sway of her hips in the slim-fitting jeans she wore. She walked like a runway model, her hair swinging across her back as she moved.

He slowed his footsteps to follow her but not necessarily catch up to her. He was enjoying the view so much that a groan of disappointment slipped out when she turned the corner and disappeared from his sight.

He hurried then to catch her. But as he rounded the corner, something struck his shins, making his legs fold beneath him as he fell to his knees.

Maybe he'd had no business agreeing to this assignment. Like he'd told his sister and brother-in-law, he wasn't an investigator.

Clearly, he wasn't observant enough. How the hell had he gotten blindsided? Again?

Before he could get to his feet, a hand struck his shoulder—holding him down. "What the hell do you think you're doing? Stalking me?"

Trick looked up into Henrietta's beautiful face as she leaned over him. Her skin was flushed with anger, her dark eyes bright with it. "I'm not stalking you," he assured her.

"You were following me," she pointed out.

He couldn't deny that. "I think we're both just going to the same place," he said.

Her dark eyes narrowed with suspicion. "How do you know where I'm going?"

"I'm just guessing," he admitted, "that we're both parked back at the firehouse."

She released a shaky breath, and her hand slid off his shoulder. But his skin felt like it was still there, like she'd branded him somehow. "I am."

"Are you staying in the bunkroom again tonight?" he asked.

She shook her head, tumbling all that long black hair around her shoulders. His fingers itched to reach out and touch it, to savor the softness of it. But when he got to his feet, she stepped back—out of his reach. "No. I'm heading home."

"No more nightmares?" he asked.

She shook her head.

"Because if you need someone to hold you, I could make that sacrifice," he offered. And he stepped closer to her—so close that his chest bumped against her breasts.

She was tall and strong but soft and feminine, too. And so damn sexy...

His body hardened—like it had when his thigh had pressed against hers in the booth. He'd felt such heat then—from her and inside himself.

Such damn desire...

It overwhelmed him now, and he slid his arms around her. She lifted her arms, too, and closed her hands over his shoulders. He waited for her to push him away.

Last night she'd been half asleep when she'd touched his face. She'd been scared and vulnerable. Tonight she was wide-awake and, since she'd only been sipping soda at the bar, completely sober. He braced himself for her to spit in his face or push him to the ground again.

Instead her lips curved into a smile. "I should take you up on that," she mused. And when he tensed, she laughed. "I'm kidding. There's no way I would ever sleep with you."

He grinned now and leaned down so that his mouth was just a breath from hers, and whispered, "There is no way you'd sleep if you were in my arms."

No way he would sleep either—with her that close to him. His body ached now. He wanted her so damn much.

She chuckled again. "You are so cocky," she said. "So sure of yourself."

She had no idea. He must have been better at faking than he'd realized. But then, he'd had years of experience faking that he was okay; he'd had to—for his dad, for his siblings...

He hadn't wanted anyone to worry about him. They'd had more than enough to be concerned about without worrying about him, too. And eventually, after faking it long enough, he had been okay.

"Want to find out why I'm so cocky?" he asked, and he wiggled his eyebrows to tease her.

She shook her head. "I wouldn't want to risk being disappointed."

He chuckled at her teasing him back. Not that she was necessarily teasing him. "I would not disappoint," he promised her.

She laughed again before she pushed him back; then she turned to walk away.

And he clucked at her. "Chicken..."

She turned her head and glanced back at him over her shoulder. "You're calling me a chicken?"

It was pretty ridiculous, given how often she put her life in danger for her job. But, from experience, he knew it was a hell of a lot easier to risk your life than your heart.

Not personal experience...

But his dad's experience had been close enough for him to feel and see his pain, no matter how hard Dad had tried to hide it from them, how hard he'd tried to be brave and strong for them, just like Trick had tried for him.

"You're the chicken," she said.

And he laughed.

"I know your reputation," she said. "Everybody does."

He furrowed his brow. "What?" She wasn't the only one who routinely put her life on the line. He did, too. And not just to fight fires...

This investigation for Braden had nearly taken him out a couple of times. The people who'd tried to kill Owen and Luke hadn't appreciated Trick getting in their way.

"You never stay with any team for long," she said. "And it's because you can never stay in any place for very long."

Maybe she did know him better than he'd realized.

But then she continued, "So you must be afraid of something, like falling for someone..."

He snorted. "I've never fallen for anyone."

She nodded. "Exactly...because you run."

"I. Do. Not. Run," he insisted, his pride prickling at her accusation, however well-founded it probably was.

She shrugged. "It doesn't matter to me," she said. "I doubt that you're going to be around Northern Lakes for very long."

That was his plan. To find out who the hell Braden's saboteur was and move on to the next team. He agreed with everybody who thought working for his brother-in-law was a bad idea.

It was.

A very bad idea...

And he wasn't even doing a good job at investigating. He was too distracted. Henrietta Rowlins was distracting him...with the desire she inspired in him.

He'd been so distracted that he hadn't even noticed

that feeling, the one he'd had since he'd shown up in Northern Lakes—that feeling he was being watched. It raced down his spine now with a sudden chill.

It was possible someone had followed them from the bar like he'd followed her. Or maybe Michaela had turned around and was behind them.

Either way, he had that prickly sensation between his shoulder blades, so much so that he turned around. Nobody stood on the sidewalk behind them.

Maybe he was just imagining it. But then he glanced across the street. A light must have burned out on that side because he could see only a shadow. Maybe it was just a shadow from the buildings along the street or from one of the cars parked at the curb.

He would have turned back toward Henrietta. But then he saw a flash from that shadow. And he realized what it was too late—just as the gunshot rang out.

THE MINUTE TRICK left the bar, the group had seemed to turn on Owen, maybe with resentment that he wanted to include the new team member. Some of the guys slipped away to the back room to play pool, while others claimed they needed the restroom, leaving Owen alone. He'd rather be with Courtney, so he got up from the corner booth and headed toward the door. And as he did, something caught his attention. He tilted his head and listened. Music blared out of the jukebox in the corner of the bar. But that wasn't what he'd just heard.

His heart pounded too fast and too hard; his body tensed. The noise he'd heard hadn't come from a song. It had come from his nightmares, from his flashbacks of when he'd been on the front lines as a Marine medic.

Acting on instinct, Owen rushed out the door, but

when he stepped outside, the night was eerily quiet. He couldn't even hear a cricket or a cicada. Had he been wrong? Had he just imagined the sound?

He peered around the area. No one was there. Then he walked around the corner. Two bodies were lying on the sidewalk.

He'd been right. But he wished like hell now that he hadn't been. That there had been no gunshots...

Hoping he wasn't too late, he rushed toward the bodies.

Chapter Four

A scream burned the back of Hank's throat. But she couldn't utter it. Trick knocking her to the ground had knocked the breath from her lungs. She couldn't breathe. She couldn't move either, with his big, muscular body lying heavily on hers.

Too heavily...

She grasped his shoulders like she had earlier. But instead of pushing him away, she clutched him to her. And finally she found her breath and her voice. She held in the scream and rasped, "Are you okay?"

He was still and quiet.

She gripped his shoulders harder, shaking him slightly. "Trick!" she exclaimed. "Are you okay?"

Fear gripped her. Fear for him...

Why wasn't he talking?

"Are you hit?" she asked. "Did a bullet strike you?"

And finally he moved, his chest shaking against her breasts. But words didn't escape his lips, which were close to hers. Chuckles rumbled out.

She shoved at him now, pushing against him. "You're laughing!"

Before she could move him off her, running footsteps announced someone else's arrival. Maybe the shooter...

She tensed and clutched at him again as fear rushed over her, chilling her skin.

"Are you two okay?" a deep voice asked.

She recognized the voice and the concern in it. "Owen!"

"Hank!" he exclaimed. "Are you hurt?"

"No," she said. At least, she didn't think so, but she had struck the concrete sidewalk pretty hard when Trick had knocked her down.

"Trick?" the paramedic asked.

"He's lost it," Henrietta said as his chest continued to shake against hers—until he finally moved.

Lifting his weight off her, he surged to his feet. Then he reached down to help her up. But she swatted his hand aside and took Owen's instead. As the paramedic helped her up from the ground, she said, "He thinks this is funny."

"It is," Trick said.

"Getting shot at?" she asked with a shudder. "I don't think it's funny at all. We could have been killed."

"By a car backfiring?" he scoffed. "That's all it was."

Owen's brow furrowed. "That's not what it sounded li—"

"I know," Trick interjected. "I thought it was a gun-shot at first, too. That's why I overreacted and knocked Hank down." His green gaze swept over her body—so thoroughly that she nearly shivered again. "I didn't hurt you, did I?"

"I would have been hurt worse by a bullet," she said and sucked in a breath as she realized he'd saved her life.

"Yeah, I would have, too," he said. "That's why I know it was just a car backfiring. Otherwise I would be full of holes."

She had heard more than one bang. "A car wouldn't have backfired more than once," she pointed out. At least, she didn't think so, but Grandpapa had only taught her the basics about vehicles, like how to check her oil and change a tire. He'd wanted her to be self-sufficient, maybe because he'd known he wouldn't be around as long as she needed him. It didn't matter how self-sufficient she was; she still needed him.

"Then it must have been fireworks," Trick said. "Probably some kid shooting them off in one of the alleys around here." They were near an alley, so near that the sound of fireworks would have echoed like the sounds she'd heard.

He chuckled again. "Can't believe what an idiot I was for reacting like that," he said. "This is Northern Lakes—not Detroit or Chicago. Why would there be a drive-by shooting here?"

She released the breath she'd drawn as a ragged sigh of relief. He was right. There were no gangs in Northern Lakes; hunters were the only ones who fired shots. Except for Louanne Brown, Dirk's widow, who'd tried killing Owen but had wound up shooting herself. And Trooper Marty Gingrich, who had shot at Luke and Willow Garrison. Gingrich was the reason she wasn't pulling out her cell to dial 9-1-1. Had Marty had a colleague helping him cover up his crimes? Was that why he'd nearly gotten away with it? After everything that had happened lately, Hank found it hard to trust anyone. Even the police…

Maybe everything that had happened lately had made her paranoid. Because really, why would anyone shoot at them? Neither of them had a treacherous spouse like Dirk's wife, Trick because he had never stayed in any one place for long, and Hank because she'd returned Greg's ring—not because she'd thought him treacherous, but because she'd felt like she was the treacherous one, that she'd accepted his proposal for the wrong reasons.

Loneliness instead of love. She'd missed Grandpapa so much, missed his stories and his cooking and fishing with him…and his smile and laugh.

"It's understandable you reacted like that," Owen said. "There's been a lot of stuff happening in this town that shouldn't be."

Trick sighed. "That's probably why we're all so on edge—imagining the worst…"

But Northern Lakes was too small to have any other dangerous people in it. It wasn't a big city rife with crime despite recent events. It must have been some kid playing with fireworks in the alley like Trick had suggested.

Owen shook his head. But if he disagreed with Trick, he didn't voice his doubts aloud. He just looked them both over more closely. "Are you sure you're not hurt?"

"Not a scratch," Trick assured him. "Hank broke my fall. Thanks."

She snorted. And she was glad now that it hadn't been gunshots they'd heard. She would hate owing him for saving her life.

"Want to go back in the bar?" Trick asked. "I'll buy you a beer."

She glared at him. "No thanks. I'm going home."

As she turned to walk away, he made that clucking sound again. And she was even happier that he hadn't saved her life. Ignoring him, she waved goodbye to Owen before heading back to the lot at the firehouse.

She pulled her keys from her pocket and clicked the fob to unlock her SUV. After opening the door, she slid beneath the steering wheel and put the key in the ignition. Then she turned it and started the engine. As it rumbled to life, she shivered as she realized she hadn't heard that sound earlier.

If that blast had been a car backfiring, why hadn't she heard the engine?

Because it hadn't been a car. It could have been fireworks, but she hadn't heard kids running away either...

But if it had been gunshots she'd heard, why would someone be shooting at them? She could think of no reason that someone would want to hurt her. But what about Trick?

Had that bucket coming apart been an accident? Or was someone trying to kill him?

FURY GRIPPED TRICK. He'd had a lot of things happen to him during all his years as a Hotshot, even more since taking on this special assignment for Braden. But getting shot at was new and not something he wanted to repeat, especially when he was with Henrietta.

He shuddered as he considered how she could have been hurt, too. But even though a bullet hadn't hit her, she would probably have bruises from how hard he'd knocked her to the ground.

He glanced in the direction she'd gone. And like when she'd left the bar, he felt compelled to follow her. But now it wasn't because he wanted to kiss her. He wanted to make sure she stayed safe. But she would probably stay a hell of a lot safer if he stayed away from her. He was the one at whom those shots had been fired. That was what those notes had meant about how he wasn't going to get away with whatever the hell the person thought he was trying to get away with—because they were going to kill him.

"Backfiring car my ass," Owen grumbled.

"Then fireworks," Trick said. That was a more plausible explanation, if he hadn't seen that shadow and the flash.

"You might have fooled Hank into believing that, but I know what a gunshot sounds like," Owen said and then shuddered. "All too well…"

Trick shook his head and very pointedly said, "You did not hear gunshots."

Owen narrowed his eyes. "Did you lose your mind like Hank said? Hit your head on the sidewalk or something?"

Trick let his lips curve into a slight grin. "No. I'm thinking very clearly."

Which he wouldn't have been able to do if Henrietta hadn't left. She distracted him too much—so much that he'd nearly reacted too slowly.

He'd felt the bullet whiz past him just as he'd pushed Henrietta to the ground. He could have been hit. Worse yet, she could have been hit. It had come too close.

Too damn close…

That was why he needed to stay away from her—even though his body physically ached over letting her walk away from him. He wanted to make sure she was truly okay. "Do you really want to help me?" Trick asked Owen.

The paramedic nodded. "Of course." He fished out his cell phone from his jeans pocket. "I'll call the—"

Trick took the device from Owen's hand. "No. I don't

want the police, and you shouldn't either after what happened with Marty Gingrich."

"He's in jail now," Owen said.

"Because of us," Trick pointed out. "Not because any of his coworkers discovered what he was doing. How could he have fooled every one of them?"

Owen's eyes widened and a breath escaped his lips as if Trick had sucker punched him. "I hadn't thought about that, that someone could have been covering for him…"

Trick shrugged. He wasn't as concerned about that as he was about his brother-in-law. "That's the least of our worries right now," he said.

Owen nodded. "Obviously."

"Getting shot at must mean I'm close," Trick pointed out. "And we need to find this saboteur quickly and quietly or Braden might lose his job."

Owen sucked in a breath. "I didn't think about that…"

That was because the paramedic probably didn't know about the letter Braden had received; Trick wasn't certain that he was supposed to know. His sister was the one who had shared that information with him, so Trick hadn't shared his threats with his brother-in-law. He hadn't wanted to put any more pressure on him or, worse yet, have Braden fire him in order to keep him safe. He knew how worried Braden was that he'd put Trick in danger, but Trick was more worried about putting Braden in danger. Braden had more to lose than Trick did. His happiness with Sam and his job.

"If we call the police and an investigation is opened, everything else might come out, too, about the sabotage. That would tip off the person responsible that we're aware of what's going on," Trick pointed out. "It also might hit the news and attract reporters to Northern Lakes. The US Forest Service would probably not just demote Braden then but fire him, too."

Owen nodded. "You're right. I won't say anything about the gunshots."

"Thanks," Trick said. "I know you all think about Braden like he's a member of your family, too." Trick was under no illusion that Owen was keeping quiet because he'd asked.

"You're a member of our family," Owen said. "You're on the team now."

Trick appreciated the sentiment, but he knew it wasn't true. Nobody had accepted him, and they didn't even know why he was really here. One of them must have figured it out, though—the one responsible for those accidents and for firing those gunshots.

"Will you do a favor for me?" he asked Owen.

The paramedic sighed. "Maybe I shouldn't have said we're family…if you're going to take advantage."

Owen wasn't the one Trick wanted to take advantage of…

Not that he wanted to take advantage of Henrietta. He didn't want her to be vulnerable and scared like the night she'd awoken screaming from her nightmare. He wanted her to want him as much as he wanted her.

But that wasn't very damn likely to happen. She didn't even like him. He liked her, though. Too much to put her in danger ever again.

"I want you to check on Hank," he said. "Make sure I didn't hurt her when I knocked her to the ground."

"You probably saved her life," Owen said.

Trick shook his head. "I put it in danger."

And that was why he couldn't check on her. He had to stay away from her—far away.

"The shooter did that," Owen said. "Not you..."

But the shooter hadn't been firing at her.

Trick was the target. And that had to mean that he was getting close...

"You're sure you're all right?" Braden asked, his heart pounding with fear as he studied his brother-in-law's face. He jumped up from his chair and leaned over his desk.

Trick nodded.

"And Hank?"

"She seemed fine, but I sent Owen to check on her and make sure," Trick said, sounding more concerned about her than he did himself. "I wasn't going to say anything to you, but I started thinking that Hank might..."

"Why wouldn't you want to tell me?" Braden asked. "And where are the police?" He hadn't heard any sirens yet, but sometimes it took a while for a trooper to come to Northern Lakes from the closest state police post.

"They're not coming," Trick said.

"Why not?" Braden asked. He wouldn't have thought anybody at the state police post harbored a grudge against them over Marty Gingrich getting arrested. Marty had been the one who'd harbored the grudge—against Braden—from childhood and high school athletic rivalries.

"I didn't call them," Trick said.

"Why the hell not?" Braden asked.

"Because I don't want anybody to know about the gunshots, and neither should you," Trick said. "I think I convinced Hank that it was a car backfiring or kids setting off fireworks. Owen's going to support that story."

"Why in the world would you lie about this?" Braden asked. "Somebody tried to kill you tonight."

And they hadn't even bothered trying to disguise it as an accident—like the bolts coming loose that held the bucket on to the crane.

Trick clenched his jaw so tightly that a muscle twitched in his cheek. "I know," he said through gritted teeth. "Believe me, I know."

"Then why cover it up?" Braden asked. "Are you protecting someone?"

Trick clenched his jaw more tightly, as if he struggled to hold in a response.

Braden said, "You wouldn't protect the person trying to kill you." Not Trick. He was too much like his sister; he would want justice and probably dole out a little of his own. So if Trick wasn't protecting the shooter…

Realization dawned, and Braden sank heavily back into his chair. "You're protecting me."

Trick sighed and dropped onto a chair in front of Braden's desk. "You can't afford your bosses finding out about the shooting. And they will if we report it. Hell, the media might even do a story since not much happens around here—until lately, anyway."

Braden groaned. The last thing he needed was a reporter investigating what had been happening with the sabotage and for how long. There had been reports about the arsonist, but that coverage had died down. And Dirk's death had been just a small article, with a follow-up after Louanne had been found culpable. Everything had been kept quiet about Luke and Willow, probably because the police had worked hard to hide their own corruption.

Braden had figured it was just Marty, but now he wondered... Had he had help? With how big an idiot Marty had always been, he'd almost had to have had help to keep his guilt hidden for so long.

"You're barely hanging on to your job as it is," Trick reminded him.

Needlessly.

Braden was well aware that he might lose his team. But he was too proud to want anyone else covering for him. "Don't do me any favors."

Trick chuckled. "Then what the hell am I doing here?" he asked. "I believe your exact words when you called and asked me to come to Northern Lakes were 'Can you do me a favor?'"

Braden tried to hold back a laugh, but it slipped out along with a curse.

"So let me do my favor," Trick said as he jumped up from the chair.

Fear gripped Braden at the thought of Trick going back out there—where someone had already tried to shoot him.

"Be careful," he advised his brother-in-law. "I don't want you getting killed."

But he hadn't been able to stop the accidents, so he didn't trust his ability to protect Trick. He had to trust that Trick would be able to take care of himself.

Because even if he fired Trick, he doubted the man would stop investigating and leave Northern Lakes. He was too invested now.

Too determined to find out who was trying to kill him...

Hopefully his investigation wouldn't cost him his life.

Chapter Five

Before pushing open the door to step outside the firehouse, Trick drew in a deep breath. He may have assured his brother-in-law that he had everything under control, but he hadn't convinced himself. Even as unpredictable as they could be, fires were easy for Trick to handle—because he had so much experience.

But this…

Getting shot at…

He didn't want to get experience in that. He wanted nothing to do with that. A shooter was even more unpredictable than a fire. Someone could shoot from anywhere. A car. The street—like earlier…

Maybe he should have reported it. But what would the police do that he wasn't already trying to do? Launch a big investigation or try to cover up their own complicity? He wasn't sure he could trust the police now, not after what Marty had done. No. It was safer to handle this on his own. He'd go back later and check out the scene, see if there were any security cameras in the area. He must have been getting closer than he'd thought to discovering the identity of Braden's saboteur, or someone wouldn't have fired those shots at him. That had to be who'd tried taking him out.

Someone who didn't want Trick exposing him or her. But who?

Not Henrietta. She'd been with him when the shots had rung out and could have been hit. He shuddered at the thought.

Where was she now? Was she okay? He wanted to call her. No. He wanted to go and see her. But it was better that he'd sent Owen to check on her. After giving him some time to do that, Trick would call the paramedic to make sure she was okay.

He let the door swing shut behind him, and the lock clicked as it closed. He peered around in the darkness like he had earlier, his body tense.

But all the streetlamps burned, dispelling the shadows here. He was safe.

For the moment...

But whoever had fired those shots would probably try again once they realized he was not going to stop investigating. He couldn't stop...until he had stopped the saboteur.

And he would.

He'd eliminated another one of his suspects from the twenty-member Hotshot team—Henrietta. He breathed a sigh of relief over her not being responsible. Hell, he was more than relieved; he was happy as hell. And he wasn't sure why he was so happy.

It wasn't as if he could actually get involved with Henrietta. They worked together. And even if they didn't...

He wouldn't be here, in Northern Lakes, long enough to date her. He would be switching to another team with an open position and then another...

He couldn't stay anyplace too long, couldn't risk getting attached to that place or, worse yet, to the people.

Despite what Owen had said about Trick being part of the family, he knew nobody else saw him that way. So it was better he left soon, before he got in any deeper, which was why he needed to find Braden's saboteur fast. Despite the superintendent's unwillingness to believe it, it had to be a member of his team.

All of them—but Braden—had been at the Filling Station. Hank and Michaela had left before Trick had. But Michaela could have circled back around and shot at them.

And what about the rest?

Who had stayed in the bar and who had left after they had? He glanced at his watch. It wasn't that late yet, so the bar was still open. While he could have walked back there, he remembered that area where the streetlamp had either burned out or been shot out, and he headed toward his truck instead.

He didn't intend to give the shooter another chance to hit him. He parked on the street right in front of the bar and slid across the seat to push open the passenger's door. When he stepped onto the sidewalk, he ducked low and moved quickly to the bar's front door.

"Cluck, cluck," he muttered to himself. Who was the chicken now? Maybe that was karma for teasing Henrietta like he had. She'd been smart to reject him, smarter than he'd been flirting with her, flirting with the danger she could pose to him.

He was already in enough danger as it was. He felt like ducking when he stepped inside the bar and everybody turned toward him. Everybody that was left. And there weren't very many.

Ethan Sommerly. Trent Miles. Rory VanDam. Carl Kozak. They all sat in that corner booth in the back.

But just because they were still here didn't mean that they hadn't left for a while—long enough to shoot at him and Henrietta.

Instead of walking toward that booth, he headed to the bar.

"You're back," Charlie remarked with slight surprise.

Was he surprised because he'd been the one who had shot at him? Even though he was tending bar, there were plenty of other staff. And as he was the owner, nobody would have questioned him stepping away for a bit. He could have slipped outside unnoticed. Hell, he might have even kept a gun behind the bar to ward off robbers.

But why shoot at Trick? Unless Charlie was the one sabotaging the equipment. But how? And why? Just because of what the arsonist had done to his bar? Could he really blame the Hotshot team over that, even though they had been the arsonist's intended target?

"Yeah, I'm back," Trick said. And if he'd been much of a drinker, he could have used one after nearly getting his head shot off. "Anybody else come back?"

The barkeep's mouth curved into a slight grin. "Hank hasn't come back."

So she wasn't the only one who'd caught Trick watching her. "I wasn't talking about Hank." But he needed to call Owen soon.

He'd barely had the thought when Charlie pointed at the door. "Somebody else came back…"

And Trick turned to see Owen walking in. The paramedic joined him at the bar.

"How is she?" he anxiously asked.

Owen shook his head. "I couldn't find her. She's not picking up her cell phone either."

Charlie had said she hadn't returned here, but Trick

glanced around the bar anyway. The crowd had thinned even more. The Hotshots who'd remained were gone now, either slipping into the restroom, a back room or out a back door. Was that because it was near closing time? Or because of him?

Or because of Hank?

Had she called one of them? Were they going off to meet her? Where the hell was she?

HENRIETTA HAD BEEN halfway home before she turned her SUV around and headed back to Northern Lakes. In the throes of her initial fear and shock, she'd accepted Trick's explanation of the noises and his reaction to them. But once she'd gotten away from him and cleared her head, she'd begun to question his claims that it had either been a backfiring car or fireworks. And she wondered if he really believed what he'd told her.

"He's not getting away with it," she murmured to her reflection in the rearview mirror. She was not going to let him lie.

Why would he even want to?

If somebody had taken a shot at them, wouldn't he want to find out who had done it and why? She sure as hell wanted to know what had really happened.

It couldn't have been a car backfiring—not when she hadn't even heard one running. But it might have been fireworks. Maybe a kid had tossed some down and run off before the fuse had ignited them. Maybe that was why she hadn't heard anything. But she could find something…some wrappers left behind…and that was why she'd turned around—to investigate. She had to know the truth.

And she didn't trust Trick McRooney to give it to her.

Not that she had any real reason to mistrust him. All that anyone who'd worked with him in the past had said about him was that he didn't stick around, but there must have been a reason for that, a reason he didn't want to stay. Was he running from something? Hiding something?

Even if Braden didn't have that rule prohibiting romantic relationships between team members, Hank wouldn't have been tempted to get involved with him. She'd already lost too many people she cared about: her parents, Grandpapa... She wasn't going to risk her heart on someone she knew she couldn't rely on.

Maybe that was why she'd accepted Greg's proposal. Because she'd known that she could trust him, that he was dependable, honest, kind...

Too kind for her to stay engaged to him when she hadn't loved him like he deserved. Her pulse had never quickened in his presence; she'd never pined for him when she'd been away from him for weeks on end fighting wildfires. She'd never felt about him the way he'd felt about her. She'd hurt him when she'd returned his ring, and she felt a pang of guilt over that. But if she'd gone ahead and married him, that would have been so much worse for them both. Hopefully he would find someone who would love him like he deserved, whose pulse would quicken when he walked into a room—like Trick McRooney made hers quicken. She sucked in a breath with the realization.

How could she be so attracted to someone she couldn't trust? Needing to know if she could trust herself and her own instincts, Hank headed back to that area where he'd knocked her to the ground.

Her shoulder throbbed from the contact with the concrete. But bruises were the least of her concerns. If someone had shot at them, she damn well wanted the person caught.

And that wasn't going to happen if the shooting didn't get reported. She would have called the police to do that herself…if she had no doubt that it had been a gunshot she'd heard.

But Trick had worked so hard to convince her and Owen that she wasn't entirely confident now. Yet. She would be once she looked around the scene. When she turned onto the street around the corner from the bar, darkness enveloped the SUV, which was weird since it usually seemed so much brighter—even at night—in the village.

Where she and Michaela lived, there were no streetlamps. But many lights were scattered through the village of Northern Lakes…if they weren't burned out.

That must have been what had happened, and no one had replaced the bulbs yet. Someone at the firehouse would probably have to do the job—with the aid of an engine or the boom truck, if it had been repaired. She flinched as she remembered how the bucket had dangled off the crane.

And how Trick had dangled off the bucket…

But that had only been a nightmare. He hadn't really fallen to the ground. So maybe she had only imagined that shot earlier.

Maybe he had been telling the truth and her over-active imagination and anxiety had made it sound like something else in her head. That was why she hadn't called the police. Yet.

But once she found proof…

First, she had to find a parking space, though. There weren't many public lots in the village, so people usually parked along the curb for the businesses and the bar and for the apartments above those establishments.

She had to drive a distance down the street before she found a spot big enough to pull her SUV in next to the curb. At least the streetlamp wasn't burned out down here. But she had to walk back to find the place where Trick had knocked her to the ground.

He'd covered her body with his. So if anyone had been shooting at them, he would have taken every bullet. Maybe because he knew those bullets had been meant for him.

But what if they hadn't been...?

She shuddered at the thought of someone wanting to hurt her. No. That wasn't possible. She had no enemies. The only person she didn't get along with was Trick McRooney.

She glanced down at the concrete where he'd knocked her to the ground. They hadn't been hit, so there was no blood. She was surprised, though, that the ground wasn't black from the heat that their entwined bodies had generated. Despite the cool breeze blowing around the buildings, that heat streaked through her again as she remembered the feeling of his body on top of hers.

So hard...

So strong...

She missed the weight and the warmth of it—of him. He'd moved too quickly, had gotten up too fast. When Owen had joined them...

He'd heard it, too. Had he been inside the bar? Or outside? He'd seemed just as skeptical as she was of Trick's claim that it had been a car backfiring or fireworks.

Where would those have been? What alley? She crossed the road to the buildings across from where Trick had knocked her to the sidewalk, and she found that there was a space between the buildings. It was even darker in the shadows of the alley, so she couldn't see anything, let alone the remains of any firework wrappers. She pulled her cell phone from her pocket and tried to turn on the flashlight feature.

But the screen was black. And cracked.

It must have broken when Trick knocked her down. She cursed and shoved it back into her pocket. She wasn't just mad that she would have to get a new phone. She hated the feeling of being cut off. What if someone had been trying to call her?

What if she needed to call someone?

A shiver chased the heat from her body, leaving her chilled, with a prickling sensation between her shoulder blades and goose bumps rising on her skin. Feeling as if someone was watching her, she glanced around the street.

Someone could have been sitting in one of the parked cars. The windows were dark, and the lights off. The buildings were dark, too, as was the sidewalk where that lamp had burned out.

Or had it burned out?

Curiosity compelled her to inspect it. The glass wasn't burned out; it was broken, like her phone.

Had someone shot out the light?

Grandpapa had taught Henrietta how to shoot years ago—when the gun had been nearly as big as she'd been. He hadn't taught her just for protection, but so that she would be able to take care of herself another way—by hunting.

But Henrietta had had too soft a heart then—and now—to kill another living being. She hadn't been able to shoot an animal; she couldn't imagine having the capacity to take a human life.

She shuddered again and hoped that Trick was right, that it had just been fireworks that they'd heard. But when she moved her foot, something rolled across the concrete beneath the sole of her shoe. She bent down and felt around the ground, and her fingers brushed across something small and metallic. A spent shell...

Somebody *had* taken a shot at them, or at least at the light. And now she had proof. But with her broken phone, she couldn't call the police. She couldn't even call Trick to gloat over proving him wrong.

Where would he be? His apartment was around here somewhere. She remembered him saying he'd found something close to the firehouse. She wasn't sure exactly where; until now, she hadn't wanted to know. She'd had no intention of ever going there.

Not that she would now either.

But it was tempting...to show him the shell.

Maybe he'd gone back to the bar. Even if he hadn't, she could use the phone there to call the police. If the Filling Station was still open...

Her cell was also what she used as a watch, since she didn't like wearing jewelry. With her job, it wasn't safe; watches, rings and necklaces could get caught on equipment.

She wasn't far from the bar and might as well head there, but then she remembered how far away she'd had to park, and she got that prickling sensation between her shoulder blades again, along with a rush of cold that chilled her flesh.

She was not alone.

She whirled around, searching the street for someone else. But she saw only shadows. Her imagination again?

She started back toward her vehicle, but as she moved, she heard footsteps echoing her own. Somebody else was definitely out there, hiding in the darkness.

Following her…

MICHAELA PACED THE small confines of the apartment she shared with Hank above the firehouse in the village of St. Paul. But Hank wasn't there.

Where the hell was she?

She couldn't have been that far behind her. Her SUV had just been parked at the firehouse. But Michaela hadn't noticed any lights behind her on the road. And there was only one route that led from Northern Lakes to St. Paul, where she and Hank staffed the firehouse with the help of some volunteers.

They shouldn't have split up when they'd walked out of the bar. Even a small town like Northern Lakes had its share of dangers…

Like Trick McRooney. The way he looked at Hank made him a danger to her—to her job and to her heart. Had he followed Hank out of the bar?

Was that where she was?

Michaela shook her head. No. Hank was too smart to risk her heart, or her job, for someone with Trick's reputation for leaving. If only Michaela had been as smart…

She shrugged off the thought. The past was the past; she couldn't change it, no matter how much she wished she could. Like leaving with Hank…

They should have verified they both made it to their vehicles tonight. Michaela punched the contact for Hank on her phone, but her call went straight to voice mail, as had all the other calls she'd placed in the past hour to her friend and roommate.

So she scrolled through her contacts and punched in another number—one she wouldn't have input in her phone if the Hotshot superintendent didn't insist that every team member have every other team member's contact information.

That person answered immediately.

She didn't bother identifying herself. "Are you with Hank?"

"No."

She should have been relieved that he wasn't, but a curse slipped out of her lips instead. At least then she would have known where Hank was. "She's not here," she said. "She didn't get home yet."

"And you're worried."

She wasn't sure why. "She might have just gone back to the firehouse to sleep again." Even though she'd said she wasn't going to? That wouldn't have been like Hank at all. Hank was open and honest to a fault. Or at least that was what the woman's ex-fiancé believed. Michaela had heard enough of Greg's grumbling over their breakup to know that he would have preferred it if Hank had lied to him and married him, even though she hadn't loved him.

"I was just there and didn't see her," Trick admitted. "But I'll check again."

And Michaela heard it in his deep voice as well, the concern and the urgency. She wasn't the only one worried about Hank.

Where the hell was she?

Chapter Six

His hand shaking slightly, Trick slid his cell phone back into his pocket.

"Who was that?" Owen asked. Even sitting on the stool next to him, he wouldn't have been able to hear the caller over the noise in the bar as the staff wrapped up for the night, tossing chairs onto tabletops to sweep up the peanut shells. While they worked, the jukebox blasted.

"It was Michaela," Trick replied.

Owen widened his eyes with shock. "She called you?"

Trick would have made some crass joke about why she'd called him, but he was too damn worried. "She wondered if Hank was with me," he explained. "She didn't make it back to the place they share."

Owen cursed now. "You were right to worry about her…"

A pang of guilt struck Trick's heart. "Maybe I did hurt her when I knocked her to the ground."

"Do you think she hit her head?" Owen asked.

Trick sucked in a breath. "I don't know…" He'd been more worried about her getting it blown off than striking it against the concrete. "Oh, my God. What if she lost consciousness while driving home…?"

The road to St. Paul wound through the national forest, with sharp curves and big trees lining it. If she'd gone off the shoulder…

He jumped up from his stool, but his legs were shaking so badly they nearly folded beneath him. "We have to find her."

Owen was on his feet, too. "I'll drive her route home," he said. "You check around town. Maybe she didn't leave Northern Lakes."

He hoped she was here—that she was close. He nodded in agreement and rushed toward the door.

Owen was with him every step of the way. "I'll call you when I find her," the paramedic said, as if he expected to discover her unconscious alongside the road.

That pang of guilt struck Trick again. He'd wanted to protect her, not harm her. What if she was hurt because of him? Too choked up to speak, he just nodded at Owen again. He would call, too, if he found her. But he wasn't as certain as Owen was that he would, or that she was still in Northern Lakes.

And if she was, where should he look for her first? While Owen rushed off toward his truck, Trick stood frozen on the sidewalk outside the Filling Station. He'd told Michaela that he would check the firehouse again, so he started toward his truck.

He wanted to find Henrietta at the firehouse, lying in one of those bunks with her hair down around her shoulders, like it had been last night. He wanted to weave his fingers through that soft hair and tip up her face to his. And he wanted to kiss her this time.

Deeply. Passionately.

He shook his head—hard—to dispel those thoughts. Before he could even pull open the door of his truck, he heard the scream. It sounded so much like the one he'd heard the night before—full of terror. He couldn't tell from which direction it had come, but he knew from whom it had come: Henrietta.

THE SCREAM HAD slipped out the minute Henrietta had started to run, and the footsteps following her had pounded against the concrete as the person ran after her. She'd had no doubt then that someone wasn't just stalking her; they were chasing her.

Why?

Had they seen her pick up that shell? Was it evidence? If it was, then someone must have intentionally fired at them.

Hank clutched the small piece of metal tightly in her hand. But she wished she had something besides the spent shell, like a can of pepper spray. But she'd left that in the glove box of her SUV.

If she could get to that...

At least she could lock herself inside her vehicle. Not that it would be much protection against a person with a gun. They could shoot out the windows.

Hell, they could shoot her now. In the back...

The footsteps pounded behind her, sounding even louder now. They had to be gaining on her.

Like all the Hotshots, Hank had to be in peak physical condition, so she ran a few times a week. But that wasn't the same as running for her life, which had her heart beating so hard she thought it might break through her chest.

But no matter how fast she was able to sprint, she wouldn't be able to beat a bullet if the person chose to fire the gun at her again. So she had to duck and weave and find her way into the shadows for protection.

She turned quickly, darting between two buildings. She was probably getting farther from her SUV, but her greatest concern was getting farther from the person chasing her. She couldn't hear the footsteps now between the tall buildings. Maybe the pursuer hadn't seen her turn.

She wasn't even certain where she was. An alley?

She kept walking, more quietly now so the stalker wouldn't hear her moving. But she had no idea where she was; there was no light at the end of the alley from the streetlamps on the other side.

Was it a dead end?

Then she walked a little farther and the alley widened into some sort of courtyard. With the space between the buildings wider now, the shadows were a little thinner. She could make out a concrete fountain with gurgling water and some patio furniture.

She'd found a more residential area. If she screamed now, someone would hear her—would call for help. But would it arrive in time?

Something scraped against the concrete behind her, and she knew she had not outrun her stalker. She opened her mouth to scream, but a big hand covered it.

She struggled against the hand, clawing at it with her fingers so that she could scream and so that she could breathe. She'd already been panting from running. Her lungs burned with the need for air.

"Shh… Henrietta," a deep voice murmured.

She stilled as she recognized that voice. His hand slid away from her mouth, and she gasped for air. "Are you okay?" he asked, his voice a low whisper of concern.

Hank drew in another deep breath before turning and nodding.

"Why did you scream earlier?" he asked.

She smacked his shoulder. "Because you were chasing me!"

"Shh," he cautioned again. "I wasn't chasing you."

"But if it wasn't you…" Then who had been following her?

"That's why you need to be quiet…"

Because whoever had been chasing her was still out there, maybe somewhere close.

THE EARLIER GUNSHOT had been intended as a warning only—since Trick hadn't heeded the warning of the notes. Since he hadn't left Northern Lakes, he clearly hadn't taken those notes seriously. Even *he* should have taken a gunshot seriously… But since the police hadn't shown up, he hadn't even reported it. So he hadn't taken getting shot at as a real threat either…

Maybe the only way to stop Trick McRooney from making mistake after mistake was to kill him. And this was the perfect opportunity. With him and the woman trapped in the courtyard, he had no way of dodging the bullets.

It would be like shooting fish in a barrel.

Easy…

A metallic click echoed off the walls of the buildings as the gun cocked.

Chapter Seven

Henrietta was shaking, her body trembling against Trick's as he wound his arm around her and pulled her into the building with him. The door clunked shut behind them, automatically locking.

He was shaking, too, and had been ever since he'd heard her scream. But moments ago, when he'd heard that telltale click in the courtyard, he'd started shaking harder—so hard that he'd barely been able to punch in the code for the security lock on the back door of the building where he lived.

The handle rattled as someone tried to open the door behind them. And Henrietta gasped.

"They can't get in," Trick assured her. But he'd feel better with more than that steel door between them and whoever had been chasing her. So he guided her up the stairwell to the third floor. He had to punch in another code to open the door at the top of the steps.

Henrietta asked, "How did you get in?"

"I live here," he said. And it was damn lucky that she'd ducked into that courtyard. But then, Northern Lakes wasn't very big, and several buildings shared that space, so it wasn't that unlikely of a coincidence.

She tensed and pulled away from him, hesitating outside the door he'd just opened. But the handle of the exterior door three floors below rattled again, and she rushed inside with him. He shut his door and breathed a sigh of relief when it locked as well.

"He's not going to get to us," Trick assured her.

"He?"

He shrugged. "I don't know…" It could have been a woman, he supposed. He hadn't seen anyone. He'd only heard Henrietta's scream and then that telltale click. "Did you see who it was?"

She shook her head. "I just know that what happened earlier wasn't a car backfiring or a kid setting off fireworks." She held out her hand toward him, a shiny shell lying on her palm. "Why the hell did you lie about it?" she demanded. "Why didn't you call the police?"

He tensed now, uncertain what to tell her. He couldn't trust that she wouldn't share whatever he told her with the rest of the team. In fact, she'd probably share everything with them, because just like Owen, she considered them family. She wouldn't believe that one of them could be responsible for the "accidents" and for the gunshots. And if the saboteur knew for certain that Trick was investigating him, those attempts on his life were bound to increase. So he shrugged. "I don't know for sure that anybody was shooting at us."

She shoved her hand toward him. "This proves it."

"Where did you find it?" he asked, his heart clenching with dread that she'd been fired on again—without him present. But she appeared to be fine…just furious.

"Underneath the streetlamp that was probably shot out."

He shrugged. "That's your answer, then. Some kid

probably shot out the light and that's the shell from that bullet. He wasn't shooting at us at all. Just the light."

"Stop it!" she yelled at him. "Stop lying to me!"

"It's not a lie if it's possible," he said. "And you know that it is."

"It's also possible that this shell is from one of the bullets that were fired at us earlier this evening," she persisted. "Why don't you want to admit that—" she gestured at his locked door "—especially now?"

"What's special about now?" he asked—besides her being inside his apartment. That was special; he'd wanted her here. Hell, he just wanted her.

But not like this…

Not trembling and scared.

"You heard it, too," she said. "You heard that gun cock."

He tilted his head. "I'm not sure that's what I heard…"

"You heard it, or you wouldn't have hurried me up to your apartment," she continued as she looked around his place. She was able to see most of it from where she stood just inside the door, since it was a studio with one small bathroom, and the door to that stood open.

He'd also left the Murphy bed down from where it folded out of a wall of built-in cabinets. The sheets were tangled, and the blanket lay on the floor. He hadn't slept well last night—after that intense moment with her in the bunkroom.

His internal debate raged over whether or not to trust her with the truth. It was one thing if she would keep it to herself, but she was certain to share it, at least with her roommate. And Michaela could possibly be the saboteur and even the shooter. Maybe that cell call had been meant to flush him out and into her trap.

He felt a little trapped now with Henrietta, and whenever he felt like that—that vulnerable—he reacted with humor.

"I had another reason for wanting to get you up here," he said, teasing her as he stepped closer to her. "Alone…"

Her eyes widened with shock as she stared up at him. "You are incredible…"

"I'm glad you noticed," he replied.

"That you're an incredible idiot?" she scoffed. "It's hard to miss. You don't hide it—like you're trying to hide whatever's really going on." She whirled around and gripped the door handle, but before she could pull it open, he covered her hand with his.

Like the last time they'd touched, awareness and attraction jolted him. That was only partially responsible for a sudden rush of panic, though.

"You can't go!" he exclaimed—because even though he hadn't admitted it, he was pretty damn certain that had been a gun cocking in the courtyard. And he didn't doubt that someone had been chasing her. Why had they been chasing *her*?

He was the one who'd been receiving the threats. Unless she'd been receiving some, too…

But everyone seemed to love and respect Henrietta. He could understand why. She was hardworking and sympathetic and loyal and so very sexy.

But now she might also be in danger. He couldn't let her leave. But if she stayed, he might be the one in danger. Of revealing too much, and maybe of feeling too much…

FURY COURSED THROUGH HENRIETTA. She jerked at the handle, trying to pull open the door. But Trick was stronger than she was. He easily held it shut, trapping her inside with him. A shiver coursed down her spine, but this one wasn't of fear.

Being alone with Trick McRooney was exciting. Having him standing so close to her that she could feel the heat and hardness of his big body against hers—that was exhilarating. She wanted him.

But she wanted the truth even more. "If you don't let me out of here, I am going to start screaming," she warned him.

"I wouldn't mind that," he said. He leaned so close that his lips brushed across her earlobe as he added, "If you're screaming my name..."

She tried to hang on to her outrage, but a laugh slipped through her lips. He really was incredible. "Can't you be serious?" she wondered. "And honest?"

"I'm seriously attracted to you," he said. "That's the truth."

Her heart flipped and then began to pound almost as furiously as it had when that person had chased her down the street. But remembering that chase had the fear and the anger rushing back over her. She spun around and pushed Trick back. "I don't think you know what the truth is."

And maybe that was why he wouldn't admit that they'd been shot at; maybe he really didn't know for certain. She opened her hand and stared down at the shell in her palm. It was possible that it was from the bullet that had shot out the streetlamp at some earlier time, since it had already been dark when Trick had knocked her to the ground after that noise.

There had been no car around when they'd heard that, nor had she found any firework wrappers in the alley.

Of course, she hadn't been able to see anything in the shadows, so they might have been there. But somebody had been chasing her; she was certain of that. Had it been Trick?

Was he messing with her for some reason? Gaslighting her?

Her head began to pound in sync with her heart now. She flinched and touched her fingers to her temple, where the pain throbbed.

"Are you okay?" he asked, his handsome face tense with concern. "Did I hurt you when I knocked you down earlier? Did you hit your head?"

Before she could answer, his hands moved through her hair, running over her scalp as if he was checking for bumps. But his fingers didn't just probe—they stroked and massaged, and she nearly moaned with pleasure.

She never reacted like that when her hairdresser washed and massaged her head, and Tammy Ingles was very good at her job. Trick McRooney was very good, too.

"I am fine," she assured him. But she didn't push his hands away like she should have. "Or I will be fine when you start being honest with me."

"I just was," he reminded her. "I told you that I'm attracted to you."

"That's not why you brought me up to your apartment and you know it," she said. "That's not why you won't let me leave."

"I don't want you going out at night alone again," he admitted, almost begrudgingly.

"Because you know someone was out there—someone with a gun."

He shrugged. "I don't know that…"

She wanted to smack him again, like she had in the courtyard. She pulled his hands down from her head. "Stop it!" she said. "Stop lying to me!"

"Did you see anyone?" he asked.

"I heard footsteps," she said.

He shrugged again. "Could have been someone out for a walk."

"It sounded like they were running."

"Out for a jog, then," he said.

She shook her head. "No. Someone was chasing me."

"Why would someone chase you?" he asked. Then his lips curved into a slight grin. "Well, someone besides me?"

"Was it you?" she wondered again.

"No," he said.

"Then how did you show up when you did?" she asked as suspicion chased down her spine with a shiver.

"I heard you scream," he said, and he shuddered now. "I was looking for you anyway, though."

"You were?" Her pulse quickened. "Why?"

"Michaela called to find out if you were with me," he said. "She was worried that you weren't home yet. Why didn't you go home?"

She held out her hand again. "I came back to look for this."

"And you didn't pick up your phone?" he asked. "She tried calling. So did Owen."

"Owen?"

"He's looking for you, too," he said. "He's worried that you might have been hurt when I knocked you down." A muscle twitched in his cheek; he must have been clenching his jaw.

Had he been worried about her, too?

A warm sensation rushed over her heart at the thought that he might actually care, at least a little.

"You did break something when you knocked me down," she admitted.

He cursed—undoubtedly at himself—and reached for her, gently cupping her shoulders in his hands. While he didn't hold her tightly, he'd found what must have been a bruise, and she flinched at the sudden pain of contact.

But of course, she didn't feel just pain. She felt that annoying tingling sensation of attraction and desire.

He jerked his hands away and fisted them at his sides. "Oh, my God, you need a doctor!"

"That's just a bruise." Or it would be; right now her shoulder was just swollen and sore. "I'm fine." She pulled out her phone and showed him the cracked screen. "This is what got broken."

He chuckled, looking relieved. "I'm sorry. I'll buy you a new one."

She shook her head. "That's not necessary." Especially now that she believed someone had purposely fired at them. "You probably saved my life."

And she hadn't thanked him for that. But that was his fault—because he kept lying about what had really happened, about how much danger they'd really been in.

He shrugged off her gratitude the same way he kept shrugging off her questions and her concerns about what the hell was going on. And that fury streaked through her again, the fury that he wasn't being honest with her.

"If my phone wasn't broken, I would have called the police," she said. "And I will the first chance I get." Was that why he was keeping her here? He didn't want her contacting the authorities? But why? He hadn't fired those shots. He'd saved her from them.

"You think that's a good idea?" he asked.

She narrowed her eyes and studied his face—his too-handsome face. "Of course it is. Despite all your denials, I think you know someone took a shot at us. And then that someone chased me down the street when I went back later—probably so I wouldn't turn this over to the police." She held out the shell again. That made sense. Maybe there were fingerprints on it or something…

Of course, now hers were all over it, along with the perspiration from her running with it clenched in her hand. She'd probably smeared whatever other prints might have been on it. But DNA… Wouldn't crime-scene techs be able to find some that wasn't hers?

"So, yes," she concluded. "I think calling the cops is not just a good idea, it's necessary."

"And you trust the police who missed Marty's criminal activities to figure out what really happened tonight?" he asked. "They couldn't even figure out what *he* was up to, or worse yet, maybe they knew and were helping him…"

She shuddered at the thought. "You really think another trooper could have been helping Gingrich?"

He shrugged. "I don't know. But I sure as hell don't trust them. Not with an investigation and not with the media."

She furrowed her brow as she struggled to follow his train of thought. "Media? What are you talking about? What media?" Dawson Hess was married to a reporter who'd covered their team once, but her focus had been on the arsonist, and on Dawson in particular. She'd since been promoted to a major network, and her only interest now in Northern Lakes was her husband.

"About one of the troopers talking to a reporter," he

explained. "Do you really think that kind of publicity is good for the team? For Braden in particular?"

She tensed. "What are you talking about?"

He shrugged again. "I probably shouldn't tell you this…" he murmured.

She sighed. "Now you sound like the old ladies gossiping at Tammy Ingles's beauty salon." She hated gossip—hated listening to it and, most of all, hated being a topic of it. Maybe it was better if she didn't hear whatever else he was about to say. Maybe it was better that she just left before anyone found out she'd been here—in his apartment. Not that she'd gotten much farther than the door.

"I'm sure they've been gossiping a lot about the Hotshots," Trick remarked. "And everything that keeps happening around them. That's not good for Braden, and it's especially not good for Braden's job."

She gasped as realization dawned. Trick was protecting his brother-in-law.

He confirmed it when he added, through gritted teeth, "He's already been warned that he'll be removed as Hotshot superintendent if things keep happening to members of his team."

"Damn it," she murmured. They couldn't lose Braden—he was the best superintendent she'd ever had. He treated her with respect, which was a rarity in the male-dominated field of firefighting, but especially of Hotshots. And more than that, Braden clearly loved his job and his entire team. Even if he kept the job at the fire station in Northern Lakes, it wouldn't be the same as running the Huron Hotshots. But she wasn't just cursing the devastating news Trick had shared. She was cursing the fact that Patrick McRooney was a better man than anybody realized he was. Well, maybe not anyone; Owen and Luke certainly appreciated his having their backs during their recent brushes with death. He'd also quickly become Braden's right hand at work. Maybe that was why everyone resented him so much and had thought he was taking advantage of his sister's husband. But he was actually protecting him.

Like he'd protected her on the street—twice…

But realizing that made her even more determined to get out of his apartment, because now it wasn't just him she didn't trust. She didn't trust herself not to act on her attraction to him. And if she did, Braden wasn't the only one who would be in danger of losing his job on the Hotshot team.

She would be, too.

But losing her job might be the least of her concerns. She couldn't lose her heart, too. Not to someone who probably wouldn't stick around; too many people she loved were gone. That was why she'd tried so hard to focus only on her job. She had to get away from him… before she did something stupid, like let him get any closer than he already was.

THE CELL PHONE vibrating on Braden's bedside table jolted him awake. A call at night was never good news. Especially not lately, with his team in danger over and over again.

As Sam murmured in her sleep, moving her head against his shoulder, Braden reached for the phone. "Zimmer," he said.

"It's Owen," the paramedic said.

Braden jerked upright in bed, his heart pounding with anxiety. Owen had called him too many times over the past several weeks with bad news. And Trick had told him that he'd sent Owen to check on Hank. "What is it?" he asked. "Is Hank all right?"

"You know about the shooting?" Owen asked, with a sigh of relief as well as concern. "I didn't think Trick was going to tell you..."

Braden cursed, wondering what else his brother-in-law might be keeping from him. He would have to deal with Trick later. Right now he was most concerned about Hank. "He told me that they were fine, but he was worried enough to send you after her..." So that worried him, too. "Is she okay?"

"She seemed to be at the time or we wouldn't have let her leave..." Owen's voice trailed off.

Braden's concern notched up to a higher level. "What's going on?"

"I don't know," Owen said. "I don't know why someone would shoot at Trick. I don't know why he didn't want to call the police..."

Braden knew. Because of him—Trick had been protecting him. And he suspected that Owen knew that, too.

"I don't know what the hell's going on," Owen continued. "But now we can't find her..."

Hank was missing?

Chapter Eight

She was so beautiful that Trick couldn't help but stare at Henrietta, especially with her standing so close to him. But because he was staring, he noticed the moment that panic flashed through her dark eyes.

"What?" he asked, and his pulse quickened with his own panic.

Had she heard something?

The shooter couldn't have followed them into the building unless they had the code to the door. There was an outside fire escape, though, that wound up from the courtyard.

He'd forgotten about that. He usually forgot everything when he was close to Henrietta—like his real purpose for joining this Hotshot team…

Like the fact that someone didn't want him here. Hell, none of them wanted him here.

"What's wrong?" he asked her.

"I need to get home," she said. "Michaela must be really worried if she called you."

He was well aware that Michaela didn't like him, so he knew how hard it must have been for her to reach out to him. So instead of being offended, he felt a twinge of guilt and cursed. "I should have had you call her once we got inside the apartment." And he needed to call Owen to let him know Hank was okay.

Just as he was thinking about contacting the paramedic, his phone began to vibrate in his pocket. When he reached for it, Henrietta reached for the door. Ignoring the call, he pushed his hand against the door, slamming it shut before she could fully open it and escape.

And he was aware that was what she was trying to do. Escape. That panic he'd seen flash through her dark eyes hadn't been because she'd heard something or someone outside. If so, she wouldn't have chosen to rush out to them. No. He was the someone she was trying to escape.

But he wasn't the danger, and he needed her to accept that. "You're not going to make it home if you rush out there alone," he warned her.

She tensed, then turned to glare at him. "So you do admit there's someone out there stalking us. Or me. Or you…"

"I don't know for certain," he said. "But I'm not willing to take the chance that someone's out there waiting for you to leave. Someone who might hurt you if you go back out alone."

"I'm not spending the night with you!" she exclaimed, and the panic was in her voice now as it rose.

He pressed a hand to his chest, where his heart pounded fast and hard at the thought of her staying with him, of her really spending the night with him. "I'm wounded. Don't you trust me enough to stay here?"

"No," she said, but her lips curved into a slight smile of amusement over his question.

She was smart. Despite his best intentions, he doubted he'd be able to keep his hands—as well as other body parts—off her if she spent the night at his place.

He uttered a heavy sigh. "You don't have to stay here, but I will make sure you get safely back to your place."

"Acting like a gentleman seems out of character for you," she mused, and her big dark eyes narrowed as she studied his face. "So you must be really worried."

He was, and not just because he had that sudden sensation tingling between his shoulder blades again, that chill of an icy gaze watching him. He was worried because of her—worried that he was putting her in danger, and worried that he was beginning to care too much about her. And now the panic was all his, making his heart pound even harder and faster.

THEY HAD ESCAPED, but not for long. For a split second, it had seemed like they'd disappeared into the darkness, until the door had opened and spilled light into the courtyard. Not enough light to shoot, though, and not enough time to pull the trigger. Yet. But then the damn door had locked behind them.

Locking them inside.

But the interior stairwell wasn't the only way up the building. A fire escape wound up the side of it from the courtyard. And it was easy enough to find them again.

And now it would be even easier to kill them…

"DAMN YOU," HENRIETTA MUTTERED.

Trick's big body tensed, and his brows lowered. "What? Why?"

"I don't like you being sweet and concerned about Braden, and especially about me," she said.

He arched one of his brows now. "Why don't you like that?"

"Because it makes it harder for me to remember that you're really an ass," she explained.

He grinned. "I really am."

But she didn't believe him now. "I wish you were…"

She'd been drawn to him when she'd thought like everyone else that he hadn't earned his spot on the team, that he was taking advantage of his brother-in-law and her boss. But now that she knew there was more to Trick McRooney than she'd realized, she was even more attracted to him—so much so that she was the one who moved closer, who pulled his head down to hers, who kissed him.

She skimmed her lips across his, just a soft caress at first. But then he groaned and kissed her back. His mouth moved passionately over hers, deepening the kiss.

And she moaned as her body pulsed and throbbed with desire. She couldn't remember ever wanting anyone this much—not even her former fiancé. But she'd realized long ago that she'd loved Greg more as a friend than a lover. And even though he'd begged her not to break off their engagement, he'd deserved more. He'd deserved to feel like this.

Trick wasn't her friend and probably never would be. But he was her coworker, so getting involved with him would be stupid. Hell, it would be career suicide given the superintendent's rule against romance between team members.

What about sex?

Could they get away with that? Could they have a fling with no feelings?

Henrietta wished that she could—that she was like that—but she always thought she felt more than she actually did. She always wanted to fall in love, even when she wasn't.

The last time she'd already had a ring on her finger before she'd realized it wasn't real. She'd given it back but, unfortunately, had broken the heart of a good man when she'd broken their engagement.

She was already trying to talk herself into thinking Trick was a better man than she'd originally thought he was. By the time she realized her feelings for him were just lust—because she would never feel friendship for him—she would probably get herself fired.

No. No matter how wonderfully he kissed or how much she wanted him, it wasn't worth it to risk her heart or her career on him.

She pressed her palms against his chest, which vibrated with the mad pounding of his heart, and summoning all her willpower, she pushed him away from her.

He panted for breath like she did. His pupils had dilated, swallowing his green irises, so his eyes were dark as he stared down at her. His face was flushed, a muscle twitching along his cheek.

"What's wrong?" he asked, as if she had to have a reason to stop.

And she had—self-preservation.

But before she could say anything, he grabbed her. For a split second she thought that he might be the ass she'd hoped he was, that he wasn't going to take no for an answer and stop, and she braced herself to fight him. But as a shot rang out around them, he dragged her to the floor. Shot after shot fired into the apartment, shattering the glass of the windows, knocking stuff from the walls.

It was definitely not a car backfiring or fireworks going off as the gunshots blasted out all around them.

Her heart pounded hard with terror, and a scream burned the back of her throat. But she couldn't utter it. She couldn't move with Trick pressing her flat against the hardwood floor as he covered her body with his. With so many bullets being fired into the apartment, it was only a matter of time before one of them struck him.

Once again, he was sacrificing his safety—maybe even his life—to protect her.

Chapter Nine

Adrenaline coursed through Trick, along with rage. He'd heard the rattle of the fire escape just seconds before the blast of gunfire. It had given him time to pull Henrietta to the floor but not to get her out of the apartment. And with it being only a studio, there was no place to hide. Even if they could have made it into the bathroom without getting shot in the back, the door was too flimsy to withstand a barrage of bullets.

But he still had a chance of getting struck—if the gunfire continued. He braced himself, his body tense with anticipation of that bullet. Of that pain…

But all he felt was the adrenaline and anger that gripped him so intensely. Finally the firing stopped, leaving an eerie silence.

"Are you okay?" he whispered in Henrietta's ear.

"Yes…?" she murmured, but as more of a question than an answer, like she wasn't certain herself. "What about you?"

He was fine—just furious. And when he heard the metallic creak of the fire escape, he jumped up. He was done ducking and running from this bastard. He was going after them.

Henrietta reached out and clutched his jeans, trying to hold him back. "Stay down. Call the police."

They'd been called. Probably a neighbor had dialed 9-1-1. Trick could hear the whine of sirens in the distance. Maybe that was why the shooter had stopped firing, so they had time to get away. Trick couldn't let that happen.

He pulled away from her and headed toward the shattered window that led to the fire escape. Glass crunched under the soles of his shoes, and shards of it scraped against his clothes and skin as he climbed through the broken window onto the fire escape. The metal stairwell rattled beneath his weight.

Then it shuddered, with a loud thump, as someone jumped from the ladder at the bottom onto the concrete courtyard. The sound of running footsteps followed, like Henrietta must have heard earlier.

This bastard had gone after her too many times already tonight. Trick was not going to give them the chance to go after her again.

His feet barely touched the steps as he careened down the escape. When he got to the ladder at the bottom, he slid down the rungs and dropped onto the concrete. There was only one way out of the courtyard, and running as fast as he could, Trick headed toward the alley. It was so dark, though, that he bumped into the edge of the fountain.

Pain radiated up his leg, but he ignored it and continued running. The only footsteps he heard now were his own. Had the person stopped?

Was he waiting somewhere in the shadows, getting ready to take another—*closer*—shot at Trick? A shot that wouldn't be able to miss...?

HER HEART POUNDED so frantically that her entire body shook. Henrietta wanted to jump up like Trick had, wanted to chase him out the window like he had chased the shooter. But she could barely move. She rolled to her side and pressed her palm against the floor to push herself up. But her hand slipped on the hardwood, and something wet dampened her skin. She turned her hand over and stared down at the blood on her palm.

She was pretty sure she hadn't been hit. Trick's big body had covered her completely—had protected her while putting himself in danger. With all the bullets that had been fired into the apartment, she would have been more surprised had he not been injured.

But how badly was he hurt?

He had jumped up. He'd run out.

So he could move. Or had that been just adrenaline and anger fueling his movements?

Fear—for Trick now—fueled her movement, and she easily jumped up from the floor. Blood trailed from the small puddle, which she'd put her hand in, over to the window near the fire escape. The trail was thin, but then, he'd been moving fast to pursue the shooter.

She could only hope that he hadn't gotten shot again. She hadn't heard anything but the sound of her heart pounding and the distant wail of sirens. They were growing louder now. Help would be here soon, but would it arrive in time?

She had to find Trick, had to make sure that he wasn't seriously injured. But she hesitated over stepping onto the fire escape. The shooter could have been waiting down there for Trick and now for her.

Instead of heading out the window, she hurried to the door, and this time there was no one to stop her from opening it and rushing out. She hurried down that stairwell to the door that opened onto the courtyard. But that wasn't the only way out. A long hall went the other direction, most likely to the front of the building on the street.

She could have gone out that way; it was undoubtedly where the police would park when they arrived. But Trick wasn't there. He'd gone to the courtyard. So she pulled open that door and stepped into the darkness.

She froze for a moment, scared to move until her eyes adjusted. But the courtyard was more illuminated now because of the lights turning on in the windows of apartments around it. The gunfire must have woken up everybody.

Now she could see the patio furniture and grills and that concrete fountain. She could also see the blood smeared across the edge of it. Trick had passed it.

But he wasn't there, and the only way out—besides through the buildings—was the alley. She drew in a deep breath and headed toward it. But once she stepped into the shadows, she knew she wasn't alone.

"Trick?" she whispered, hoping against hope that it was him. But if it wasn't…

Strong hands gripped her arms, tugging her deeper into the shadows. She opened her mouth to scream, but with the sirens wailing louder now as the police vehicles drew closer, Henrietta wasn't certain that anyone would hear her in time to save her.

OWEN PUSHED OPEN the door of the paramedic rig and stepped onto the sidewalk. He'd had no sleep yet, but that hadn't stopped his shift from starting. He probably could have called in—could have gotten someone else to cover for him. But he'd known he wasn't going to sleep until he was sure that Hank was safe. He hadn't found her during his search.

And if Trick had found her, he hadn't called to let Owen know. He hadn't even picked up when Owen had called him, which had compelled Owen to make that call to the Hotshot superintendent. Now he was worried about Hank *and* Trick. He felt a twinge of guilt for piling on to Braden's already-overflowing burden of concerns.

He blew out a ragged breath and focused on the present situation. Whatever that was…

"What's going on?" he asked the trooper who held open the door to a brick building not far from downtown Northern Lakes. He recognized her from other incidents, mostly vehicle crashes, to which they'd both shown up as first responders. Wynona Wells's red hair spilled out from beneath her beige hat and brushed the shoulders of her beige uniform.

"Report of shots fired," she said.

"When?" he asked. Had someone called in the shooting from hours ago when those shots had been fired at Trick and Hank? But that had happened closer to the Filling Station than this building.

"Just a short time ago," she replied.

"Has the scene been secured?" he asked. "The shooter apprehended?" He hoped like hell the person had been caught this time.

She shook her head. "No."

"But someone's hurt?" he asked.

She nodded. "There's blood in the apartment."

"What about a body?" he asked. "A victim?"

She shook her head. "We haven't found one yet. But like I said, there's blood. Someone got hit. We're searching for a body now."

She touched the radio piece in her ear and gasped. "The landlord just told me the name of the tenant whose apartment is all shot up. It's someone you know—"

Owen tensed, because he had a suspicion even before she continued.

"—Patrick McRooney."

Now he knew why Trick hadn't answered his call. He'd been getting shot at and maybe worse. Where the hell had he gone? How badly was he hurt?

Chapter Ten

Trick had run out of the alley into the street. But he'd heard nothing except for that distant whine of sirens. He hadn't been willing to give up yet on finding the shooter. The person hadn't just disappeared into thin air. They had to be somewhere close unless they'd gotten into a vehicle and driven away.

They could have parked anywhere along the street— or farther down it, closer to where they'd shot at them earlier, where Henrietta had found that shell. Trick shuddered as he thought of her.

He'd left her alone back in that apartment. What if that was what the shooter had been waiting for? What if they'd waited until Trick had run out of the alley and they'd turned around and gone back for her?

Maybe Trick hadn't been the target at all. People other than the saboteur had gone after Owen and Luke in recent weeks. Their problems had had nothing to do with the accidents the team had been having. So maybe these shootings had nothing to do with the notes Trick had been receiving. Maybe the shooter had been aiming for Henrietta earlier. That was why she'd been chased when she'd gone back for that shell casing—not because she might have recovered evidence, but because she was the one the shooter wanted.

And Trick had left her unprotected.

Panic clutched his chest, making it hard for him to breathe. His lungs were already aching from running after the shooter. He panted for air now as he turned and ran back to the apartment. Lights flashed, illuminating the night as he neared the front of the building.

Had the police arrived in time to help Henrietta— since he'd abandoned her? Guilt weighed heavily on him, but he hurried toward the front entrance. A police trooper blocked the doorway to the foyer.

"You can't come in here," the man told Trick.

"I live here," he said.

The trooper narrowed his eyes beneath the brim of his tan hat. "You're not allowed in the building until the scene has been secured."

"The scene is my apartment," he said. "It's my place that was shot up."

The man tensed and reached for the radio on his lapel. "I have the tenant here," he murmured into the receiver. Static emanated from his earpiece, but he must have been able to understand it because he told Trick, "You can go up."

Trick headed for the stairs, but when his foot hit the first step, his leg nearly folded beneath him. He grabbed it and realized he was bleeding. He'd been hit.

"Are you okay?" the trooper asked from behind Trick.

Before he could answer the officer, Owen rushed down the stairs toward him. "Are you wounded?"

Trick stared at his leg, at the blood staining the denim of his jeans. "I guess I was hit…" He hadn't felt it then, but the wound stung now. That pain was nothing in comparison to his panic over leaving Henrietta alone. "How about Hank?" he asked. "Was she hit?"

Since Trick had been able to run just fine, the bullet must have merely grazed him without doing any damage. Maybe, after it had passed Trick, it had struck Henrietta, though.

Owen's blue eyes widened with apprehension. "She was here?"

Fear gripped Trick. He had been a fool to run off like he had, leaving her unprotected. "She's not here now?"

Owen shook his head. "No. Just that blood on the floor. I hope it was all yours."

"Me, too," he murmured. But if she'd been shot, surely she couldn't have gotten far. That would have only made it easier for the shooter to catch her this time. "We have to find her."

"I didn't realize you had," Owen said. "You were supposed to call me. I was so worried when I didn't hear from you that I called Braden."

Trick flinched. He was supposed to be helping his brother-in-law, not adding to his worries. And Trick putting another team member in danger was certain to worry the Hotshot superintendent. Instead of being distracted by Henrietta's closeness, he should have been making certain that she was safe, that no one had come up that fire escape.

Owen stepped forward and grabbed his arm. "Hey, let me treat that wound."

Trick shook off his grasp. "Not until we find Henrietta." Where the hell could she be?

Hopefully the shooter hadn't circled back while Trick had been chasing them and gotten a hold of Henrietta.

But she was strong. She would have fought him. If she'd been able…

"WHAT THE HELL'S going on?" Braden demanded to know from where he stood in the doorway to Trick's place. His heart had been pounding like mad ever since he'd gotten the call from the state trooper that there had been a shooting at his brother-in-law's apartment.

Another shooting…

But the trooper didn't know that. And Braden wasn't certain what to tell her. He had no damn idea what was going on, and that infuriated him.

And scared the hell out of him…

He'd brought in Trick to help him, but the man had been in peril pretty much since the minute he'd shown up in Northern Lakes. Those other times had been because he'd been trying to protect Owen and Luke from the threats to their lives. Now his life was the one being threatened. Was he being targeted by the same person targeting the team, or was it someone else? He'd thought the person mentioned in the note had been focusing on Owen and Luke at first, but Louanne and Gingrich had been behind the attempts on their lives.

And was Trick the only target this time?

While Braden had been trying to answer the trooper's questions about the shooting, Owen had rushed downstairs to check on Trick the minute they'd heard he'd shown up at the entrance to the building.

"I need to check on my brother-in-law," Braden told Trooper Wells. He needed to know if the blood trail across the hardwood floor was Trick's.

A curse rang out from below, propelling both Braden and the trooper down the hall to the stairwell. "Are you okay?" he asked Trick.

Blood stained one leg of the man's jeans. But if he had a bullet in him, it hadn't slowed him down. He climbed the steps with ease, except for the muscle twitching along his tightly clenched jaw.

"You have to let me treat that wound," Owen persisted as he followed Trick up the stairs.

"It's fine. I ran after the shooter with it, no problem," Trick said.

"You saw the shooter?" Trooper Wells asked.

Trick shook his head. "No."

"You didn't?" The trooper sounded skeptical, and her green eyes narrowed as she stared at Trick.

"I was too busy keeping my head down so it wouldn't get shot off," Trick remarked resentfully.

"But what about when you were pursuing them? Why did you risk that?" she asked, and she seemed as suspicious of the shooting as her predecessor, Martin Gingrich, had been of anything that had happened to a Hotshot. He'd always suspected Braden's Hotshots of wrongdoing. Or maybe he'd just been desperate to pin something on them, like he'd tried framing Luke for his crimes, to make the Hotshots and Braden look bad.

Braden had hoped Wynona Wells would be more open-minded, but he wasn't surprised that she wasn't, since Marty had trained the young officer. She probably felt some loyalty to him, enough that she might have helped him cover up his crimes, or she might have even helped him frame Luke.

Trick had been right that they couldn't really trust the troopers that had worked with Marty. So Braden wasn't going to share with her everything that was happening to the team just yet—not until she proved herself unbiased and trustworthy. He was finding it hard to trust anyone right now but his wife and a handful of his team.

"Because he finally stopped shooting," Trick replied.

"He?" Wynona repeated. "So you did see the shooter?" Braden grimaced at her line of questioning.

"I'm guessing," Trick admitted. "I don't know if it was a man or a woman." He shrugged. "I'm sorry I can't be of more help." And he sounded sincere.

But Braden couldn't help wondering if his brother-in-law was keeping something back. Like the first shooting...

Trick didn't volunteer anything about that. And, not wanting to get his brother-in-law in trouble for not reporting it sooner, Braden said nothing about it either.

"Were you alone?" Trooper Wells asked.

"Yes," Trick replied quickly.

Too quickly?

Braden narrowed his eyes and studied his brother-in-law's face. He looked exhausted; after the night he'd had, that was no surprise. But more than exhausted, he looked worried.

He wasn't sure his wife would forgive him if something happened to her brother, and Braden was even more unlikely to forgive himself. There could be no more attempts on Trick's life, because sooner or later, the man's luck was going to run out.

"I SHOULDN'T HAVE let you rush me out of there," Henrietta told Michaela when they entered their apartment above the firehouse in St. Paul.

"Out of a crime scene?" Michaela asked with a snort. "You were in danger."

"The police were arriving," Henrietta reminded her. The state police SUVs had been pulling up to the front of the building as Michaela had driven her away from the alley at the back of it.

She was the one who'd grabbed Henrietta in the dark. Henrietta had recognized her just in time to swallow the scream she'd been about to release.

"But just because the police were there doesn't mean you would have been safe. Look at how Trooper Gingrich nearly killed Luke and Willow."

"But Owen showed up, too," Hank reminded her. She only knew that now, after Michaela had called him on the ride back to St. Paul to let him know that she'd found Hank and was bringing her home.

"Braden was there, too," Michaela said. "Which is another good reason for you getting the hell out. You can't be seen at McRooney's place."

Being seen there was the least of her concerns at the moment, and should have been the least of Michaela's concerns for her.

"There was a shooting," Henrietta told her. Again. "I should have stayed and talked to the police." Unless Trick was right—unless they couldn't trust them because one or more had been working with Marty.

"Did you see who did it?" Michaela asked.

She shook her head. It could have been one of the troopers. It could have been anyone but Trick, who'd saved her once again. She remembered the blood trailed across the floor, and panic clutched her heart again.

"Then you had nothing to tell a trooper," Michaela said. "Nothing to do but risk your job if you stayed. Or, worse yet, your life. You don't know where that shooter was, where they went. We had to get out of there."

Henrietta was well aware of how much danger she'd been in—how close she'd come to being shot, if not for Trick shielding her. But at what cost to himself? How badly had he been wounded?

"I should have stayed to make sure Trick is okay," she said. Her voice cracked as she added, "I think he got shot, Michaela."

"Not so badly that he didn't run off and leave you alone," Michaela reminded her—like she had when Henrietta had wanted to stay and check on him before leaving the scene.

She must have still been in shock then since she'd let Michaela convince her to leave. But her friend had been so scared for her—for them—and so determined to get Hank to safety that Hank hadn't argued with her. Until tonight, she'd never had anyone shoot at her. She trembled now with the terror that had gripped her then.

"And when I talked to Owen just a little bit ago, he said Trick came back alive."

Did her friend sound disappointed?

Suspicion snaked inside Henrietta's mind, and for a second she wondered… Could her roommate have been the one who'd taken those shots? After everything that had happened to the Hotshots over the course of nearly a year, it was getting harder and harder to trust anyone. The arsonist had seemed like a sweet young man. Dirk had seemed to have a good marriage. And Luke…poor Luke… He'd come under such suspicion.

A wave of guilt swept away Hank's suspicion of her friend. There was no way that Michaela would hurt anyone. Despite her tough exterior, the blonde Hotshot was very sweet and sensitive. Maybe too sensitive sometimes.

While Michaela had certainly never been a fan of Trick, Henrietta was confident that her roommate hadn't ever wished him dead—just that he would quit the team, because his sudden arrival, and relationship to Braden, made everyone uneasy and suspicious. Michaela wasn't the only one who'd expressed the wish that Trick would leave.

Henrietta had as well. And now, after he'd kissed her, that wish was even more fervent. Because if he didn't leave the team, she could never act on the attraction she felt for him. She wouldn't risk losing her job, but then, he was unlikely to stick around anyway, so it was better that she protect her heart. Her heart still ached with the loss of her parents and Grandpapa.

But just because she didn't want to get involved with Trick didn't mean that she couldn't care about him—as a teammate. "How badly did Owen say that Trick was hurt?" she asked.

"He's fine," Michaela said.

"No, he's not," she said, cringing as she remembered the blood that had smeared on her skin. His blood. "He must have been hit."

Michaela shrugged. "Owen didn't say. He was more worried about you—since you'd gone missing." Her face flushed slightly with color, as if she was embarrassed for rushing Hank away from the scene.

"You overreacted," Henrietta said. And she'd let her friend's urgency and fear for their safety compel her into Michaela's pickup instead of staying to make sure that Trick was all right.

"And you're underreacting," Michaela said. "You need to be worrying about yourself—not Trick McRooney. You could have been killed because someone was shooting at him!"

"Maybe it wasn't Trick's fault we were shot at," Henrietta suggested, voicing her fear aloud. "Maybe the person was after me."

Michaela snorted. "You don't have an enemy in the world," she said.

"Neither did Owen or Luke," Henrietta reminded her. "And Trick helped them." Just like he'd helped her tonight. And instead of staying to make certain he was okay, she'd taken off to protect herself. Shame weighed heavily on her already-aching shoulders. "And tonight he saved my life. Twice."

Michaela snorted again, and her face was probably flushed with anger—not embarrassment. "Because he was the one who put you in danger."

"You don't know that."

"You really think that bucket coming loose from the crane was an accident?"

Henrietta tensed. "Of course it was."

Michaela arched a blond brow in skepticism.

"Of course it was," Henrietta repeated. "We've been having problems with the equipment."

"Like the winch truck for Dirk?" Michaela asked.

Henrietta gasped. That hadn't been an accident. "Dirk's wife rigged that to break."

Michaela nodded. "Exactly."

"Louanne is dead," Henrietta reminded her. "She can't be behind the bucket mishap."

"She could have given someone the idea," Michaela insisted. "Or maybe whoever's been causing all the equipment failures we've been having gave her the idea."

"Martin Gingrich?" He'd been having the affair with Dirk Brown's devious wife. "He's in jail now." Awaiting trial. And there was no doubt that he would be convicted of trying first to frame, and then to kill, Luke Garrison. "You think someone could have been helping him?"

"I don't know what to think," Michaela said. "I just

know that you'll be safer the farther you stay away from Trick McRooney. Someone's obviously targeting him now, like Owen and Luke were targeted."

Maybe her heart would be safer; Henrietta wasn't so certain that her life would be, though. "We work together," she reminded her roommate.

"You won't do that much longer if you wind up dead, collateral damage like Courtney and Willow nearly were just because they were too close to Owen and Luke. You need to stay away from Trick," Michaela cautioned.

Henrietta released a weary sigh. She was too tired to argue any longer. "I'm going to bed." But as tired as she was, she knew that she wouldn't sleep until she could be certain Trick was okay.

Fortunately, they had a landline in their apartment, with a phone in both their rooms as backup to their cells since northern Michigan didn't have enough towers to ensure reliable cellular service. Also fortunate was the fact that their rooms were on opposite sides of the living room. Michaela wouldn't hear Henrietta calling Trick because she headed toward her bedroom at the same time.

But the minute Henrietta stepped into her dark room, she knew that she wasn't alone. Her curtains rustled at the open window, through which a cold breeze blew. Goose bumps rose on her skin, and she shivered. She had not left that window open. Someone else had. And that someone was inside, standing in the shadows.

Chapter Eleven

"Is it really you?" Henrietta asked, her voice just a raspy whisper as she stared at him.

Trick nodded as he stepped out of the shadows. And then she was in his arms, trembling against him. Trick didn't want her to be scared, but when he'd arrived at the front door, he'd heard her and Michaela talking and hadn't wanted a confrontation with the blonde Hotshot. So he whispered in her ear, "It's me…"

"Thank God you're all right," she murmured.

He hugged her closer to the heat of his hard body for a moment before releasing her. Because if he kept holding her, he might not let go. And that wasn't why he'd come here. At least, he didn't think it was.

After eavesdropping on her conversation with her roommate, he knew it could never be the reason. Michaela was right; he probably was putting her in danger just being near her. He shouldn't have come here. But when he turned and walked back toward the open window, he closed it instead of stepping through it to the fire escape outside.

"Bet this isn't the first time you've snuck through a woman's bedroom window," Henrietta remarked.

"This is the first time I've done it without an invitation," he said. "I hope I didn't scare you."

She had already been through enough for one night. Maybe he shouldn't have come here, but he'd had to see for himself that she really was all right. And considering how fast he'd driven away from his apartment building, there was no way anyone could have kept up and followed him to her.

She chuckled. "Scared? I'm not sure what it feels like *not* to be scared lately."

"I'm sorry," he said.

"It is your fault," she said.

He flinched.

He'd heard her defend him to her roommate, but that must not have been how she really felt about the situation. Clearly, she didn't think much of him, or she wouldn't have left like she had—without checking to see if he was really okay. Now he was tired and vulnerable, like she'd been the night she'd awakened screaming from that dream. He felt like the little kid he'd been all those years ago, when his mother had cut and run on the family.

Except for a couple calls and letters over the years, she'd rarely checked on them to see how they were all doing without her. Maybe she hadn't wanted to know; maybe she just hadn't given a damn.

Had Henrietta given a damn about him? He doubted it, or she wouldn't have let Michaela whisk her away. So why was he here?

Why the hell did he give a damn about her?

"I was scared that you were badly hurt," she said, "when I saw that blood on the floor."

He shrugged. "Just a scratch."

She snorted. "Scratches don't bleed that badly."

"There was no bullet in my leg," he assured her. "Owen wasn't even sure that one grazed me. It might have been the glass that was flying around when the window got broken." The paramedic had called him some choice names for chasing the shooter. Because of the adrenaline, he hadn't noticed the wound then, but he had when Owen had cleaned it up and bandaged it. It throbbed now, like his heart pounded in his chest. He stepped closer to Henrietta and stared down into her face.

With the curtains open and dawn approaching, her bedroom wasn't as dark as it had been when he'd climbed up the fire escape and jimmied open the window. He could see her better now, could see that dark circles of exhaustion rimmed her beautiful eyes.

He needed to let her get some sleep. But he had to make sure first that she was really okay. "You didn't get hit at all, right?" he asked.

She shook her head, tumbling her long waves of black hair around her shoulders. "No," she said. "You saved my life." She took a step closer to him. "And I didn't thank you…"

"You didn't stick around," he remarked and winced as he heard that damn vulnerability slip into his voice. He hated feeling this way—hated feeling at all. Forcing a laugh, he said, "Not that I blame you. Michaela's right. You need to stay away from me."

And he'd made a mistake coming here. A terrible mistake, like when he'd run after the shooter earlier and left her unprotected. He wanted to run away now—to protect himself. He turned back toward the window and reached for the sash. But before he could slide up the pane, a hand wrapped around his arm.

He tensed at her touch, his body aching with need. But it wasn't just a physical need he felt; this went deeper and scared him nearly as much as the shooter had.

HENRIETTA COULD FEEL the tension in Trick's body. But it was what she'd heard in his voice that had her reaching out to him to stop him from leaving. He was hurt, and not just physically.

Had she hurt him? Could she?

Despite working together for the past several weeks, they barely knew each other. She suspected he let few people get close enough to really know him. Maybe that was why he moved from team to team so often. He didn't want to be vulnerable to anyone; she understood that all too well, the pain of loving someone and losing them.

"I took off like that because I was in shock," she said. "And I was scared. I didn't know if that shooter was still out there, waiting to try again." She shuddered. "That's why I left with Michaela, so she and I would both be safe."

"And what about me?" he asked, and there was that slight break in his voice again, that vulnerability.

Her pulse quickened, and she murmured, "You're definitely not safe…" At least not to her, to her heart.

He turned back then and stared down at her face. "No, no, I'm not," he agreed, his voice gruff.

"Are you talking about the shooting?" she wondered aloud. Or her? Of course he had to be talking about the shooting. She shuddered as she remembered. "We were shot at twice tonight…" The sky was growing lighter and lighter outside her window, so she amended, "… last night…"

She waited for him to argue and try to pass off the

first shooting as fireworks again, but he just shuddered as well and remarked, "Until tonight, I've never been shot at before…"

She arched a brow to tease him. "Really? No jealous husbands or boyfriends have tried to kill you before?"

Instead of laughing, he tensed again and lifted his chin with pride. "I make sure there are no husbands or boyfriends before I go out with someone."

"You didn't ask me…" she murmured.

"We're not going out," he replied.

She flinched now as if he'd slapped her. Had he just been teasing earlier—when he'd hit on her, when he'd kissed her? Well, she'd kissed him first, but he'd kissed her back.

He continued, "Because you're too scared." Then he made the clucking sound again, but softly. "And you're smart to be scared. I shouldn't have even come here."

"Why did you?" she asked.

"To make sure you're really okay."

"Even though Michaela talked to Owen, who said you were fine, I was going to call you and check on you myself," she said. "To make sure you weren't hurt."

He nodded, but his face was still tense, as if he didn't believe her.

"I was," she insisted.

"Your phone's broken," he reminded her.

"There's a landline in here."

He looked skeptical but replied, "I saved you the trouble."

"You are trouble," she murmured as her heart began to pound faster and faster. He was so damn good-looking. But beyond his appearance, there was something about him that drew her—that excited her.

He didn't argue with her but just nodded in agreement. "Michaela's right. You should stay away from me."

"Why?" she asked. "Do you have a jealous wife or girlfriend?" She was teasing now, because from what other Hotshots on that last wildfire call had told her, he hadn't stayed in any one place long enough to have a serious relationship with anyone who'd care enough to go after him.

He chuckled and shook his head. "No jealous wife or girlfriend." His lips curved into a grin. "Why are you asking?" he queried. "We're not going out."

"I'm asking because someone shot at us twice when we were together," she said. "Maybe it was a jealous ex."

He shook his head. "Not mine."

"And not mine," she said. While Greg had been upset when she'd broken their engagement, he wasn't the type to hold a grudge. In fact, he'd reached out several times to make sure that she was all right and probably to see if she would change her mind.

Trick's green eyes narrowed as he studied her face, as if wondering if she was lying to him.

She wondered the same. "You really have no idea who was shooting at us?"

He shook his head. "No…" Then he glanced toward the window. "I should go. I probably am putting you in danger."

He was. She couldn't argue about that. But she didn't want him to go either. After tonight, after how close they'd come to getting seriously wounded or worse, she didn't want to be alone. "Or you could stay…"

He sucked in a breath.

She stepped closer to him and had to tip up her head to hold his gaze. She wasn't used to that; there weren't many people she had to look up to since she was so tall herself. "I owe you a huge thank-you," she said. "You saved my life. Twice."

He tilted his head. "I'm not so sure about that," he said.

Now her pulse quickened with annoyance. "Don't try to pass off that first shooting as fireworks," she warned him. "You know that it wasn't."

"I know," he finally admitted. "But maybe all those could have been warning shots since we didn't get hit."

"You got hit," she reminded him.

"Grazed," he said, dismissing the wound. "And it could have been just some broken glass."

"And if your body hadn't been covering mine, I would have gotten hit, too," she said. Or worse…

She shivered.

And as if unable to resist, he reached out and wrapped his arms around her. "You're fine…" But he drew her closer, as if he needed to assure himself of that as well.

Maybe that was why she didn't want him to leave. In just the course of one night, they'd been through so much together. But they'd cheated death even before that… with the bucket accident that could have taken his life.

If it had been an accident.

Henrietta had already had nightmares about that; she couldn't imagine what dreams she would have now. Maybe that was why she didn't want to sleep. Or maybe it was just that she knew there was no way she would be able to sleep—because the adrenaline was rushing through her body now. But it had nothing to do with the shooting and everything to do with Trick holding her.

"I'm grateful," she said. "I hope you know that." And she rose on tiptoe to press a kiss to his mouth.

He froze, his lips stiff beneath hers. He pulled back. "I don't want your gratitude. That's not why I came here."

"You came to make sure I'm okay," she said. "You're a good man, Trick McRooney, no matter how many people want to think otherwise."

He chuckled. "Maybe all those other people are right, and you're wrong. Because if I was a good man, I'd leave right now."

"I don't want you to leave," she said.

"And that's why I should," he said.

She entwined her fingers with his and tugged him away from the window, toward the bed. "I want…" She rose on tiptoe again and brushed her lips across his.

They weren't stiff and cold anymore. They moved beneath hers.

But she pulled back and whispered, "…you. I want you."

He shuddered now. "Henrietta…"

She liked that he called her that—instead of the masculine nickname everyone else used. She didn't want him to think of her like the other male members of the team did—like a buddy. Like one of the guys…

She was female—all female—and she wanted Trick to know and appreciate that. So she pulled out of his arms and reached for the hem of her sweater. When she tugged it off over her head, he audibly sucked in a breath.

Her heart thudded hard with excitement. He seemed to like what he saw.

But then he stepped closer and touched his fingertips lightly to her shoulder. "I did hurt you," he murmured. "Your shoulder is swollen and red."

She shrugged off his touch and his concern. "I'm

fine." She'd forgotten all about the injury, forgotten all about the shooting—about anything but him.

He drew in another breath and nodded. "Yes, you are fine. You're beautiful…" And now he touched her again, his fingertips skimming over the swell of her breasts pushing against the cups of her lacy bra. "So damn beautiful…and sexy…"

He was the sexy one—with his big, muscular body and cocky grin. The grin was gone now, though. He looked very serious as he stared into her eyes. "Are you sure?" he asked, and his voice was gruff.

She stepped back, shucked off her jeans and then unclasped her bra so she wore only the thin lace of her G-string.

Trick pressed his hand to his chest, which rose and fell with heavy breaths. "You're killing me…"

She shook her head. "Not me…"

But someone was trying to. The thought of something happening to him…

"Your leg? Are you okay?"

He nodded—vigorously. "Oh, yeah, nothing's going to stop me from being with you…"

Hearing those words made her want him so much. She reached for the button of his jeans, undid it and tugged on the tab of his zipper. When the teeth of it lowered, a hiss escaped—from his lips, between his tightly clenched teeth. She rubbed her fingers over his erection, which strained against his boxers.

He groaned. "And yes, you are killing me. I want you so badly…"

"I know…" She could tell from his erection, which pulsated beneath her fingers. And she could feel it in the tension in him, see it in the heat of his green eyes. "I want you, too."

He moved then, shedding his shirt and the rest of his clothes until he stood before her, naked but for a bandage wrapped around his thigh.

She gasped when she saw it.

He shook his head. "It's really not bad at all."

She didn't know if she believed him. But then he proved how healthy he was by lifting her off her feet. And she wasn't light. She was too tall, too muscular, to be easily carried, and yet he carried her easily to the bed. When he laid her on the mattress, she looped her arms around his neck and tried pulling him down onto her.

But he held back. Then he walked away.

"Where are you going?"

He bent over the pile of clothes they'd left on the floor. She admired his muscular backside, the ripple of his smooth skin. But he straightened up too quickly, a packet clutched in his fingers.

She smiled. And seeing her smile, he sucked in a breath. "You are so beautiful…"

He walked back to the bed, leaned over and pressed his mouth to hers. He kissed her deeply, passionately. That passion coursed through her, making her hot and restless. She clasped his broad shoulders, trying to tug him down onto her.

She needed his body covering hers again, but this time the only danger was what she felt for him. Too much…

She'd never wanted anyone with this intensity. She didn't just want him; she needed him. Even though she tugged harder on his shoulders, he didn't budge. He was too big—too strong—and pulled away from her instead.

But he didn't move away from the bed. He moved farther down her body—skimming his mouth from hers, down her neck, over the swells of her breasts. Then he moved back up and closed his lips around a nipple.

Pleasure shot from that contact directly to her core. She arched up and moaned. She tunneled her fingers into his thick auburn hair, holding his head against her chest. Her heart hammered inside her breast while his mouth continued to drive her to madness.

He moved again, farther down her body. His lips skimmed across her navel before moving lower yet. He tugged off her panties before making love to her with his mouth. His fingers stroked over her nipples while his tongue stroked over the most sensitive part of her body.

The tension inside her spiraled out of control. She writhed and moaned as the tension finally broke and pleasure crashed through her body. She shuddered at the force of it. But he kept moving his mouth over her skin, kissing and tasting every inch of her—driving her out of her mind again.

The tension built inside her. But she wasn't the only one feeling it. His body was hard and tense as she ran her hands over it, caressing his muscles and skin. She closed her hand around his erection.

But he pulled back. Plastic ripped as he tore open a condom. Then he joined her on the bed, kneeling between her parted legs.

She clutched his butt and then his erection, guiding him inside her. He was so big, so engorged, that he barely fit. She arched and took him deeper and deeper inside her.

He pulled back before moving inside her again. He stroked in and out, teasing her to madness once more. She wrapped her legs around his lean waist and her arms around his body, matching his thrusts. And she skimmed her lips along his shoulders and neck, where cords of tension stood out.

He gritted his teeth, groaning. "You feel so damn good…"

So good…

She kissed his lips now, and he deepened the kiss, plunging his tongue inside her mouth like he plunged inside her body. The tension inside her wound tighter before breaking with an orgasm that had her body shuddering with pleasure. She'd never felt so much before—so much that tears stung her eyes as emotions overwhelmed her.

He tensed, then choked back a growl as he reached his climax, his body shuddering against hers. She wrapped her arms around him and held him now, wanting him to remain inside her, filling an emptiness she tried to forget she had.

He didn't try to pull back either. He slid his arm around her back and rolled to his side, taking her with him—against him. Then he wrapped both arms around her and held her, as if he didn't want to let her go either.

But he would—eventually. He would leave, just as he had every other team he'd worked with. She doubted this team, even with his brother-in-law running it, would prove an exception for him. Especially if Braden lost his job as superintendent…or if Trick lost his life…

She couldn't come to care about him and lose him, like she had too many others. This had to be just sex and nothing else.

How the hell had every bullet missed?

It wasn't fair that he'd escaped unscathed once again. It wasn't fair. And it couldn't continue.

Trick McRooney couldn't continue living. He was never going to learn—never going to change his manipulative ways. He hadn't heeded any of the warnings.

Not even the gunshots fired at him on the street.

But the ones into his apartment, those hadn't been warnings. Even that hadn't fazed Trick—hadn't stopped him from running out.

He would never learn.

The only thing that was going to stop Trick McRooney was death. He had to die.

Soon.

Chapter Twelve

Guilt weighed heavily on Trick as he snuck out of Henrietta's bedroom the same way he'd snuck in—through the window. The only thing that was different now was that instead of scaring her, he was the one who was scared—scared by the power of what they'd shared.

He had never felt like that before.

And he wasn't sure he wanted to feel like that again.

It was so much, so intense…

And what was even scarier was how badly he wanted to stay with Henrietta, how badly he wanted to hold her until she awakened and then make love to her all over again. But he couldn't do that; he couldn't be seen with her any more than she could be seen with him.

Because when he dangled from the last rung of the fire escape ladder, he saw the paper fluttering beneath his wiper blade. He doubted anyone in this town—which was even smaller than Northern Lakes—had anything to advertise with a flyer.

It had to be another damn note.

The shooter had followed him here—to Henrietta. And he'd thought he'd been so careful. But he'd put her in danger yet again, just being near her.

Danger had been this close—close enough to leave

another note. His hand shook a little as he reached out to grab the slip of paper. He unfolded it and read the bold black letters printed on the page: *Next time you're dead.*

Now he knew for certain that the shooter and his note writer were one and the same. And it was clear how the person intended to *stop* him now—by killing him.

Trick barely resisted the urge to crumple the note in his hand. He wanted to wad it up and set fire to it. But he might need to use it one day—for evidence—if he could ever figure out who the hell was sending them. Who had shot at him and Henrietta the night before…?

Dare he trust Trooper Wells with the notes? Dare he trust anyone right now…but his brother-in-law and sister and Henrietta…? But Trick didn't want to tell Braden about the notes because he knew he'd get fired—his brother-in-law would send him far away from Northern Lakes to keep him safe. And if he refused to leave town, Braden would worry even more than he was already worrying. And the guy had been through too much in the past several months, had too much else on his mind for Trick to add to his concerns.

Trick had a lot on his mind now as well. He glanced up at Henrietta's window. There was no movement there, but he caught a swish of curtains at another window on the same floor. He swallowed a groan, hoping that Michaela had not seen him. She was already giving Henrietta a hard enough time about him.

What would she say now?

Would she protect her? Or would she tattle on them to Braden?

How good a friend was she to Henrietta? And how much did she dislike Trick? Enough to be leaving the notes? Could she be the person responsible for the accidents? It had to be someone on the team…although the equipment wasn't under guard. Even at the firehouse, they just had the friendly sheepdog/mastiff mix as more of a mascot than protection.

It wasn't just the equipment that needed protection, though. Not now…

The thought that Henrietta could be living with such a devious, dangerous person as the shooter, or saboteur, chilled Trick more than the early-morning breeze.

Maybe staying away from Henrietta wouldn't keep her safe. Maybe it would put her in more danger—if she was living with the enemy.

Moments ago he'd been anxious to get away from her and from all those feelings she'd brought out in him.

Like that vulnerability the night before. And then, when they'd made love, he'd felt an intensity of passion and pleasure he'd never experienced before. Hell, he'd never even known it existed. Maybe that had just been the culmination of all the adrenaline and fear they'd felt earlier.

Nothing more…

It couldn't be anything more. He wasn't looking for anything but Braden's saboteur. Could she be living with Henrietta?

As he stared up at the window where he'd seen the curtain swish, his cell vibrated in his pocket. He pulled it out and hit Accept when he saw his caller. "Hey—"

"Where the hell are you?" Braden shouted into the phone, making the speaker crackle and birds fly up from the trees around him.

He had no intention of telling his boss the truth, and maybe Braden knew that, because before Trick could say anything, he continued, "You better be in my office ASAP."

Because Braden was his boss, Trick didn't argue. He disconnected the call and shoved the cell back into his pocket along with that note. Then he pulled out his keys, unlocked the door and started his truck.

But before he drove off, he glanced up at the second story of the firehouse one more time, and he saw curtains move again. But this time it was Henrietta's window where someone stood, staring down at him.

His pulse quickened and his skin tingled, and he knew she was the one watching him. He wanted to go back, wanted to climb back into her bed, into her arms…

But the best thing he could do for her—and for himself—was to stay far away. They had no future together. Hell, if the person who'd sent him the note had his way, Trick would have no future at all.

BRADEN STARED AT the clock on the concrete-block wall of his office.

Where the hell was Trick? What was taking him so long to get to the firehouse?

He hadn't spent the night at his apartment. Even if the police had released it as a crime scene, the windows had been shot out, and in northern Michigan the temperature dropped pretty low at night, even this late in the spring. Despite his invitation, Trick hadn't come back to Braden and Sam's house, and none of the beds in the bunkroom looked like they'd been used last night either.

So where the hell had he gone?

"Maybe I should have taken him into custody," Trooper Wells murmured as she paced in the small space in front of Braden's desk. She wasn't a very big woman, so she didn't need much space.

But Braden knew better than to underestimate her because of her petite size; he knew how many people had made that mistake with his wife, including her dad and brothers. Sam was tough, and Braden had a feeling Wynona Wells was, too. But was she trustworthy? Or had she been closer to Marty than anyone had known, like how close Marty had been to Dirk Brown's wife?

"What do you mean 'into custody'?" Braden asked. "You think you should have arrested him for getting shot at?"

"I think I should have arrested him for withholding information," she said. "For hindering an investigation."

Braden felt the same way—that Trick hadn't told either of them everything—that he was keeping something to himself. But he felt compelled to defend his brother-in-law and asked, "Do you have any proof that he did that?"

Wynona's face flushed nearly as red as the tendril of hair that had escaped from beneath her hat and trailed down along her cheek. "No…but he must know more than he's saying."

He did. But for that matter, so did Braden. He wasn't going to bring her in on everything that had been happening to his team—about all the *accidents* or about that note he'd received.

No. Braden couldn't risk the team's safety, especially Trick's, with someone he didn't trust. Hell, of his team, Trick was one of just a handful he trusted. The other guys were too close to each other and the situation to objectively investigate what was going on. So he'd brought in Trick for that job.

And the plan must have been working, or why else

would someone shoot at Trick? He was getting close. To whom, though?

Hank? She wasn't the shooter, since she'd been shot at with him at least once. Had she been with him the second time, too?

Was that what he was keeping from Braden and Trooper Wynona Wells?

"Did you miss me?" a deep voice asked as Trick pushed open the door to Braden's office. "Is that why you…" He trailed off as he noticed the female trooper. "Oh…"

"Surprised to see me, Mr. McRooney?" she asked.

He nodded. "Yeah, I was thinking it might take you longer than a few hours to find the shooter. Guess you are damn good at your job."

Her face flushed that bright red again. "I would be," she said, "if people were honest with me."

"Yeah," Trick said with a sigh. "Guess nobody's going to outright admit to a crime, huh?"

She narrowed her eyes as she stared at him. "Have much experience with the habits of criminals, Mr. McRooney?"

"Nope," he said. "I'm a firefighter—not a police officer."

But that hadn't stopped him from agreeing to investigate for Braden. Braden had known he'd put his brother-in-law's life in danger, but after the shooting Trick couldn't deny his special assignment was too damn risky—riskier than being a Hotshot. But even knowing that, Braden couldn't quite bring himself to confide in the trooper.

"Why would someone shoot at a firefighter?" Wells asked.

Trick shrugged. "I have no idea," he replied.

But Braden knew Trick had some idea—the same damn idea Braden had. Whoever was behind the accidents had figured out the real reason Braden had brought Trick on the team.

"Why don't I believe you?" Wells asked.

Because she was smart, far smarter than her predecessor had been.

Trick shrugged again. "I don't know, Officer. I don't know you."

And he wasn't acting as if he wanted to get to know her, which surprised the hell out of Braden. Even as a happily married man, he acknowledged that the female trooper was beautiful.

"I don't know you, Mr. McRooney," the trooper said, "but I need to if I'm going to find the person who fired those shots into your apartment."

"Not much to know about me," Trick told her. "If I were you, I'd probably check into who rented the apartment before me. That's probably who the shots were meant for."

"You think it was a case of mistaken identity?" she asked.

And he nodded. "Has to be. I have no enemies."

"I don't know you," she repeated. "But I have a feeling that's not true."

Trick chuckled. "Ouch…"

A fresh wave of red flushed the trooper's face, and she glanced at Braden for confirmation. "Even you had an enemy, Superintendent."

He nodded in agreement. "Marty Gingrich didn't go after me, though. He went after my team." And he really wanted to ask her if she'd helped him, but he doubted she would willingly admit it.

"Do you think someone could be going after your brother-in-law to get to you?" she asked.

"It's definitely possible," he admitted. Especially if they'd figured out why he'd brought Trick on the team.

"What about your enemies?" she asked Braden then.

He shrugged now. "Other than Marty Gingrich, I don't know..." But there was someone else out there, someone who'd sabotaged the equipment and was threatening Braden's job and the lives of some of the team.

"Maybe it is still Marty," Trick suggested with a pointed stare at Wells. "Maybe he had help, like he helped Louanne Brown."

The trooper returned Trick's stare with a hard one of her own. "I don't know of anyone who would help Marty."

"Maybe check to see who Marty has been calling from jail or who's been visiting him," Trick suggested. "He still could have put this all in motion."

The trooper nodded. "I'll look into it," she agreed, but then she conceded, "I understand why you both may be reluctant to trust me after what Gingrich did to Luke Garrison, but I'm not like him. I am a good officer. You can tell me whatever you're holding back." She waited a long moment for either or both of them to speak up, but when neither said anything, she sighed and walked out of Braden's office without another word.

"She is good," Trick admitted after she'd gone. "She knows we're not telling her everything."

"She's not the only one," Braden said.

"You're keeping secrets from the team, too," Trick remarked.

"You know why," Braden said. He hadn't told many of them about the note, about the warning that one of them was not who they seemed to be, because he didn't want to tip off whoever that was, since he had no idea who… "I'm talking about you now, about what you're withholding from me."

Trick chuckled, but his face flushed a bit. "You're getting paranoid."

"Where did you sleep last night?" Braden asked.

"I didn't," Trick quickly replied, and the dark circles beneath his eyes backed up his claim. "So if you want to interrogate me like the trooper just did, can you wait until after I crash for a while in the bunkroom?"

"Trick—"

His brother-in-law's yawn interrupted him. The guy was clearly exhausted. He was also clearly keeping something from Braden.

"Go," he told him. "Go to bed. But we're not done."

"No, we're not," Trick agreed. "We won't be done until we catch the person responsible for all the accidents and for the shootings."

So Trick believed that person was one and the same. After what Owen and Luke and he and Sam had gone through recently, Braden wasn't so sure. The only thing he was convinced of was that Trick was keeping something—or someone—from him.

Why?

HENRIETTA STOOD BEFORE her window again—like she had just a couple of hours ago, after Trick had snuck out of it in the same way that he'd snuck in. She waited for a surge of embarrassment or regret. But there was no way she could regret the pleasure she'd experienced with him.

She had never felt anything like that—anything that

powerful, that earth-shattering. Would it have been like that, though, if not for all the danger earlier?

Maybe it was just the adrenaline from being shot at that had intensified her feelings. Maybe it had had nothing to do with Trick, with his kisses, with his touch, with how perfectly he'd fit her...

She shivered and wrapped her arms around herself, but she was too chilled to get warm on her own. She needed Trick's big arms around her, like they'd been just a short time ago. But he was gone.

And she needed to get out of her bedroom, so she would stop thinking about him, stop longing for him. But she'd been waiting for Michaela to leave before she left.

Once she heard the apartment door slam behind her roommate, she ventured out. Even if Michaela hadn't overheard them the night before, she would have probably figured out what had happened just from looking at Henrietta's face.

Henrietta wasn't embarrassed, but she was tired—too tired to listen to another of Michaela's lectures, complete with warnings to stay away from Trick. She didn't need anyone telling her what she already knew.

He was a danger to her career, maybe even to her life, and most certainly to her heart. She couldn't get used to being with him, to sleeping in his arms.

She couldn't fall for him only to suffer another loss, another heartbreak.

Because he wasn't staying...

He never stayed, according to the team members who'd worked with him in the past.

She couldn't stay either—in her bedroom or even in the apartment. She had to get a cell phone—not that she was expecting Trick to call her. But she needed it for work—for the local department and the Hotshot team to contact her.

As long as no one was hurt, she would almost welcome a fire now. She needed the distraction, so that she would stop thinking about Trick and about last night. Those gunshots, his wound…how much worse it could have been…

He could have died. And even though she knew he wouldn't be staying in Northern Lakes, she didn't want to think of a world without him in it. It wouldn't be quite as bright or exciting.

She hurried down the steps from the second-floor apartment to the small firehouse beneath it. They had one engine and, with the exception of her and Michaela, only volunteer workers. But if they needed it, they had the Northern Lakes Fire Department as backup. They rarely needed it. The only blaze she'd battled recently out of this firehouse had been a bonfire that had gotten out of control.

Actually, the teenagers who'd started it had been more out of control than the fire. But she and Michaela had handled it with just their crew of retirees.

One of those retirees sat in the garage now, sipping coffee from a thermos. "Hey, Hank," he called out to her. "You rushing out like Michaela?"

Michaela had probably hurried so that she didn't get sucked into the volunteer's boring stories about the good old days. They had both heard them way too many times.

Henrietta forced a smile for the old man. "Unfortunately I have to, George. I broke my cell last night and need to replace it ASAP."

He sighed. "People can't seem to live without those

damn things anymore." Despite his disdain, he carried one, too, as required for his being a volunteer.

"Can you watch the place until I get back?" she asked.

He nodded. "Of course. Nothing else to do…"

His wife had passed away a couple of years ago. If not for the firehouse, he probably would have died of a broken heart. But having the responsibility of firefighting kept him in good physical and mental condition. She felt a pang of guilt over leaving him alone as she rushed out the door. When she returned, she would listen to his stories.

In a hurry to escape him and get a new phone, she quickly unlocked her SUV and climbed inside before she noticed it. The slip of paper fluttered beneath the wiper on the driver's side. "What the hell…?" she murmured.

Had Trick left her the note? Had he thanked her for a good time?

Had he had a good time?

She thought the intensity of their passion and their pleasure had shaken him as much as it had her. Maybe that was why he'd snuck out like he had—because it had been too much, too dangerous…for so many reasons. She suspected he didn't want to get attached to her either. She didn't take it personally. He probably moved so often because he didn't want to get attached to anyone.

So leaving a note didn't seem like Trick's style. Just leaving was his style.

Hank rolled down her window and reached out with a slightly shaking hand to grab the missive. When she unfolded the slip of paper, she was surprised to find the crude block letters written across it.

And what it read surprised her even more: *You made a terrible mistake. And you're going to die for it…*

Chapter Thirteen

He hadn't lied to Braden—about needing to sleep—although at the time, Trick had doubted he would be able to without Henrietta clasped in his arms. But once he showered, he collapsed onto a bunk and crashed. Usually one sleepless night wouldn't have taken such a toll on him. Maybe it had been the rush of adrenaline from getting shot at and chasing the shooter that had exhausted him.

Or maybe it had been Henrietta. The intensity of that passion with her had rocked him to his core. That intensity must have depleted his energy, because he slept for much longer than he'd thought he would.

When he awoke, it was closer to sunset than sunrise. And he might not have woken up even then if not for the loud rumblings of his stomach. As well as being exhausted, he was also starved. And not just for food.

He wanted to see Henrietta again—wanted to be with her like he'd been the night before. But that would be a mistake. He would only put her in more danger. Remembering the note on his windshield brought him fully awake with a surge of anger. He'd been followed to her—had led danger right to her.

Unless the danger had already been there...

He needed to figure out who the hell was after

him—who was behind the accidents and the notes and the shootings. And now it wasn't just his favor for his brother-in-law motivating him to get to the truth; it was his anger and his concern for Henrietta.

Was she okay?

Was she furious with him for sneaking out like he had?

She had to know that her roommate was right; it was too dangerous for her to be around him. But even knowing that, moments later, when he walked through the door of the Filling Station, disappointment flashed through him when he saw that she wasn't there.

Most of the other Hotshots were. At the meeting the day before, Braden had informed them that they were on call for another wildfire out West. If it wasn't contained soon, they would head out to work a stint on it.

Fighting fires was in his DNA, so usually the thought of working one had excitement coursing through him. He never felt more alive than when he was doing his job—until last night. And it wasn't just because he'd cheated death when all those bullets had missed him. Or mostly missed him. He'd taken off the bandage when he'd showered, and the denim of his jeans rubbed against his scratch as he walked toward the bar. He'd had a change of clothes in his locker at the firehouse, but he needed to go back to his apartment and pack more stuff—after he ate.

The moment he'd never felt more alive was when he'd been making love with Henrietta Rowlins. Maybe that was because they had both cheated death. Trick couldn't put her in the position of having to do that again. Sure, she did it herself every time she fought a fire. But that was different.

A fire was more predictable than some psychopath with a gun.

He needed to find out who the hell that psychopath was. Was he here?

Settling onto the stool at the bar, Trick swiveled around and took account of everyone inside the place. That corner booth where the Hotshots always gathered was full, despite Henrietta not being there. In fact, she was probably the only one not present, which sent a chill running down his spine.

Where was she?

In danger?

No. She had to be safe— because she was nowhere near him. Still, his fingers twitched with the urge to call her, to check on her. But he'd broken her cell the night before. Had she gotten it fixed or replaced?

Did she have any way of calling for help if she needed it? Of calling for him if she needed him?

His body ached with wanting hers again. And a groan slipped through his lips.

"Heard you had a rough night last night," the bartender/owner, Charlie, remarked as he placed a chilled mug of beer in front of Trick.

That was why Trick had had to be careful about what he'd told the trooper and Braden. Gossip spread fast in a town like Northern Lakes. He didn't want anyone gossiping about Henrietta being with him on the street and then later in his apartment. He didn't want to put her in danger of losing her life, or even her job.

Trick grinned. "If it gets me free drinks, I'll have a rough night every night." Especially if it ended like it had last night—or this morning—in Henrietta's bed, in Henrietta...

"The first one's on the house," Charlie said.

One was all Trick usually drank, which they both knew. "I'd like to order a burger, too," he said, "with the works." His stomach rumbled again at the mention of food.

Charlie chuckled as he put in Trick's order on the computer behind the bar. "So who was shooting at you? Jealous husband or boyfriend?"

"Why does everyone think that?" he asked. Before last night, he couldn't even remember the last time he'd gone out on a date. Not that he and Henrietta had gone out...

Or that they were dating...

But Charlie was already moving down to someone else at the bar and didn't answer his question.

Instead, a female voice did. "Don't take it personally. It doesn't take much to get a reputation in this town."

He swiveled the stool around to find the local hairdresser standing behind him. Tammy Ingles was a beautiful woman, but she probably took a lot of time to get her hair and makeup just right for herself, like she did for the customers of the salon she owned. She reminded him of his sister's old college roommate. Colleen had always taken such care with her appearance, too. While she'd been nice, she hadn't seemed real to him. Henrietta was real, with a natural beauty that seemed to radiate from the inside out.

"It's not the whole town," he conceded. "Just Charlie. And Hank..." But Henrietta was the only woman he'd hit on since coming to Northern Lakes—since probably even a while before that.

But whatever this was between them couldn't continue. They couldn't repeat what they'd done—no matter how amazing it had been. He didn't want Henrietta to get hurt because of him, and he definitely didn't want to hurt her. He'd learned long ago that it was better to stay detached, to not get emotionally involved. He didn't want to wind up like his dad, brokenhearted. And he didn't want to break anyone's heart either.

"Hank being rough on you?" Tammy asked with a teasing smile. "And Charlie has no room to talk. He's a bigger flirt than I am."

Trick was aware that the hairdresser had a reputation for being a bit of a firehouse groupie. But he'd never seen her hanging around the firehouse, bringing by cookies or even offering free haircuts. When she was in the bar, she joined them for drinks, but he suspected that was because her best friends were engaged or in romantic relationships with firefighters—not because she wanted to be. Through her friends, Tammy Ingles knew the team very well. Maybe she could offer some insight into who might be the saboteur.

"Join me?" he asked, gesturing toward the empty stool next to him.

She narrowed her eyes. "Just so you know, the rumors about me aren't true."

"I know," he said. "That's why I feel safe talking to you. I know you're not actually going to eat me alive."

She chuckled but hesitated. "What about you?"

He shook his head. "I'm no threat."

He was the one being threatened—with those stupid notes and now the gunfire.

"You're not to me," she agreed as she finally sat down next to him. "But I've seen the way you look at Henrietta." Her eyes twinkled with amusement.

He tensed.

"Didn't you realize you were being that obvious?" she asked.

He shook his head and gestured for the bartender to bring Tammy a drink. He wanted her comfortable enough to talk to him, but not too inebriated to understand. She could prove a great resource for information on the team. But he found himself interested in only one member at the moment. "So tell me about Henrietta."

Tammy giggled. "I knew it…"

And Trick knew that Henrietta was not responsible for anything he was investigating: the sabotage, the notes, the shootings…

There was no reason for him to learn more about her—except that he wanted to know.

"I've seen the way you look at Ethan Sommerly," he said, teasing her back.

Her face flushed with color. "That's just curiosity," she said defensively. "I wonder what he looks like underneath all that hair and that bushy beard."

Trick glanced toward the booth in the corner and found Ethan's gaze on them. What was the guy hiding? Because it was almost as if all the hair was some sort of disguise…

If anyone was not who they seemed, as Braden's note had warned, it was probably Ethan Sommerly. What or whom was he hiding from behind that beard? And how desperate was he not to be found out? Desperate enough to leave the threats Trick had been receiving? Desperate enough to shoot at him?

"What do you know about him?" he asked.

Tammy shook her head. "Nothing. He doesn't talk."

Trick would need to do some more research on him, figure out what his story was. But there was another man in that booth that had a story. "What do you think about Trent Miles?" The Hotshot from Detroit was the stereotypical good-looking firefighter who'd probably posed for those cheesy calendars. And if he really was a former gang member, he had that whole bad boy vibe some women liked, so he might have been more Tammy's type than Sommerly.

"He talks too much," she quipped.

"Rory VanDam?" he asked. His light blond hair was kept short in a buzz cut, and his blue eyes were eerily pale. He was like Ethan Sommerly, minus the beard and long hair. He spent most of his time alone on some ranger station on a small island in Lake Michigan. Was he hiding from something out there?

She giggled. "Are you asking all these questions just to prove that Henrietta isn't the only person you're interested in?"

No. He was doing his job—well, his special assignment for his brother-in-law, but, as always, thoughts of Henrietta distracted him. He sighed. "What do you know about her?"

"More than I do about the guys you just mentioned," she said. "After her parents died, Henrietta came to live in Northern Lakes with her grandfather."

"Her parents died?"

Tammy's mouth pulled down into a frown, and she nodded. "Yes, car crash when she was seven. It was terrible. But her grandfather took good care of her and she of him. They were so close…"

"He died, too?"

Tears of sympathy sparked in her eyes as she nodded. "Just a couple of years ago…"

"And she has no siblings?"

"No. Not even aunts and uncles. She's completely alone now."

A pang of sympathy clenched his heart. His mom had taken off years ago, but he still had his dad, who, despite the demands of his job, was always there for him. And he had his siblings—pains in the ass that they sometimes were. Except for Mack—his oldest brother had been pretty much MIA since his last deployment with the Marines. He'd come back alive, but not the same. He was even more reclusive than Ethan Sommerly and Rory VanDam.

Unlike Trick, Henrietta was all alone—except for the team, which was the only family she had now. He couldn't stem his curiosity about her. "She's always been alone?"

"She has tons of friends," Tammy said defensively.

"I mean more than friends," he said.

Tammy sighed. "She was engaged a couple of years ago."

Trick felt a pang of something he'd never felt before. It couldn't be envy that he had never come close to anything that serious. He'd wanted it that way—whereas Henrietta had once wanted to spend her life with someone…*else*.

"What happened?" he asked.

Tammy shrugged her slender shoulders. "You'd have to ask her. She gave the ring back."

"So that means she broke the engagement, right?" Trick asked. He had friends who had broken engagements—especially Hotshot friends whose fiancées hadn't been able to handle their careers and had returned their engagement rings. Mack had also been engaged once and had gotten the ring back just as he'd left for his last deployment. He flinched, remembering his brother's pain.

He was so like his namesake, their dad, Mack. And watching the men he'd admired suffer like that had made Trick even more determined to never risk that kind of pain. That was why he'd never had a serious relationship, and didn't intend to ever have one.

Yet he couldn't stop thinking about Henrietta. Maybe that was just because he was worried about her.

"What about this fiancé?" Trick asked. And something twisted in his chest as he said the word—that word—in regard to Henrietta. She had been engaged. She had been in love…

Some emotion washed over him, making him feel sick, so that when Charlie placed a plate with his juicy burger in front of him, his stomach roiled instead of rumbled.

"What about him?" Tammy asked.

"Was he fine with her breaking the engagement?" Trick wondered. He wouldn't have been fine—had he been with Henrietta and then lost her.

Tammy shrugged again. "I don't know. Like I said, you'll need to talk to her about that."

Maybe he needed to, but only because it was possible that her ex was the one sabotaging the equipment and sending those notes—out of jealousy. Out of unrequited love.

Maybe her ex didn't want Henrietta to be with anyone else. Maybe he didn't want Henrietta to *be*.

Trick needed to make sure that she was safe.

"Here's your chance," Tammy remarked. "Hank just walked in."

And as she did, she walked right past him, without

even glancing his way—like he didn't exist. Like last night hadn't happened…

Did she regret what they'd done? Or was she angry that he'd slipped out the window without saying goodbye?

She had to understand that it was too dangerous for him to be around her—too dangerous for them to be around each other, and not just because of the gunshots fired at them…

In her presence, Trick's heart started pounding so fast and hard in his chest that it was difficult for him to draw a deep breath, and his entire body tensed and tingled with awareness.

In another pair of slim-fitting jeans and an oversize sweater, she was impossibly sexy, impossibly beautiful—and impossibly uninterested in him.

Had she forgotten all about last night? About the pleasure they'd given each other?

Or hadn't it been as powerful for her as it had been for him?

He wanted to ask her. Hell, he wanted to do more than that—he wanted to experience that all over again. But he had to force himself to stay away from her.

For her sake.

And his…

HENRIETTA HAD NOT missed Trick sitting at the bar. She'd noticed him the moment she'd opened the door to the Filling Station. Her pulse had quickened, and her skin had heated. And she'd wanted nothing more than to walk up and slide her arms around him and press her body against his.

But she would never be able to do that. He wasn't her

boyfriend. He was her teammate, and because of that, last night never should have happened. And could never happen again...

And after nearly being shot, she shouldn't want to be anywhere near him. The note proved those gunshots hadn't been a fluke. They had been meant for him, and now for her, too.

She needed to tell someone about the note. But she hadn't said a word all day—not even when Michaela had returned to the firehouse. Thankfully, George had stuck around, too, so Michaela hadn't had a chance to lecture Henrietta about her late-night visitor. And from the look in her friend's eyes, she knew that Michaela knew...

But surely Henrietta could trust her to keep it secret. As the only two women on the team, they had bonded immediately and were closer than the others. They looked out for each other.

Which was probably why Michaela jumped up from the booth as Henrietta approached and stopped her before she got within hearing range of the others. "Did you see him?" she asked.

She didn't need to ask who, and Michaela didn't give her time to ask before she continued. "He's hitting on Tammy at the bar." Then Michaela's brow puckered, and she slowly, almost reluctantly added, "Well, she walked up to him first. So maybe she's hitting on him."

She winced at the sudden pain that jabbed her heart. Or was it in her back? Tammy was a friend. Henrietta had known her even longer than she had Michaela. But it wasn't as if Tammy was betraying her, because she didn't know about Hank's infatuation with her fellow Hotshot. Only Michaela knew.

"Tammy often buys us drinks," Henrietta reminded

her. Her friend did well with her salon and appreciated the Hotshots' heroic efforts to keep the town safe, as well as their help in battling fires across the country.

Michaela pointed toward the bar. "He's the one paying."

Henrietta flinched. Had he snuck out of her bed to try to climb into Tammy's? Heat rushed into her face, but it wasn't from embarrassment. She was furious—with him.

Obviously he hadn't been as affected as she'd been. Or maybe he'd been just as overwhelmed and this was his way of running away, like he had from every other team, from every other city. Why didn't he stay anyplace?

Because she knew he didn't, she never should have gotten involved with him at all. Sleeping with him was obviously the horrible mistake she'd made. But why did the note writer think she needed to die for it?

It wasn't as if she was ever going to repeat it. Not now. Not ever.

The mistake she'd made last night hadn't necessarily been sleeping with him. It had been in romanticizing him. Just because he'd saved her life last night didn't mean he was a knight in shining armor.

"Somebody should warn her," Michaela remarked. "Like I warned you..." And she stared hard at Henrietta.

She shivered. "Did you...?" Could her roommate have left that note? But why?

Michaela's brow furrowed. "You know I did. I told you to stay away from him. And look what happened."

She'd had the most exciting night of her life. But she could have done without some of that excitement—like the shootings.

"Did you ever go out with him?" Henrietta wondered in a whisper. There had been quite a few nights recently when Michaela hadn't come back to the apartment they shared, but Henrietta hadn't wanted to pry. Until now...

Michaela snorted. "Oh, God, no. Not Trick McRooney."

But there had been someone...

Who?

Was it another team member? Was that why Michaela was so insistent that she not date Trick? She didn't want Henrietta risking her career as well? But it wasn't just Henrietta's job that was on the line when she was around Trick McRooney; after being shot at twice, it was also her life. Maybe that was what that note had meant; that she was going to pay for the mistake of getting involved with Trick—with her life.

LEAVING THE NOTES might have been a bad idea. Especially since Trick hadn't heeded them anyway.

Henrietta Rowlins might. She'd been obviously shaken. And earlier tonight when she'd walked into the bar...

She'd realized the mistake she'd made.

But it was too late.

And it was too late to get that note back from her. Not that it mattered, since the only fingerprints on it would be Ms. Rowlins's. The earlier notes, though, the ones left for Trick...

Those might have prints on them because emotion had been overruling self-preservation then. So those notes had to be destroyed. Where the hell had Trick put them?

He obviously hadn't reported them to the police yet, because they would have tested them for prints. The notes had to be disposed of before Trick turned them over to the authorities. Had he given them to his brother-in-law?

If he had, Zimmer probably would have turned them over to the police. Or his wife…

No. The notes had to be somewhere at Trick's place. And after the shooting, he wasn't there. This was the perfect opportunity to search it. Hence, the impromptu visit to the apartment. The police hadn't released the crime scene yet, but they weren't guarding it either. While there was a lock at the door, the windows weren't secured beyond some hastily tacked up pieces of plywood.

One of those came loose easily enough—enough to slip inside and begin searching. But the search had just begun when footsteps echoed in the stairwell outside the apartment door.

Somebody was coming.

The flashlight flipped off, but before it could get shoved into a pocket, it slipped and tumbled onto the hardwood floor. But then the gun came out, clasped tightly—finger near the trigger.

Whoever was coming was going to get a hell of a surprise—in a bullet…

Chapter Fourteen

Trick ignored the crime-scene tape strewn across the doorway to his apartment—just like whoever was inside had ignored it. As he'd climbed the steps, he'd heard the crash of something tumbling over inside his place. The landlord had shown up the night before to tack up plywood over the broken windows, so the wind couldn't have blown over anything. It had to be a person who had knocked down something.

Trick probably should have gone back downstairs and called the police. But the same impulse that had compelled him to chase after the shooter compelled him now to unlock his door. He wanted to find out who the hell had broken into his apartment and why. He didn't want to wait for cops. The intruder could be gone by then.

What the hell did they want—besides him dead?

Of course, walking into the place gave the shooter the opportunity to try again. And knowing that he might get shot at had Trick ducking low as he pushed open the door.

He heard the telltale click he'd heard in the courtyard the night before: the metallic clink of the gun cocking. And he dropped entirely to the floor. But the gun just clicked and clicked again.

Either it was empty or jammed.

And he was damn lucky.

He rolled to his knees to get up from the floor, but before he could stand, a shadowy figure rushed from the darkness, brandishing something. The object whacked him across the back, sending pain shooting down his spine.

He tried to reach for the weapon, but it was swung again—this time at his head. It hit Trick hard, and pain radiated throughout his skull. He dropped to the ground again and rolled onto his back, trying to peer up at the figure standing over him. But everything went black as consciousness slipped away.

HENRIETTA HAD KNOWN the minute he left the bar, and not just because a few of her fellow Hotshots remarked about it. She knew because her pulse slowed down and her skin stopped tingling. But she was still tense, still achy with wanting him, even while she fumed with anger and frustration over how easily he'd ignored her.

As if last night had never happened…

She'd wanted to pretend that it hadn't either. She would like to forget about the shooting. But the sex…

She wasn't likely to ever forget that. Or the shooting…

Her head began to pound as she tried to make sense of it all.

"The spy has left the building," Ethan Sommerly quietly remarked with a ragged sigh of relief.

Was that why someone had been shooting at them? Because they thought he was a spy? But what were they worried that he might discover? What were they trying to hide?

Trent Miles chuckled, but it sounded hollow, not as

deep as his laugh usually was, as if the thought made him uneasy, too. "You really think he's spying for the boss?"

"You don't?" Rory VanDam was the one who asked the question now.

Trent shrugged. "I don't know what to think about him. He held his own on our last job out West."

"And he held on when that bucket nearly slipped off the boom a couple of weeks ago," Ethan added with almost reluctant admiration.

Henrietta shuddered as she remembered how close a call that had been for him. Was Michaela right—had that not been an accident at all? Had anything that had been happening to them been accidents? She knew for damn certain the gunshots hadn't been.

"That wasn't your fault," Trent assured her.

The bucket incident or the gunfire? But few people seemed to know about the gunshots. Or were they just not talking about it…?

"We need some new equipment," Carl Kozak remarked. "It's all older than I am."

"And that's old," Trent said, teasing the most senior Hotshot.

Carl was in amazing shape, though, muscular and strong, with a bald head that had earned him the nickname Mr. Clean.

Carl laughed but flipped off Trent. "Yeah, so old that it's past my bedtime."

It wasn't late, but if they were going to be sent out to a wildfire soon, they needed to get their rest. So everybody filed out together. As they parted at the door, Michaela turned to Henrietta and asked, "You coming right home?"

"Of course." She had no place else to go. Well, she

should head to the state police post and turn over that damn note and the spent shell she'd found the night before. It was probably already too late to get any evidence from that shell, and if Marty Gingrich had been working the case, he would have arrested her for tampering with evidence and withholding information. There was a strong possibility that the trooper's former coworkers might do the same. She did not want to go to jail like Luke and Trick had when Marty had had them arrested.

"Do you just want to ride home together?" Michaela asked.

Henrietta shook her head. "I'm fine. I'll see you soon," she promised as her roommate walked out. But before she could slip through the door, someone grabbed her arm—lightly.

It wasn't Trick's strong grasp. This hand was small and perfectly manicured.

"Can we talk?" Tammy Ingles asked her.

At least her friend hadn't left with Trick, but that didn't mean she wasn't meeting him later somewhere. Like Michaela had said, maybe Tammy needed to be warned about Trick McRooney.

Still… Henrietta hesitated, reluctant to talk at all.

"Please," Tammy implored her.

Henrietta nodded and turned away from the door. She followed the petite woman back to the bar and took the stool Trick had vacated when he'd left the salon owner alone.

"Drink?" Tammy asked.

Henrietta shook her head. She needed to drive herself back to her apartment tonight. Alone.

"This is why we need to talk," Tammy said.

"Because I'm not drinking?" Henrietta asked, and she forced a smile. "Is this some kind of reverse intervention?"

Tammy giggled and shook her head. "No. This is about you being mad at me."

"I'm not."

"I saw your face when you walked in and noticed that I was sitting with Trick McRooney," Tammy said.

Hank shook her head. "I didn't even look your way." Except for a fleeting glance. She hadn't wanted Trick to see her looking at him—wanting him—when she knew it would lead only to disappointment and potentially worse…if she got too attached to him…

Or if she was in too much danger being near him. Maybe she needed to warn Tammy to steer clear of him, too. At least until the shooter was caught.

Her friend reached out and squeezed Henrietta's hand. "I noticed your look," Tammy said. "I recognized it."

"I'm not jealous." She refused to acknowledge that sick feeling churning her stomach.

Tammy smiled. "You shouldn't be," she said. "You have no reason to be."

"Of course not," Henrietta said. "I'm not interested in Trick McRooney."

"He's interested in you," Tammy said, and her hazel eyes twinkled.

Henrietta shook her head. "No, he's not." He had been last night, though—completely interested in pleasing her and taking pleasure from her. A rush of heat streaked through her as she remembered the passion that had burned between them.

Tammy tilted her head. "Then I wonder why he kept asking all kinds of questions about you."

Henrietta tensed. "What was he asking about me?"

Tammy smiled. "He wanted to know about your love life. Exes, boyfriends…"

Heat rushed to Henrietta's face now. "What did you tell him?" she asked, aghast at his audacity.

"To talk to you," Tammy said. But then her face flushed slightly. "I did admit that you were once engaged, though. I'm sorry."

So was Henrietta. She never should have accepted that ring. But at the time she hadn't known there was more than what she'd felt for Greg. Then she'd seen some of her friends fall in love—really in love—and she'd realized what she'd felt wasn't the same.

Greg had insisted that her affection for him was enough, that he would be happy, and that he would make her happy. That was why she hadn't been able to maintain her promise to stay friends, because every time they'd talked, he'd pleaded with her to reconsider. Even now he sometimes called or stopped by the firehouse, asking to take her out for dinner or a movie or just to talk. She wished he would move on…

Like Trick moved on, from team to team. But he was still here. Was he spying like the others suspected? Was that why he'd asked about her?

Or did he think whoever had shot at them had been aiming for her? She needed to show Trick that note she'd received. But if the shooter had really been aiming for her, then she was the one who had put Trick in danger.

And seeking him out to show him that note would put him in danger all over again if he was near her. She didn't know what to do, and the indecision must have shown on her face because Tammy clutched her hand more tightly. Like Michaela, she was stronger than she looked.

"He's really interested in you," Tammy said.

"That's not good," Henrietta murmured. For either of them, and for so many reasons.

Tammy tilted her head again as she studied Henrietta's face. "I think it could be," she said. "If you're careful—if you keep it secret so you don't get in trouble with the superintendent."

Tammy knew all the Hotshots so well that she could have almost been one of them. She knew about the boss's rule prohibiting romantic relationships between team members.

"I would be the one getting in trouble," Henrietta said, "since Trick is Braden's brother-in-law."

"I know everybody thinks that's the reason he got the open spot on the team," Tammy said. "But I don't think that's it…"

Henrietta wondered, too, why Trick had come to Northern Lakes. He could work on any Hotshot team anywhere. Why here? Had he wanted to be closer to his sister? But as a premier arson investigator, Sam was so busy that she traveled often. She wasn't in Northern Lakes as much as Trick had been since he'd arrived in town. Or had he just been doing a favor for his brother-in-law, and was only temporarily filling the open spot on Braden's team, just as he'd temporarily filled spots on so many other teams?

"It doesn't matter why he's here," Henrietta said. "I don't intend to have anything to do with him."

"You work with him," Tammy said.

"That's all I intend to do." Now. And if she wanted to keep working, she had to make certain that what happened last night never happened again. And that nobody found out about it. She slid off the stool.

But before she could turn to leave, Tammy caught her

arm again, like she had at the door. "He was going back to his apartment to get some stuff," she told Henrietta.

That sick feeling churned in her stomach again and she found herself asking, "Does he want you to meet him there?"

Tammy shook her head. "Not me…"

"Not me," Henrietta repeated.

Tammy's lips curved into a smile. "He's interested in you," she persisted. But her smile turned down at the corners. "It was almost as if he was afraid to admit it, though."

After what had happened the night before, he had every reason to be afraid. And so did Henrietta. But she suspected he was scared for another reason.

"He was shot at last night," she said. While nobody else had been talking about it, she bet Tammy had heard about it, like she heard about everything that happened in Northern Lakes. "He should be scared."

"I think he's more scared of his interest in you than he is of whoever shot at him," Tammy speculated.

Maybe that was because he thought his interest in her was why he'd been shot at; that would explain why he'd asked about her love life. They'd teased each other about jealous exes the night before, but maybe Trick hadn't been teasing. Maybe he thought her former fiancé could have been the one who'd fired at them.

She couldn't imagine Greg ever hurting anyone, but most especially her. But then, he'd never had to see her dating anyone else. Not that she and Trick were dating…

And not that Greg had probably seen him. As the principal of the St. Paul elementary school, he spent more time there than he did in Northern Lakes, and until last night, Trick hadn't been to St. Paul.

"He needs to be worried about the shooting," Henrietta said. "So do you."

Tammy's brow creased. "What do you mean?"

"Just that I don't think Trick McRooney is safe to be around," she said.

Tammy smiled. "I don't have to worry about that. You do."

MAYBE TAMMY HAD guessed where Henrietta was going, even though she hadn't been sure herself until she'd said goodbye and left the bar. A short while later she found herself standing outside the front door of his apartment building. She tipped her head and stared up at the third story but noticed no lights on inside his apartment. Maybe he'd already gone back to the firehouse or to Braden's.

Or her place? Despite his ignoring her at the bar, he'd apparently been pumping Tammy for information about her.

Why?

Because he was genuinely interested in her? Or was he the spy that the rest of her team thought he was? And what was he spying on them to learn?

She had to ask him, so she reached for the intercom next to the security panel and rang the bell for his apartment. The sound of it eerily echoed down the quiet street. She glanced around her at the shadows in the darkness and shivered as she remembered that note.

The threat.

She was going to pay with her life. Was the shooter out there waiting to try for her again? She needed to get inside—soon.

But nobody answered the intercom in Trick's apartment. She reached for the door to the foyer, and surprisingly it opened. Had it been left unlocked? Or had someone unlocked it from their apartment?

Trick might not have said anything into the intercom, but he still might have let her in. She hurried through the foyer door and let it swing shut behind her. But it didn't click and lock behind her like the door to the courtyard had locked behind them the night before.

It looked like the same kind. So why hadn't it locked? Had someone tampered with the door?

She shivered again as her uneasiness increased. She'd been lucky the night before. Trick had protected her. But she didn't know where he was now.

He'd told Tammy he was coming here, so Henrietta continued up the stairs to his apartment. She didn't have to worry about anyone unlocking this door for her; it stood wide open, a strip of crime-scene tape dangling from the jamb.

"Hello?" she called out as she hesitated in the doorway. The apartment was dark, except for the faint light that spilled in from the stairwell. But that light only illuminated a tiny half circle of the hardwood floor inside the door.

The rest of the apartment was all shadows. Of furniture? Or was someone inside the place?

"Trick?" she called out.

A faint groan emanated from the darkness. Somebody was inside, and that somebody was hurt. Knowing that it was probably Trick, she rushed over the threshold without thinking about her safety.

Trick had saved her life the night before—more than once. She needed to help him. But as she entered, something swung at her from out of the darkness. And she didn't have Trick to block the blow from striking her like he'd blocked the bullets the night before.

She threw up her arm and screamed.

KNOWING THAT THEY might get called out to a wildfire soon, Owen should have been spending as much time as he could with Courtney and getting some rest. But after the shootings the night before, he knew his friends were in danger, and so he'd actually picked up this paramedic shift to be on call in case something happened again.

Therefore he wasn't surprised when his rig got dispatched to the same address it had been sent to the night before. But he was scared—damn scared—that he might arrive too late.

"How badly is he hurt?" he asked the dispatcher.

"How'd you know the patient is male?" Evelyn asked.

"I know the address," he said.

"Male isn't the only victim," Evelyn said. "A female has been injured as well."

"Gunshot wounds?" he asked through the huge lump of emotion that had welled up in his throat.

"The trooper who called it in didn't provide many details," Evelyn said. "Only that the male was unconscious."

So Trick was hurt badly. And the female? It had to be Hank. How badly was she hurt?

"Hurry," Owen told the driver. But no matter how fast his partner drove, they might not make it in time. Owen didn't want to lose another teammate. Even though he hadn't known Trick long, the man had become a friend.

And Hank...

She was like his sister; she was family.

They had to be okay...

Chapter Fifteen

"*Trick...*"

The voice drew him out of the darkness, out of oblivion. "No!" he wanted to shout, but the word burned in the back of his dry throat.

No. Don't come in! It's too dangerous...

He'd wanted to say all those things, but all that slipped out of his lips was a weak groan. And then he'd slipped into oblivion again, drowning in the waves of pain crashing through his head. He hadn't been able to warn Henrietta to run, to try to escape the killer hiding in the shadows of his apartment.

What had happened?

He fought his way back now, trying to regain consciousness. Battling his way out of the darkness, he dragged open his eyelids and winced at the bright lights overhead. A curse slipped out between his lips as he squeezed his eyes shut again.

"You're alive," a deep voice murmured.

He opened his eyes again to see Owen leaning over him. "You're the paramedic," Trick said. "You tell me..."

"You're alive," Owen confirmed. "You probably have a hell of a headache, though."

Trick groaned with the pain reverberating throughout

his skull. "Hell is right," he murmured. "Are you sure I'm not dead?"

"Yup. But I need to get a CT scan to see how badly that blow scrambled your brains."

Something snapped across Trick's waist, and his entire body rose as Owen raised the stretcher beneath him. And then he snapped back to reality.

"Henrietta!" he said, and he looked around the brightly lit apartment.

Owen and his paramedic partner were not alone. Trooper Wells and a male trooper also walked around the studio apartment. But Trick didn't see any sign of Henrietta.

He grabbed Owen's arm and asked, "Where is she?"

Had she already been taken to the hospital? How badly had she been hurt?

Owen shrugged. "She left before I got here."

While Trick was still unconscious? Hadn't she cared enough to wait for him to get treatment? To make sure he was okay?

She'd left the night before when he'd been out chasing the shooter. She couldn't have made it clearer either time that she didn't give a damn about him.

So why the hell did he care so much about her?

"You need to make sure she's okay," Trick urged him.

"After I take care of you," Owen said. "You're the one with the head injury."

Trick lifted his hand to his head and found his hair sticky and damp with blood. His blood.

"Yeah, you're going to need stitches this time," Owen said, and he and his partner started pushing the stretcher toward the doorway.

"Stop!" a female voice said.

But it wasn't Henrietta's.

Wynona Wells leaned over him instead. "You're awake."

He was tempted to shut his eyes and pretend he'd passed out again. But he needed to know what had happened, and maybe the trooper could answer his questions.

Before he could say anything, though, she asked, "Do you know what happened?"

He nearly laughed. He might have, if he didn't think the sound would shatter his skull. He pointed toward his head. "I got hit."

"I figured that out," she replied. "Did you see who did it?"

"It was dark," he said. "I don't know."

The trooper's eyes narrowed with skepticism. Clearly, she didn't believe him. "What were you doing here?"

"It's my apartment."

"It's a crime scene."

"I was going to pack up some of my clothes and stuff," he said. "But when I came inside, somebody else was already here. They jumped me."

"They?" she repeated.

He wished there had been more than one, but he suspected the intruder had acted alone. "I don't know..."

"I have already questioned Ms. Rowlins," she told him, as if that would influence his replies at all.

"Is she okay?" he asked anxiously.

The trooper nodded.

"The dispatcher said she was injured, too," Owen shared. "Why isn't she here?"

"I took her statement already and she declined to have medical treatment."

But was she hurt?

"Maybe you should have waited until a medical professional could determine that she didn't need treatment," Owen advised.

The trooper glared at him. "She refused it," she told him. "I couldn't force her to seek treatment."

"You could have forced her to stay," Owen suggested.

Another twinge of pain jabbed Trick, but this time it moved through his heart, not his head. He hated thinking of Hank being forced to stay. That reminded him too much of his mother, who'd been dying inside as a wife and mom, who hadn't been able to wait to leave them, just like Henrietta hadn't been able to wait to leave him, even when he'd been hurt and unconscious. He shuddered, and a groan slipped through his lips.

"I need to get him to the hospital," Owen said. "He needs a CT. He could have bleeding on the brain."

He would rather his head bleed than his heart. This was why he never got serious about anyone. It hurt too much to care about someone who could just walk away without even looking back.

Not that he cared about Henrietta. He barely knew her. But he didn't want her hurt.

So it was good that she was gone. He didn't want her in any more danger because of him.

But why had she been here?

What had she wanted?

SHE KEPT LOOKING over her shoulder—on that short walk from her vehicle to the Northern Lakes firehouse. She glanced back into the shadows. Was someone there like they'd been in Trick's apartment, waiting to jump out at her from the darkness? Maybe she should have gone back to St. Paul, but she wanted—she needed—to talk to Braden. She wanted him to make certain that Trick was all right. She'd gone by Braden's house first, but nobody had been home, so he was probably here. Or maybe he was already on his way to Trick's apartment, or to the hospital…

She shivered, despite the thickness of her oversize sweater. She wasn't sure anything could warm her up after that attack—except Trick. His arms wound tightly around her could heat and comfort her.

But she'd had to leave him.

The trooper had given her no choice. She'd wanted Henrietta gone before he regained consciousness. She hadn't wanted them comparing stories—like they were the suspects and not the victims.

Now she knew how Braden had felt when Trooper Gingrich had treated him like a criminal rather than the hero he was. The disgraced officer had trained Trooper Wells, apparently, to be as suspicious and closed-minded as he'd been. Was she also a disgrace to her badge? Could she be trusted?

Because Henrietta couldn't decide, she hadn't told her much. She'd denied being there the night before, during the shooting, and she hadn't shared anything about the threatening note left on her windshield either.

Maybe the officer had suspected that Henrietta had been withholding information. Maybe that was why she'd seemed so mistrustful of her. She hadn't even seemed to believe her when Henrietta had assured her that she was fine.

Sure, she'd been struck on the arm. But the blow had glanced off. It had probably left a bruise, but it hadn't broken anything. And instead of striking her again, the intruder had run out of the apartment. Maybe her scream had scared him away.

Or her...

She couldn't be sure. Like she'd told the trooper, she'd seen only a shadow in dark clothes—no face, no figure...

She shivered again and rushed the last couple of steps to the firehouse. Because she usually arrived after someone else, she never had to unlock the door, so she automatically reached for the handle. But because it was so late, it should have been locked, so she gasped as the door opened, just as the exterior door of Trick's apartment building had earlier that evening.

Was that same someone inside the firehouse?

No. Braden might not have been contacted yet about Trick; he could be working late, as he often did. That was why she'd decided to come back to the firehouse, on the off chance that he might be here. But maybe it was Stanley, the kid who did odd jobs around the firehouse. A few weeks ago he'd been staying in the bunkroom. The former foster kid had no family of his own, and all of them treated him like a kid brother now.

She pulled open the door and stepped inside, calling out, "Stanley?"

Her voice echoed off the fire engines parked in every bay of the garage. But no other voice echoed hers.

And no bark. If Stanley was here, his dog, Annie—the firehouse mascot—would have been, too. The sheepdog/mastiff combination loved people too much not to have rushed to Henrietta to jump on her and lap at her face with her huge tongue.

No. Stanley wasn't here, but he might have forgotten to lock the door when he left earlier. He was a sweet kid and a hard worker, but he could be easily distracted.

And Annie, with all her puppy exuberance, was often a distraction.

"Braden?" she called out hopefully. She really needed to talk to her boss. Again only her own voice echoed back at her.

Braden was probably with Trick, and a pang of envy struck her heart as she wished she could be with him to make sure he was okay. The trooper had assured her that his pulse was strong and his breathing fine. He probably just had a concussion.

But concussions could be serious.

She should have refused to leave him. Despite the trooper's insistence on wanting them apart, Henrietta was determined to see him. She would just wait at the firehouse for a little while before going over to the hospital. He would have to be taken there.

And eventually the trooper would leave. It wasn't as if Trick was a suspect. Was Henrietta? Was that why the trooper had wanted to keep them apart?

She shivered again as the image of him lying on the floor passed through her mind. Blood had dampened his auburn hair from the wound where he'd been struck. He hadn't been able to deflect the blow like she had. And he must have been hit hard to lose consciousness.

The only way she should have left him was if the trooper had carried out her threat to arrest her. For what? For being a victim?

Henrietta certainly couldn't have hurt Trick. Sure, she'd been angry with him earlier. But she would never wish him harm—even if he had been hitting on Tammy. But he hadn't. He'd only been asking about Henrietta.

And about Greg.

Could Greg have had anything to do with the attempts on Trick's life? On hers?

They'd broken up a while ago, so it didn't make sense for him to act out now. But then, she hadn't been involved with anyone else since they'd broken up. Could he know about Trick? Could he have been following her? Could he have noticed how attracted she was to the new team member?

She was attracted to Trick—more so than she'd ever been to anyone else. Even Greg… Especially Greg.

She shook her head. No. It didn't make sense.

It was much more likely that Trick was the one with the enemy. With the exceptions of Luke and Owen, nobody else on the team liked him.

She wasn't sure that she liked him. Desired him, yes. But liked…

A smile tugged at her lips as she thought of some of their conversations, of his quick wit and wicked grin.

Yes, she liked him. Too much…

But other team members resented the hell out of him, mistrusted him and thought he was spying for Braden. Could one of them want him gone badly enough to try to kill him, though?

She shivered again as she considered it. That one of her team could be capable of trying to kill someone…

And that someone had nearly killed her as well, and had threatened her. Did they think her attraction to Trick was a betrayal?

Was that what the note meant?

The mistake she'd made.

Could it be a member of her team? They had all left the bar shortly after Trick had. Any of them could have followed him back to his apartment, or maybe even beaten him there, if they'd known where he might be going...

She didn't want to think it—didn't want to believe it. But if someone had sabotaged that bucket like Michaela had suggested, that person would most likely *have* to be a member of their team. How else would they have known that she and Trick would be using it the next day? How else would they have known how to sabotage it so that it wouldn't be noticed until it was already being operated?

The thought chilled her to the bone, making her shiver yet again. She'd left a jacket in her locker, so she headed up the stairs to the second story. The locker room was near the bathrooms and the bunkroom. As she passed the bunkroom, she glanced inside—just to see if anyone was using one of the beds.

A lot of the out-of-towners like Trent, Ethan and Rory crashed there when they were on call for a wildfire, like now. But the room was empty.

Where had they all gone after the bar? Where were they staying?

Were they avoiding the place because they suspected Trick might be staying there and they didn't want to room with him?

She shook her head now and sighed. With Dirk dying the tragic way he had, nobody who took his place would have been easily accepted. The team was all hurting too much over his sudden loss, but Braden had made the situation worse by bringing in his brother-in-law. Now they all felt as if their boss didn't trust them, as if he wanted an inside man on the team, and because of that, Trick would never be accepted.

Colder now, she hurried into the locker room—anxious to find her jacket. She flipped on the lights and illuminated the big space. Her and Michaela's lockers were in the same room as the guys'. Braden had offered to give them a separate space, but they'd said having their own bathroom was enough. They could share the locker room. And as they all treated each other like family, it wasn't a big deal. Or it hadn't been, until Trick had arrived.

She didn't even notice the other guys, but she was painfully aware of him. He wasn't like a brother to her and never would be.

Her locker was in the back of the room, so she had to pass the other rows of them on the way to hers. One of the locker doors stood open at an awkward angle, like it had been bent. Curious, she walked over to it and noticed the name scrawled on it across a piece of masking tape. Before reading the name, she knew whose locker it was. Everybody else had metal placards with their last names. Only Trick had the masking tape with McRooney jotted on it.

His metal placard hadn't arrived yet. Had Braden even ordered him one? Trick had a reputation for never staying long with a team. A hollow ache yawned inside her as she thought of him leaving, or getting hurt, like he was now.

As she moved closer to his locker, her foot struck something lying on the floor in front of it. She cursed at the sudden jolt of pain, and the clatter of metal as the crowbar rolled against the bottom of the lockers echoed her. Someone had used that to pry open the locker. What had they been looking for?

She peered inside and noticed his bloodied jeans spilling out of a duffel bag on the bottom. Even if the person had taken whatever they'd been looking for she would have no idea what was missing. But maybe they hadn't broken in to take something.

Another piece of masking tape, probably ripped from the end of the one with his name, held a sheet of paper against the open locker door. A note had been written with the same crude block letters on the one she'd received, and nearly the same message: *Next time you are going to die...*

What if he was already dying? The head wound could have been more serious than the trooper thought. Henrietta needed to go back to his apartment, or to the hospital…

But at the moment she couldn't do anything but stare at that note. The person who'd written it had been inside the firehouse, inside the locker room.

They must have come right here after attacking Trick and Henrietta. Maybe with that crowbar, which was probably what they had used to get inside Trick's apartment. Was the intruder gone now?

Or were they hiding somewhere inside the firehouse, like they'd hid in the shadows of the apartment, waiting to attack her again?

Then she heard it—the creak of a door and the sound of footsteps coming up the stairs. She was not alone.

HENRIETTA WAS ALONE. Here was the chance to finish what had been started at Trick's apartment when the female firefighter had warded off the blow and uttered that blood-curdling scream.

It had been so loud that someone had certainly heard it and probably called the police. Leaving had been the only option then to avoid being caught.

But now—here at the firehouse—there was the option to finish this with Henrietta Rowlins. Coming back here after the skirmish at Trick's place had been just to search his locker, to find what hadn't been found at his house.

The notes…

They weren't here either. So another one had been crudely scribbled out and taped to the locker, as a warning. As a message…

Maybe it was too late to send that message to Trick. He might already be dead. There hadn't been a chance to finish him off for sure before Henrietta had shown up there. And then she'd screamed like she had…

The note writer gripped the gun in gloved hands. No prints would be found on anything. Now to wait in the shadows for Henrietta…

Her coming here was more than an option to finish her off. It was a serendipitous opportunity…

To get rid of Henrietta Rowlins once and for all.

The gun had jammed earlier, when Trick had stepped inside his apartment. There had been a bullet stuck in the chamber. It had been cleared now, so it would fire properly. And Henrietta would not be able to ward off a bullet.

Chapter Sixteen

"You haven't changed a bit," a female voice remarked. The curtain around his stretcher opened just enough for a petite blonde to slip through. "Still doing whatever you can to get all the attention."

Trick chuckled, just like his sister probably wanted him to, but she was clearly the one who needed to laugh. There were dark circles beneath her blue eyes and worry lines in her usually smooth brow.

"Hey, it got you running over here," he said as he curved his lips into a grin.

His siblings had always been there for him. Hell, Mack would probably even surface from wherever he'd disappeared to if he knew Trick needed him. But Trick didn't want to admit that. He could handle his cowardly attacker on his own.

Or he would…once his head stopped pounding. First, he had to find Henrietta and make sure that she was really okay. So he tried swinging his legs over the edge of the stretcher, as he had earlier, but his vision began to blur yet again as oblivion threatened. Before he could fall back on the stretcher, small hands pushed him down.

"That's why I'm here," Sam said. "My husband called me so I could get my idiot brother under control."

If Braden hadn't arrived at the apartment when he had, Owen probably wouldn't have gotten Trick into the ambulance. Despite his pounding head, he'd been insisting that he was fine so he could go off and find Henrietta.

But Braden had insisted he get the X-rays Owen wanted him to have—to make sure there was no bleeding on his brain. There wasn't, and the cut on his head had been stitched up.

"I'm fine," Trick insisted.

"You have a concussion," Sam said. "But clearly it hasn't knocked any sense into you."

He sighed. "No, it hasn't…" If he had any sense, he wouldn't be so damn worried about a woman who clearly didn't give a damn about him. She'd just left him…bleeding on the floor. Clearly, she cared more about her career than she did him. She'd taken off before Braden had seen her at his place, with him.

"What's wrong?" Sam asked, all traces of humor slipping away to leave only her stark concern for him.

He touched his fingers to the stitches on his head. "I have a concussion, remember?"

She snorted. "You've had those before, and worse than this one seems to be since you're already conscious. What's really bothering you?"

"Besides the fact that someone's trying to kill me?" he asked.

"Oh, you're pissed about that," Sam said. "I am, too."

That was the McRooney thing—no matter how much they teased each other, they also defended and protected the hell out of each other from outsiders. That was why Trick had agreed to act as Braden's mole. He'd done it for his sister more than his brother-in-law because he knew anything that hurt Braden hurt her even more.

He didn't want his sister getting hurt any more than they'd already been when their mom had taken off all those years ago. That had been hardest on Sam—growing up without a mom as the only female in a house of men.

Sam reached out, and instead of smacking him like she usually did, she gently touched his cheek. "You're also upset about something…" She narrowed her eyes and studied his face. "About somebody…"

He shrugged and tried to look away from her scrutiny. But she moved her hand from his cheek to his chin and forced him to meet her gaze. She looked the most like their mother, with her petite build, blond hair and blue eyes, but she acted the most like their father. It was that ability to see right through people that made her such a damn good arson investigator.

"I'm not a suspect," Trick said. "Stop interrogating me."

Sam smiled slightly, but her eyes remained narrowed and her gaze focused fully on his face. "Stop hiding something from me."

"Hey, I'm not the brother who hides stuff," he insisted.

She nodded in agreement. "No, you're not. That's what makes this so weird. I expect Mack not to tell us stuff—even Rand keeps stuff to himself. But you never do."

"Are you saying I have a big mouth?"

She nodded. "Yes, usually you do. So spill."

He sighed again—in resignation—because he knew how damn relentless she could be. "But you can't tell Braden."

"I don't keep secrets from my husband," she said.

"You can tell your *husband*," he allowed. "But you can't tell the *superintendent* of the Huron Hotshots."

She sucked in a breath. "What did you do? Or should I ask *who*?"

Damn. She knew him too well, so well that heat rushed to his face.

She groaned. "I'm right."

"It's not like that," he said—even though it was exactly like that, or it had been the night before. "I just need to know if she's all right."

"Who?" she asked. "And why? What happened? What did you do?"

"Nothing," he insisted. "I just went to my apartment for some clothes when I walked in on the intruder."

She touched his head now. "And got blindsided."

That hadn't actually been the case. And Sam must have figured that out from his hesitation because she cursed. "You didn't get blindsided! You knew someone was in your place and went inside anyway! Damn you, Trick, you could have been killed."

He might have been—had that gun not jammed. But he wasn't about to share that with his sister. "I could have also caught the son of a bitch like my boss hired me to do."

"He doesn't want you risking your life anymore," she said.

Trick suspected that was another reason Braden had called Sam to the hospital. "Is he firing me?"

"I can only speak for my husband," she said, "not for the superintendent of the Huron Hotshots. You'll have to talk to him about that."

Panic pressed on Trick's heart. He didn't want to leave

the team—even though he hadn't really become part of it and probably never would be accepted as one of them.

"I will," Trick said, although he had no idea how he would convince Braden to keep him on the team, especially if his boss found out about him and Henrietta. He was reluctant to say too much to Sam, but he needed to know if the other Hotshot was really okay.

"Who do you want me to check on?" Sam asked him, as if she'd read his mind, or at least his face.

"Henrietta," he said.

She nodded, as if she'd already figured it out. And maybe she had. Tammy Ingles had picked up on his interest in the beautiful firefighter, so he wouldn't have been surprised if his sister had as well. Even as busy as she was, Sam knew him so well that it wouldn't have taken her long to see his attraction to Henrietta.

"I'm worried about her because she showed up at the apartment tonight," he said. "I think the intruder attacked her, too."

Sam sucked in a breath. "Was she brought to the hospital?"

He shook his head and flinched as pain reverberated throughout his skull. If not for this damn concussion, he would have already left the ER and gone to find Henrietta himself.

"So she must not have been badly hurt," Sam said, as if offering him reassurance.

He wasn't reassured. "I don't know why she left," he said, and a twinge of pain struck his heart now. "She may have just not wanted Braden to see her there."

Sam nodded. "Okay…"

"It's not like that," he said again. But his sister probably knew he was lying.

She didn't call him on it, though. Instead she re-marked, "You don't seem to know much about what happened with her. Did she leave before you regained consciousness?"

He sighed—an utterly ragged sigh. "Yes."

Sam nodded again, and her small jaw was tense, as if she was clenching her teeth.

"She left before Owen got there, too," he admitted. The paramedic had promised that he would check on Henrietta for him, but Trick hadn't seen him since Owen had pushed him through the doors of the ER. So now he was even more worried. Had she been hurt worse than she'd thought?

Where was she?

"She doesn't seem to care enough to make sure you're okay," Sam remarked, her voice sharp with disapproval. "So why do you give a damn about her?"

Heat rushed to his face again. Maybe he was a fool. "She's a team member," he said. "It's my job to care..."

"It's hers, too," Sam said.

"But I'm the one putting her in danger," Trick said. "It's me this person is after."

"Why are you so sure she's not the person?" Sam asked. "Even Braden thinks it's a member of the team—though he hopes it isn't."

"I think it is, too," Trick said. "But it's not her. She was with me both times that somebody shot at me. So it can't be her."

Sam sucked in a breath.

"But you can't tell the superintendent of the Huron Hotshots that she was at my place," he implored her, "or he might think something was going on between team members if he found out about that."

"The superintendent already has somebody on his team keeping secrets from him," she said, probably in reference to the note Braden had received. "He brought you on to find out who that is—not to keep secrets of your own from him."

Guilt formed a lump in Trick's throat, and he nodded. "I know..."

"Why would you worry more about someone who didn't even care enough to stick around until you regained consciousness than you do about keeping your promise to your brother-in-law?" she asked.

Trick swallowed down that guilt. "My promise was to investigate his team," he reminded his sister. "My investigation proves that Henrietta is not responsible. That's all I'm obligated to tell him."

Sam shook her head.

"Please," he pleaded with her. "Just find Henrietta and make sure she's really okay."

Sam clenched her jaw again, but finally, after a long hesitation, she nodded. Then she added the caveat, "But only if you'll stay here for observation like the doctor ordered."

"Sure," he said. But like when they'd been kids, he had crossed his fingers to belie the promise. He had no intention of staying in the hospital. Once his head stopped pounding and he could stand without falling on his face, he was getting the hell out of there.

HENRIETTA BRACED HERSELF for the attack, but she had no hope of warding it off. She staggered back under the onslaught, banging into the lockers behind her. Then a wet tongue slobbered across her face, and she grimaced.

"Annie!" she exclaimed as she petted the huge dog's

massive head before pushing her equally massive paw from her bruised shoulder.

"I'm sorry," Stanley said, panting for breath as the curly haired teenager joined them in the locker room. "She just took off running when I opened the door."

Henrietta breathed a sigh of relief and pressed a hand against her madly pounding heart. "She surprised me," she admitted. But it had been a good surprise—unlike the one at Trick's apartment, where she'd found him bleeding on the floor. "I thought you were gone..."

He bobbed his head in a quick nod. "Yeah, but I think I left my phone here." He glanced around the room and must have noticed the door to Trick's locker had been pried open. Color rushed into his face, and he looked away from her.

"I didn't do that," she assured him. "I came in and found it that way. Was it like that when you left earlier?"

He shook his head. "No." Then his brow furrowed. "I don't think so. I'm not sure if I came up here, though."

Stanley was sweet but so easily distracted.

She reached out and squeezed his skinny arm. "That's okay," she said, not wanting to worry him. But she had to know. "Was anyone else here when you left?"

His head bobbed another big nod that made his curls bounce. "Pretty much everybody but you..."

So maybe everybody else had been staying here. But where were they now?

She had an odd feeling, as if they weren't alone. And as if Annie felt it, too, she whined and looked toward the door.

Henrietta shivered.

"Why'd you come back?" Stanley asked. "Are you staying here tonight, too?"

She shook her head. "I—I came up here to get a coat from my locker, and I found Trick's like this…"

Stanley shook his head. "I'm sorry I didn't see anything." His lips pulled down into a frown. "I never see anything that can help…"

When the state trooper had been framing Luke, Stanley had wanted but had been unable to alibi him. The kid could not tell a lie.

"It's okay," Henrietta assured him again. "Let me help you find your phone." She pulled her new cell from her pocket to call his and realized she must have had her ringer turned off, because she'd missed a number of calls—from Owen. And her hand began to shake.

Had Owen been trying to call her about Trick? Maybe he'd had a paramedic shift tonight and had arrived at the apartment. Maybe he knew how Trick was really doing.

She shouldn't have listened to the trooper. After what Gingrich had done to Luke Garrison, she shouldn't have trusted Wynona Wells. She could only trust her team. Then she glanced again at Trick's pried-open locker and wondered. Should she trust her team? Or had one of them opened that door and stuck the note to it?

Had one of them hurt Trick tonight and tried to hurt her as well? They all seemed to think he was a spy, but which one of them was worried about Trick exposing their secret?

"Are you okay?" Stanley asked.

She nodded now. "Yeah, yeah…"

"Should we call the police?" Stanley asked.

"No!"

Stanley jumped, and his brown eyes went wide with shock. Even Annie barked.

"I—I just think we shouldn't do anything until we

find out what really happened," she said. "Maybe Trick forgot the combination and pried it open himself." She was not about to tell Stanley about the note. She didn't want to scare him. The former foster kid had already been through too much in his life when the Northern Lakes arsonist had tried to frame Stanley for his crimes.

"Is Trick here?" Stanley asked.

He should have been—probably would have been—had he not been hurt. She needed to call Owen and see if he could find out how badly Trick had been wounded. But she didn't want to make that call in front of Stanley.

"No," she said. "And we probably shouldn't be either…" She guided him toward the door. Annie rushed out ahead of them, bounding down the stairs as if she'd heard somebody moving around like she must have Henrietta.

Or maybe she just sensed when someone was close. Despite being untrained, the dog had some good instincts. She had once saved Stanley and another Hotshot's girlfriend from one of the arsonist's fires.

A chill chased down Henrietta's spine, making her shiver.

"You forgot your jacket," Stanley said.

"I'll be fine," she said. She wanted to get out of the firehouse, and she wanted Stanley out of there as well—in case the person who'd pried open the locker was still around. She quickly punched in the contact for Stanley to locate his phone. Music began to play faintly in the distance.

His face reddened, probably because it was show tunes playing out of his phone instead of rap or whatever else he might have considered cooler music. She smiled reassuringly at him.

"There you go. You must have left it downstairs near the trucks." And he probably would have found it already if Annie hadn't run up the steps to her.

She clicked off her phone and the music stopped, but Annie's barking would have drowned it out anyway. As they descended the steps to the garage level, Henrietta saw the dog scratching at the service door Stanley must have closed behind them.

"She wants out," she said.

Stanley ignored the dog to grab up his phone. "Thanks for helping me find it," he said. Then he asked, "Should I call Braden about the locker?"

"Let me talk to Trick first," she said, yearning to talk to him, to see him, to make sure he was all right. She needed to call Owen and find out if Trick was still at the hospital. She needed to see him ASAP. "Maybe there's nothing to tell Braden and no reason to get him involved."

Stanley nodded again. "Yeah, he's already got a lot on his mind."

She wasn't sure to what the kid referred. Dirk's death? Owen's and Luke's and now Trick's near misses? The Hotshot superintendent certainly had a lot of things that could have been weighing on him.

She didn't want to add to that, but she had wanted to talk to him about the shootings and the note she'd received, and now the one she had found threatening Trick. After Trooper Wells had forced Henrietta to leave Trick's place, Hank didn't like, let alone trust, the female trooper.

Because she could tell Stanley was worried, she cupped his shoulder and reassured him. "Everything will be fine." And she hoped she was telling the truth.

He didn't look any more convinced than she was. He just shrugged and moved toward the door and his dog. When he pushed it open, Annie ran out into the darkness.

Stanley started running after her.

"Wait!" Henrietta called after them both—worried about what or whom the dog was chasing now.

A killer?

She had no more than considered it when a shot rang out and a bullet struck the wall of the firehouse next to her head. She ducked down and screamed just as more shots rang out. And she could only hope that none of those bullets had struck sweet Stanley or his dog.

BRADEN WAS STILL with Trooper Wells at Trick's apartment when she got the call. "Shots fired?" he asked, his heart pumping fast and furiously with fear. "Where?"

She sounded almost sympathetic when she murmured, "The firehouse."

Braden groaned with despair. Some members of the team were probably staying there while they waited to see if they were called to fight the wildfire out West.

"Was anyone hurt?" he asked. Like Trick had been hurt tonight.

Fortunately he hadn't been shot.

But he had a feeling, as the trooper hesitated to answer him, that someone had been shot—someone Braden cared about.

"Who?" he demanded to know. "Who was hurt?"

Chapter Seventeen

"You stubborn son of a bitch," Owen grumbled as he drove toward the firehouse.

He was more right than he knew. But Trick had always kept his feelings about his mother from everyone else—even from his family. They had enough of their own stuff to deal with without handling any of his.

He shouldn't have asked Sam to help him tonight— shouldn't have put her out there, potentially in danger. But he was worried—with good reason—about Henrietta.

"I did not need to stay in the hospital," Trick assured his friend.

"That's not what the doctor thinks," Owen reminded him.

"He's being overly cautious," Trick said. "I'm fine. I've taken harder hits than that before and never had any issues—just ask my sister. She was probably the one who delivered them." Sam was freakishly strong. So he shouldn't have been too concerned about sending her to find Henrietta—except that he had not heard from her either.

"That's the problem," Owen said. "You've had concussions before. That puts you in even more danger of complications from this one."

This one hadn't been quite as bad as some of the others. He only wished he'd regained consciousness sooner. But it had still been faster than that time he'd been drugged. While he had been protecting Owen, Dirk Brown's widow had snuck something into his coffee at the café. He was lucky she hadn't killed him like she had her husband, and like she'd tried to kill Owen.

She was dead now, and her real accomplice was behind bars, so they had nothing to do with the attempts on Trick's life. It had to be someone else—someone on the team…

"My complications have nothing to do with my head," Trick said. And everything to do with another organ he tried even harder to protect: his heart.

"Your complications have to do with how damn stubborn you are," Owen remarked as he peered through the windshield into the darkness the headlamps on his truck barely penetrated.

Once his head had stopped pounding so hard that he'd thought his skull was going to burst, he'd managed to get off the gurney without passing out. And he'd been about to call a cab when Owen had shown up.

With bad news…

"Why isn't she answering her cell?" he murmured to himself.

"You're sure she replaced it?" Owen asked.

"She had to," Trick said. "Braden requires us all to carry cells."

Owen snorted. "Like you follow every rule of the boss's…"

He hadn't. But he wished like hell now that he had—

that he hadn't gotten Henrietta caught up in the danger surrounding him.

Frustration gnawed at Trick, sharpening his temper and his voice when he replied, "Don't tell me you're like the others and think I can get away with anything I want just because I'm the boss's brother-in-law."

Owen snorted again. "I know Braden better than that. I know it won't matter to him that you're his brother-in-law."

Because Owen had guessed, like Luke had, why Trick had really joined the team. And it hadn't been just to fill an empty spot. His main concern now was to make sure another spot on the team did not open up.

Henrietta's spot.

Owen's cell vibrated from its place in the console between their seats. He breathed a sigh of relief. "That's probably her now, calling me back."

But when he pressed the accept button and the call linked up to the Bluetooth in the truck, it was Braden's voice that emanated from the speakers.

"Did you get called to the firehouse?" he asked, his voice gruff with emotion.

"I—I finished up my shift," Owen said.

Trick snorted now. He suspected Owen had called someone in to take over for him so that he could babysit Trick for all the signs of complications of his concussion that the doctor had warned him about.

"Why?" Owen asked. "What's going on?"

"I'm on my way to the firehouse," Braden said. "There's been another shooting there. Trooper Wells is heading there now, too."

"Anybody hurt?" Owen immediately asked.

"I don't know," Braden said with a heavy sigh. "She

was acting weird and wouldn't answer me right away when I asked that. Then she admitted that the same person who called to report the shooting is the one who reported the attack on Trick earlier tonight."

Fear jabbed Trick's heart. Henrietta…

She'd been shot at; he just knew it. This person—whoever it was—wasn't just after him anymore. He was after Henrietta, too. What the hell was going on?

Braden echoed the question. "What the hell's going on, Owen?"

"Why do you think I know?" Owen asked defensively.

"Because you and Luke are the only ones who've actually befriended Trick since he's joined the team."

Trick flinched as if Braden's words had struck him. But it was the truth. Nobody else liked him. That was probably as much his fault as theirs, though. He had a tendency to be extra cocky when someone didn't like him. But that didn't excuse someone trying to kill him.

Or Henrietta…

"Owen doesn't know anything," Trick said, defending one of his few friends.

Braden's curse echoed from the speakers now. "You better be talking to me from your bed at the ER."

"I'm in Owen's truck, and we're on our way to the firehouse," Trick said—because he knew that even though the paramedic wasn't on duty any longer, there was no way he'd be able to stay away if he thought a team member needed him.

The shooter must have fixed that damn gun. Trick cursed now as he thought of the opportunity he'd missed. He'd been so close to catching the person, so close to ending all of this danger.

"I was wrong," Braden said. "You're not his friend, Owen, if you couldn't keep him in the hospital."

"Have you met him?" Owen asked. "He was leaving with or without me. I figured if I left with him I could keep him from falling on his face."

"I'm fine," Trick insisted. But he wasn't—he was a wreck worrying about what had happened to Henrietta earlier tonight at his apartment and now, if she'd been at the firehouse. He suspected she had been, or there wouldn't have been another shooting.

"What did you do to your sister?" Braden asked with sudden urgency in his voice. "She was supposed to talk some sense into you."

He tensed as he realized that Sam might have been with Henrietta when the shooting occurred, if she'd found her like he'd asked her to do. A groan slipped through his lips.

"What?" Braden asked. "What did you do?"

He groaned again before admitting, "I asked her to find someone for me…"

Braden sucked in a breath before he even asked the name. He must have already guessed. "Hank," he said, then swore again as he realized what Trick already had—that Sam could have been at the firehouse, too.

Guilt pressed heavily on Trick's chest, making it hard for him to draw a deep breath. His sister was tough, though. She was all right. She had to be.

"Hurry," he said, urging Owen to drive faster. He was tempted to straddle the console and push down on the accelerator himself. But the paramedic was already speeding, so much that the tires squealed as he turned the corner onto Main Street. As he neared the firehouse, he had to slam on the brakes to stop before he collided with one of the state police vehicles blocking the street.

Before Owen put the truck into Park, Trick pushed open the passenger's door and jumped out onto the street. His legs shook slightly beneath his weight—either with fear for his sister and Henrietta or because of the concussion. He held on to the door for a moment to steady himself, and as he did, Braden rushed past him. His brother-in-law must have parked elsewhere on the street.

He rallied and raced after Braden, but both of them had to stop at the door, at which a trooper stood guard. "This is my firehouse," Braden told him. "You need to let me in."

"This is Northern Lakes firehouse," Trooper Wells corrected him as she walked up behind her fellow law officer. "You just operate out of it."

"I'm the superintendent," Braden said. "I'm responsible for the house and the firefighters. So I need to know if everyone's all right."

"You didn't need to bring a paramedic," she said as Owen joined them at the door. "Maybe a vet…"

"Annie," Braden murmured. "Was she hurt? Was Stanley?"

Trick knew that if that dog had been hurt, the kid would be devastated, whether or not he'd been struck with a bullet as well. The dog must have heard her name being called, though, because she pushed past the female trooper, nearly knocking her over as she bounded up to Braden. She jumped up, planting her paws on his shoulders. Usually the boss pushed her down, but instead he gripped her furry head in his hands and stared at her. "You all right, big girl?"

"She probably saved my life," a familiar voice remarked as Henrietta stepped out of the firehouse door. Like the dog, she nearly knocked the smaller woman aside. "She went after the shooter, so he only got off a couple of shots."

"She was a hero again," Stanley chimed in. He'd slipped out with Henrietta as if she'd been holding on to him.

She squeezed his arm now. "Yes, she was. You really shouldn't have run after her, though."

"Are you okay?" Braden asked them all.

Stanley gave one of his vigorous nods.

Henrietta forced a smile. "Yes, I'm fine. The bullets didn't come close."

Trick didn't know her well, at least not as well as he would have liked to, but he could tell she was lying. And the splintered jamb of the service door provided confirmation of her lie.

"And once again," Trooper Wells said, her voice gruff with frustration, "nobody saw anything." She obviously didn't believe them.

"Were you the only ones here?" Braden asked.

Stanley bobbed his head again. "Just me and Hank and Annie."

Braden opened his mouth, then closed it before saying anything more. Sam wasn't here, so he probably didn't think there was any point in mentioning her name.

While Trick didn't want his sister in danger, he wished she had been here. The super-observant arson investigator might have actually seen something—or someone—so this crazed shooter could get caught.

"I asked what they were doing here at this late hour," the trooper remarked. "One was retrieving a phone and the other a jacket." She looked at Henrietta with suspicion. "Yet she isn't wearing one."

"She was going to get it," Stanley said in defense of the female Hotshot. But Henrietta sent him a pointed glance.

It was too late, though. The trooper followed up his remark with a question. "And what stopped her?"

"Stanley can't speak for me," Henrietta said. "And I already told you. I changed my mind and just wanted to head home. And unless you are going to follow through on your threats to bring me into custody, I will be leaving now."

"You've threatened to arrest her?" Trick asked the trooper. Was that why she'd left the apartment earlier? "For what? She can't be shooting at herself, can she?"

Wells glared at him, clearly not happy with him basically calling her an idiot. But fury coursed through him. "You're no better than Gingrich, are you?"

And now the trooper sucked in a breath.

Trick wondered if he'd been right to be suspicious of all the troopers. Just as Gingrich had tried to carry out what Dirk's wife had started, could Wells be carrying out Gingrich's agenda—to take down the Hotshots?

Braden must have considered the same thing but dismissed it because he said, "She and I were still at your apartment when this shooting occurred."

So she couldn't have done it. Unless she was working with someone else…like one of the Hotshots.

"Why are you here?" Henrietta asked him. "Why aren't you in the hospital?"

"Because he insisted on leaving," Owen said, "against doctor's orders. He's supposed to stay overnight for observation for his concussion."

"You need to bring him back," Henrietta said—as if she actually cared.

His heart moved with hope that she did. But would it matter? They had no future together. Unless they caught the shooter soon, neither of them might have a future— together or apart.

ALL THE WAY back to her apartment, the vehicle followed behind her. Every time she glanced into the rearview mirror, it was there—its lights burning brightly through the darkness. Its presence should have reassured her; it was actually a state police trooper, ostensibly for her protection. But she wondered if that was really the case.

Was she a suspect?

Trooper Wells certainly treated her like a criminal every time that they met. The woman was smart, though, so she obviously knew that Henrietta wasn't telling her everything. For instance, she hadn't told her about what she had found in the locker room—about the note to Trick.

She wanted to tell him about it. She wanted to be with him. But he'd needed first to heed his doctor's orders and return to the hospital. Hopefully Owen and Braden had talked him into going back for observation. To make sure he had no complications…

Since coming to Northern Lakes, his life had gotten complicated while he'd helped Owen and Luke, and then with the boom truck incident, and now the shootings. And was that note she'd found his first, or had he received others?

She needed to talk to him. But she hadn't wanted to do that in front of the trooper or her coworker and boss. She would ask him once he'd rested and recuperated from his head injury. And once she got some sleep.

But when she pulled up on the street next to the firehouse where she and Michaela worked, lights burned in the windows of the second floor. She wouldn't be able to sneak in and head to her bed. Michaela obviously wanted to talk.

Once upstairs, she found that Michaela was not alone. The woman with her could have been her sister. Sam McRooney-Zimmer certainly looked more like Michaela than she did her brother. But Henrietta hadn't realized the two women were even friends.

"You have a visitor," Michaela said as she yawned into her hand. "And I have my bed waiting for me."

Henrietta had worried about Michaela lecturing her again. But apparently her roommate wasn't the one she'd needed to worry about. Michaela's bedroom door clicked shut behind her as she left Henrietta alone with Trick's sister.

She'd talked to Sam before—while the woman had been investigating the fires and at Hotshot events she'd attended since with her husband. While they'd always been friendly with each other, they weren't friends.

Sam didn't look as if she'd come here to change that either. Her blue eyes were quite cold as she stared at Henrietta. "So you are okay," she said. "My brother had no reason to worry about you."

Henrietta shivered as she remembered the shooting at the firehouse. He'd had reason to worry, but she would let Braden tell his wife about that. "Trick was worried." It wasn't a question. She'd seen the concern on his handsome face when he'd shown up at the firehouse—the concern and the pain. Hopefully he'd returned to the hospital.

"Were you worried about him?" Sam asked.

"Of course," Henrietta replied. She was still worried about him.

"Then why'd you take off before he even regained consciousness?" Sam asked, and the coldness was in her voice as well as her eyes now.

Henrietta shivered again. She really should have retrieved that jacket from her locker. "I wasn't given a choice," she said. "Trooper Wells ordered me to leave once she'd taken my statement."

Sam wrinkled her nose as if she didn't believe her. "And if you had been given a choice…?"

"Of course I would have stayed," Henrietta said, but then heat rushed to her face. Nobody was supposed to know about them, but especially not the boss. And telling this woman would be just like telling Braden. "Because he's a team member, and he's hurt."

"He was hurt that you left," Sam said. "And if you were just a team member, I don't think it would have bothered him that you'd abandoned him."

"I didn't abandon him," Henrietta said, even though guilt weighed heavily on her that she hadn't fought harder to stay.

"I'm sure he didn't see it that way," Sam said, "after our mother did the same damn thing to us when we were little kids."

The McRooney family was legendary for their father being the most esteemed trainer of smoke jumpers and for raising his kids on his own. Henrietta hadn't realized that was because their mother had left; she'd thought the woman was dead.

"I'm sorry," she said. "I didn't know…"

"That's why Trick is the way he is," Sam said. "Why he always leaves first—so he's not the one left."

"I—I don't know why you're telling me this," Henrietta said. And she wished that Sam hadn't shared that with her. She didn't want to know Trick better, didn't want to understand him, because that only made her want him more. And she already wanted him too much.

Sam shrugged. "I don't either. It's obvious you don't care about him."

Henrietta sucked in a breath, and tears stung her eyes. They were probably just tears of exhaustion or frustration or anger. Because anger shot through her now, and she found herself saying, "It's none of your business what I feel for your brother."

"You're right," Sam readily agreed. "But it is his. And he doesn't need to get hurt worse than he already is."

"I agree," Henrietta said. "But I'm not the one hurting him. You should be looking for the person who's been shooting at him. Not me."

Sam nodded. "You're right again. But once that person's caught, Trick will probably leave again…like he always does." And sadness dimmed the brightness of her blue eyes. "It's too bad. I was hoping that once he came to Northern Lakes, he might find a reason to stay."

Did she think Henrietta could have been that reason? "You just said that he always leaves first," she reminded his sister. "Do you really think he's going to change?" The question wasn't rhetorical. She really wanted to know the answer.

But Sam left without replying.

And Henrietta knew that he wouldn't.

THAT DAMN DOG!

If not for it charging out of the firehouse, Henrietta Rowlins would have died. The bullet had come so close to the target—so close to killing her. But then the dog had rushed forward, getting so damn close. It should have been shot. But it had been moving too fast, and the sound of the gunshots hadn't stopped it.

The shooter had had to run…so the dog wouldn't stop them. All those years of training in how to shoot… and yet nobody, not even the damn dog, had been hit…

But it was much easier to shoot targets than people. People moved. They ducked. They ran.

Or they fought back.

There had to be an easier and more effective way to get rid of Henrietta and Trick McRooney for good. A way that could not miss—because they both had to die, and the sooner the better…

Chapter Eighteen

Trick studied the bent door to his locker. He hadn't noticed it the night before—not in all the excitement of yet another shooting. After Henrietta had left, and the rush of adrenaline had drained from him, he'd barely made it up the steps to the bunkroom—let alone the locker room.

Owen had insisted on babysitting him throughout the night, which had meant he'd woken him up every hour or so to blind him with a light burning into his eyeballs. Even now, hours later, black spots fluttered in and out of his field of vision. But he could still see that the door had been forced open, and inside someone had stashed the crowbar that must have been used to do it.

Henrietta?

Had she come back here to go through his stuff?

He peered inside and cataloged the contents. Nothing was missing. The only difference was the addition of the crowbar. But then he pushed the door all the way open, against the lockers next to it, and he noticed the thin scrap of masking tape stuck to the inside of the door. Something had been taped up there.

A note...

Another damn, cowardly note.

He doubted Henrietta had left him one of those, that she'd left him any of those. But had she taken this one?

Or had she stumbled upon the note writer as they'd been leaving this one?

It had to be someone with whom he worked—a member of the team he'd been brought here to investigate. Which one? They were all in town now—since they were on call—so it could have been any of them.

And what had happened to the note?

Had the writer taken it with him when Henrietta had walked in, or did she have it?

His gut clenched with worry. He didn't want her getting any more involved than she already was. She'd barely escaped injury too many times because of him.

She was fine, though. He'd seen her last night, and although she'd seemed shaken by another near miss, she hadn't been hurt. And a trooper had followed her back to her place for protection.

She was safe.

Safer without him than with him.

He flinched over the pang in his chest at that thought. He missed her. His body missed hers so much that it ached. He ached.

"What are you doing here?" a deep voice asked.

Trick turned away from his locker to focus on his brother-in-law. "I work here."

Braden tensed but didn't say anything.

And Trick was compelled to ask, "Don't I?"

Sam had acted strangely the night before—like Braden had come to a decision about Trick's special assignment. Had he decided to end it?

"I don't think bringing you in was a good idea," Braden admitted, his voice heavy with regret and guilt.

"I wasn't sure either," he shared. He wasn't like Sam; he wasn't an investigator, and he'd made that clear to them both. "But I must be getting close or someone wouldn't be trying to take me out."

"It's the trying to take you out thing that I don't like," Braden said. "I didn't want to put you in danger."

"We're dealing with a dangerous person," Trick said. "So it was going to happen whether we wanted it to or not." What he didn't like was that Henrietta had been drawn into the danger as well. But that was his fault, not Braden's.

He didn't want to add to his brother-in-law's guilt. Nor did he want to admit to how involved he'd become with his fellow Hotshot. He didn't want to get her in trouble with their boss—didn't want to put her job in jeopardy any more than he already had her life.

"Maybe it's time we brought in the police," Braden said, "that we told them everything."

Trick shook his head. "I don't think that's a good idea…" Not when he was so close.

"Trooper Wells already suspects we're keeping stuff from her," Braden said. "That's why she's being so tough on you and Hank."

"You think you can trust her?"

"She's not Gingrich," Braden said.

"No, she's not. But he trained her," Trick reminded him. "And even if she's not like Marty, she's still trying to make a name for herself. She could bring in the press. Then you'll lose your job for sure."

Braden flinched. "I'd rather lose my job than lose another member of my team."

"Dirk's death had nothing to do with whoever's been

sabotaging the equipment. That was a domestic situation you knew nothing about."

"Exactly, and a good man lost his life because he didn't share what was going on with anybody else on the team," Braden said. "Maybe it's time to quit the secrets." He stared at Trick now—as if he knew that Trooper Wells wasn't the only one Trick hadn't been completely honest with.

Trick shook his head. "We're too close now. We've just got to ride this out."

"You may not survive this assignment," Braden told him. "This maniac has gotten too close to taking you out."

Trick grimaced at the dull pounding in his head. "I've been through worse," he insisted. But he wasn't being completely honest about that either.

This was different because he wasn't worried just about himself. He was worried about Henrietta, too. He needed to talk to her—needed to find out if she'd taken anything out of his locker, like another threatening note.

Maybe she'd even seen who might have pried open his locker to put the note inside it. That put her in more danger.

A trooper had followed her home last night, but had he stayed outside her apartment to protect her? Or was the shooter out there now, waiting for another opportunity to take her out?

"Even Sam's worried about you now," Braden said, "and she knows you better than anyone else does."

Trick tensed—because he knew his brother-in-law was right. Nobody knew him like Sam did. But because of that, he suspected she wasn't just worried about him getting physically hurt. She was worried about him getting emotionally hurt as well—by another woman like their mother, one who didn't care about others.

Like Henrietta obviously didn't care about him—even after that powerful experience they'd shared. But maybe it had only been powerful for him.

He shrugged off his sister's concern. "There will be no reason to worry once we catch this bastard."

Braden smiled at the thought. But then he admitted, "Maybe that's what she's worried about—that you'll leave once we catch him."

"That's always been the plan," Trick reminded him. "I'm just filling in here. I'm not staying."

He hadn't heard anything, so he had no reason to look toward the doorway. Except that he'd felt it, that sudden tingling awareness…

And sure enough, when he looked around his brother-in-law, he saw her standing there.

Henrietta…

HE WASN'T GOING to stay. She'd already known that, of course. But hearing him confirm it caused a strange feeling of panic to press on her heart, squeezing it so tightly it seemed to miss a beat.

Or maybe that was just because he'd looked at her—in that way that seemed to see right inside her soul. He'd gazed at her like that last night, but he'd seemed so exhausted, so wounded.

He didn't appear much better today. Dark circles still rimmed his green eyes, and his hair was mussed and nearly standing on end like he'd been running his hands through it or he'd just rolled out of bed.

Maybe both.

"Hey, Hank," Braden said as he turned and noticed

her, too, probably because of the way Trick had been staring at her. "Are you okay?"

"Yes," she said. But she wasn't—not with Trick staring at her, staring inside her. She felt more vulnerable than she could ever remember feeling before. And she didn't like it. "Or I will be once Trooper Wells calls off the guy she has following me around..."

"Are you sure it's a trooper?" Trick anxiously asked.

"Yes. And I don't understand why he's following me."

"How can you say that—after last night?" Braden asked. "You were attacked and shot at. You're in danger."

She shook her head, and her thick braid slapped from one shoulder to the other. "I think I was just in the wrong place at the wrong time."

With the wrong person...

With a person who wasn't going to stick around anyway. She'd made a mistake the other night—when she'd slept with him. And she'd made a mistake going to see him last night.

But if she hadn't shown up when she had, would he be here? Or would his attacker have finished him off?

She shivered as she thought of it—of Trick dying. And she hated the thought of that much more than she hated the thought of his leaving.

"Why don't you go now?" she asked him. "Since you don't intend to stick around anyway?"

His brow furrowed for a moment, then he nodded. "I have to give Braden time to find my replacement, which would be hard now that the season's already getting started."

And they would probably be leaving soon to fight another wildfire. Usually the thought of dropping in somewhere, of battling a big blaze, filled her with excitement.

But now she felt only fear—not of the fire, but of fighting it with a team she couldn't entirely trust.

Because she'd found that note here in the firehouse, she believed it had to have been one of them who'd put it in his locker and probably on her truck as well. The block letters were too crudely similar to not have been written by the same person. Last night she'd intended to tell Braden everything, but now she wasn't sure that she should say anything to the boss until she had proof.

There was always a chance it was someone outside the team who knew them and their haunts, and she wasn't about to jump into planting suspicions about all her fellow Hotshots after what they'd been through in the recent past. The culprit alone deserved the blame, and she'd not point fingers until she was sure she was targeting the wrongdoer.

Which one of them might have crossed the line from resenting Trick to wanting to kill him? Ethan? Rory? Trent? Carl? They'd all been at the bar the night before… until Trick had left. And then they'd all curiously left as well. Why? To ambush him at his apartment? To come back here and pry open his locker?

"I'll get to work on finding someone else for Dirk's spot," Braden offered.

Trick flinched.

He obviously hadn't expected his brother-in-law to be so eager to replace him. But after the attempts on his life, he should have been relieved to leave Northern Lakes.

She would be relieved—that he was no longer in danger, and that he was no longer a danger to her. But a twinge passed through her heart, forcing her to admit that losing him would hurt, too.

Even though she'd never really had him.

"I'm glad you're both here," Braden said. "I've been wanting to talk to the two of you."

Now she felt a twinge of panic—that the boss had found out about them and was going to fire her. But if Trick was leaving anyway...

Nonetheless, she'd broken a rule, so she would have to face the consequences of her actions—of their actions—on her own. She braced herself.

But then Braden's phone rang and vibrated inside the pocket of his shirt. He pulled out his cell and murmured, "I need to take this..." And he walked off to do just that.

"Maybe that's your replacement now," Henrietta told Trick.

She'd expected him to grin and heave a sigh of relief. Instead his brow puckered as if the thought bothered him, as if he wasn't ready to leave yet.

But then he said, "Let's get out of here." And he wrapped his big hand around her arm.

A jolt of awareness shot from that contact all the way to her heart. She tugged her arm free of his grasp.

He must have thought she was going to argue with him because he continued, "You know we can't talk here, and we need to talk." He looked pointedly at his pried-open locker then.

He must have guessed what she'd found inside it. And he probably wouldn't have guessed if he hadn't already received other notes.

"Yes, we definitely need to talk," she agreed.

"But not here," he said. "And we can't go back to my place."

"Or mine," she said. Michaela might still be there, and after getting shot at, Henrietta wasn't willing to trust anyone. Not even her roommate.

"But I know a place," she said, even as her stomach churned at the thought of bringing Trick McRooney there since it was truly her home. "It's just a few streets over from here, on one of the little lakes just outside of town."

There were several little lakes in the area—thus the name Northern Lakes. Her grandfather had lived in a cottage on one of them. And even after his death, Henrietta hadn't been able to part with it. She had too many happy memories there. Weekly rentals during the summer paid all the expenses to keep it and then some.

But since it was still spring, she didn't have it rented yet.

"Can you drive?" she asked.

He nodded. "Yeah, I'm fine."

She gave him the address, but before she could start out of the locker room, he caught her arm again.

"Be careful," he told her. "Make sure you're not followed."

"You, too," she said. She knew Northern Lakes so well that it would be easy enough for her to lose the trooper and anyone else who might try following her. The last thing she wanted was to lead the shooter back to her grandfather's cottage—to her home.

WHO THE HELL did they think they were fooling? Driving separately—taking circuitous routes. It was clear they were meeting up—somewhere.

After thoroughly checking out Henrietta Rowlins, it wasn't difficult to figure out where she was going. So instead of trying to follow them and risk being caught—why not drive there first and wait as they both arrived?

This was good. It would be easier to kill them now—when they were together—easier to get rid of both of them.

Forever...

Chapter Nineteen

The brightly painted cottages stood close together between the winding road and the glistening lake. The
driveway was too short to fit both their vehicles, and
Henrietta had already pulled up beside the sunny yellow
cottage, so Trick parked his truck on the street.

If not for her SUV in the driveway, he might not have
believed this was the place where she'd meant to meet
him. She hadn't even been able to tolerate his hand on
her arm, so why would she want to be alone with him
in a beautiful setting like this?

The note…

She must have found one in his locker and wanted to
show it to him. He didn't need to see it to imagine what
it said—some menacing kind of new threat.

He pushed open the driver's door and stepped out.
As he started toward the cottage, his pulse quickened
with anticipation—not in reading the note, but in being
alone with Henrietta again. Not that they would be like
they'd been that night—in her bedroom. He couldn't risk
being distracted like that again, putting her in danger
and his heart there as well. He was leaving soon; it was
the smart thing to do, the safe thing, because he couldn't

get any more attached than he already was. He couldn't wind up like his dad.

"Hurry up," she said as she opened the door for him. "Get inside…" And she peered around the cottage, as if looking for the shooter. Or maybe for the trooper that Wells had assigned to her.

"We weren't followed," he assured her. He'd been so careful—*for* her. Now he needed to be careful *of* her.

But she didn't relax. She just stepped back and anxiously gestured for him to step in, and he realized it wasn't just the shooter she was worried about. She was worried about anybody seeing them.

The other cottages looked empty, though. They might not have been opened for the season yet. Once he walked across the threshold, she slammed the door shut behind him.

"Are we breaking and entering?" he asked. "Or are you just ashamed to be seen with me?"

"Anytime I'm with you I get shot at or somebody swings something at me," she said. "So it's safer for me if we're not seen together."

He flinched, but he couldn't argue with her. She was right. "You really weren't hurt last night?"

"You saw me at the firehouse," she said. "I didn't get shot."

"At my apartment," he said. "You didn't get attacked."

She flinched now and shrugged off his concern. "I was fine."

Doubtful, he snorted.

"You were unconscious," she said. "And whoever it was took off right away."

"Without trying to hurt you?" he asked, still skeptical.

She sighed. "Like I said, it's really not safe for me

when we're together. But I think I was in as much danger of being arrested as of being physically hurt. That's why I left. Trooper Wells threatened to arrest me if I didn't."

He shook his aching head. "Why would she do that?" Unless she was involved somehow…

"I don't think she wanted you and me to have a chance to compare notes and concoct a story for her."

He released a ragged sigh. "She's smarter than I thought." And if she'd been helping Marty, it explained how he'd nearly succeeded in framing Luke and killing him and Willow. "Maybe too smart…"

"She knows we've not been completely honest with her."

"We can't be," he said.

"You really don't think we can trust her?"

He shrugged. "I don't know. After what Gingrich pulled on Luke Garrison, I have my doubts. I also don't want the media getting wind of a story and descending on Northern Lakes. The last thing Braden needs is any publicity about what's been going on."

She studied his face in the glare of the sun shining through the windows that looked out over the lake. "You're worried about him."

He nodded. "His job's in danger."

"*You're* in danger," she said. And she pulled a slip of paper from the knapsack-like purse she carried slung over a shoulder. "I took that from your locker."

"And if you told Trooper Wells that, she'd think you put it there," he suspected. "Is that why you didn't mention it to her last night?"

"I wanted to show it to you first." Her brow furrowed. "But you haven't even looked at it."

"Since my arrival in Northern Lakes, it's not the first one I've received," he admitted.

She gasped. "You got more?"

He nodded.

"But not until you showed up here?"

He nodded again.

And she closed her eyes as if trying to hide her suspicion. But she must have come to the same realization that he had, the one he spoke aloud now. "It has to be a member of the team."

She shook her head. "They are like family to me..."

It was especially hard for her to believe that one of them would try to hurt him, let alone her. He found himself reaching out and closing his arms around her shoulders. "I'm sorry..."

"I want to blame you," she said. "I want to think this is all your fault—that you stirred everything up. But..." She reached up and locked her arms around his shoulders and clung to him. "But you've just stirred me up..."

He tensed and pulled back slightly so that he could study her face—her beautiful face. "What?"

Her mouth turned down at the corners with unhappiness. "I want you so badly..."

"And it makes you miserable," he surmised.

"It scares me," she said. "I'm not just risking my job hanging out with you. I'm risking my life, too." As if she'd come to her senses, she pulled away from him.

And he had to let her go. He knew he was a danger to her. But then she pulled another note from her knapsack purse. "I found this on my vehicle the morning after you and I..."

This note he read, shuddering at what the blocked letters spelled out. Someone definitely wanted her dead now, too. "I'm sorry," he said again. "I had one on my windshield that morning, but I didn't think to check yours."

"Why is someone threatening you?" she asked. "Why are they threatening me now? What is this all about?"

He wanted to tell her everything—wanted to admit Braden's reason for bringing him on to the team. But if he told her, she might tell someone else—someone who shouldn't be told, maybe even the person who was trying to hurt them.

He shrugged. "I don't know. Maybe somebody on the team really hates nepotism."

Amusement tugged up her lips but only into a slight smile. She was scared. And he hated that she'd been put in danger as well.

He lifted his hand to her face, cupping her cheek in his palm. "And they don't want you *hanging* out with me," he said. He drew in a deep breath, bracing himself to do the right thing even though his body ached with wanting to stay, with wanting to be with her. "So I should go…"

But he couldn't quite pull his hand away from her face, or from the silkiness of her skin. He wanted to lean down, to close the distance between them and brush his mouth across hers. With a groan burning the back of his throat, he jerked his hand away and forced himself to step back—toward that door.

If he kept staring at her, he wouldn't be able to leave, so he glanced around the cottage instead. The lakeside home was all tall windows and bright sun. The rest was warm knotty pine walls, floor and cabinets.

"Nice place," he murmured as he turned toward the door that opened on the street side. He closed his hand over the knob, but he hesitated before turning it. Then he drew in a deep breath and braced himself.

Before he could pull open the door, he heard a soft whisper. Just one word...

Stay...

HAD SHE SAID it aloud? She'd been shouting it inside her head, and it had echoed inside her madly pounding heart. But the word must have slipped out of her lips as well, or why would he have stopped? Or had he just read her mind, or her heart?

He turned back toward her, his body so tense it looked as though, despite all the muscle, it might snap. But when she said nothing—or nothing else—he turned back toward the door.

And the word slipped out again—this time loudly and clearly. "Stay!"

She'd already told him that she wanted him, but it was more than desire. She needed to be with him again— needed to feel alive in the exhilarating way he had made her feel. But more importantly, after finding him unconscious the night before, she needed to feel that he was alive and well.

"I want to," he said, his voice gruff with that desire. "I want you...so badly...but I don't want to put you in any more danger."

"We were careful," she said. "Nobody followed us. Nobody knows we're here."

"Where is here?" he asked as he glanced around the place.

She smiled. "Home."

He tensed. "Then the other Hotshots might look for you here."

She shook her head. "I don't think anybody knows that I kept it after my grandfather died." She'd always felt so safe here—with Grandpapa—that she couldn't believe she would ever face danger here.

Then Trick locked the door and started walking back toward her, and she realized that he was the danger, the greatest threat to her, in so many ways. But instead of turning and running away, she rushed toward him and threw her arms around his neck, clinging to him. His heart thudded in his chest, beating as fast and furiously as hers.

"Thank you for sharing this place with me," he said. "I know your grandfather meant a lot to you…"

"Grandpapa," she murmured wistfully. Tammy must have told him about her guardian.

"I'm sorry about your parents," he said. "About how that must have felt to be…"

"Orphaned," she said. "Not abandoned. They didn't choose to leave me."

He groaned. "Sam did find you last night. She told you…" His face flushed, and he looked down—as if he had any reason for shame.

She clasped his handsome face in her hands and tilted it up, so he had to meet her gaze. "I'm sorry for what your mother did…"

He shrugged. "I'm fine. I have my dad. My sister. My brothers. I'm lucky."

"You are," she said.

"I am," he reiterated as he moved, as if to sweep her up in his arms.

But she resisted. "No," she said.

And he tensed. "You've changed your mind?"

"Hell, no," she said with a laugh. "I just don't want

you falling on your face from trying to lift me. You have a concussion."

"And I'm fine," he said. As if to prove it, he moved again and easily swept her off her feet.

Too easily...

She knew better than to risk her heart on a man like Trick, a man who never stayed. But, at the moment, she had no control over her feelings—over her desire—for him. She wanted him so badly—she needed him so badly—that she wouldn't let herself think about his leaving.

Not yet...

She would deal with that later. And at least she would have this when she did—memories of the two of them together. She linked one arm around his broad shoulders and pointed her other toward the direction of one of the bedrooms.

This one had been hers, but a brass, queen-size bed had replaced her twin one with its pink canopy. Her grandfather had always called it her princess room. He'd known that even though Henrietta was as tough as a boy, she was still feminine. Not many other men had noticed that about her—until Trick.

He treated her like a princess, too, as he carried her through the door as if she weighed nothing. Instead of laying her on the bed, he set her on her feet. Then he kissed her—touching just her lips with his, softly, sensually...

She moaned as passion overwhelmed her, as he overwhelmed her. And she reached out, tugging at his clothes, trying to undress him. She needed skin against skin. She needed to be with him, needed him inside her, filling that hollow spot that ached for him.

But he stepped back, and then he began to undress her. And even though his hands shook, he took his time, and every inch of skin he exposed he kissed as softly and sensually as he had her lips.

She moaned against the onslaught of passion, the ache of desire. Tears stung her eyes as frustration gnawed at her. She needed that release—that powerful release—that he'd given her, or she felt as if she might snap in two now. Her legs trembled beneath her, threatening to fold, and as if he felt it, he lifted her again. This time he laid her down on the bed, but when she tried to tug him with her, he pulled back.

He shed the last of his clothes and grabbed a condom packet before joining her. Skin slid over skin now as they rolled across the bed, their mouths fused together—their hands stroking.

She pushed him onto his back and skimmed her mouth from his lips down his throat to his muscular chest. But before she could move her head lower, he caught her and pulled her back up.

His green eyes were dark, totally dilated with desire. "I want you so damn badly."

She took the condom from his hand then and tore it open with her teeth. Then she sheathed his pulsating erection.

And he groaned, his teeth gritted. "So damn badly…"

Then she guided him inside her. His hands locked around her hips, but he didn't lift her off him. Instead he helped her move.

But she needed no assistance to find what felt best—for both of them. To find the rhythm…

His hands slid from her hips up her torso to her

breasts. As she moved, he cupped the mounds in his palms and stroked his thumbs over her sensitive nipples.

She came a little, moaning at the sensation, even while the tension built more with each stroke of him inside her. He touched her so deeply, filling her completely.

She leaned down and kissed his lips. Their mouths clung together, their tongues mating like he moved inside her, driving deeper and deeper.

Making her fall harder and harder...

Finally the tension broke as she began to come over and over again. She screamed his name at the power of the orgasm, of the connection between them.

Then he clutched her hips again, moving her as he drove deep before his body shuddered beneath hers. And he cried out as pleasure overwhelmed him.

She dropped down onto his chest, her body limp against his. And her head automatically went into the nook between his head and his massive shoulder, as if it had been made for her. As if he had been made for her.

But he wasn't hers to keep. He wasn't anyone's for keeps.

WHERE THE HELL had they gone?

Braden had slipped away for only a few minutes to take that call from Sam. But when he returned, they weren't around. And he suspected that, even though both their vehicles were missing, they had left together.

What the hell was going on between them? Or was it better that he didn't know for certain? Not that he cared all that much about their breaking one of his rules. What he cared about was the fact that their lives were in danger...

And they'd gone off somewhere alone—where he

couldn't protect them from the threat to their lives. But he wondered if that was the only threat they faced, or if they had another—a threat to their hearts.

Chapter Twenty

Trick awoke with a start to darkness. At first, he didn't know where he was, until Henrietta murmured against his shoulder. Then he knew…he was where he belonged.

No. That was silly. He'd never belonged anywhere. He didn't want to belong. He wanted to leave.

Usually…

But lying here, with her, felt so damn right—felt like home in a way no place had since his mother had taken off on them all those years ago. This was Henrietta's home; that was what she'd called it. And he was humbled that she'd brought him here. He could tell it meant a lot to her—that her grandpapa had meant a lot to her.

She shifted against his shoulder and murmured again. "We fell asleep…"

After what they'd done—and how many times they'd done it over the past few hours—he wasn't really surprised. Except that he shouldn't have fallen asleep, not with the danger they were in. But he'd felt safe here—with her—which should have scared him even more.

"You said nobody could find us here," he reminded her. And fortunately, nobody had, since she must have fallen asleep like he had. How long had they been out? It was so dark…until something clicked, and a small circle of light glowed from the bedside lamp she must have turned on.

A phone buzzed, vibrating against the floorboards from beneath the pile of clothes they'd discarded. That must have been what had awakened him.

Henrietta groaned. "We need to answer that. We might have gotten called out to that fire."

Trick cursed. He'd forgotten about that. His special assignment had taken his focus from what had always mattered most to him: fighting fire. No. It wasn't his special assignment that had done that; it was Henrietta.

She slipped naked from the bed and every thought slipped from his head as his body reacted with need. Despite how many times they'd made love—how many releases he'd had—he wanted her again.

He needed her.

She bent down and rummaged through the pile of clothes before pulling out a cell. "It's yours," she said as she walked to the bed and extended it to him.

Instead of reaching for it, he reached for her, pulling her down on top of him. Her skin was so silky, her flesh so warm and now flushed with desire. She wanted him just as badly as he wanted her. He could feel her heart thudding against his chest, feel the tightness of her nipples rubbing against his skin.

A gasp of pleasure escaped her lips, but she shook her head. "It's the boss."

Trick cursed again. The last thing he wanted to do right now was rush off to fight a fire. He'd rather do Henrietta. But he'd come here not just as a favor to his brother-in-law, but also to fill a hole on the Hotshot team. He had to do his job. Both of his jobs…

So he took the phone from her and clicked the accept button. "McRooney here…"

"Where the hell is here?" Braden asked.

He was not about to tell his boss that. "Close," Trick said. "Have we been called up to that fire?"

"Not yet…"

"Then why are you calling me?" Trick asked. "Did you find my replacement already?" He doubted it, but he felt a pang of regret—of loss—over the thought of leaving.

Usually he couldn't wait to move on from a team to the next. To the next location. The next adventure…

But he'd found more excitement in Northern Lakes than he'd ever experienced before. More than he'd wanted. He'd also found something else that he hadn't been looking for, that he hadn't believed he wanted…

Henrietta…

And whatever this powerful feeling was between them, this attraction, this passion, this pleasure…

He didn't want to give it up. Not now. Not yet…

"No," Braden said. "I didn't find your replacement. But I'm worried about you. You have a head injury."

"I'm fine." And he was today. Last night he'd thought his skull had been shattered, but today it hadn't even pounded. Much…

"I'm not sure you should go if we get called out," Braden said. "I'll have to make sure you're medically cleared."

"I'm fine," Trick insisted. He wasn't going to let down the team—even though they obviously hated him. But at least on that last wildfire out West they had worked with him, however begrudgingly.

"I'm not sure you'd be safe," Braden admitted.

Trick realized they weren't talking about his medical condition anymore.

Henrietta tensed against him, and it was clear she'd overheard enough of the conversation to come to the same conclusion.

"I might be safer at the fire," Trick said. "We'll all be together. Harder to try for me then."

"Or easier to make it look like an accident," Braden suggested.

"They're not trying to make it look like an accident now," Trick reminded him. Not with the shootings, with the attack at his apartment…

He didn't even want to think about what his stalker might try next.

"Fire," Braden murmured in a strange-sounding voice.

And despite the heat of Henrietta's body lying atop his, Trick shivered. "What? We *are* being called up?"

"No," Braden said. "I just have a feeling…"

Braden Zimmer was legendary for those feelings— for that strange premonition he seemed to get when a fire was about to start.

"Then we're probably going to get called up soon," Trick remarked. "That's probably what you're feeling…" But he had an odd sensation of his own now. He'd just been wondering what the stalker might try next.

Arson?

Not Henrietta's little cottage. It clearly meant too much to her—so much that she hadn't parted with it even after her grandfather's death. They needed to get out of here.

Now.

"I'll head back to the firehouse," Trick said.

"It's getting late. And you won't be alone there,"

Braden murmured. "Come back to the house. Sam's worried about you, too."

Trick suspected his sister wasn't just worried about his safety. He'd revealed his vulnerability to her the night before—when he'd asked her to find Henrietta. She knew he was getting in deeper than he ever had in the past, that he was risking more than he ever had.

Not his life. He willingly put that on the line all the time.

This was his heart that was in jeopardy—because of Henrietta.

And because of that, he needed to stay away from her—not spend more time with her. He just kept getting in deeper and deeper and putting her in more and more danger.

He had to leave her before his stalker found them together. "Okay," he told Braden. "I'll see you soon."

"What about Hank?" the boss asked.

"What about her?" Trick asked.

"Is she with you?"

She jumped up from his body then, from the bed, and moved toward the window. The bedroom was on the street side, not the lake, so he wasn't sure what she was looking at, but her body tensed.

Was someone out there?

Had he already left too late?

"I have to go," he said as he clicked off the cell without answering Braden.

"What is it?" Trick asked, even as he jumped up to join her at the window.

"You're not going to be leaving now," she said. And she pointed out the window at the glow of a fire…inside his truck.

He cursed. Then he pulled her back from the window. The stalker had found them. "Get down," he told her as he ducked low himself.

He wasn't just avoiding bullets, though. He was grabbing up his clothes from the floor.

Henrietta dressed quickly, too, and pulled her phone from her pocket. "We need to call 9-1-1."

He cursed again. It was his truck on fire, but Henrietta was going to lose more than a vehicle. Especially if this psycho after them started her cottage on fire next. "You call. I'm going out there." Maybe this time he would catch the cowardly son of a bitch.

"NO!" HENRIETTA SHOUTED as she grabbed Trick's arm. "You can't go out there. You know it's a trap. The minute you stick your head out that door, that maniac will try to shoot it off."

Trick shrugged off her hand and her concern. "Lucky for us they're a terrible shot…"

Now she slammed her hand into his shoulder. "This isn't funny." And her voice cracked with the tears burning the back of her throat and her eyes.

Trick turned back then and cupped her shoulders in his hands. "I don't think this is funny at all," he said. "I'm pissed, and I want to put a stop to all of this."

But she worried that the shooter would put a stop to him. So she implored him, "Please don't go out there. Wait for the police."

He shook his head. "I don't want the shooter coming in here. This place means too much to you."

She felt a flash of panic—but at the thought of the shooter coming after them. "This is just a house." Her grandfather was what had made it a home for her, and he was already gone.

She didn't want to lose Trick, too. Not like this…

"It's more than that," Trick said. "And you're more…" His voice trailed off before he said what she was.

More to him than his own life?

She shook her head. "You can't go out. Wait for the police." Remembering she should have called them, she clicked the emergency button on her cell. While the call distracted her, Trick pulled away.

"No!" she screamed again.

"What?" the dispatcher asked with concern. "Are you in danger?"

"Yes," Henrietta said. "Hurry. Please hurry."

But it would be too late for Trick. He was already slipping out one of the lakeside sliders onto the deck. He had no weapon. No protection.

Nothing to block the bullets from striking his body.

She cringed, bracing herself for the shots that she was certain were to come.

"Where did he say that he was?" Sam asked as she stared out the bedroom window of the small house she shared in town with her husband. Braden had bought it before they were married, after the divorce from his first wife and because of its proximity to the firehouse.

Braden cursed. "Close. That was all he would say."

Which, Sam suspected, meant that he was with Hank and he hadn't wanted to admit it to their boss. Last night, after the way she'd left him, Hank hadn't proven herself very worthy of Trick's concern for her—when she hadn't been worried enough about him to stick around.

But then she'd told Sam about the trooper's threats. And she'd seemed genuinely upset and concerned about Trick.

Did she care about him?

Was she falling for him?

Sam was worried about them both now—for many reasons. Not just her brother…

She was also worried about her husband.

He restlessly paced their small bedroom and she could feel the tension in him. He sensed that a fire was coming.

Maybe it would prove to be just a call to go out West to fight the wildfire. Or maybe…

She had no chance to consider the alternative as she heard Braden's phone echoing the siren she could hear from the firehouse.

There was a fire.

Here. Somewhere close…

She didn't have Braden's sixth sense about things, but she damn well knew that the fire was wherever her brother was.

Chapter Twenty-One

Trick had braced himself—for bullets or another physical attack. But nothing came.

Nothing happened, which left him even more on edge than he'd been when he'd slipped out of the slider. Where the hell had the shooter gone? Why set the truck on fire if it hadn't been a trick to draw him out of the cottage?

When he noticed the lights on in the cottage next to Henrietta's, he understood why. The cottage was too close, with more windows overlooking the street. Somebody else had noticed the fire before he and Henrietta had.

And that someone had called the police, as well as tried to get a hose out of his garage. But Trick held the person back from moving any closer to the street.

"It's too dangerous," he told the older man. Loudly. So he could hear.

The elderly man bristled beneath Trick's hand on his arm. "I can handle a little fire, son."

Trick shook his head. "I'm sure you can, but I just filled the gas tank on that truck. It could blow up."

And as if to demonstrate his point, a blast rocked the street, and the two men, as the truck exploded. Glass and bits of debris came flying, so Trick pushed the man down to the ground. The guy trembled against him—maybe more with anger and pride than fear.

"Are you okay?" another voice asked—a female one—as Henrietta joined them.

Her dark eyes were wide with fear, and a tear had even rolled down her cheek.

Trick nodded. "Yes."

"I thought you were out there…" She shuddered, but then stepped forward to help her neighbor to his feet.

"I was going to put it out," the old man told her. "But I called the fire department first."

"Thank you, Uncle Ernie," she said.

He already knew she had no family, so she must have adopted the old man like she had the members of her Hotshot team.

"Thought those vehicles might belong to some of those weekenders you rent the place to," he said. "Didn't realize you were here…"

He must have missed the US Forest Service emblem on Trick's truck. Or maybe it had already been burned off before the old man had noticed the fire.

Was that all he'd noticed?

"Did you see anything else?" Trick asked him. "Anyone hanging around?"

He nodded and squinted, as if trying to remember or trying to see again, and Trick noticed the foggy look to the man's irises, probably an indication of cataracts.

"Yeah," Ernie said, "another vehicle pulled up behind it for a while. I couldn't see who was inside, though…"

Trick swallowed a curse of disappointment. He was just happy that the old man hadn't been hurt over what he had witnessed. He had already put Henrietta in peril from being around her. He didn't want to endanger anyone else.

"You two should get inside," Trick urged them—just in case the shooter wasn't gone like he'd thought.

Maybe they were still out there; they'd just wanted to flush out Henrietta, too, before they started firing. Over her neighbor's head, she met Trick's gaze, and must have read the concern in his eyes.

She nodded. "Yes, Uncle Ernie, let's go back inside…"

But before she could turn him toward his cottage, sirens wailed from the street as fire engines arrived.

"Took them long enough," Ernie sniffed.

Since the tank had just blown, Trick figured the fire hadn't been burning very long before they'd arrived.

"Got here too late, though," Ernie continued. "There's nothing left of that truck." He reached out then and grasped Trick's arm. "And if you hadn't stopped me from going out there, there'd probably be nothing left of me either."

"Or you," Henrietta murmured. "If you'd run out there, too."

And maybe that had been the trap. Setting the fire so that Trick would see it and rush out to his truck just as it exploded. But who would know that might happen?

A fellow firefighter would have. It had to be a team member—the notes, the locker, the gunshots, the attack in his apartment and now this…

It was all too damn much—so much that his already-frayed temper snapped. Now he rushed out to the street—but not to his truck that already stood like a black skeleton of the vehicle it had once been. Instead he approached the firefighters who'd answered the call.

"Which one of you started it?" he asked.

These were the guys to ask. Trent Miles, Ethan Sommerly, Rory VanDam and Carl Kozak had shown up. They must have been bunking at the firehouse and decided to go out on the call. They were also all in the first truck. But another fire engine was pulling up behind it.

"What the hell are you talking about?" Trent asked. "You're the one who's here. What the hell are you doing here?" He glanced at the cottages.

Had Henrietta gone inside? Did it matter if she had? Her SUV was parked in her driveway. Everybody was probably going to figure out that he'd been with her.

Again.

"That's my truck," Trick said. "Or it was my truck."

Carl snorted. "I've been on this team longer than anybody and I still don't have a US Forest Service truck…"

Now neither did Trick. Was that why someone had set fire to it? Because they resented him for having it? "I came with the truck," Trick reminded him as he'd had to when he'd first shown up with it and some of the team, like Carl and Trent, had made remarks. He'd gotten the truck years ago—for agreeing to be a Hotshot sub, joining whatever team needed a member and didn't have time to deal with new recruits.

"You don't have it now," Trent remarked with an unsympathetic chuckle.

Sommerly worked the line, rolling out the hose. "We still gotta put it out and make sure it doesn't spread." He glanced at the cottages, too.

Trick stood in his way. "You should have thought of that before you lit it."

Ethan bristled, his eyes burning with rage within his hairy face. "I didn't light anything. Now get the hell out of my way."

"What's wrong with you?" Rory asked him. "You're talking nonsense."

"What's wrong with me?" Trick fairly roared the question back at him. "Somebody's trying to kill me. That's what the hell's wrong with me. And I want to know which one of you is doing it!"

"You're losing it," Sommerly remarked as he stepped around him.

Trick reached out to grab him, but before his hand could close over his shoulder, somebody pulled him back. Owen had rushed up from the second truck.

Trick jerked away from him. "What about you, Miles? Isn't arson your thing, working your regular job where you do?"

Trent Miles snorted. "I do put out a lot of arson fires. I don't start them." He shoved Trick out of his way as he helped Sommerly with the line.

Trick lunged at him, but before he made contact, Owen and Luke Garrison pulled him back.

"Calm down," Luke told him. "Calm the hell down."

Trick tried to wrestle free of the grasp of about the only two guys he really trusted on the team. He was sick of having to watch his back every day, of not knowing whom he could trust, especially among his own teammates. "You know how this feels," he reminded Luke. "You know what it's like when somebody's trying to take you down."

"We both do," Owen said, answering for him and Luke. "But we were wrong when we thought it might have been someone on the team. And you're wrong, too."

Trick shook his head. His friends didn't know everything. They only had their suspicions about the real reason he'd joined the team.

They didn't know about Braden's note concerning one of them not being who he or she seemed to be. How could a firefighter set a fire like this, a fire that could have taken him out—and Henrietta, and even her elderly neighbor?

But from Sam's job, Trick knew that occasionally firefighters became arsonists and killers. He knew that it had to be one of them. But which one?

Who wanted him dead?

"MAYBE I SHOULD just kill you myself."

Braden was angry. But he wasn't the one who'd hurled the threat at his brother-in-law. Instead, he almost felt sorry for him as Trick withstood Sam's angry tirade.

"Then I wouldn't have to keep worrying about you," she went on.

Trick grinned. "You don't have to worry about me now. I'm fine."

"You could have been blown up," Sam said. "Like your truck."

Trick shook his head. "It was just because I filled the tank recently."

Sam shook her head. "No, it wasn't. I found an incendiary device in the box. Somebody figured on that truck blowing up—probably just as you rushed up to put out the fire."

Trick cursed. "It's not like I thought it was an accident…"

"No, it wasn't," Braden said. "But you still shouldn't have gone after all the first responders."

Trick snorted. "You know it was one of them."

"No, I don't," he said. "And neither do you."

"Bull—"

"You have no proof," Braden reminded him.

He wished like hell that he did—that they knew who was behind all these attempts on Trick's life.

"I told you before that I'm not a damn investigator," Trick said. "You brought me in to give you my impression of everybody on your team—"

"Objectively," Braden reminded him. "You were supposed to be objective. I think I brought in the wrong man for the job. I think it's time for you to leave."

Trick sucked in a breath as if Braden had punched him. "You can't get rid of me until you bring in a replacement. You can't run your team short."

Braden cursed now—because his brother-in-law was right. It wouldn't be fair or safe for the rest of the team if they got called out to one of the wildfires. "I can stop your investigation," Braden told him.

But Trick cursed now. "Like hell you can!"

Before Braden could say anything else, his brother-in-law stormed out of his office. The door rattled in the frame from the force of Trick slamming it.

The door wasn't the only thing that was rattled. Trick was, too. And not just because of his truck. "What the hell's going on with him?" he asked his wife.

Sam knew her brother better than anyone else. And she was clearly just as worried as Braden was. "For the first time in his life, Trick is feeling something—it must be terrifying for him."

"Anger?" Braden remarked. He couldn't believe the redheaded firefighter had never been angry before.

Sam shook her head, and a slight smile played around her beautiful mouth. "No. Something far more dangerous…"

And Braden knew what could unsettle a man even more than someone trying to kill him could.

Falling in love…

SHE COULD HAVE stayed inside the cottage and hidden from her teammates. But once she'd settled down Uncle Ernie and made sure the excitement hadn't been too much for him, she headed outside. They'd all been too busy then to ask questions, but she'd seen the shock and the recrimination on their faces.

She could have avoided them after that—could have waited until the next team meeting, or until they were called out to that wildfire. But she knew that if she didn't say anything, they would all speculate. They'd gossip.

And they'd draw their own conclusions. They'd probably end up with the right one—that she and Trick had crossed the line.

So she'd gone down to the Filling Station to…

Lie?

She wasn't a liar. But then, she'd never had anything to lie about before she'd met Trick. From the first moment she'd seen him, she'd started lying—to herself. She'd told herself that he wasn't that good-looking…

That charming…

That smart…

That hardworking…

That damn irresistible.

Despite her lies, she'd been unable to resist him—unable to resist the overpowering attraction she'd felt for him. She had never wanted anyone the way she'd wanted him—not even her ex-fiancé. Especially not Greg…

She'd broken up with him when she'd made herself

face the truth of her feelings. And now she'd had to face the truth again.

While she was being honest with herself, she wasn't ready to be honest with her coworkers—not when she was pretty damn sure one of them had tried to kill not only Trick but also her.

Somebody on the team wasn't being honest with any of them. And to find out the truth about that person, she would have to lie. She would have to act like she still trusted all of them.

But she didn't. She couldn't after finding that note in Trick's pried-open locker. It had to have been one of them, hadn't it?

She forced herself to push open the door to the Filling Station and walk inside, where most of them had gathered after the fire. While the guys from the second rig—Owen and Luke—had said they were going home, everybody from the first rig on the scene had agreed to come back to the bar. After that, they'd head to Carl's house, where they'd all been staying while his wife was off visiting one of their kids at college. Henrietta suspected they hadn't wanted to share the bunkroom with Trick.

She'd promised to meet them at the Filling Station and buy them a drink for coming out to her grandfather's place.

And she'd acted then like it was no big deal that Trick had been at her place. That was how she had to act now, when all conversation stopped the second she approached that booth in the back corner of the bar.

"You actually showed up," Michaela said with surprise. She hadn't been at the fire with the others, but she'd obviously heard about it—and Henrietta's promise to join them all later.

"You did, too," Henrietta remarked as a wave of suspicion swept over her. Where the hell had Michaela been earlier? She was one of the few Hotshots who knew about the cottage—who'd been there before. "Haven't seen much of you lately…"

Sommerly looked back and forth between them like he was watching a ping-pong game. "Thought you two were roommates…"

"We are," Michaela said. "Or at least I think we are."

The bearded Hotshot shivered and murmured, "This is why I live alone…"

"Catfight?" Trent Miles asked almost hopefully as he set a full pitcher of beer on the table. He must have been playing waiter for the group.

Henrietta glared at him. "Not at all…"

"You missed it earlier," Miles told Michaela as he slid into the booth beside her. "There was just about a fight at the fire."

Henrietta doubted this was the first Michaela had heard of what had happened tonight. It was just being retold for her benefit, for her reaction.

"Really?" Michaela asked, but instead of turning toward Trent, she studied Henrietta's face.

"Yeah, McRooney went after Ethan."

Michaela glanced at the bearded Hotshot. As everyone was aware, Ethan was the quietest, most mild-mannered one of the group. "Why would he do that?"

"He was ranting and raving about somebody lighting up his truck," Trent continued. "Even accused me and Rory."

"And me," Carl chimed in. "He's a hotheaded lunatic."

Something snapped inside Henrietta. She couldn't lie or hide anything. Not anymore…

Not when they were all acting as if Trick had no reason for acting the way he had. "And how the hell calm would you all be if somebody was trying to kill you?" she wondered aloud. "How trusting would you be of people who've treated you like the enemy since the day you showed up here?"

Michaela sucked in a breath, obviously surprised that Henrietta would defend the man. But Hank didn't care—not right now.

"He *is* the enemy," Rory remarked, his blue eyes cold and hard.

"Why?" she asked. "Why do you think that?"

"He's a spy," Ethan said. "The boss hired him to spy on all of us."

"Why?" she asked. "And if that's what you think, why aren't you all mad at and mistrustful of Braden?"

Sommerly shrugged. "He's the boss…and we've known him longer."

Long enough to know that if Braden had someone spying on them, he had a damn good reason, like he couldn't trust one of them. Her skin chilled as she realized that; Braden and Trick were probably already aware that someone on their team wasn't really a team player.

"Why would it matter if he did?" she wondered aloud. "We shouldn't be hiding anything, right? We shouldn't have any secrets that could risk our job?"

"Are you the person who should be asking that question?" Michaela asked.

Henrietta sucked in a breath with a twinge of pain over the remark of her roommate, a woman she'd once considered a close friend. Hell, she'd once considered all of them close friends. But not anymore… "I don't blame Trick for not trusting any of you," she said. "I blame myself that I have." With tears of frustration and disillusionment stinging her eyes, she turned to leave.

But before she could walk away, Trent grabbed her arm. "Wait," he said. "Why would you say that?"

She blinked away the tears as anger surged through her, and she turned back and glared at all of them. "Trick isn't the only one that somebody's been trying to kill. Someone's taken a shot at me a couple of times, too. And with the way gossip spreads in this town, you have to know that."

From their faces, it was clear that nobody was completely surprised. While she and Trick had tried to keep it quiet, someone had obviously seen them together and spread that news. Maybe Michaela had? Or the person who'd shot at them?

"It's bad enough you're all heartless enough to not give a damn that somebody's gone after him," she said. "But you don't give a damn about me either!"

She tugged free of Trent's grasp and ran for the exit. Tears burned her eyes and blurred her vision, but she managed to find and push open the door.

She could barely see the steps, though, or the street as she started across it to where she'd parked her SUV. But she heard the other vehicle. She heard its engine rev just before it headed straight toward her. But now, with its lights blinding her, too, she didn't know where to turn—where to run.

Chapter Twenty-Two

In that second, seeing Henrietta frozen in the beam of the vehicle's bright lights, Trick's life passed through his mind.

His life with her...

It hadn't been long. There weren't many memories. But the ones they'd made together were more monumental than anything else in his life.

While those images flitted through his mind, he wasn't frozen. He moved, rushing off the curb to push Henrietta out of the street. They fell to the pavement, but he rolled them—just out of the way as the vehicle's tires squealed across the asphalt.

Brakes grinded as the vehicle slowed for the corner. He glanced up, but there wasn't time to read the plate before it careened over the curb as it turned onto the other street and disappeared. A curse burned in his throat, but he couldn't utter it. He couldn't move.

He'd knocked the breath from his own lungs. Or maybe seeing Henrietta standing there, about to be run over, had knocked the breath out of him. He was certain his heart had stopped for a moment as it had threatened to break. It pounded hard now with the fear that had yet to subside.

She lay so limp and still in his arms. Alarm filled him with air, and he asked, "Are you okay?"

She was quiet for another moment, so quiet that he surged up and leaned over her. Her face was deathly pale in the glow of the streetlamp.

"Henrietta?"

Voices echoed his. "Hank! Hank!"

Running footsteps grew louder as people rushed from the bar.

"Are you okay?" he asked again. Or had he hurt her more than the car would have?

Her long thick lashes fluttered as she blinked, then finally nodded. "Yeah, yeah…"

Then those other voices echoed his question. "Are you okay?"

"What happened?"

"What the hell did you do?" That question was hurled at him.

But he didn't have to answer. It was Trent Miles who replied for him. "He saved her life. And he could have died trying." The firefighter's big hands reached out and helped Trick up from the ground as the others aided Henrietta.

"I'm sorry," Sommerly murmured as he steadied her when her legs nearly folded beneath her.

A surge of something Trick barely recognized passed through him, and he wanted to go at Ethan again like he had earlier. This time Luke and Owen weren't around to pull him off either.

Ethan, Trent and Michaela had rushed out to join them. Maybe they'd been on their way out of the bar already.

"Me, too," Michaela said as she shuddered. "I'm sorry."

None of them could have been behind the wheel of that vehicle. Or could they?

He supposed it could have been parked around the corner and they could have run up with the others, feigning concern. But this felt genuine, their apologies and their concern.

"Why are they apologizing?" he asked Henrietta. He could guess it had to do with him, with how they'd judged her for getting involved with him when they all considered him public enemy number one.

"Because we've all been acting like jackasses," Trent answered for her now.

Trick wasn't about to argue about that—not here, not right now. Not when the shooter could be out there somewhere or even closer, like one of them. "We need to get out of here," Trick told Henrietta. "It's too dangerous."

The others looked around, peering down the street as if waiting for the car to return.

"Did any of you catch a plate?" he asked.

"There was mud smeared across it," Ethan said. "But the bracket around the plate was for a car rental company."

So it hadn't been someone's personal vehicle. Probably because their personal vehicle could easily be traced back to them, especially if it belonged to a firehouse or the US Forest Service.

"What about the driver?" he asked. "Anybody see who was behind the wheel?"

"It was already going around the corner when I came out," Michaela said.

"I was out first," Trent said. "I saw it bearing down on Hank." He shuddered. "If you hadn't pushed her out of the way…"

SHE COULD HAVE DIED. She would have died—if not for Trick coming to her rescue, once again.

He tried to carry her off after the near miss, probably to hide her away from the next attempt. And there was certain to be a next attempt. She knew that as well as he did.

But Trent, Ethan and Michaela talked Trick into coming back to the firehouse—once they'd all made sure that Braden was gone for the night.

And in the conference room on the third floor where Braden usually called their meetings, only part of his team had called this one—without him. They'd called in a few others, though, like Rory and Carl. Hank felt a flash of guilt for excluding the boss. But just as she'd wondered at the bar, it was clear Braden had lost some of their trust, just as he'd lost it for them.

Or maybe the team had excluded Braden to protect her and Trick's jobs, in case it came out during this impromptu meeting that they were involved. Clearly they'd all realized that they were. And if they cared enough to protect her job, she doubted any of them would have tried to take her life.

She felt another flash of guilt for her earlier suspicions of them. They'd all apologized to her. But she finally found her voice and said it now. "I'm sorry…"

"For what?" Trick asked. He hadn't been there when she'd gone off on everyone at the Filling Station. And clearly, he hadn't had the revelation she'd had when that car had nearly run her down—when it would have run her down if not for Trick saving her life.

"For accusing them of trying to kill you," she said. "And me…"

He looked around the room where they'd all taken seats. "Why would you apologize for that?"

"You think so, too." Ethan mumbled his remark; it wasn't a question. The suspicion was apparent on Trick's handsome face and in his green eyes as he studied all of them.

"I get it," Trent said. "We've not exactly rolled out the welcome mat for you."

"More like rolled it up," Henrietta remarked.

"But, Hank…" Michaela murmured, her husky voice even raspier with hurt. "How could you think that any of us would try to harm you?"

Henrietta swallowed down the lump of guilt and pain that had risen in her throat. And she blinked back the tears stinging her eyes.

"Somebody has been trying to kill her!" Trick shouted the reminder. "What the hell do you think she's been thinking? That someone wants her dead for no other reason than that she's been with me."

Heat rushed to Henrietta's face along with his admission. But nobody looked surprised. They'd all figured out that she and Trick had crossed the line from just team-mates to something more.

What the hell were they, though?

Lovers?

She felt a flash of panic at the thought—of loving him. Maybe it was just gratitude for all the times he'd saved her, but she felt something for him—something warmer and more powerful even than the passion they'd shared.

"Maybe she shouldn't be with you, then," Michaela suggested with resentment.

Henrietta felt like withdrawing her apology. "Don't blame him!" she said. "He's saved my life over and over—"

"After putting it in danger," Michaela argued.

Trick sighed and nodded his agreement. "I know. I've put her at risk—"

"Bullshit!" Henrietta exclaimed. "Whoever tried to run me down in the street put me at risk. Not you. I didn't even know you were there until you saved my life. Again."

"So what the hell's going on?" Michaela asked. "Which of you is this psycho after and why?"

Henrietta had already considered that once and dismissed the thought. But what if it was true?

"Could someone be after me?" she wondered aloud, her voice cracking. She'd dismissed the thought before because it didn't make sense. She could think of no enemies.

Trick slid his arm around her, offering her comfort and support. Despite their audience, she leaned into him for just a moment, taking that comfort. Then she pulled away from him.

The others acted as if they hadn't noticed.

"Ex-boyfriend?" Trent asked.

"Ex-fiancé?" Ethan asked.

The bearded Hotshot was the most reclusive of the team, yet he seemed very well-informed about the rest of them. Since he wasn't a talker, maybe he was a very good listener instead.

"You asked me about Greg," Henrietta remembered, and she turned toward Trick.

His jaw was tightly clenched. What was it about her ex that bothered him? Was he jealous?

She shook her head, dismissing the thought. He was just worried that someone was trying to kill her and him, too.

But he shook his head, too. "I don't think your ex has anything to do with this." It was clear that he still considered one of the team to be the primary suspect.

"No," she said. "I've thought, too, that it might be one of us, especially after your locker was pried open, but we all know that Stanley rarely remembers to lock that door. It could be someone else…" She hoped like hell that it was an outsider, especially now that they were all supporting her. It was clear from their faces and their actions that they didn't mean her any harm. But Greg couldn't either, not when he'd professed to love her so much.

"It has to be one of the team," Trick said. "It's the only thing that makes sense."

None of it made sense.

"Why?" Ethan asked the question. "Tell us what the hell's going on."

Trick clenched his jaw so tightly that a muscle twitched in his cheek. He shook his head again.

Now she reached out for him, sliding her arm around his waist. "We need to tell them," she said.

"Why?" he asked.

"Because maybe they can help."

Trick stared down at her, and he was clearly torn between keeping secrets and opening up.

"Please," she implored him.

WHERE THE HELL had Trick come from? Was he never far from the female firefighter?

Was that why—once again—he'd been able to rescue her? This attempt would have worked. The woman had frozen in the street, unable to move.

She would have died, or at least been seriously

wounded—if not for her white knight showing up to save her again.

Damn it!

If only he hadn't moved quite so fast…

Next time he wouldn't. Next time he wouldn't be able to save Henrietta Rowlins. Next time he wouldn't even be able to save himself.

Chapter Twenty-Three

Trick studied the room, watching them all watch them. The heat of Henrietta's arm didn't just wrap around his waist; it wrapped around his heart, too.

Maybe that was why he took the leap.

But he had to do it his way. "You think one of them will confess?" he asked her.

"And he wonders why we didn't roll out the welcome mat," Trent Miles remarked.

"I didn't wonder," Trick asked. "I wasn't looking for it—not coming in like I did, to take over for a dead team member."

"Is that the only reason you came in?" Ethan Sommerly asked, his dark eyes narrowed so much that they nearly disappeared in his bearded face.

The guy was smart, or just suspicious out of guilt. If anyone looked like he was hiding who he really was, this guy was the one.

"What other reason would I have?" he asked. "I'm a sub with the US Forest Service. I fill in on teams that are down a member until they can find permanent replacements."

"Why don't you ever want to stay with a team?" Michaela asked.

Henrietta turned her head so that she was staring up at him, and it was almost as if she held her breath, waiting for his answer.

He shrugged. "It's just what I do because I like to move around."

"You don't like to stick around," Michaela murmured, and she shot a glance at Henrietta. A warning glance.

He'd already made that clear to Henrietta, just as he had to every other woman he'd dated. Not that he and Henrietta had actually gone out on a date, though.

Until tonight she hadn't even wanted to be seen with him. So Henrietta wasn't the one Michaela had to worry about—at least, not emotionally.

Physically she was in danger. And that was the only reason Trick had decided to open up with the team. Somewhat. He wouldn't tell them everything that Braden had asked him to keep quiet.

He was actually only going to tell them what Braden didn't know. And he felt a pang of regret over not leveling with his brother-in-law. But Braden would have tried to get rid of him sooner if he'd known how soon the threats against him had started.

"So we didn't welcome you with open arms," Trent Miles said. "That doesn't mean we've been trying to kill you."

"Like Henrietta said, the threat could be to her life," Ethan added. "Maybe her ex…"

Trick wished it was; then he'd know for certain that the guy would never convince her to give him another chance. But he couldn't let her ex-fiancé take the rap for something he hadn't done, and Trick doubted he was their man. He'd already lost enough when he'd lost Henrietta.

Trick sighed and shook his head. "Somebody started

leaving me threatening notes pretty soon after I got to town," he said.

Henrietta turned to him again. "You've gotten more than the one?"

He nodded. "They're usually left on my truck. One in my mailbox, but there was no postage on it."

"What has Braden said?" Trent Miles asked.

Trick shook his head. "I didn't tell him. He's got enough on his mind without worrying about me." But it was too late for that now. Braden was worried and so was Sam. And they didn't even know about the notes.

"Wow," Sommerly murmured as he ran a hand over his bushy beard. "We really did have you pegged wrong."

Trick chuckled. "I'm not the narc you thought I was?"

Miles chuckled, too. "You gotta understand why we'd think that. The boss is married to your sister and your family is notoriously tight-knit."

Trick snorted. "I don't remember the last time I saw my oldest brother, but sure, we're close." And they were. If he reached out and asked Mack for help, his brother would come to the rescue. So would his dad.

But Trick didn't want to ask that family for help. He wanted to ask this one—if they could act like the family that Hotshot teams were supposed to be.

"Braden's had a lot on his plate the past several months," Trick continued. "I wanted to relieve his burden, not add to it." He uttered a ragged sigh. "So much for that with the damn shootings and that fire and…"

"Someone hitting you over the head after breaking into your place," Henrietta added, as if he could have forgotten.

After his tumble in the street, his head had begun to

pound again. But it was more from tension and fear than the concussion. He'd come so close to losing her.

Again.

"That happened after the shooting," Michaela said. "The place was already a crime scene. You weren't supposed to go back there. How did they know you would?"

"He told Tammy," Henrietta said. That was why she'd gone there. Had Tammy told someone else? "Or had the person gone there to leave a note like they had in your locker?"

"Is that why your locker was all jammed up like that?" Ethan asked. "I thought somebody was trying to get something out of it—not put something in it."

Trick tensed as realization dawned. "That night—at my apartment when I got hit over the head—it sounded like someone was searching the place before I got there…"

"For what?" Miles asked.

"Maybe the notes," Henrietta suggested. "Do you have them all?" Excitement lifted her voice. "Maybe there's a clue in them."

If there was, he hadn't seen it. But maybe if everybody looked at them, one of them would recognize the crude writing or a turn of phrase.

But when he hesitated, Henrietta sucked in a breath. "They weren't in the truck, were they?"

He shook his head.

"The locker?"

"No," he said.

Ethan Sommerly stroked his beard and remarked, "The break-in, the truck fire…it does sound like somebody wants to destroy those notes…" And he actually glanced at the other people in the conference room. Then he laughed. "Now I get it—why you're so suspicious."

"Yeah, how did somebody else get into the firehouse locker room?" Trick asked.

Miles snorted. "Stanley never locks that door. And Braden had to remove the automatic lock from it because Stanley locked himself out every time he let Annie out. So if Stanley leaves last—which he usually does—then he usually leaves the place unlocked."

"Yeah," Carl said. "This house isn't run like it used to be before that kid showed up."

The short hairs rose on the nape of Trick's neck. *That kid...*

He'd never really looked at Stanley as a suspect. But it was about the time he'd been hired that the accidents had started happening to the team.

"Don't," Henrietta cautioned. "Don't even think it. Stanley was already falsely accused once when the arsonist tried to frame him. It nearly destroyed him. And he was with me when those shots were fired at me after I found your locker pried open."

So Stanley couldn't be the shooter. But he could still be the saboteur, if they weren't one and the same. Trick wanted to believe the kid was innocent of that, too. But sometimes people were capable of things that even those closest to them would have never guessed—like his mother. He would have never guessed that she could so easily abandon her family to go off and find her bliss, or whatever the hell she'd called it.

"So do you have the notes?" Michaela was the one who asked the question now—a bit anxiously.

"Yeah," he said.

Knowing he would eventually need to turn them over

to Braden, who would probably turn them over to Sam for processing, he'd sealed them in a plastic bag. And so nothing would happen to it, he'd carried it on him this entire time. He pulled the soft plastic sandwich bag from his pocket, pulled it open and spilled the notes across the conference table. "My fingerprints are already on them, but none of you should touch them," he said as he unfolded each note and laid them out for the others to read.

"Maybe your note writer was worried he left a print on one of these," Ethan remarked as he peered over Trick's shoulder. "That's why he tried getting them back."

"She," Henrietta said softly. "Your note writer is a woman."

Trick studied her face, which had suddenly gone as pale as when she'd been lying in his arms in the road. She looked as scared now as she had then.

"How do you know?" he asked, and his heart pounded with fear.

"ARE YOU CONFESSING?" It was Michaela who asked, but the question was also on Trick's face, in his tightly clenched jaw—in the dread in his green eyes.

Despite the panic pressing on her chest, Henrietta managed a short chuckle. "No."

But she was scared that someday—soon—she would feel the same pain Trick's note writer had felt when she'd penned those threats.

"An ex-lover wrote these," she said. And she pointed toward the ones that were more worn, the paper thinner from having been carried around in that bag in Trick's pocket for so long. These must have been the first ones he'd received, and they seemed more personal. More accusatory:

How could you do this?

Who do you think you are?
You're going to regret this.
You're never going to find what you're looking for...
You're going to be miserable.

While Trick might not have considered them personal, Henrietta recognized the anger and the pain in them. Greg had said things like this to her in those early days of their broken engagement. He'd added more, like *Nobody else will ever make you as happy as I can. Nobody will love you like I will...*

You're going to miss me. You're going to be so lonely without me...

Rory whistled between his teeth. "Damn, I think she's right. These sound like notes my old high school girlfriend used to slip into my locker after we broke up."

"A stranger didn't write these older-looking notes," Ethan agreed. "The person knew you. Until tonight, I don't think any of us actually had."

Because they hadn't given him the chance. And she saw now that they all regretted it, like Henrietta was regretting how close she had gotten to him—because she knew when he left, she would be hurt, just as this woman had been hurt.

Trick shook his head. "It doesn't make sense."

"With all the moving around you do, you must have left somebody behind, must have pissed someone off," Michaela said with disapproval.

"I'm always clear about the fact that I'm not sticking around," Trick said. "I don't lead people on. I don't lie about my intentions or my feelings."

Michaela's lips curved into a smile, but there was something almost heartbreakingly sad about it. "Some women might see that as a challenge, might think that they can be the one to finally make the playboy settle down…" She turned toward Henrietta. "But that woman is only fooling herself. You can't change other people."

Henrietta suspected Michaela was talking with the voice of experience. Was that why her marriage had ended? She'd never talked about it before. Or was this experience more recent? Henrietta moved closer to her and squeezed her hand. Now she understood why her roommate had been so disapproving of her spending time with Trick. She'd been worried she'd get her heart broken, too.

And probably rightfully so.

Trick shook his head again. Henrietta nearly laughed over his reluctance to accept that a woman could fall for him despite his warnings. She could have told him how wrong he was, that she was already beginning to fall for him despite knowing that he could leave anytime. Or die anytime…

She shuddered at that horrible thought.

"I think they're right," Rory VanDam said. "I think you pissed off somebody and maybe it wasn't recently."

"But why go after Henrietta?" he asked. "Why not just me?"

Michaela snorted. "Nobody likes being replaced."

Heat rushed to Henrietta's face.

"Don't worry," Ethan assured her. "We won't tell Braden."

"You won't tell Braden what?" a deep voice asked as the boss walked into the conference room.

Henrietta's stomach sank. Trick was leaving anyway, so Braden might not fire her, too, for breaking the no-romantic-fraternization rule. But just as Trick had always made it clear he wasn't sticking around, Braden had always made it clear that he didn't tolerate any team member breaking the rules.

Was she about to lose her lover and her job?

BRADEN DIDN'T KNOW whether to be furious or relieved over finding this part of his team holding a secret meeting in the conference room. These members had been the ones who had resented Trick's addition to the team the most. But just because they were meeting together didn't mean they were all getting along.

But there seemed to be something in the room that he hadn't felt in a long time within his team—a sense of solidarity.

"I don't remember calling this meeting," he gruffly remarked.

"Then why are you here?" Trick asked him, his green eyes twinkling with amusement.

Braden was not going to be goaded into laughing at his unrepentant brother-in-law. "Because I'm about to call a meeting..."

Hank's throat moved as if she was struggling to swallow. She looked shaken and afraid. What the hell had he missed?

"We got called up," Braden continued. "We have to report out West."

Everybody had gathered around the conference table, but they were standing so he couldn't see what was on it. And as he approached, they moved closer together, as if to hide whatever was there.

Trick stepped away, allowing Braden to see the profusion of notes. "You'll need to get these to Sam to have someone process them for fingerprints," he said.

"What the hell are they?" But he could see them now, so he read the threats.

"I've been getting them since I got here," Trick admitted.

Braden cursed. What the hell kind of situation had he brought his brother-in-law into? "You don't know who's been sending them?" He glanced around the room at those members assembled.

Had Trick called them together to confront them? To get the note writer to confess?

Trick's face flushed with color, and he mumbled, "Everybody else thinks it's probably an ex…"

Braden waited for a surge of relief that never came. He wasn't as convinced as the others seemed to be. He'd received that note he had long before Trick's arrival—the one that had warned him about the team.

Dare he send them all out together on this call? Or should he have turned it down?

He had a horrible feeling that they might not all make it back to Northern Lakes. That he might lose Trick.

Chapter Twenty-Four

With how quickly the team had to fly out West, Trick hadn't had time to think about Henrietta's suspicion about those notes. No. Not suspicion. Conviction.

She was convinced those notes came from an ex. He wasn't as certain. But, on the plane ride back to Northern Lakes, he was too keyed up from the adrenaline of successfully battling that fire to sleep, so he started scrolling through his phone.

He found more women than he'd realized he'd dated. Most had been just one date, though, just a coffee or a drink. Nothing romantic. He'd even gone out with Sam's old college roommate a few months ago when he'd worked with a team stationed out in DC, where she lived. She was a fire investigator like Sam. He'd always wondered if the woman had been a little obsessed with his sister. Since most of the team was still awake like him, Trick shared with them what he'd gleaned from his phone. He even made the remark about Colleen that he'd been thinking, that Sam's roommate had been a little too Single White Female.

Ethan Sommerly shook his head and murmured, "That's why I prefer to live alone..."

"You prefer to live alone because nobody wants to

live with a grizzly bear like you," Trent Miles said, teasing him.

Ethan's beard moved, so he was probably smiling. It was hard to tell, though.

Henrietta wasn't smiling. She sat across the aisle with Michaela, who was sleeping.

Braden stood in the aisle, leaning over Rory's seat as he listened to their conversation. "Are you talking about Colleen?" he asked.

Trick nodded.

Braden smirked. "I think she calls to ask Sam more about you than she asks about Sam."

A suspicion began to niggle at Trick. "Any word back from Sam on the notes?" he asked his brother-in-law.

Braden shook his head.

"I thought Sam could get a rush put on processing," he said. But they had only been gone a week.

"Is that why you didn't want me to give them to Trooper Wells?" Braden asked. "Or could she be the note writer? Has she shown any interest in you since you got to town?"

Trick shivered. "Not like that. She'd probably like to arrest me like Marty arrested me and Luke. I still don't trust her."

The others could have been wrong about those notes; they might not have been that personal. Maybe Wells had sent them because she didn't want him finding out that she'd been helping Marty sabotage the team. But why would she have gone after Henrietta, too? No. It made more sense that the team was right—that someone was after him and that Henrietta had just gotten in the way. Or maybe, if it was someone obsessed with him, like

Henrietta and the others thought, that they were jealous of her now.

Could they have noticed even before he had how very attracted he was to the gorgeous female Hotshot? He was beginning to worry that it was more than attraction…

HENRIETTA CLOSED HER eyes and acted as if she was sleeping for the remainder of the plane ride home. But she kept rereading those messages in her mind.

The pain.

The recrimination.

It was personal to the writer of those notes, but it clearly hadn't been personal to Trick. He had no idea who could have sent them, yet he'd probably broken that woman's heart.

And when he left, he would break Hank's, too.

She'd told herself that it was just attraction she felt for him. Desire…

Sure, she was grateful for the times he'd saved her life. But she felt so much more than gratitude for him. She was falling for him. Sometime during the past several weeks since he'd joined the team, he'd started to mean more and more to her.

Maybe it had started when he'd nearly fallen out of that bucket to his death and she'd thought about what a loss it would have been, never getting to know him better.

Intimately.

But now that she knew him intimately, she knew better than anyone else why he would leave. She knew about his past, about his mother's abandonment.

"He's gone," Michaela whispered.

And even though she hadn't really been sleeping, Henrietta jumped—startled. Was he gone—gone?

She opened her eyes and noticed that everyone else had already disembarked the plane, leaving only Michaela and her in their seats. She'd been so deep in thought that she hadn't even noticed their landing and the others leaving.

Michaela reached for and squeezed her hand. "I'm sorry…"

"Sorry you were right?" Henrietta asked, and she forced a smile for her friend.

"Sorry that you're hurting," Michaela said.

She sighed. "Unlike the rest of you, who worried that he was going to try to be Dirk's permanent replacement, I always knew he was leaving." And now she even knew why.

"He's not gone yet," Michaela said. "He's just left the plane, not Northern Lakes."

Henrietta turned in the seat to stare at her friend. "What are you saying?" Was the pessimist actually offering her hope?

Michaela shrugged. "I don't know." She shook her head. "Forget it. Thinking like that was what got me married and divorced. I knew better then, and I damn well should have known better now…" Her husky voice trailed off with emotion.

Henrietta wondered if her friend was talking about her and Trick now or about herself and someone else… Who?

She hadn't been around the apartment much more than Henrietta had the past few weeks. "Is there something you want to talk about?" she asked.

"Want?" Michaela shook her head. "But I might need to… Just not yet…"

"Whenever you're ready," Henrietta said. "I'll be there for you."

"You don't think I'm trying to kill you anymore?" Michaela asked, but she was smiling.

Guilt struck a pang in Henrietta's heart. "I'm sorry that I accused you all of that, but especially you..." They were friends as well as roommates.

Michaela shook her head. "Hell, after getting shot at like that and getting that note, I would have started suspecting everybody around me, too. I didn't give Trick a chance—just because he reminded me of..." She shook her head again. "My mistake."

Now Henrietta had made the same mistake—falling for a man who wouldn't change. At least she had her friend back. And her team.

She had a feeling she would need to lean on them heavily when Trick left. He was going to leave a hole in her heart. He was also going to leave a hole in the team.

This was the second wildfire they'd worked with him. And it had gone even better than the first. He'd fit in like he'd been with them for years, not just weeks.

He'd seemed to belong.

Had he noticed it?

No. If he had, he'd probably get so scared that he would leave even sooner.

But maybe leaving would be a good thing—for him. It might keep him safe from whoever was stalking him. It might keep her safe, too.

Then she'd only be losing her heart—not her life.

HENRIETTA ROWLINS HAD to die. First. She was the reason Trick hadn't left Northern Lakes and come back to DC for her. At first, Colleen Conrad had been angry with him that he still couldn't see what she had all those years ago, that they were perfect for each other. When he used to visit Sam at college, he'd treated Colleen like she was his sister, too. Maybe that was her fault; she'd tried to be like Sam, who was so smart and so pretty. All the men had wanted Sam, but Colleen hadn't had to compete with her for Trick, since he was Sam's brother. And he was even more perfect than his sister...

They were perfect for each other, and if he'd stuck around DC, he would have finally figured that out. Maybe he already had, since he'd finally asked her out for dinner. But then he'd taken off so quickly, after a call from Sam. She'd asked him to come up here, and he would do anything his sister wanted. But Colleen had overheard him telling Sam that he wasn't an investigator. And so she'd thought if she followed him up, discreetly, without anyone noticing, and if she left him a few notes, that maybe he would give up and leave. And come back to her...

Then she'd seen the way he'd looked at Henrietta Rowlins. The way he'd never looked at Colleen. He really saw Henrietta. He was interested in her in a way that he'd never been interested in Colleen. She'd finally realized that, and that was why she'd tried to kill him. Out of rage. But the female Hotshot kept getting in the way, kept forcing Trick to come to her rescue.

Well, he wouldn't be able to save her this time. This plan would work. Colleen glanced around Hank's bedroom at the spartan furnishings. It reminded her of Trick's apartment...although he didn't know Colleen had been inside it. Her investigator's card granted her access to a lot of places. If she didn't get back to work soon, though, she was going to lose her job. So she had to end this now.

Rage coursed through her, and her finger twitched against the trigger of the gun she held. No. She couldn't fire a shot now.

Not yet...

Someone might hear it.

And they couldn't hear her yet. Not until it was too late.

This plan was going to work—was going to play out perfectly. She'd thought of everything this time.

There was no way that Henrietta was going to avoid getting shot. She was dying tonight. But she wasn't the only one...

Chapter Twenty-Five

Colleen...

It had to be Colleen. The more he'd thought about what Braden had said on the plane, the more convinced Trick had become.

"You're right," he told his brother-in-law as he paced the small confines of the superintendent's office. "Colleen is obsessed with me." When he'd scrolled through his phone, he'd noticed the texts from her at all hours. At first he'd thought nothing of his sister's friend offering to show him around the city he'd just moved to, but now he wondered how she'd known where he'd moved and where he lived.

Sam, who sat on the corner of her husband's desk, flinched. "I always knew she asked a lot of questions about you, but I guess I didn't realize how much information I was giving up to her. And I was used to, growing up with older brothers, every girl in school always asking me about you guys. But still..."

"Don't beat yourself up," Trick said. "She's a trained investigator, too. She knows how to get people to talk. I even told her more than I should have..."

"About what?" Sam asked.

"About Northern Lakes, about the team, about why

my brother-in-law needed my help, and I gave her the perfect scapegoat in the saboteur." But instead of helping Braden, he'd brought more danger to the team.

To Henrietta…

His body tensed and ached at the thought of her. And not just his lower body…

Thinking about her made his heart hurt. He'd felt a sharp pang when he'd forced himself to deplane without stopping at her seat, without waking her up. But Michaela had waved him off the plane.

She didn't want him putting her friend in any more danger.

Trick didn't want to do that either.

Sam shook her head. "I know Colleen always had a thing for you, but I never thought she could go this far. Trying to kill you and Hank…" She shuddered. "That doesn't make sense…" She narrowed her eyes and studied Trick's face. "What did you do?"

Trick shrugged. "I was nice to her when we went out a couple of times in DC—"

"You went out with her?" Sam exclaimed. "A couple of times?"

"They weren't dates. I ran into her while I was grabbing coffee near my place—"

"How?" Sam asked.

"I don't know. It was innocent—"

"No, I know where she lives and works and where you live and work," Sam said. "She shouldn't have innocently run into you. What happened then?"

"She was telling me about great places to eat in the area and suggested we meet up for dinner at one of them…"

Sam groaned. "Oh, my God, she was stalking you…"

And she shuddered again. "My roommate...and I never knew..."

Trick shuddered now. "I always thought she was a little off," he admitted.

Sam looked from him to her husband, who nodded as well. Then he got up from his desk and wrapped his arms around her, as if trying to protect her. Sam had found someone solid, someone special in Braden. Despite his first wife cheating on him, he hadn't harbored resentment. He'd opened his heart up to love again, and he'd found in Sam the loyalty and the love he deserved. Despite how much she looked like their mother, Sam was nothing like her.

Trick looked at them with new interest. They were making it work—even though their jobs often separated them. They always came back to each other.

Their love was real.

It would last.

Neither was going to leave the other one. Not everybody took off.

Would Henrietta?

If he stayed, would she eventually drop him? With as much as her career meant to her, he suspected she would. Not that he expected her to choose him over her job. As a Hotshot himself, he understood that it was so much more than just a job. Even as a little kid, he'd known it was what he was meant to do—like maybe as a McRooney, it was part of his DNA. But he'd met a lot of other people to whom the job was just as important. Henrietta was one of them.

He didn't want her to give it up, but he didn't want to give her up. Maybe there was a way to make it work like

Sam and Braden were making it work. First, he had to make sure she was in no danger because of him, though.

"Do you know where Colleen is?" he asked his sister.

Sam released a ragged sigh and shook her head. "She won't answer my calls to her cell, so I checked in at her office in DC. They told me she's been off on a long leave to take care of her sick mom..."

"Did you check to see if that's true?" Trick asked.

She shook her head. "I don't need to. Her mom died before she started college."

"So it is her," Trick said. "Where the hell could she be staying in Northern Lakes that we didn't even notice her?" But Colleen was like that; Trick had barely noticed her when he'd gone to visit Sam at college. He'd always been nice to her, though. Maybe too nice...

"She could have rented a cabin on one of the lakes," Sam suggested.

"Only a few have been opened for the season," Braden said. "It's early yet..."

"And it would have to be close to the firehouse to keep an eye on me like she has," Trick pointed out. The cabins were farther out of town, and Northern Lakes wasn't big enough to have more than one hotel.

"Northern Lakes Village Inn," Sam said, as if she'd read his mind.

He nodded.

Braden reached for his phone. "I'll see if she's checked in..."

But Trick was already heading out the door. He knew that was where she was. He knew...

Ignoring the shouts of his brother-in-law and sister for him to slow down, he rushed out to the truck that had been waiting for him on his return from their most recent assignment. The US Forest Service had had it delivered. It was new, and it was fast. He pulled into the parking lot of the Village Inn just moments after leaving the firehouse.

While the concierge was still talking to Braden on the phone, telling him that he couldn't share their guest list without a search warrant, Trick stepped around the desk and peered over the man's shoulder. Despite the man's protestations, he'd pulled up Colleen's information. After seeing her room number, Trick rushed up the stairwell to the third floor, which was the top one. She must have had more money than he'd realized because the rooms were all suites up here. He scanned the door number plates and found that hers was standing open, a cleaning cart blocking the entrance.

He poked his head around the doorway and called out to the maid who was pulling the plastic bag out of the trash can. "Did Ms. Conrad check out already?" Had she realized that they were closing in?

"No. Ms. Conrad is just out for now." The maid glanced up and smiled at him. "You're on the desk."

"What?"

"Your picture," she said.

He edged around the cart and walked over to where she'd pointed. The photo on the desk was the one Colleen had snapped when they'd been out to dinner together, a selfie of the two of them that she'd said she was sending to Sam. But that wasn't the only photo. She had some old ones, ones he was certain he'd taken with Sam, but Colleen must have cut his sister out. Like she wanted to cut Henrietta out of his life now...

His gaze moved from the picture to the stack of papers and the Sharpie pen lying next to them. Colleen was definitely his letter writer. But she'd abandoned the block letters for the date and time she'd written on a scrap of paper.

It was today's date and the time their flight would arrive. She hadn't met him at the airfield. She hadn't been anywhere in sight there or at the firehouse.

So where the hell had she gone?

Seeing again how she'd cropped Sam out of those old photos, he knew. To Henrietta...

She wasn't just trying to crop Henrietta out of photos, though. She wanted her out of his life. But it wasn't just Henrietta whom she'd tried to kill; she obviously wanted his life, too, since she must have finally realized that she would never have his heart.

Maybe she'd figured out even before he had that he'd given it to someone else: to Henrietta.

HENRIETTA'S SMILE FROZE on her face while she patiently listened to George's story. As usual when she returned from fighting a wildfire, he had to share stories from his years as a Hotshot. Michaela had begged off with a headache and hightailed it up to their apartment nearly an hour ago.

Henrietta wished she would have done the same. She stretched her mouth into a fake yawn and murmured, "Sorry, George. I'm really beat. I think I better call it a night."

"Not night yet," he said with a glance at the sky outside the open garage doors of the small firehouse.

"It is for me," she said. "Still on west coast time..." Which would have made it earlier in the day, not later. But George didn't argue with her, and she finally slipped away from him to climb the stairs to the second story.

"How do you do that?" she asked Michaela as she opened the door. "How do you get away from him so easily?"

Her roommate didn't answer. Maybe she really had had a headache and had gone to her room to lie down. Henrietta hadn't been lying about being tired either. She'd only faked sleep on the plane.

But she needed to rest now. First, she needed a drink, though. Even though George had done all the talking, her mouth was dry. That tended to happen after spending all that time in a wildfire.

When she walked into the kitchen, she found Michaela slumped in a chair. A bottle of wine and a glass sat in front of her. Not much was gone from the bottle or the glass.

And Michaela, despite her petite size, was no lightweight. Henrietta rushed forward and tipped back her friend's head, which lolled on her neck like she was a rag doll. Her fingers trembling, she reached for Michaela's throat and found a pulse, albeit weak.

"Hang in there," she murmured as she reached for her cell phone. "I'll get you help."

"No, you won't," a female voice told her. "Drop that damn phone."

She nearly did; the intruder had startled her so much. The woman stood in the doorway to the kitchen, a gun clenched in her hand. The gun was nearly as big a shock as her presence. Not that she had much of a presence with the dark, oversize clothes that hung on her tall body, and with the way her long brown hair concealed most of her face. Hank had never seen her before, but she looked at Hank like she recognized her and hated her. Her brown eyes were dark with that hatred, her face flushed with anger. She might have been a pretty woman if she'd smiled, but the way she glared and growled at Henrietta was ugly. "I told you to drop that damn phone or I will drop you right now."

Clearly, she intended to do that anyway. "Did you poison her?" she asked about her roommate. She had to make sure that Michaela would be okay.

The woman shook her head. "No. Just drugged. I had some sleeping pills to spare." Using the gun barrel, she gestured at the bottle of wine. "You were supposed to drink some, too."

"Why?" she asked. "Will it make it easier for you to shoot me if I'm passed out?"

"You haven't been easy to kill," the woman resentfully admitted.

"Why do you want to?" Henrietta asked. "We've never met. I don't know who you are."

"Trick knows," she said.

"Colleen…" Henrietta murmured. He'd mentioned her on the plane trip back. "But you're supposed to be Sam's friend."

"Sam is no friend of mine," Colleen said. "Not anymore."

Henrietta nodded. "I guess not, or you wouldn't be trying to kill her brother."

The woman's face flushed more. "That's her fault. She called him up. She got him to come here just after he'd finally moved to the city where I live. We were starting to see each other, and then she made him move here."

"He doesn't intend to stay," Henrietta said, as if assuring her. "He was just helping out Braden and Sam. He would have gone back."

Colleen shook her head. "I had already waited so long.

I was so close. That's why I followed him here and left him those notes."

"You thought those would scare him into leaving?" The woman obviously didn't know Trick well.

"They might have," Colleen insisted. "If not for you…"

"What about me?" Henrietta asked. "I'm just another Hotshot on the team. That's all I am to Trick."

"Don't lie to me! I know that he's been with you…" Jealousy twisted the woman's face into an ugly grimace. "I know that he's still in Northern Lakes because of you. That's why you have to die."

"He's leaving!" Henrietta shouted before the woman could pull the trigger. "He probably would have been gone already and back in…" She didn't even know where he'd been before coming to Northern Lakes.

"DC."

"He would have been back if not for the notes," Henrietta said. "He only stayed to figure out who was leaving them."

The woman paused and tilted her head, her dark eyes narrowed. "I don't believe you."

"He's just here to fill a spot after one of the team died," Henrietta said. "Until a permanent replacement could be found. He's not staying." He was never going to stay anywhere.

Maybe Colleen knew that, too, because tears pooled in her eyes. "Sam wasn't going to stay either, but she met someone here and she fell in love. And I think Trick did the same…" She pointed the gun at Hank again. "With you!"

Henrietta held up her hand, and as she did, she tried to press the emergency call button on the phone she still held. If she dropped it, like the woman wanted, she had no chance of calling for help.

She could scream. But even if George heard her, he probably would only make it upstairs in time to take a bullet himself. "No. No. Trick doesn't love me." Maybe it was good that he didn't, because Hank had a feeling there was nothing she could do to talk this woman out of pulling the trigger, out of killing her.

COLLEEN WOULD HAVE pitied Henrietta Rowlins if she'd thought the Hotshot was wrong. She knew how painful that realization was since she'd recently come to it herself; Trick would never love her. Maybe it had been at that dinner, when she'd taken that picture with him... when she'd remembered how he'd looked when she'd "accidentally" on purpose bumped into him in the neighborhood where Sam had told her he'd moved. He hadn't been happy to see her; he hadn't even recognized her at first.

In that moment, something inside Colleen had broken. But she'd manipulated him into eating dinner with her anyway, hoping that he would see her then. Instead he'd been bored—she'd seen that—so bored that he'd taken his sister's call. Then he'd left, taking all of Colleen's dreams and hopes for a future with him away. She'd chased after him, but she'd been doing that for years. And she'd realized she was never going to catch him. That was really why she'd started threatening him. Then, when she'd watched him interact with Henrietta Rowlins and had seen how he'd looked at the female Hotshot, Colleen had finally accepted that he would never look at her that way.

So she hadn't wanted him looking at anyone anymore. Killing Henrietta wasn't going to make him fall for Colleen. Nothing would. But killing Henrietta was going to make her feel better, before she killed Trick and then herself...

She moved her finger to the trigger and pulled.

Chapter Twenty-Six

The shots startled the old man who'd been blocking Trick's way to the stairs. Trick darted around him and ran, his feet tripping over the steps as he rushed up to Henrietta's apartment. What if he was too late? He drew in a deep breath, bracing himself for what he might find as he kicked open the door.

The gun barrel turned on him, and Colleen fired a bullet that struck the jamb near his head. Before she could squeeze the trigger again, she crumpled into a heap on the kitchen floor. Henrietta stood behind her, a wine bottle in her hand.

"Are you okay?" he asked as he rushed forward.

Henrietta just nodded. "But call an ambulance for Michaela…"

He didn't see his other teammate until he looked around the kitchen. She lay limply on the floor, as if she'd spilled out of the overturned chair next to her. "Has she been shot?"

Henrietta shook her head. "No. I knocked her to the ground when that bitch started shooting. Colleen drugged the wine."

"I take it that you didn't drink any," he said. She was

clearly alert and strong and so damn amazing that a lump rose in his throat, choking him.

She shook her head. "Nope. George waylaid me downstairs."

"Me, too," Trick said. "Then I heard the shots and I thought I was too late. I already called the police. They're on their way."

Sirens whined in the distance. They would have been too late…if not for Henrietta.

She glanced down at the woman lying at her feet. "Guess her wine knocked her out, too," she said with a short chuckle. Then she began to shake.

Trick realized shock was setting in for her. He stepped over Colleen, pausing only to pick up the gun she'd dropped to the floor when Henrietta had taken her down. Then he closed his arms around the woman he loved, holding her close to his madly pounding heart.

"You are so damn amazing," he said, and tightened his arms around her trembling body. "It's no wonder I've fallen in love with you."

She tensed in his embrace. But maybe that was because of the footsteps pounding up the steps. He whirled toward the doorway, keeping his body between hers and whoever was charging up the steps. And he faced down another gun barrel.

A woman held this one, too. Trooper Wynona Wells. And even when she saw them, she didn't lower it. For a fleeting second he wondered if Colleen had been responsible for *all* the attempts on his life. Or if there had been someone else…

HOURS LATER, IN the hospital checking on Michaela, Henrietta still wondered: Had he said what she'd thought she'd heard? No. She could not have heard him correctly. Her pulse had been beating so hard that it must have been the sound of her blood rushing through her veins that she'd heard.

He couldn't have said that he'd fallen for her.

It was good that Trooper Wells had shown up when she had, or Henrietta might have done something stupid, like told him she loved him, too. Admitting that would have been certain to send him running.

Now she wouldn't be the only one missing him. All the Hotshots had come to the hospital to make sure that Michaela was okay. Nobody had blamed him for putting her and Michaela in danger. But him…

Guilt weighed heavily on him as he slumped his broad shoulders and bowed his head. He kept telling everyone that he should have figured it out sooner. But they'd all slapped his back and reassured him that he'd done nothing wrong.

Henrietta believed that as well. He hadn't led Colleen Conrad on; the woman was delusional. The trooper had already ordered a mental evaluation for her based on what Trick had found in her suite at the Northern Lakes Village Inn. She'd been stalking him for years.

But she wasn't a threat any longer. The only threat to Henrietta now was Trick himself—when he left and took her heart with him.

She was strong at the hospital—for Michaela. Her friend was dealing with so much more than Henrietta had realized. She vowed that she would be there for her from now on; she even offered to stay with her, since they wanted to keep her overnight.

But Michaela insisted that Henrietta go home. And so she went—back to the cottage she'd shared with her grandfather. Usually when she stepped through the door, a wave of warmth washed over her—filling her heart with fond memories and love.

Now other memories rushed in—memories of Trick and her together...

Would they ever be that way again?

When knuckles rapped against the door, she wasn't surprised. She'd noticed him leaving the hospital when she had; she'd seen the lights in her rearview mirror. She opened the door and leaned against the jamb. "Are you stalking me?"

He shuddered at the thought, or the memories of being stalked himself. "I'm sorry..."

"It's fine," she said as she stepped back and let him cross the threshold.

"Not about following you," he said. "I'm sorry about Colleen."

"It wasn't your fault," she said. "She got fixated on what she couldn't have." Henrietta could understand that.

"What about you?" he asked.

She tensed. "What do you mean?"

"Can I have you?" he asked.

She wanted him—so badly—even if it was just this one last time. So she linked her arms around his shoulders and pulled his head down for her kiss. She moved her mouth hungrily over his.

He growled in his throat and deepened the kiss before he pulled back. Panting for breath, he asked again, "Can I have you?"

"Yes," she said. And she linked their hands, tugging him toward the bedroom. The bed was still mussed from the last time they'd made love in it. She released him and reached for her sweater, pulling it over her head. But when she reached for the button on her jeans, he stopped her—his hands over hers.

"I don't mean just now," he said.

"What are you talking about?" she asked.

"Forever," he said. "I'm talking about the rest of our lives and how I want to spend it with you."

Shocked, she dropped her arms to her sides. "What?"

"I told you that I've fallen in love with you. Didn't you hear me?"

"I didn't think I heard you right," she said. "I didn't believe…"

"I can't believe it myself," he admitted. "I always vowed that I would never let it happen, that I would never fall in love and risk being left, like my mom left my dad. But I want to stay here…with you…if you'll have me…"

She would have thought she was dreaming if her heart hadn't done a quick flip in her chest as it swelled to bursting with love for him. She threw her arms around him again. "Yes, I'll have you…"

"Are you sure?" he asked, his face tense with concern. "I don't know how we'll work it out with the job—"

She pressed her fingers over his lips. "We'll work it out." They had to; they were meant to be together. She knew it, and she would convince the rest of the team and Braden of it as well. And even if Braden had begun his search for Trick's replacement, it might not be for naught. There was a chance they would need another member before too long. But that wasn't Henrietta's news to share.

"We'll make Braden change his rule," she vowed.

His breath hissed out between his lips. "You are amazing—so damn strong," he murmured, and he looked as if he was in awe.

Of her…

She smiled as pride filled her. This wasn't just attraction between them. While it might have started that way, it had grown so quickly to more.

So much more…

"I love you," she said. Now she cupped his face—his perfect, handsome face—in her palms. "And I will never leave you."

He smiled. "I know."

"Pretty cocky, aren't you?" she teased. But she knew he wasn't, that he was more vulnerable than he liked to admit.

"No," he said. "I trust you."

She knew that wasn't easy for him—to trust. She was awed now—by how much he loved her. And she knew that no matter what happened with the team, they would be together.

Always…

This time when she reached for the button of her jeans, he didn't stop her. He was too busy shucking off his own clothes, dumping them onto the floor. She tugged him toward the bed as he was reaching for a condom.

He laughed as he tumbled onto the mattress with her. "You're impatient."

"No," she said. "No. I've been patiently waiting for you all my life. For my knight in shining armor…"

He pushed back the hair that had fallen across her face and said, "And I've been looking for you all my life. That's why I kept moving around… I was looking for you."

She smiled. "Liar."

"I didn't know it," he said. "But my heart did. And the minute I got close to you, it knew…"

Tears stung her eyes. She never would have considered him capable of such romantic words. But she knew he wasn't just charming her. He was speaking from his heart.

From his love...

He showed her that love with how gentle and passionate he was. He caressed her everywhere. Kissed her everywhere. Then finally, when she writhed on the mattress, nearly begging for release, he joined their bodies. He filled her—with himself—with his love.

They moved together so perfectly, and she knew without a doubt that they were meant for each other. For always...

"I'M THE BOSS!" Braden said, and he slammed his fist down on the podium at the front of the conference room.

A couple members of the team jumped at his unusual show of anger. But he wasn't angry. He was actually quite thrilled. He couldn't show that—not now. Not yet...

"I am the one who makes the rules," he continued.

A couple rumbles of disagreement emanated from some of the members. Surprisingly the sounds came from Ethan Sommerly and Trent Miles—surprising because they had struggled the most to accept Trick as part of the team.

But he'd been fully embraced now. And everybody already adored and respected Hank.

"So I am the only one who can change them," he said.

There had been a hell of a lot of lobbying for him to do just that. He'd heard it. But he wanted to be sure. "Before I consider that, I want to make certain that nobody has a problem with Trick and Hank working together on this team."

But everybody knew they weren't just working to-gether. That they were so much more than that.

"No problem at all," Michaela said. "I feel safe with them both."

She should. Hank had saved her life.

A chorus of "me toos" rang out from the rest of the team. He'd already known from all the one-on-one lobbying that everybody was in favor. He'd enjoyed his wife's lobbying the most.

Too much...

His body was completely satiated from how hard she'd lobbied for her brother and Hank to remain on the team. And maybe they'd started that family she'd told him she was ready to start now with him.

"So I'm changing the rule," he said. "Romantic frat-ernization will now be allowed."

Trent Miles heaved a huge sigh of relief, reached over and clasped Ethan's beefy hand in his. "We can stop sneaking around now, my love."

Ethan tugged his hand free and slapped at Trent. But he was laughing.

They all laughed.

Except for Trick, who'd dropped to his knees in front of Hank. And in his hand, he held an engagement ring. "Henrietta Rowlins, will you let me spend the rest of my life with you, as your husband, your partner in work and everything else?"

Tough Hank blinked furiously, but tears spilled through her thick lashes despite her best efforts. "Yes," she said. "Yes, I will." She leaned forward and pressed her lips to his.

And the room erupted in applause.

Sam was going to love this. Love that her brother had found his happiness in Northern Lakes.

If only he'd found the traitor, too.

That person was still on the team. When Trooper Wells, and then Sam, had questioned Colleen, she'd made it clear that she hadn't been responsible for everything that had happened to Trick. She hadn't sabotaged the bucket on the boom truck. She'd claimed she wouldn't have had the first clue how.

She'd even claimed that she hadn't set his truck on fire, that seeing Hank's neighbor was home in the next house had scared her off from making any attempt on their lives there. Neither Trick nor Sam, nor even Trooper Wells, had been certain she'd been telling the truth about that.

But Braden believed her about the truck. He believed that he still had someone on his team that he couldn't trust—no matter how much he loved them all. And now he was more determined than ever to find that person—to make sure that nobody else got hurt.

* * * * *

COMING SOON!

We really hope you enjoyed reading this book.
If you're looking for more romance, be sure to
head to the shops when new books are
available on

Thursday 8th December

To see which titles are coming soon, please visit
millsandboon.co.uk/nextmonth

MILLS & BOON

THE HEART OF ROMANCE

A ROMANCE FOR EVERY READER

MODERN
Prepare to be swept off your feet by sophisticated, sexy and seductive heroes, in some of the world's most glamourous and rom locations, where power and passion collide.

HISTORICAL
Escape with historical heroes from time gone by. Whether your pas for wicked Regency Rakes, muscled Vikings or rugged Highlanders the romance of the past.

MEDICAL
Set your pulse racing with dedicated, delectable doctors in the high sure world of medicine, where emotions run high and passion, com love are the best medicine.

True Love
Celebrate true love with tender stories of heartfelt romance, from rush of falling in love to the joy a new baby can bring, and a focus emotional heart of a relationship.

Desire
Indulge in secrets and scandal, intense drama and plenty of sizzling action with powerful and passionate heroes who have it all: wealth, good looks…everything but the right woman.

HEROES
Experience all the excitement of a gripping thriller, with an intens mance at its heart. Resourceful, true-to-life women and strong, fea face danger and desire - a killer combination!

To see which titles are coming soon, please visit

millsandboon.co.uk/nextmonth

LET'S TALK
Romance

For exclusive extracts, competitions
and special offers, find us online:

JOIN US ON SOCIAL MEDIA!

Stay up to date with our latest releases, author news and gossip, special offers and discounts, and all the behind-the-scenes action from Mills & Boon...

 @millsandboon

 @millsandboonuk

 facebook.com/millsandboon

 @millsandboonuk

t might just be true love...

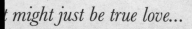

GET YOUR ROMANCE FIX

Get the latest romance news,
exclusive author interviews, story
extracts and much more!

blog.millsandboon.co.uk

MILLS & BOON

MODERN

Power and Passion

Prepare to be swept off your feet by sophisticated, sexy and seductive heroes, in some of the world's most glamourous and romantic locations, where power and passion collide.